PENGUIN MODERN CLASSICS

THE ANGELIC AVENGERS

Isak Dinesen was the pen-name of Karen Blixen, who was born in Rungsted, Denmark, in 1885. After studying art at Copenhagen, Paris and Rome, she married her cousin, Baron Bror Blixen-Finecke, in 1914. Together they went to Kenya to manage a coffee plantation. After their divorce in 1921, she continued to run the plantation until a collapse in the coffee market forced her back to Denmark in 1931.

Although she had written occasional contributions to Danish periodicals since 1905 (under the *nom-de-plume* of Osceola), her real début took place in 1934 with the publication of *Seven Gothic Tales*, written in English under her pen-name. In 1937 she published, under her own name, *Out of Africa* (Penguin 1954), an autobiographical account of the many years she spent in Kenya. Most of her subsequent books were published in English and Danish simultaneously, including *Winter's Tales* (1942, Penguin 1983) and *The Angelic Avengers* (1946), under the name of Pierre Andrézel. Among her other collections of stories are *Last Tales* (1957), *Anecdotes of Destiny* (1958), *Shadows on the Grass* (1960, Penguin 1984) and *Ehrengard* (1963).

Baroness Blixen died in Rungsted in 1962.

ISAK DINESEN

(KAREN BLIXEN)

The Angelic Avengers

PENGUIN BOOKS

Penguin Books Ltd, Harmondsworth, Middlesex, England
Viking Penguin Inc., 40 West 23rd Street, New York, New York 10010, U.S.A.
Penguin Books Australia Ltd, Ringwood, Victoria, Australia
Penguin Books Canada Limited, 2801 John Street, Markham, Ontario, Canada L3R 1B4
Penguin Books (N.Z.) Ltd, 182–190 Wairau Road, Auckland 10, New Zealand

First published simultaneously in the U.S.A. and Canada by Random House, Inc. 1946
First published in Great Britain by the University of Chicago Press 1975
Published in Penguin Books 1986

This edition is published with the permission of the Rungstedlund Foundation

Printed and bound in Great Britain by
Cox & Wyman Ltd, Reading

contents

"You serious people must not be too hard on human beings for what they choose to amuse themselves with when they are shut up as in a prison, and are not even allowed to say that they are prisoners. If I do not soon get a little bit of fun, I shall die."

PAGE 110

PART ONE

rose-strewn roads and thorny paths

*

1. a lonely young girl

A YOUNG girl, whose name was Lucan Bellenden, on a spring evening sat deep in thought by the window of a fine big English country house. After the fashion of the 1840's, her rich golden hair was hanging down her neck and shoulders in long ringlets. She had on a plain, black frock that fitted tightly round her delicate bosom and arms, but was amply folded and draped below the slim waist. From time to time she gently pressed or wrung her fingers between these black folds; this was her only movement.

Lucan was an orphan and sadly situated in life. Already as a child she had lost her mother, and a year ago, at her father's death, she had seen her home dissolved and her little brothers placed in the house of those of her relations who could provide for them. She herself must also try to earn her bread. For some months she was companion to a rich old lady, who in her young days had been a beauty, and whose heart still sent off wild sparks of jealousy when her white-haired or bald old beaux neglected their game of whist or their glass of punch to stare at the lovely young face and figure of the girl who moved about in the room. Lucan had been lonely in this rich house, and had felt as if no human being there, and not even the parrot in the cage or any silk-covered armchair or sofa, was kindly disposed toward her. But she was so young that, through solitude and depression, in her heart she preserved an invincible faith in something beautiful and happy which must be awaiting her somewhere in the world. "It will soon all be otherwise," she thought. When her old lady suddenly died from a stroke, she went to an employment office in London, and through it obtained a situation as governess at the house in which she was now sitting.

The master of the house was a businessman, a successful and respected gentleman, stately and proud, but reserved and chary of words. He was a widower with three children, two girls and a boy. His wife had brought him a large fortune, but she had been delicate and ailing, so that at the birth of each child her life had been in danger. Mr. Armworthy, before anything else in life, wished for a son who might in time carry on the big firm which he himself had founded. He had felt it a heavy trial that his two first children were daughters. At last, after many years' traveling on the continent and sojourns at baths, his wife gave birth to the deeply coveted son, and paid for him with her life. A still sadder misfortune was to befall the lonely man: it soon became apparent that the pretty little boy was blind. The father now more and more withdrew himself from the company of other people, and became almost entirely absorbed in his business. Only rarely, and for a period of a day or two, did he come out to his country house "Fairhill," and to his children.

Lucan's father had been a scientist, a highly gifted botanist, ahead of his time, and therefore but little appreciated by it, and opposed by certain of the clergy. He had many friends among French and German scholars. One of them was the French man of science, Dr. Braille, who invented the system of writing for the blind. Lucan had seen the famous man in her home, and had listened as he developed his ideas. She had learned a little about blind-writing herself, and this was why Mr. Armworthy had engaged the girl, among numerous applicants, as governess to his children. In her heart, Lucan thanked her father for her good fortune, and felt sure that his kind eyes even now were following her. The little boy was as yet too young to learn to read, but Lucan played with him, taught him little rhymes and songs, and soon came to love the talented, unhappy child who reminded her of her own small brothers. She felt freer and lighter of heart here in the country than in her first situation in town. Even in the winter months, when the garden and park were white with rime, every day, on her promenades with the children, she had rejoiced in the beauty of the landscape, and here, too, for the first time after her father's death, she herself could laugh and play. Now summer was near, and it seemed to her as if it were to be that beginning of the happy time to which she had so long looked forward. Each day from now on was to bring her a keener and sweeter delight.

She understood that the father of the three children had come to notice and appreciate her work with her pupils and her affection for them. A couple of times he had discussed his son's future with her, and this, surely, must be a proof of his trust in her, for the old housekeeper, when she first arrived, had informed her that it was a subject which Mr. Armworthy would never approach, and which she must take care to avoid. It had surprised and flattered her, that a man, who was almost as old as her own father, and so much wiser and more experienced than herself, should thus listen to her with attention, when she told him of her little observations and designs. When at times he smiled at her, a faint, wondering compassion ran through her whole being; the smile appeared on his face stiffly and with difficulty. He must, she reflected, long ago have got out of the habit of smiling. He now gave more of his time and interest to his children, and within the last month he had twice prolonged his stay in the country a day or two. As the weather grew milder, he sometimes took the boy and his governess with him on a drive in the neighborhood, where other handsome houses stood in their parks and gardens. Lucan had never before driven in a comfortable carriage, with a pair of fine horses. Through her father, she had knowledge of plants and flowers, and she looked forward to seeing the grounds around Fairhill, and all the lovely landscape, unfold and blossom, and, on her walks and drives, to find those wild flowers which she loved best of all.

Last Saturday, Mr. Armworthy had arrived at his country-house earlier than usual, and had had his small son brought down to the drawing-room. For an hour he patiently listened to the child's eager tales of what he and his governess had been doing in the course of the week, and to the pretty little songs which Lucan had taught him as she accompanied him on the piano.

When the nurse again fetched the boy back to the nursery, he asked the young governess to remain with him and keep him company for a while. He began to question her on her own home and childhood. Lucan told him how, when fourteen years old, she had been fetched home from the boarding school to her mother's death-bed, and how, ever since, she had kept house for her father, and endeavored to console him in his great misfortune. She was like her mother, people told her, and therefore, better than anybody else, she had been able to cheer him up when he was sad or depressed. It was so long a time since Lucan had talked to anybody of her home that she forgot her shyness of the big, silent man, and freely recounted to him her walks and talks with her father and her happy games, adventures and travels of discovery with the little brothers. In the end she broke off, embarrassed at having talked so much about herself.

Mr. Armworthy sat quite still and looked at her benevolently. "I understand," he said, after a short silence, "that your youth, your kind heart, and your confidence in your fellow-creatures may bring back faith in the happiness of life, even to those who have long lost it in this world." He took her hand, which rested on the sofa arm, and gently carried it to his lips.

She rose, deeply moved and silent. He rose with her and chivalrously followed her to the door. As he was holding it open for her, she had to pass him closely, and for a moment he placed his arm round her shoulder, and lightly pressed her toward him. Her father had been wont to hold her like this when she was saying good night to him. It now seemed to her that it was her father himself who caressed her. For a brief moment she yielded to the gentle touch. Immediately afterward, she walked out of the door and, slightly dizzy, up the stairs.

When, the next morning, after Mr. Armworthy had left the house to go to town, she came out of the school room, where she had taught the two little girls to write a really neat and well-proportioned letter, his valet brought her a letter from him. He wrote briefly and gravely that he asked her to forgive him if, within an uncontrolled moment, he had forgotten himself, and frightened or perhaps even offended her, than which nothing had been further from his intention. It was his wish to explain himself to her, and he begged her, on Saturday next, to allow him an interview in the drawing-room, after he had dined, and the children had been brought to bed. He had much on his heart which he could not express till then. He concluded the letter with the assurance of his respect and devotion.

At the first moment the letter made no particular impression on the girl. But in the course of the week its significance seemed to grow upon her. She had known but few men, and never in her life had she received a letter of proposal. "It is my future, it is all my life which is at stake here," she thought.

She had wondered at the fact that a man of experience and influence, of whom everyone thought with respect, should consult her on serious matters, on his children and their future. But she did not wonder at the idea that he should love her. She knew, or felt, in her heart that to a man any innocent girl might mean all the happiness of the world.

Only when, about four o'clock of the afternoon, she heard the carriage, which brought back the master of the house, roll up on the gravel by the entrance door, she was seized by a violent agitation at the idea that she must tonight, and all on her own, decide upon her destiny. While she sat by the window, gently squeezing her fingers in her lap and waiting to hear the clock above the stable door strike nine, she tried to conquer the disorder of her thoughts and to make up her mind.

2. Lucan's resolution

"NAY, it is impossible. I cannot marry him, for I do not love him."

This had been Lucan's first thought, when she had read Mr. Armworthy's letter. But here by the window she grew restless. It seemed to her that all the people she knew, if she had told them about his offer, would have advised her to accept it. "No, Father would not have advised me so," she thought, but immediately afterward remembered how, at the approach of death, her light-minded, unconcerned father had grieved about the future of his children, and above all about the future of his only daughter. If he had known that a wealthy and respected man would ask her to become his wife, he might have left the world with an easier heart. She wished that she could have walked out of the house and down in the park, as if there, underneath the big trees, she would have found a solution to her problem, or would have been free from brooding on it any more. But it was already evening, and she must stay indoors.

She remembered how often her father had laughed at her, because, like her mother, she could only view a case from one side. "The very first faculty, my girl," he had said, "which one requires in order to behave like a reasonable and sound-minded person, is imagination." She now tried to use her imagination, to figure out all possibilities, and to consider and weigh Mr. Armworthy's proposal. Like Robinson Crusoe on his island, she thought, she would draw up her account, and faithfully enter each plus and minus upon its pages.

As now her thoughts sought for a starting point, they fell upon the blind boy who was at this moment asleep in the room next to her own. He had been confided to her charge, and during these months had been in her mind every day, but if now she refused his father, she could no longer remain in the house, and they would have to part. She tried to strengthen herself against the pain which this outlook caused her. "There are many others," she thought, "who can bring him up better than I. But," she sadly continued her course of thought, "will they understand him as I do? He is self-willed and capricious. Will they be patient with him?" Her mind strayed from the blind boy to her own little brothers, who were now scattered in houses and amongst people strange to them. As the wife of a rich man she would be able to help them in the world. The eldest of them had ardently wished to become a scientist like his father, and had wept bitterly when he had realized that he would have to give up his school, to learn bookkeeping, so that he might in time get a position in some office. If once Mr. Armworthy saw and understood how good and talented her boys were, it was impossible but that he would take an interest in them, and have them placed in good schools. What joy and bliss would it not be to visit them there, and in the holidays see them run about in the park with Mr. Armworthy's own children! She remembered the old maid-of-all-work of the family, and how broken-hearted she had been when she had taken leave of them all—how happy, how proud would she not be, if she could see the big, fine house and her own darling as mistress of it!

"God," Lucan thought in great alarm, "all this I throw away! Am I, then, a selfish and narrow-hearted girl, who thinks only of my own feelings? What is it, in marrying Mr. Armworthy, I so dread and shudder to lose? Happiness? But many of the things I have here thought of are what people understand by happiness. What is it that I demand of life and I have always longed and hoped for?" Her own heart at once answered her, clearly and loudly, "It is love!"

Her father and mother had loved each other, and their deep feeling had made them happy, even in adversity and hard times. She herself had never imagined the possibility of a loveless marriage. At the idea of such a marriage she grew cold, as if she had descended into a cellar. "Is it then not at all possible," she thought, "that I can love Mr. Armworthy?" No, it was impossible. He was so much older, so different from her in everything; he had been married before. "It is that, most of all," she reflected, "which makes it impossible that I should marry him. He might be still older than he is, his voice drier, his eyes more lifeless, and it might yet be done. But he has already once kissed a girl and put a ring on her finger; he has already once, many years ago, driven home from church with his bride. And what does it mean, then," she thought after a time, "to give up love?"

Without any effort of her own, as if it had been shown to her by another person, the dismal picture drew itself before her eyes. Never more would she, as Mr. Armworthy's wife, dare to open those books of poetry which, till now, had been her consolation in sorrow and loneliness, never more would she dare to listen to music, never more enjoy the beauty and fragrance of flowers. For all this spoke of a charm and an enchantment in life, which would then no longer exist for her. Could one go on living without these things? "No," she whispered, "no, life is not such a desert. The glory of which I have dreamed is a reality. I will, I must believe in happiness!" As she listened to her own low whisper, like an echo of it Mr. Armworthy's words came back to her: "Your fresh youth and your kind heart may restore the faith in happiness even to him who has lost it long ago."

She was deeply moved. Then it was, in reality, she herself who had something to give! It was the rich man, the master of the fine big house, who was destitute, and who needed her, and could not do without her. His life had been barren. Now he came to her, and begged her to make it flower and bear fruit. His heart had been so cold, even toward his children. Now he brought it to her, so that she should warm it.

It seemed to her that she could, at this moment, look both backward and forward, and that many things, which till now she had not understood, here lay clear before her. It was the world of rich and successful people, the powerful world which used its power without mercy, the world which had denied her father, and by continuous distress had laid her mother in the grave, and which had eyed her herself with ice-cold arrogance, when she had tremblingly entered its service. It was this world which, tonight, in the form of a lonely and sad man, came to her and begged for her help! And in return, it was prepared to give her all that it had boasted of before: riches, power, and the esteem of men!

In the deep quiet of the spring evening, her whole nature filled with a new satisfaction and pride. The present offer from this proud world held a satisfaction which did not apply to herself only, but to her father and to all his friends. But she gently and slowly shook her head at it. Her father had been prepared to give the work of his life for the acknowledgment of this hard world; her mother had given her life itself. Now it offered her its riches for something less than these things, for she was not a highly gifted person like her father, not angelic or unselfish like her mother. But tonight, for once, that haughty and cold world was to learn the meaning of a refusal. Tonight it would know how it felt to beg and to be refused. She remembered the old lady, in whose service she had first been engaged. Many things which had happened in her house came back to her, and a kind of triumph ran through her.

"No," she thought after a while, "it is not right; it is not worthy of my father's daughter to think like this. I will show that rich, poor man that I understand him, and am grateful to him. I am prepared to call his offer an honor for me. I will make peace with all that world which he represents. But I will not marry him. No, if Father himself came into the room and told me to do so, I would not marry him."

She looked out at the park. It might have been hers. It had, so to speak, really been hers for two hours. The whole house, with all that it contained, had been hers! Lucan had but little experience of what a big house, and the position which it gives to its owner, does really mean. But she was a young girl, and she could not fail to know that she was pretty. She suddenly bethought herself of a frock which a lady had worn at one of the parties of her old mistress, and of which since then she had often dreamed. This frock was made of thick pink silk, and its many rich flounces had been edged with fine lace. Such a pink frock she might herself, as Mr. Armworthy's wife, have worn. It would have been laid out in her room, only waiting for her. For a few minutes she kept standing by the window, slowly letting her hands run over her old black merino frock, and she seemed to feel, within her fingertips, the sweet sensation of running them over the surface of smooth, heavy satin.

At that same moment the clock struck nine. She grew very pale, and without a single glance in the looking-glass or arranging her long tresses, she walked out of the room and down the stairs.

3. converse in the evening

THE big drawing-room, with its heavy, dark curtains and furniture, was only dimly lit by a lamp, but in the fireplace the flames were bright and clear. Above it hung a portrait of Mr. Armworthy's late wife, and in the light of the flickering flames it appeared to be moving faintly. Lucan met the picture's eyes, which seemed to rest gently and sadly upon her face. They were, perhaps, two against one in this room. And on which side was the dead woman?

Mr. Armworthy was sitting by the fireplace with a book on his knee, but he had not been reading. He rose, as the girl entered the room, and led her to a chair opposite his own. He hesitated a few moments before he spoke. His words came slowly, and with some difficulty.

"I am grateful to you, Miss Lucan," he said, "because you have been good enough to come here to have a talk with me. All during this week, whatever I have been doing, you have been in my thoughts." He made a short pause. "I have likewise," he said, "in my mind, carefully gone through that talk which I am now to have with you. And first of all, and even before I begin it, I have a request to make to you! It will not be easy for me to express myself as openly as I shall now have to do—and you yourself should run no risk of deciding before you have had ample time to consider my question. Therefore you must consent to hear me out without interrupting me. It must be our bargain that, like a good, obedient child," he smiled slightly at his own words, "you sit still while I speak, and later leave this room in silence, to think matters over."

He looked away. Lucan thought: "It is difficult for him to beg for anything! He has never done it till now."

"My life," Mr. Armworthy began, after another pause, "has been without romance. I have never imagined that I should come to feel any inclination or sympathy for such a thing. But at a time when I almost believed my real life was behind me, your youth and innocence have been brought on my path! The strength of my own feelings have surprised and alarmed me. It is to me an extraordinary thing to realize that my whole destiny, if I may use that word, should depend upon another person, and, at that, upon a young girl! And still, at the same time, I feel grateful to Providence, because, through this, I have conceived the possibility of a kind of happiness altogether different to any I have known or dreamed of. I shall," he added, "tonight have to speak of facts which must appear to you prosaic. But, believe me, the very last thing I want to do is to hurt that richness and tenderness of heart, that sweet faith in the ideals of life which, first of all, in you have moved and touched me, and from which I myself now expect or hope a new, late felicity.

"But a long life has taught me how much the purely external and material circumstances of existence do mean to all human beings. You yourself, Miss Lucan, have gone through much to which you ought never to have been exposed, and on the idea of which I have often dwelt with pity: loneliness, insecurity, hard work—because your existence has had no proper firm material foundation. I now wish to give you such a basis, precisely because I imagine that within secure and happy surroundings the fullness of your nature would unfold, to the happiness of those who understand and appreciate it. Nay, do not interrupt me, my dear child," he said, and took her hand, on the arm of the chair. "You must remember our bargain.

"You are young, and your life lies before you. It is my wish at once, and from the beginning, to safeguard your existence. I do not know how you will imagine such a happier way of life. Perhaps you do not know it yourself. Maybe you will have dreamed of traveling on the continent. With what great pleasure would I show you the treasures of art of Florence, or take you through the ruins of Rome! Or you might wish to perfect your pretty talent for music, which indeed would give me much pleasure. Or I imagine that works of charity, toward the unfortunate of this world, would satisfy your kind and generous nature. Of all this we shall speak in time. Whatsoever you will choose, I pride myself on being able to give it to you, in ampler measure than you yourself will ever, till now, have imagined.

"It will be my happiness to protect and guide you. I understand that you have a sincere love of the country, of gardens and flowers. I have been planning to give you a pretty house, after your taste, out of town . . ."

"Out of town?" Lucan exclaimed in surprise.

"Yes," he said, "so close to it that my journey out there shall not be too long. And yet, I dare not, as you will understand yourself, make it too close. I know that you will turn it into a true place of rest and refuge to the man who has met with much affliction in life, and to whom your inexperience and ignorance of the world have a particular attraction in themselves. I shall be happy to give every free hour to the small paradise which you will be creating for me there."

His eyes rested upon the young girl's form. Within the firelight her hair shone like gold; her cheek and throat took on a deep, delicate glow; the blue eyes with their thick eyelashes were wide open, and met his with an inquiring, glassy brilliance. He felt, at this moment, proud, both of her, who was so lovely and innocent, and of his own power over her. Once more he turned away his eyes, so as not to be tempted to take her in his arms, and to press that delicate, pure and blooming young body to him.

"You see, Lucan," he said, moved as he felt that he might now allow himself a more familiar form of address, and further moved by the deep, fatal shiver, which, at his words, ran through the young girl, "I have been placed in a peculiar position." He was silent for a short while. "However highly I respected my noble late wife, there were between us none of the feelings which young girls like yourself call romantic. After her death my home was lonely to me. Under other circumstances, I might have tried to make it happier through a new marriage with a lady of my own circle. But as you know, I am tried by a sad misfortune: my son is blind! He is, as you yourself have realized, an unusually intelligent child. I have not given up the hope that, in spite of his affliction, he may still, by careful training, become capable of carrying on my firm. But if I had had a younger son by a new marriage, a conflict might become inevitable, and I might be compelled to wrong my eldest, unhappy son."

He went on in a changed voice. "All the same you must not doubt that I will stand by you under all circumstances. You have spoken to me of your young brothers. I gather that these boys are very dear to you. . . ."

"No," Lucan interposed, abruptly and in a low voice, "you must not talk of my brothers."

"Yes, my child," he said softly, "I particularly want to speak to you of your brothers. They are, I understand, talented, brilliant boys without any practical sense, just like your father. . . ."

"No," Lucan once more whispered, "you must not name my father."

"Aye, believe me," said Mr. Armworthy, "I respect your father. I have been making inquiries about him, and understand him to have been worthy of a happier lot. At times," he continued, smiling blandly to himself, "I have compared the tenderness I feel for you with his. Believe me, you may trust me, and feel convinced that in all that may ever happen to you, I will show the same care for you as he himself would have wished to give you, had it been possible. When I declare that I will help your brothers where I can—and my help may not be quite without value to them—you will gather from this that anybody near you shall at the same time be near and precious to me myself."

He suddenly broke off, looked away, and once more back at the girl. After a moment he rose, and seemed to expect that she too should rise. When she kept sitting in the chair, absolutely immovable, as if she had not realized that he had changed his position, he gently lifted her up toward him, and it seemed to him that she was wavering on his arm. Her emotion communicated itself to him.

"And now," he said, "you must let this night pass, before you give me your answer." His voice broke, and she felt the same shiver run along his arm. "Good night, good night, my dear," he said. "It is hard to have to part from you in this way. A good-night kiss might perhaps be no more than my right. But I will not claim this right here, and not at the present moment. Soon —soon, I hope, in surroundings that may prove to you the sincerity of my feelings, I may be claiming even more than . . ." He stopped. The face of the sedate and reserved man colored into a deep, burning red; his high fine stock suddenly appeared to have become too tight for him; he grew silent, and forgot to accompany the girl to the door.

While he remained standing immobile in front of the fire, staring after her slim figure, without a word, and without any intimation of either consent or refusal, she walked out of the room.

4. flight

LUCAN came up to her own room in such confusion and anguish as if someone had given her a hard slap on each cheek. The most terrible, the bitterest thing to her during the first minutes was that she had not shown Mr. Armworthy how deeply she resented him. She sat down on onc chair, rose, and sat down upon another. Her face burnt, and then again she grew very pale. Before she had gone down to the conversation with Mr. Armworthy, she had summoned within her mind her father and her friends to advise and help her. Now it seemed to her that there were no other people in the world than the man who had offended her and herself.

She went to the window, and in the dusk once more took in the outlines of the big trees in the park. Slowly all the meditations which had gone through her mind, while she had been gazing at these groups of trees an hour ago, now came back to her.

An hour ago she had asked herself if she could ever possibly come to love Mr. Armworthy. "And if I had loved him," she now thought, "might I then have done what he wanted? No, it would then have been a hundred times worse. If I had been ready to give him my whole life, and he, in return, would have offered me a small part of his own, the time and the feelings left over from more important matters—then I should have died at the thought of such a proposition."

While she was thus repeating his words to herself with trembling lips, and searching her mind for the answers she ought to have given him, she had already, deeper down in her consciousness, decided to leave the house. She had even opened a drawer and taken out a few things from it: her purse, in which was the three months' salary that had just been paid out to her, a night-gown, and a pair of gloves. Now she stood quite still, and tried to concentrate her whole being upon the task before her.

She would not for anything in the world again meet Mr. Armworthy face to face. She must go away tonight. Very methodically, as if she had for a long time prepared herself for the journey, she now packed the most necessary clothes into an old leather traveling bag which had belonged to her father. But she dared not walk down the stairs to get out of the house; she might wake up some of the servants, or Mr. Armworthy himself might hear her, open his door and come out. She was not certain either if, by herself, she would be able to open the heavy lock of the entrance door.

She would have to find another way out. Outside her window was a balcony, and an old ivy twined its strong stems all the way from the ground to the balustrade. She had, before now, playfully pictured to herself how, by these, as by the steps of a ladder, Romeo might climb to her room. She did not know of giddiness, and she had no other way out.

She could not climb down from the balcony with her bonnet on because she then could not look sideways. She fastened it to her traveling bag by the long bonnet-strings, and then with her shawl fastened the bag to her waist. As she stepped onto the balcony and felt the night air round her, she closed her eyes for a minute. Her thoughts went to the sleeping children; she wished that she could have said good-bye to them. But it would be too risky. And then, she reflected, they were Mr. Armworthy's children, and might some day have given her as terrible a surprise as their father had! She collected all her courage, lifted her knee onto the balustrade and fumbled for a foothold in the twisted branches of the ivy.

The traveling bag knocked against the wall a couple of times, and nearly made her lose her balance. Her skirt was caught in the twigs and the foliage, and was lifted high over her knee, so that, in the dark, with burning cheeks, she thought, "It is a good thing that nobody can see me!" On the next floor, below her own room, there was another balcony. She would have liked to have rested here for a moment, but she saw a light behind the door, remembered that this room was Mr. Armworthy's bedroom, and in great haste threw herself over the broad rail. A branch at this moment caught her hair, as if it had been Mr. Armworthy himself who seized it and tried to stop her, but it broke off, and a few minutes later, stretching her foot as far down as possible, she felt the ground below it.

Twigs and leaves from the ivy were hanging in her long curls, her right hand was bleeding, and one of her stockings was torn. She was glowing with exertion and triumph, but her legs were trembling, so that for a moment she sat down on the ground with her head on her knees. Then she got up, unfastened the bag and put on her bonnet.

The heavy iron gate to the garden was locked at night, but from her walks with the children she knew of a small door in the wall which was closed only with a hook on the inside, and she quickly walked toward it. As she closed this door behind her, she closed an epoch of her life, the happy light-heartedness of the last months, the irresolution of the last few days, and the panic of this evening. She was robbed now of some hopes and illusions, poor as before, or poorer, but she was free!

She had known, already when she pulled out the drawer in her room, which way she would take, and she at once made for her destination. At half past eleven the night coach passed a cross-road not more than a mile from Mr. Armworthy's house, and stopped here, if there were passengers to take up. The four strong horses would quickly carry her far away, and her whole mind clung to them and to the postilion who would be driving them. A couple of times she had to stop and put down the heavy bag. She became afraid that she would be late for the coach, and walked on as quickly as possible, but she would not run. Mr. Armworthy should not force her to that! But as, quite out of breath, she reached the cross-road, she heard the clock of the village church strike eleven, and realized that she was in time and was saved.

The moon was now up, and the landscape around her lay in a

silvery mist. There was a great view over the open, undulating country. The grass was wet with dew. Lucan had but rarely been out so late, and never alone. But she was not afraid. Like a person who has escaped from prison and from the abhorred presence of an enemy, she was longing solely for wide space and solitude.

Only at this moment did it occur to her that she did not know where she meant to go from here. Her resolution to get away from Mr. Armworthy's house had brought her to the stopping place of the coach. Her thoughts had not traveled any further. In the course of the night, she knew, one coach was going north, and another south. Sad and sick at heart, she reflected that she might just as well take the one as the other. There was nothing in her existence which could decide for her.

Her relations would be dismayed, should she take refuge with them as a fugitive from a situation of which she had spoken with joy in her letters. If she were to look for another situation, she would have to give references, and this might once more bring Mr. Armworthy into her life. And all the same, she realized, she would have to go somewhere.

Alas, she thought, her father had been right, and imagination was indeed a necessity in life. But she herself was an inexperienced girl, without imagination. She became as afraid to see the carriage approach before she had made up her mind as, a short time ago, she had been to miss it.

In her distress she could think of no other resort than going through the alphabet from beginning to end in the hope of stumbling on the name of a person or a place she could throw herself upon. She had almost come all through it without result, and was about to despair, when in the last moment, at the letter Z, a name struck her and kindled a sudden bright light in the darkness around her. Zosine! "God! Zosine," she thought. "Dear Zosine. I had not thought of you for such a long time. But now you must help me."

Zosine had been her best friend at the boarding-school. This school was somewhat above Lucan's own social sphere, and was for the greater part frequented by girls of noble and rich families.

But her father's sister, who was its headmistress, had obtained admission for her, and Lucan had passed a few happy years there. When it became known that she and Zosine were born on the very same day, the other girls in the class had christened them the "Twins."

The two girls at that time had vowed an eternal friendship, and Zosine had often invited Lucan to spend her holidays with her in her father's house "Tortuga." She had even written: "Nothing of all the things which I have got to amuse myself with at Tortuga gives me any pleasure whatever, now that you will not come and share them with me." But after the time when, at her mother's death, Lucan had been fetched home from school, they had not met, and slowly their correspondence had ceased.

It was as if, during her years of worry, of poverty and dependence, she had shunned the radiant picture of her former friend, and had not cared to approach Zosine, or to appear before her, even in thought. But now, in the hour of real distress, this friendship of her childhood, with all the happiness, warmth and life that it had contained, stood up before the lonely girl at the crossroad, and she caught at it and clung to it.

The picture of Zosine came to the lonely girl at the cross-road as a radiation of life and warmth. "Surely," she thought, "it must be all Zosine's schemes of flight and adventure, and our secret nocturnal walks, which now make me think of her."

At the same moment she heard the noise of the carriage, and at a turn of the road the lanterns of the coach appeared and approached.

5. fellow-travelers

THE coach rattled on steadily through the moonlit landscape, with its freight of sleepy passengers, who nodded beneath the dim lantern, coughed and rubbed the window-panes to see how far they had gone.

In a corner a young girl sat breathless and motionless with her traveling bag beside her. She now realized that she was deadly tired and that her limbs ached. From time to time her heart beat violently, as it had when she had been hanging in the ivy on her flight down the wall.

But she was no longer alone, she had a fellow-traveler with her: Zosine sat beside her. Everything that belonged to Zosine was childlike, pretty and gay. Zosine had possessed elegant frocks, bonnets and mittens, which she had lent to Lucan, when they went to church or promenaded with her schoolmates. She had boxes with candied fruit sent from home, and shared them with her friend. The dream of the unknown house, from which all these treasures came, had occupied and intrigued Lucan, when she was twelve years old. Now she once more tried to picture to herself how it would look, and how it would receive her, when on her flight she should seek shelter there.

She knew that Zosine, like herself, had lost her mother, and that, like herself, she loved her father above everything on earth. Mr. Tabbernor was a tremendously rich merchant, probably, Lucan thought, what one called a millionaire. He owned great properties in the West Indies; his father and his grandfather had owned them before him, and had been married to heiresses of noble birth. Zosine's own mother, however, had not been rich, but Lucan knew that she had been a beauty, a Frenchwoman by birth, that she had come from Santo Domingo, and that it was from her that Zosine had her foreign name. From all that Lucan had ever heard, Zosine's home must be an earthly paradise of a unique and fantastic nature. Many tropical trees and shrubs had been brought from far away and had been planted in the park. There were hothouses with rare flowers and fruit, and a big glass house with small monkeys and parrots. A strange and exotic figure within the house itself was the old Negress, Olympia, who was so fat that she could hardly get in through any of its doorways. She had been the nurse of Zosine's Papa, and, thus, must be as old as the hills, but she belonged to a particular tribe which never did age; she was still as lively and garrulous as a parrot, and would surely live to the age of a hundred. When Zosine's Papa himself, as his daughter said, was as big and heavy as an elephant, it was all due to the supernatural power of his nurse's milk. Olympia, Zosine said, was a real angel, and at the same time something of a devil. When some time Olympia's flow of speech should come to a stop, then the end of the world would be near.

Zosine herself as a child had been to the West Indies; later on she had traveled with her Papa in France, Germany and Italy, and she was gaily looking forward to other great journeys. "There must not be any sky in the world," she proclaimed, "which has not looked down on Zosine Tabbernor." She had two riding horses, the names of which Lucan still remembered. In the memory of her friend she had all the look of a butterfly, forever fluttering in the sun.

As she drove on, Lucan remembered more and more things connected with Zosine. There was her Aunt Arabella, Mr. Tabbernor's cousin, an elderly, tremendously rich and tremendously ugly maiden-lady, who in the old days, before Zosine's father met his wife, had been in love with him, and therefore never had married. She was Zosine's godmother, adored her and gave her all she asked for. There was likewise her Cousin Ambrose. Ambrose's mother had been Papa's favorite sister, and had married the son of an Earl. When this splendid personage had spent all his wife's money and had died, Papa took charge of his youngest sister's only child; he placed him in a fine school, and in time meant him to carry on all his own affairs. Yes, very likely in his heart he hoped to see Ambrose married to his own daughter. But in that chapter Papa was mistaken, Zosine said, for Ambrose was nothing but a little dandy and fob, who spent money, and depended on Papa to pay his debts! All these people, who had played such big parts in the fancies of her childhood, Lucan might now come to see with her own eyes.

It slowly began to grow light through a thick morning mist. Lucan looked out upon a strange landscape. She saw the grass-fields white with dew, and the sun a dim red ball in the mist rising from the earth. It was as if the breaking morning light belonged to her flight, and to the thoughts of Zosine. She had ventured to take her destiny in her own hands—and the first effect thereof was a sunrise!

At Staines the coach changed horses, and the travelers got out. A young farmer with a gun on his shoulder, who had been staring at Lucan ever since it began to grow light, was waiting for her by the step of the coach, and gave her his hand to help her down. But she refused to enter the inn with him or the others, and kept standing outside. She shivered a little in the morning air, and drew her shawl tighter round her. Through the open window she could hear her fellow-travelers order hot drinks and bread, and felt that she herself was cold and weary, and that a cup of tea would have done her good. But she did not know how to give her orders to the waiter or the maid of the inn, for it was, surely, a highly unusual thing that a young girl should thus be traveling alone. Another coach, which came from the west and was going up to London, had now also stopped in front of the stable, and the coachmen were taking out the relays. As she had nothing else to do, Lucan kept following their movements. The mist had grown thicker, and the steam from the horses mixed with it. At the same moment she became aware of a lady who stood and looked at her.

The lady was dressed in gray, and had a small gray veil on her bonnet. She had come so noiselessly that it seemed to the young girl that she must be one with the morning mist, and had just stepped out of it. At the first moment she was almost frightened, and searched her memory to find out if the newcomer could possibly have known her before and have recognized her. But she was set at ease, when she saw the old lady smiling at her. She was sure, too, that she had never seen this face or this figure before.

The lady was probably between fifty and sixty years old. "An old maid," Lucan thought. She was small, angular and flat-breasted, with a long face and a broad, flat nose. She had such big and long teeth that there hardly seemed to be room for them in her mouth. Her face and hands were almost as gray as her hat and shawl. She kept on smiling to Lucan, but for a long time she neither moved nor spoke a word.

At last she said, "I saw you as you stepped down from the coach, my dear. I myself did arrive with the other coach. Are you waiting for somebody here?"

Lucan, a little embarrassed, explained that she was alone.

"Would it not be a good thing for you to come in and have a cup of tea?" the old lady asked. "There is still time for it." She had a deep, somewhat raucous voice, and she must, Lucan reflected, come from some distant part of the country; she stressed her words in a peculiar way. "You need not hesitate," she added. "I myself want a cup of warm tea badly, and should like to have your company."

The unknown lady was the first human being who had spoken to Lucan since Mr. Armworthy said good night to her. She took her kindness as a good omen, and accepted her invitation with thanks.

Within the big common-room of the inn a small corner by a screen had been turned into a compartment for traveling ladies. Lucan here arranged her hair and put her bonnet straight in front of the small looking-glass upon the wall. The little old lady seemed to be an experienced traveler, and not in the least afraid of the waiter. Perhaps she was also used to act as a duenna, for she appeared to be setting up a second, invisible screen round the girl, and solely by her sharp glance dismissed the rubicund young man who dawdled over the teacups to gaze at her pretty face.

"Are you really traveling all alone, my young Miss?" she asked, as she poured out the tea.

"Yes, I am alone," answered Lucan.

"But then somebody will meet you where you get out of the coach?" the lady asked.

"No, I do not think so," said Lucan, and blushed a little.

The old lady was silent for some time, but above her teacup she kept her round gray eyes on the girl. "Is it a situation to which you are going?" she suddenly enquired. "If so, I hope you will find it a nice one. You are pretty, and look sensible. You ought to be well paid. It is pleasant for a young girl to have dainty frocks and bonnets, and a bracelet or a brooch to fasten her shawl with. A new bonnet might look sweet on that golden hair at which everybody seems to be gazing. The time of youth is soon past."

The hot tea, and a fresh bun, made Lucan feel easier. She thought, "This little lady has all the look of one of the fairy-godmothers in my old book at home! What if she were now to offer me to change a pumpkin into a coach, and four little mice into horses? Nay, I forget I have got both a coach and horses to it. I hope then that she will not retransform them into mice again, so that I shall get no farther!"

"But surely people are expecting you at the place to which you are going?" the stranger persistently continued her questioning.

Lucan did not want to say "no" once more; she only shook her head. The old lady drank two cups of tea in absolute silence. As if she did not quite know what to do with all her big teeth, she seemed to have got into the habit of munching, or of rubbing them gently against each other, when she did not speak.

"Well, it is no affair of mine," she exclaimed in the end.

The other travelers had already begun to leave the common-room to get into the coach. Lucan fumbled in her pocket to pay for her tea. "That we can settle later on," said the lady, "in the coach. For can you imagine, my dear, what bad luck I have just had? I have forgotten a highly important thing—the most important of all to me—at the place from which I come! I begin to think that I shall have to turn straight back to get it, by that same coach with which you yourself are going. Then we can have a nice little chat, and get to know each other on the way."

They left the inn together. But as they walked toward the coach, with the fresh horses ready, and the postilion on the box, the old lady slackened her pace, in the end stood quite still, and with a strained and troubled face twice slowly shook her head at herself. "No," she said, "no, it will not do. It is impossible. I must say good-bye to you here, my little Miss." Lucan gave her her hand.

The old lady kept looking straight at her. "I might give you my address," she said very slowly, "in case you were to come to London later on, you know, to look for a better situation." She once more broke off, and abruptly, almost angrily cried out, "No, no, I must not do it! I have been told not to do it!" She was still holding one of the girl's fingers, and was so loath to let it go that she kept pinching it quite hard. "But it is a pity," she whispered in her hoarse voice, "it is indeed a pity. You are such a good girl, so pure and prudent, such a tender little lamb that surely he, whose will we must all obey, would smile at seeing you get what you deserve." She reluctantly let go her hold of the girl's hand, but she followed her with her light round eyes, while she got into the coach, and until the coachman cracked his whip, and it rolled off.

Now that it was getting lighter, the coach could make better speed. The inn with its many outbuildings, the high stacks of hay and the big elm trees that surrounded them soon were swallowed up in the white mist. A little later in the morning the sun broke through the veils that had covered it. The young farmer with the gun kept on staring at Lucan, so that soon she pulled down her own veil. Behind it she thought of many things: of the humiliation, which she wanted to forget, but which still from time to time drove the blood to her cheeks, and of the dim, sweet light of hope that shone before her. Once or twice she also thought of the meeting at the inn. Already now, only a mile or two from the inn, it looked strange and unreal to her. She did not know what to make of it.

6. Zosine

In Xanadu did Kubla Khan
a mighty pleasure-dome decree . . .

THE first lines of a poem that she had read with her father re-echoed in Lucan's mind as she slowly walked through the big park. She gazed round her, stood still, and again walked on. Her light face took on a still, happy radiance.

Tortuga was in reality at this time one of the most famous show places in the south of England. For a hundred years its owners, who were all great travelers with love and knowledge of nature, art, and fine workmanship, had given their time and wealth to create and perfect it. The first of them had built the house and laid out the park and the garden. The second, who had married a peer's widow, had embellished the place, in particular by a number of artificial graceful ponds and canals. The third, the present owner, who found it already finished, had, as it were, playfully, added a multitude of fresh and fantastic details, so that now novel, surprising and enchanting sights met the eye on all sides. He generously left his property open to the public on certain days of the week during summer, and on such days the park and garden were crowded with promenading gentlemen, ladies and children who had often come from distant places and who could hardly satiate their eyes with the charms of Tortuga.

Within the clear light of this early May morning, the beauty of the scenery was at its highest; the air was fresh and mild and filled with the fragrance of flowers and foliage.

Lucan walked through a long avenue of blossoming Javanese cherry trees which seemed to float above her head like clouds of exquisite rose. A little farther on, the delicate, silvery branches of a Chinese willow tree, the leaves not yet altogether unfolded, drooped like an elegant waterfall into a deep green pond, wherein black swans were floating. Here she sat down on a seat for a few minutes. She had forgotten that she did not fit in with these rich and lovely surroundings, that her frock had a long tear, and that the stocking which she had ripped in the night had become so ragged that she had pulled it off behind a tree on the road, so that now—as she had thought it better to let the other stocking follow it—she was barefooted in her dusty shoes. She was dwelling in a sphere of delight and gratitude. She thought: "It is equally wonderful that people can have the imagination to invent all these things and that they have the power to turn them into realities."

The wealth which she had known in Mr. Armworthy's house had been heavy and, as it were, self-conscious; it had not tempted her. But this was like the places she had seen in her own dreams, and it seemed friendly, almost familiar. By the big gate to the park the lodge-keeper, standing outside the lodge, had given her and her bag a little jovial nod, as if he had been expecting her. In the park she saw gardeners and boys at work. They passed her with big baskets of flowers, and they too looked at her as if she were expected and welcome.

On the other side of a broad terrace, where tall clear fountains splashed, the house itself now lay before her, luminous in the morning sun, with its colossal double marble stairway and row of white pillars. Here some people were occupied in hanging up Chinese lanterns. "Will they be doing so every night," Lucan wondered, "in order that the inhabitants of the house may sit on that terrace and enjoy the sight of the green, yellow and crimson lights?" An old servant came out of the house to give his instructions to the men. She remembered that Zosine had mentioned her father's old trusted and faithful servant John. She seemed to recognize him in the small dignified figure, and, collecting all her courage, approached him, told him her name, and asked if she could possibly see Miss Zosine.

After having looked at her attentively for a minute, the old servant told her to follow, and picked up her bag. As they came up to the house, he seemed to hesitate whether to conduct her to the main entrance or to the wing of the house, when, at the same moment, a young lady in a striped frock appeared on the top of the stair between the pillars. She cried out an order to him in a clear and sonorous voice, broke off, shaded her eyes with her hand, and, as in surprise, exclaimed, "Who have you got with you there?" It was Zosine.

Lucan stood gazing at her, while the old servant deferentially went up to her, and the young lady quickly came down a few steps of the stairway. Lucan recognized her old school friend in the slim and light figure. But she had not been prepared to find Zosine again as a grown-up, elegant and fashionable young lady; she was deeply and happily moved by the apparition. Zosine exchanged a couple of words with the old man, and then came swiftly toward her, stood still and fixed a pair of very clear eyes on her.

"Miss Bellenden?" she asked slowly. "What do you want here? Who has sent you?" Lucan was frightened and distressed to see that Zosine did not seem to recognize her. Her heart beat violently, and she felt as if her life depended upon overcoming this unexpected misfortune. For a few seconds the two young girls looked at each other gravely.

"Yes, I am Lucan," she said. "I come here because of an invitation of many years ago. Much has changed for me since then. My father is dead. I no longer have a home of my own. I have fled from the place where I was last, to come to you."

"Lucan?" Zosine repeated slowly, and immediately after, as if surprised and seized, "Fled? Did you say that you had fled? Why?"

Lucan had meant to throw herself upon Zosine's neck. She had been happy when the old servant had taken her bag, because then she had both arms free for this purpose. Now she sadly stretched out her right hand, more as a farewell than a welcome.

"Yes, I am a fugitive," she said with trembling lips. "If you will not receive me, I do not know where to turn."

Zosine's clear, wide-opened eyes were steadily fixed upon Lucan's face. She took her hand, but still held her own arm outstretched, and kept the distance between them.

"A fugitive," she repeated, with profound concern. "How does it feel to be a fugitive?" Suddenly, as if the touch had wakened her slumbering memory, her whole face colored deeply.

"Lucan," she cried out, "is it you? Are you coming here today? How is it possible that I did not recognize you at once?" She threw herself into the arms of her friend, again withdrew to look at her, and once more embraced her with all her might. "Have you come at last?" she cried. "And today of all days! You are as lovely as ever! No, you are even lovelier!" For a short while neither spoke.

"I knew you at once," Lucan said, blushing and radiant, "but how charming and elegant you have grown!"

"Me?" Zosine cried. "No, I am not charming. When they all tell me so, it is only to give me pleasure. A young lady must be charming, or it is too hard on her Papa. It is true that I have a waist which many girls envy! But you, you have a real, genuine bust!"

"Oh, it is so delightful to be here," said Lucan.

They talked for the sake of talking, as when girls gently and lightly caress each other. "It is tremendous that you have come today," said Zosine and drew her breath in deeply.

"Why today?" Lucan asked in surprise.

"It is my birthday," cried Zosine. "I am eighteen today, and Papa is giving a ball in my honor!"

"Is it your birthday?" Lucan exclaimed, and tried to collect her thoughts. "Then it must be mine too."

"Indeed, it is yours too," Zosine called out. "Had you forgotten it? And is there no one else who has remembered it for you?" She took a short step back, and regarded Lucan from head to foot. "You come here all alone," she said, puzzled and slowly. "You have no stockings on! You are so pale! Lucan, how is it with you?" The alternate distress and happiness of the last few moments had in reality exhausted the girl; everything went black and she swayed on her feet.

"God," cried Zosine in great alarm, "you are ill, you are fainting!" She threw her arms round Lucan's waist. "Lean on me," she said. "I will support you. But fetch Marie," she cried to the old servant, who still kept at a short distance. "We must carry you into the house."

"No, no, I can walk," Lucan faintly protested, but at the same moment her strength gave way. She closed her eyes, and only dimly realized what was happening round her until she found herself seated in an armchair in an exquisite little room, with Zosine anxiously holding a glass of wine to her lips.

"Thank God," Zosine cried joyfully, "now you are looking a little bit better. Now you have a little bit of color in your cheeks. You are starving perhaps, and I am sure you have walked many miles. Marie," she called out to a pretty young girl in a black frock and a small white apron who must have followed them into the room. "Go and tell Master that I have great, wonderful news for him. My best friend has come here today to help me!"

Lucan looked round. In the midst of the exotic and fantastic splendor of Tortuga, this was the most graceful and dainty little room she had ever seen. The pink walls were covered with transparent, pleated white muslin which was gathered together at the top in a small frill. The four-poster was fitted up in the same way, and the pretty chairs and sofa were upholstered in a cream material with a pattern of roses in it.

Zosine's eyes followed Lucan's in their wandering about the room. "You see," she exclaimed triumphantly, "I had this room put up six years ago, when I believed you were to come and stay with me. And you, you wicked girl, deceived me, and never came. But now I have got you, and this time you may be sure that I am not going to let you off! If there is anything you are afraid of or distressed about, then rely upon me. I will do anything in the world for you. Yes," she repeated, slowly and solemnly, "anything in the world! And if you have fled, as you tell me, I shall take care that nobody catches you. There is nothing in the whole world that I will not do for a fugitive!"

7. the pink frock

"WHAT things happen in this world!" Zosine cried. "What a terrible old villain, a seducer downrightly. Why did you not go straight to the Queen?"

"To the Queen?" Lucan asked in surprise.

"Yes, to our lovely young Queen," Zosine said. "Her Majesty is only four years older than we. It is obvious that she would not, in her own kingdom, allow anyone to treat a young girl so abominably. Or, if the matter was too atrocious for her to concern herself with, she might make the Prince Consort—a sweet man, I have seen him myself—take the monster thoroughly to task."

Lucan had been sleeping till late in the afternoon on the deep pillows, and below the silken quilt, of the big four-poster. A short time after she had gone to sleep, the sweet melody of a waltz had mixed into her dreams. She half woke up, only to be told by Zosine who was still sitting by her bedside, "It is but the orchestra rehearsing in the ballroom beneath." A little later, she was vaguely aware that Zosine and a very portly old gentleman with long, noble, white whiskers were standing by her bed. Zosine clung to him and talked in a low voice and in great excitement, but Lucan did not comprehend what they said.

And at last she woke up altogether. The curtains of the room were drawn, and everything seemed to swim in a delicate rosy mist. She gazed in surprise at her own arms protruding from sleeves of batiste and lace. Then she remembered that Zosine and her maid had undressed her, attired her in one of Zosine's nightgowns and put her to bed. Beneath Marie's penetrating glance Lucan for the first time had felt ashamed of her old clothes.

"You need not be so bashful," Zosine said. "We have slept in the same room before now. And we have surely not become any less pleasant to look at since then." Lucan also had a breakfast tray brought to her in bed, and Zosine had held the spoon to her lips, as if she had been a little child. They had laughed together, just as in their school days. And then she had fallen into a deep slumber.

Now the two young girls, Lucan in a negligée of Zosine's, were sitting arm in arm in the sofa, and Lucan had recounted to her friend all that had happened to her. It was as if her misfortune had volatilized in this gay and pleasant room. She could now almost smile at Zosine's anger and indignation.

"You are right. We will think no more of him," said Zosine. "His picture is not worthy of being kept within your sweet, pretty head. But I think," she added thoughtfully, "that you are a girl to whom many wonderful things are sure to happen in this world."

"Alas, you are quite wrong," said Lucan. "Do you not remember when, at school, you wanted me to take part in some kind of adventure, I was always too timid? I myself last night reflected that my father was right in telling me that I have no imagination."

"But perhaps that is just the way of the world," said Zosine, "and destiny will lose her interest in those people who are themselves capable of inventing things. She will leave them to have things happen to them within their own imagination. But with you she will take trouble to contrive the most extraordinary events."

"Tonight," she said after a while, "we will cudgel our brains and invent something quite exquisite. I want you to be the very loveliest lady of the ball, and we must find out which of my frocks to choose for you. They are sure to fit you. We used to be of the same height, and I believe we are so still."

They solemnly measured themselves, back to back, before the looking-glass, and found they were really the same height.

"At school," Zosine said, "my hair was just as long and pretty as yours. But I was ill last winter. That is why it has been cut off.

Still, such golden curls as yours will always be more perfect than my brown ones, and indeed I have before now been envious of your head of sunshine. But in order really to decide well," she suddenly cried, "we must have Olympia with us."

In Mr. Armworthy's house Lucan would have been horror-struck at the unexpected appearance of the old, coal-black woman, who the next moment entered the room. But here at Tortuga it was as if Zosine was quietly and playfully holding up before her every fantastic picture of a picture-book which she had already known as a child. Olympia was just the exotic and wonderful person Lucan, years ago, had figured to herself. She was as big and heavy as a hippo, so that, as she came in, she filled the whole doorway, and she seemed as placid and good-natured as a big wild animal in the zoo. She had a small, gaudy silk cap on her head. Beneath it her face broadened all the way down to the chin, so that her fat cheeks almost hid her neck. Every movement was heavy, but at the same time had a strange, serpentine, swaying grace.

But Olympia was also as dumb as a picture in a book. Zosine had once told that the old woman was as garrulous as a parrot. Now she did not open her lips, and it seemed to Lucan that her black eyes, yes, that her fat arms themselves, hanging down limply at her side, expressed a kind of wild and mute despair. "She has grown old," Lucan thought, "and surely, she is now longing for her old country."

Zosine placed Lucan in the middle of the floor, and the old Negress in an armchair opposite her. "Look!" she said. "My Papa, who knows his beloved daughter to be a little capricious, and to have her whims, has given me three new frocks for the dance tonight: one pink, one blue and one white. But I myself have thought of my poor Mama, who was a Frenchwoman by birth, although her parents emigrated from France during the Revolution, and before she was born, and she herself did never see her beloved country. Those old emigrants hated and detested the new, three-colored French flag; they stuck to the ancient, royal, white banner of France. And how could I wear either the pink or the blue frock, when they are put before me like this, in the manner of the Tricolor? It is to be the white frock for me tonight. Still the other colors are sweet too, when you take them one by one. Is not this a lovable pink, like the petal of a dewy, sweet-scented rose, that does not know itself how pretty it is? It is the very frock for you, Lucan!"

Lucan could hardly believe that she was not dreaming, as, in the frock held up by Zosine, she perceived the exact duplicate of the one of which she had so often thought. It was made of heavy, very pale rose satin, with broad lace round the shoulders and the flounces, and to make the whole thing perfect, it was trimmed with buds of moss-roses, as live and fresh as if they had just been picked in the garden. Surely it must have taken more than twenty yards of satin to make the flounced skirt alone, and as Lucan thought of this, her cheeks became as sweetly pink as the frock itself. She turned her happy, dreaming eyes toward her friend. "Yes, indeed, that is your frock," said Zosine.

In front of the looking-glass the girl, with growing excitement and delight, watched herself transformed into a great lady and a beauty so enchanting that the sight took away her own breath. As keen and eager as if she was dressing a doll, Zosine found and sent for new articles of finery. She made Marie bring forth ear-rings, bracelets, a garland of flowers for Lucan's pretty hair, a narrow black velvet ribbon for her white throat, and, to complete the whole, a pair of little white gloves with scalloped edges. She gave the old black woman more than one angry and indignant glance, because she kept sitting in her chair as silent as if she did not notice how Zosine's masterpiece was advancing toward perfection. Once only, as Zosine asked her old nurse to arrange the lace round Lucan's smooth shoulders, she lifted one of the girl's long golden curls in her hand, and seemed to wonder at its color and luster.

While the three women were in this way absorbed in their undertaking, the old footman or butler, whom Lucan had seen in the garden, came in to ask for some direction about the ball in the evening. But Zosine sent him off. "I would rather stay with you," she said. "Papa will arrange all the other matters. Alas, then he will be tired, and have to leave the ball early to go to bed.

And he shall be free to do so. For he is so terribly fat, my poor sweet Papa, that his heart cannot possibly stand any strain."

She took a step back, and drew a deep sigh of content. "You are a wonder!" she exclaimed. "I wish I looked like you."

"But it is nothing but a play, a joke, Zosine," Lucan said, "and I cannot possibly keep your frock on."

"Oh, you can have much more than that," Zosine cried out, as if struck by a sudden idea. And as if there was no longer any limit to her whims, she opened the doors of all the wardrobes, pulled out all the drawers in the room, and threw the contents onto bed, sofa, and chairs.

In a moment heaps of delicate, sweet-scented linen, silk stockings and petticoats covered every piece of furniture in the room; bonnets and shawls were hurled on top of them, together with pair after pair of little neat shoes. Lucan, quite bewildered, recalled what the old lady in the inn had said to her. Was this the effect of her magic power? She tried to hold back her friend.

"Zosine, Zosine," she cried, "stop it! Do you imagine that I would ever accept all this? You yourself would have nothing left then."

Zosine stood still and looked at her. "Listen," she said, suddenly quite grave, "I am going to tell you something. From tomorrow I will wear nothing of all this. It is better that you should have it."

It occurred to Lucan that some great change and event in the life of her friend must be about to take place. Zosine was to marry, her trousseau was ready, and this was the reason why she was so rashly giving away all her maiden wardrobe. Still holding Zosine's hand, which she had seized to stop the mad frolics, she smilingly searched her face. "Tell me," she said imploringly, "will your cousin Ambrose be here tonight?"

"Ambrose?" Zosine asked, looking straight back at her. "How does it occur to you to ask me about him?"

"In the old days you used to talk so much about him, I thought that perhaps you might still have a tenderness for him," Lucan said. "And, indeed, you must confide in me, if you are going to announce your engagement tonight."

"Alas, poor Ambrose," Zosine burst out laughingly, "he is the only one of all my friends whom you will not see tonight. He has got a most shocking cold in the head, and cannot possibly come to my ball. Yes, indeed, Ambrose is a dashing spark! But I will confide something to you: tomorrow, sure enough, he will come and tell me that he will never in his life propose to me. And I shall not die from grief at that either. I am not thinking of lovers tonight," she added gravely.

Something in Zosine's manner confused and bewildered her friend. It was as if, underneath the childish, thoughtless surface, great waves of suspense and passion were running. Lucan could not possibly imagine that Zosine had ever had any experience of care or sadness, but she thought: "If she is always in such violent emotion, and if her moods are always changing so swiftly, how can she possibly have kept alive, even until the age of eighteen?"

Zosine met her gaze as if she was reading her thoughts. "Listen," she said slowly, "you will be the queen of the ball tonight, and all our beaux will be at your feet. But you must not fall in love with any of them. Aye," she added in the same way, after a pause, "if you can make any of them so deeply enamored of you that he will declare himself at once, and that we may announce the engagement at supper, then you may do so. But otherwise not! If you care for me at all," she cried, throwing herself on Lucan's neck, "you must give me your word of honor on that."

8. zosine's birthday ball

A BALL to a young girl is not only an experience or an adventure; it is a revelation. When she dances, she realizes why she exists, and why she was born. As the poet in the moment of inspiration, transported and beautiful, sees himself as the interpreter of the universe, so does the girl, as she glides over the floor, conceive the truth both about herself and about life. The poet in such a second is solely spirit. But a young girl is eminently body, and the beatitude to her lies in the perfect harmony between matter and spirit. Her limbs themselves are inspired and winged, her small feet take command and great heavenly powers descend into the ballroom, and yield obedience.

Lucan had gone through a dancing course at school, but had never been a brilliant pupil. She had no idea that, when a large orchestra carried her, and an experienced partner led her, she could dance as if she had come into the world waltzing. Zosine had taken care that her programme was filled, or she would have taken care of it, had not the ardent young beaux on their own crowded round the girl in the pink frock. During the first waltz and the lanciers, it was the enchantment of the dance that swayed the girl, but after the second waltz, her own nature was drawn a step further, and it was to life itself that she surrendered. She was in love, but her feeling applied equally to each of her partners, so that she was indeed unable to prefer one to another, even clearly to distinguish the one elegant black figure and eager admiring face from the next. She knew that her emotions tonight were mysterious, but she did not feel them to be dangerous. She innocently apprehended that if Mr. Armworthy had offered her a ball every night of the year, she might have taken his offer into consideration. The other young ladies of the ball looked at the unknown young girl with increasing attention and jealousy. The old ladies, who chaperoned their daughters or nieces, put up their lorgnettes.

Three big chandeliers beamed down upon an undulating sea of light colors, rhythmic movements and radiating faces. The ballroom and the adjoining apartments were filled with flowers, and the silk, satin and lace frocks of the ladies were themselves as gay and varied as big bouquets. The black cavaliers seemed to be there only to set off the joyous feminine grace. A few of them, who were dressed in uniform, impressed Lucan as being at the same time chivalrously competing with, and chivalrously laying down their arms before, her own sex. The tall windows of the ballroom opened to the terrace. Here between the dances the couples promenaded below long festoons of Chinese lanterns. At the end of the room there was a winter garden. In its dim light palms, giant ferns and creepers were faintly seen, and from the midst of its marble floor, a slim jet of water played high up into the air.

Mr. Tabbernor had opened the ball with his daughter. The portly gentleman only swung her elfin figure round half the room, but within these few seconds it was made evident that he had once been a heavenly dancer, and in the smiles which his performance roused, there was a good deal of admiration. It seemed as if a majestic elephant had taken the floor for a moment.

To Lucan's eyes the master of the house, with whom she had only talked for a short while before the ball, was a benevolent protector, because, in spite of the difference in age and size, he was somehow like Zosine. The vivacity and self-confidence of the girl was also found within the colossal mask of the elderly gentleman, but it was here collected, and confirmed in a particular, grand and gentle calm. "These people," Lucan thought, "ignore what trouble and solicitude mean. They know nothing of the everyday life that others lead." She tried to represent to herself how one could possibly live in such a manner.

"This is my best friend," Zosine had declared, while they were still waiting for the first carriage to roll up in front of the mighty entrance door, and while the old servant John was directing the lighting of candles up the stairs. "Kiss her, Papa! I give you permission to do so, although in general she is exceedingly prudish, and has jumped out from a tower, and run through a wild wood at night, because an old gentleman like yourself was planning to kiss her!"

Between the dances Mr. Tabbernor walked from group to group of his guests, complimenting, or jesting with, the pretty young ladies. During one of these promenades Lucan's attention was caught by a young man, who, although she could not exactly have explained the reason for it, seemed to differ from the rest of the company. He was extremely neatly dressed, with curled and pomaded hair and whiskers, and he appeared to be following Mr. Tabbernor about wherever he went with a kind of obtrusive admiration. While the old gentleman was chatting with her, this young man joined them, had himself introduced to her, and delivered a number of exaggerated flatteries, before once more sliding off in the wake of his host. "Surely," she thought, "this is a young man in the office of Mr. Tabbernor who is all too keen to make a quick career for himself there." As, a little later, she and Zosine sat together, and the young man passed them Zosine exclaimed to her, "There you have made a conquest. And you are welcome to turn the young gentleman's head, and to make him forget his other duties tonight.

"Now the cotillion is to come," she went on, "and now I have got an earnest and humble prayer to you, Lucan. Papa cannot possibly go on all night telling us pretty things. Surely he should sit down now for a little while in the winter garden and look on, while we amuse ourselves. You would be a darling if you would keep him company there, and give him permission to smoke one of his loathsome cigars during the next dance. That is a hideous habit which people acquire in the West Indies. I know that it is a cruel thing to take you away from our young men. But I cannot myself leave my guests, nor can I let my poor Papa feel quite forsaken."

Lucan drew a little sigh because she had to give up her dance, but she was happy to do Zosine a service. She followed her and her father, who with great ceremonious charm thanked her for her kindness, across the floor into the winter garden. The hot, moist air in there was filled with the scent of earth and plants and of a multitude of exotic flowers.

Two big chairs were placed at the entrance to the ballroom, to which the glass doors were pushed open. Behind them the tall palms and creepers formed a dense, green thicket, as if one were sitting at the edge of a tropical forest. Zosine said, "Now you are to sit perfectly still, Papa, and only turn your eyes about to watch what fun I am having." Before leaving them, she turned back twice and put her arms round her father's neck.

"How those two love and understand each other," Lucan thought.

Mr. Tabbernor asked Lucan's permission to smoke, and lighted a big cigar. He sat very still, as Zosine had told him to, and with a little sweet smile followed the movements of the ballroom. "This is a pretty tune," he remarked, and told Lucan how in his young days he had played the 'cello, and had always taken great delight in all music. "When you have more than half your life behind you," he said, "you often feel that you have wasted your time in pursuits and ambitions of no actual value, while neglecting to do the things toward which your nature was truly inclined. I know your father's name," he added after a short pause. "I have read his books. They have helped me to realize how every small particle of creation confirms the unity of it. As a child, I lived in the West Indies, from where some of the plants that surround us have also come. I often long to go back there once more. During these last years I have many times reflected that the very best way of passing one's old age may well be that of the pious hermits of old: beneath the crown of a palm, with the shadows of the birds and the little monkeys up there playing before one's feet, and all the time, from every detail of the world, inferring the truth of the whole.

"Zosine is my only child," he said after a while, "I have always wished that she had had a sister. I myself had three sisters, people named them the graces of Tortuga. Alas, none of them is now alive. The two of them found happiness in the world; the third met with a sad destiny. But they always held together. When they grew up, my father gave them three fine sets of jewels, the one of opals, the second of nephrite, and the third of emeralds. They then each had three of the prettiest stones taken out, and again put together, within three rings, so that the initials of the stones formed the word 'One.' These rings they took with them into their graves. I wish that you might be such a sister to Zosine. Alas, I am afraid that my child is too much like her father."

He fell into deep thought, but tore himself away, and lighted a new cigar. "I shall bring you a rare flower," he said with a smile, "and beg you to keep it. It will be the token of my gratitude, because you sacrificed a dance for an old man."

He rose very slowly, and took a step or two in amongst the palms behind him. At that same moment, Zosine danced past them in the arms of the young gentleman with the pomaded hair. For a second Lucan imagined with dismay the possibility of Zosine being in love with this young man, and insisting on marrying him against her father's wish. Indeed, this might be the cause of her hidden agitation, and of the sadness of the old gentleman. Before she had had time to look into this distressing prospect, Mr. Tabbernor came back again, and once more took his seat beside her. Between the fingers of one hand he still held the lighted cigar, and between those of the other, a cream-colored, strongly scented flower, which, without a word, he handed to the girl.

"I know it," exclaimed Lucan, pleased at her own knowledge, "it is an orchid, the flower of the vanilla-plant. It grows in trees in damp places." She held it toward her face, and inhaled its sweet smell. "Flowers," she said, "one can always recognize. You cannot mistake one perfume for another. They cannot possibly pretend to be anything but what they are."

"No," said Mr. Tabbernor.

9. a strange dancing partner

THE varying figures of the cotillion wound in and out the ballroom and, every second, brought new and enchanting surprises. A small chariot, drawn by two snow-white angora goats, and piled with bouquets, rolled in and was surrounded and plundered, and immediately after, like an elysian torrent, hundreds of roses poured down from the ceiling. During the next figure a little gaudy and gilt pagoda was carried into the room, and a tiny Chinese distributed from it dainty fans and delicate silver bells. The big room was fluttering and twittering like an aviary. The faces of the young girls, whose arms were filled with flowers, were all on fire with the happiness of being admired and courted, and the most captivating cavaliers paraded, their chests covered with stars and ribbons, like aged deserving generals.

Mr. Tabbernor from time to time laid down his cigar on a flower pot to applaud a particularly graceful figure. Zosine had extricated herself for a moment from the long chain of dancers. Her white frock billowing round her, she ran into the winter garden, fastened a small bunch of flowers in her father's lapel, and was gone. Her example was followed by a multitude of pretty girls, and as, once more, they floated back into the dance, the old gentleman kissed his finger to them, but did not utter a word. Lucan herself had a rich collection of flowers in her lap, although she had refused to take the floor. She thought, "God! Perhaps I may stay in this house a little while yet, a month or a week! Perhaps this dream may last a little longer!"

Mr. Tabbernor cleared his throat a couple of times, held the cigar a little away from his shirt-front, and said, "Look, there

Zosine is dancing. And all these amiable young gentlemen dancing round her admire her or adore her. But some of them adore her because she is a rich girl and an heiress; others, *although* she is heiress, a millionaire's daughter. There may also be found among her cavaliers some idealistic youths, who adore her *in spite* of her being the future possessor of so many millions. But in the mind of every one of them, she is still, inevitably, in the one sense or the other, the heiress, the golden bird, in short, the big catch, and the prize! In the museums there are, as you know, pictures of female saints, painted upon a golden background. The saint will certainly remain the same, even if you remove this background. But the picture will change its character all through. The same thing would happen to our excellent Zosine, in the eyes of the world and of her adorers, if the background of golden circumstances, upon which they now observe her, should suddenly disappear."

"No, that would be impossible," said Lucan.

"Aye, believe me, I know the world," said Mr. Tabbernor, "and can one now in any way blame these exquisite young people for such a state of things? No, one cannot do so. The love of beautiful things is the instinct which has carried humanity forward from barbarism to civilization. Our entire existence is based upon it. It is imprinted on our young minds at school—somewhat inconsiderately, I have at moments reflected—and the preaching of it is conscientiously continued at the universities. You cannot, without it, be a civilized person—and it is thus open to discussion whether you can be a civilized person without getting into debt. It has taken centuries—eighteen hundred and forty years—eh?—to bring us to the point at which we really know by instinct that love without lace is but a mediocre affair. The whole lace industry, which—as you, my dear young lady, are sure to know—does employ thousands, aye, hundreds of thousands of people, is built up upon this refined and civilized point of view. Well, we have got so far, we have arrived at this conviction, and what, then, to a chivalrous man, a real gentleman, is the consequence? Answer: that he will on no account expose the woman whom he idolizes to the risk of offering her a love which—without lace—is worthy neither of him nor of herself. It is by no means a lack of reverence for woman which forces him to do so. It is, in diametrical opposition, our invincible veneration of woman in general and, in particular, of that young woman whom we happen to worship.

"Everything," Mr. Tabbernor continued, "everything for which human beings, from the barbaric stone age—of which we need speak no more here, as we are both fully acquainted with it—have labored and toiled, has in reality only striven to place woman within such surroundings as fit and agree with her, and as will be worthy of her. We have not yet, on any account, reached our goal. It will probably be another eighteen hundred and forty years before we can give to woman, the jewel of our existence, the setting to which she is entitled. For the whole world is still in an embryo state, and quite notoriously most of what is achieved is done by way of experiment. But Providence, most considerately, has given us at once a goal and a standard in your divine sex. Any young girl like Zosine or you yourself is, in reality, five hundred years ahead of the clumsy and savage male. We are aware of the fact; we take pleasure in endeavoring to make the coarse world of today come up with you, and to make it harmonize with your charms. But, in case the task becomes impossible—what then is left to the shamed barbarian? Nothing, indeed, but to take off his hat and declare, 'Thanks for the ideal with which you have graced my sphere of comprehension. The low and vulgar reality does herewith, within my sorry figure, take its leave of it, and of you. Nobody can regret it more than myself.' "

Lucan was surprised to hear the old gentleman talk in this way. Even his voice seemed to have changed. She did not know what to answer, and for a while sat on in silence. This appeared to put her partner somewhat out of tune. After a while he once more cleared his throat, and said, "Properly speaking, I ought not to discuss woman, love or lace. It is not my department. I am, as you know, a man of business, and business is what I understand. Money, assets and liabilities, accumulated interest, and so on. These are my pursuits. Only from time to time, in a free and happy moment, do I dare to occupy myself with the beauty of life. I might be tempted to tell you of my last great speculation. It would, I feel convinced, make your mind reel. The world of affairs, which is my true element, is filled with heavy problems, disappointments and delusions. Try to represent to yourself, my charming young lady, that a merchant adds to a cask of wine ten per cent of water. If he now were to add nine gallons more water, the mixture would contain as much water as it would contain wine. How many gallons of wine had he, then, at first?"

For a moment Lucan considered the possibility that the old gentleman quickly had taken a drop of something strong behind the palms while picking her flower. But he himself seemed entirely undisturbed and indeed highly pleased with his long speech, and he cheerfully went on, "If you were told the story of my childhood and youth, you would, while admiring me for what I have achieved in life, also pity me for what these results have cost me in wearing labor. A man would indeed be happier, if money were not, at every moment, such an indispensable necessity, and if he might really, as some philosophers appear to have proclaimed, live joyfully in an idyllic content without it."

No more than before could Lucan think of anything to answer, and her silence this time suddenly made Mr. Tabbernor highly uneasy. After a short pause he asked her, "What was it we were talking about before I left you to pick the flower?"

"We were talking of your sisters," Lucan answered.

"Of my sisters?" Mr. Tabbernor exclaimed. "Nay, that is impossible! And yet, by Jove, you are right, we were talking of my sisters. The one of them was to be sadly pitied—you would agree with me, if you knew her son! We were not discussing him, I suppose?"

Here the cotillion had come to an end, the music ceased, and the dancing couples spread to all sides.

Zosine came swiftly into the winter garden, still breathless with dancing. "Now, sweet Papa," she said, "you have sat here long enough, like a lovely idol, watching over us all. Now I give you permission to go to bed. But before you leave us, I will present you with the very last flower of the cotillion, to show that you are a seductive gentleman."

Mr. Tabbernor rose from his big chair, so slowly and with such difficulty that Lucan felt herself confirmed in the belief that he had had something to drink. Leaning on his daughter's arm, he walked all through the long ballroom, all the time slowly and with almost exaggerated dignity. A couple of times he stood still to exchange a few words with one of his guests. At the end of the ballroom he passed the young man whom Lucan, with so much reluctance, had seen as Zosine's dancing partner. He stopped in front of him, and smilingly took him by the lapel. "I hope," he said with pronounced kindness and geniality, "that you have had a pleasant evening. I am an old man. I have to leave you. But in my bed, here just above your head, the sweet tunes of the waltzes will still reach my ear. In my thoughts I will keep close to all these charming and happy young people, and, I give you my word, to you in particular."

His old servant was waiting for him at the doorstep, and he let go Zosine's arm to lean on John's. From the ballroom, one could still follow his heavy figure, as extremely slowly, step by step, he ascended the broad stair.

Zosine looked after him for a few seconds, and then with shining eyes turned toward the throng of the ballroom.

10. converse at dawn

THE candles in the chandeliers were nearly burnt down. Outside the tall windows the May morning made the Chinese lanterns look like strange, glowing fruits in the trees, and the grass was wet with the morning dew. The guests were taking leave. Contrary to the custom of the house none of them was to stay at Tortuga. Papa, Zosine informed them, had wished her to begin her first year as a grown-up lady with him only. She curtsied to the noble old ladies, embraced all the young ones, and fifty times let her hand be kissed by the young gentlemen. The last to leave the house was the curled young dandy. Coach after coach rolled away and the big ballroom stood empty.

"Now it is over!" cried Zosine, and drew in her breath deeply. "Thank God! Now come with me quickly." She seized Lucan's hand, and dragged her with her up the stairs. Upon the broad landing she stood still for a moment. She had grown very pale. Then she opened the door in front of them.

The big room they were entering, like the huge four-poster in the middle of it, was upholstered in crimson brocade. At the foot of the bed, like mourners at a deathbed, stood old John and the Negress Olympia. The old man's face was white. The black woman was absolutely silent, but while before her arms had been hanging down limply, she now held them crossed upon her enormous bosom. Her face was bathed in tears, but at the same time radiant with a mysterious, hidden triumph. In the four-poster, Mr. Tabbernor himself was lying, with the featherbed pulled up under his chin, so that his long white whiskers were resting upon it. He panted heavily a couple of times, but as he turned his head and caught sight of his daughter, he jumped out of bed with surprising adroitness, panted once more, and cried out, "At last!"

Zosine looked not at her father, but at John. The old servant solemnly nodded his head. "It is all right, Miss," he said in a trembling voice. "Master got out of the house without anybody in the world knowing of it. He is on his way now, and with the relays which he has got all the way, he will be on board ship before midday."

"Thank God!" Zosine cried once more, stretching up both her arms.

Mr. Tabbernor slowly walked up in front of the big cheval-glass, pulled off his black coat, and from his chest and belly loosened a couple of voluminous cushions, which he flung to the floor. He cautiously fingered his face, and made a grimace, then he undid his beautiful undulating white whiskers, and sent them the same way as the pillows. At last he lifted off all the smooth and shining crown of his head with its delicate and reverend white locks, and turned straight toward the girls. In less than a minute he had been transformed into a large-limbed, rubicund, dashing young cavalier.

"My dear," he said to Zosine, "will you now, when you think of me in the future, remember that for Uncle Theodore's sake, I stuck it a whole night, sewn up in a featherbed? I now vividly realize how I shall look in thirty years, and how, at that time, it will feel to have the face of the girl you embrace more than three feet away."

Zosine put her arms round the young man's neck and kissed him. "All my life I will reckon you my best friend in the world, Ambrose," she exclaimed. "And from now on I will never quarrel with Papa when he says that you are worth more than you look."

She gazed toward the petrified Lucan, and smiled faintly at her. "You poor little lamb," she said. "You know nothing, and may well hold me and Ambrose to have gone mad. Come and sit down by me. I am so tired myself that my legs will support me no longer. But I shall tell you everything.

"A terrible misfortune has hit Papa," she said, and once more drew a deep breath. "One of his great speculations has failed. He has lost all he possesses in this world. And as if this were not enough," she cried, "wicked people, who are envious of Papa, have tried to accuse him of being a cheat and a swindler. They meant to put my Papa in prison!" Her lips were trembling, she had to wait a minute before she could go on.

"You understand," she said, "that this must not be. Papa's heart is not strong. He might die in that prison, even before he could have the shocking misunderstanding cleared up. We had to get him away, to the West Indies, where these evil people cannot lay hands on him, and from where he will explain everything. 'Give me six months,' said Papa, 'and then the tobacco harvesting at Cuba will be finished, and I shall be a rich man once more, yes, richer than I have ever been before.' Then, indeed, his enemies will be sorry for themselves.

"Yes, Papa had to fly, like yourself, and from a more monstrous danger. We had been informed that the police would come out here and carry him away from Tortuga today. Solely because Papa has got such a fine name and so many friends, and because he has given away more money to works of charity than any other man in England, they let themselves be persuaded to wait, until my birthday ball was over. But they kept an eye on him even here, in his own house! The police had a secret spy at the ball. Oh, it serves him right to have been taken in, the silly, pomatumed braggadocio! They did not know that John, Olympia, Ambrose, and I might also have some sense when it came to saving Papa. They did not know, either, that at the back of the winter garden there is a window-pane which may be opened, and to which a ladder may be put. As Papa walked round the palm to fetch a flower for you, with John's assistance he got out through that opening and down that ladder. Fancy my own poor, fat Papa on a ladder!

"Ambrose had been hidden in the winter garden since early in the morning, dressed up as you saw him there. It was Ambrose who, at the moment when Papa disappeared, came forward and sat down with you. As long as their spy could watch Papa in his big chair and with his cigar, the police must feel convinced that they did hold him securely enough. The real crisis came when he had to walk through the ballroom. But then all the people were a little dizzy after the last figure of the cotillion. And Ambrose, as you see, is much like Papa, and played his part well. Did he play it well when he was entertaining you in the conservatory?"

Overcome with surprise, Lucan tried to recollect the conversation of the winter garden. "No," she exclaimed, "no, he was so changed that I almost imagined him to be drunk."

"In truth," Zosine cried, "he had ordered a couple of bottles of champagne in there. But Ambrose always has most sense when he has had something to drink."

She rose from the sofa, went to the window and looked out. "That is the way he went," she said. "He is now driving on out there as fast as the horses can carry him. He is perfectly quiet and confident, and thinking of me. Yes, think of me, Papa. I will do anything in the world for you."

She once more turned toward the others. "No one, no one on earth," she passionately exclaimed, "can realize what I have gone through, what I have experienced during these days and nights. It is a terrible thing to be deceiving people all round you. But at the same time it has in it some kind of fascination, a power to exert all one's faculties. It is a fatal game, it is wicked, I believe. But still it is a game, one feels as if one might go on forever. But now I am more tired than I had thought it possible to be. It is when danger is over that one sits down to die! I am happy, but my strength has gone, and I am changed. I believe I have grown old."

"You probably mean what you say," said Ambrose, "and that is all that anybody expects from a lady. But I doubt that you know what you are saying. Are you aware that tomorrow the bankruptcy court will seize the house with everything in it? You own nothing more in the whole world, my poor cousin."

"What," cried Zosine, "what does that signify, when Papa is in security?"

"I have some knowledge of creditors," Ambrose said thoughtfully. "It is not the circle I would choose to move in, if I could help it. But in this case," he added, "they are likely to let you keep your clothes and jewels, and if you tell them that the furniture of your rooms belongs to you, they will probably not take that away either. That is always something."

"And do you imagine," cried Zosine, "that I would keep anything of all that? When Papa was rich, all he had was mine. Now all I have may go away with him. I will walk barefooted, I will sell flowers in the street rather than accept anything from the people who mistrust Papa."

"Well, you will not have to go barefooted," said Ambrose. "I put my confidence in Aunt Arabella. 'Amor vincit omnia.' That is Latin, and I have learned it in school. It cannot fail us now. She has adored Uncle Theodore all her life, and she is one of the richest old maiden ladies in England. It is well known that you are in time to inherit all she has. Now I am convinced that she will joyously advance you a part of your inheritance in order that you two may sit hand in hand, and talk of Uncle Theodore.

"As far as that goes," Ambrose went on after a pause, the while carefully wiping the paint off his face with a handkerchief, as he had done during all the conversation, "things look somehow darker to me myself. Up to this lovely morning, I have been the flighty, but charming Ambrose Leppinghall, who was to be the partner and, to some extent, the heir of his millionaire uncle. But when tomorrow I shall be walking down Piccadilly or entering my club, I shall be nothing but poor worthless Ambrose Leppinghall, who, God knows, is only fit to be a warning to the frivolous young people about town. Well," he finished, with a little wry smile, "Uncle Theodore has always told me that I was a gambler by nature. If so, I shall have to see this game through. Uncle Theodore was a gambler by nature himself. He may well at this moment be enjoying his own game."

Lucan had been listening to their talk in alarm and dismay on behalf of her friend. She herself had lost her father and had been lonely and friendless. But in her own distress no shame and no doubt of or fear for the dear lost one had mingled, and such things, it now seemed to her, must be a far heavier burden. She rose in violent emotion, and put her arm round Zosine. "Zosine," she cried, "your father last night told me to be your sister. I am used to being poor. I am used to being lonely. You received me as a friend, when I was forsaken and scared. Now let me stay with you and try to help you."

11. mr. tabbernor's epitaph

EVEN after the sun had risen and had given to the young girls' ball frocks and to Ambrose's disorderly costume a tint of unreality, as if they had been figures at a masquerade, those left behind were talking of the man who had gone.

"Mr. Tabbernor," old John said solemnly, "was such a master as I shall never see the like of. The gentry do not themselves know what makes us happy and contented, or the opposite, in their service. They often think that we prefer to serve a respectable, reasonable and meek gentleman of whom you know what to expect. They try their best to be reasonable and meek with us. But you see, Miss Zosine and Master Ambrose, respectable, reasonable and meek, all that we may be ourselves, I should not exaggerate much if I told you straightaway that I were so. And that amongst people of the same kind the one should command and the other obey. That has no sense, and is unworthy of human beings.

"But nobody could tell one day what Mr. Tabbernor might do the next. In that way I could not possibly live myself. For this reason, it was grand and strange to serve him, as it is grand and strange to serve the Almighty Himself. He would suddenly take into his head to make one a present of a gold watch with diamonds in it. God knows what one were to do with it. But he would also at times, when you came to him and asked for your wages, decline to pay you, and he would not know himself why he did it, God bless him. When things went well with him he became impatient, as if he was worrying how he should manage to get rid of the money he was making. But in hard times, when millions were at stake—and I have seen such days before now—and when everybody else was trembling with alarm and fear, Mr. Tabbernor would sit and smile and purr like a big cat. And in real distress, he showed the world a radiant face. I was in his house when our dear mistress died. I am a widower myself, Miss Zosine. I did not whimper or wail. Nay, I believe I met my misfortune, as people will say, like a man. But a radiant face I could not put up.

"How, then, should I now, after having been with Mr. Tabbernor all my life, take service with a gentleman who is not really very different to me, except in so far as he has got a bigger house, finer plate, and finer clothes and carriages? It is a good thing that I have laid aside a bit of money here. Mr. Tabbernor's house was a good place for that. But all the same, if you would take me on, Mr. Ambrose, I should be happy to stay with you."

"It cannot be done now, John," said Ambrose.

John sighed deeply, and withdrew to the wall.

When he was silent, the Negress Olympia stepped out on the floor. She slowly looked round the room, beat her breast with her fist, and raised her voice. "I, I will tell you of my master," she said, "now that he has gone. All that John has said is but the praise of a white man, a thin soup. But I am a wild woman. For many years I have walked in the streets of your towns and on your roads, but still I do not like to keep to them, as if I were walking on a rope. Now I will moan and wail, as if I stood in the virginal forests of my own country. My master, who was also my child, has gone across the sea, and has not taken me with him, although it would have been good for me if I could have gone back to Santo Domingo, where first I became his nurse. If I had not become so then, I should have died from grief. Now I can die from grief here.

"When I was fourteen years old, Miss Zosine and Master Ambrose," Olympia went on and breathed deeply, "I was as pretty as a flower. I belonged to a great family in a big house, your father's grandfather's house. I was maid to the daughters of the house. I dressed them for their fine balls and parties, and then in their turn they dressed me up. When I had powdered their long, smooth hair, in jest they powdered my curly hair as well. They laced me up in their satin stays, and—would you believe it?—I had a slimmer waist than any of them. When the eldest son in the house was eighteen years old, the master gave me to him. They had that way with them in the great families, as long as the sons were not old enough to marry a white young lady out of another great family, then to give them a pretty, decent black girl to please themselves with. The sisters knew nothing of it. Nice young ladies had nothing to do with those things, the sweet angels. But when they saw that I was so dear to him, they laughed at their brother, and named me Ambrose's Venus, for he was called Ambrose like you, and Venus means sweetheart. But my old master became uneasy. Because Mr. Ambrose held me so very dear, he sent his fine son away on a journey, and in his absence married me off to a quite respectable Negro, whose name I no longer remember.

"Now there is something of which you do not know, on our island, on Santo Domingo. We have got our own customs there, at night, in the woods. We have a big snake, magic, things altogether outside your understanding. We met in the woods, and sung and danced, we sacrificed young goats to the big snake. And the one who knows the snake best and is aware of what it wishes, and whom we must all obey when he commands, is there called Papa le Roi. He is the big priest on our isle, just as here in England the Archbishop himself, God bless him. My own grandfather was our Papa le Roi until he died, a big, fat, beautiful man. But when he was dead, and we no longer had any priest, the dances in the woods were not what they had been; the big snake was not fed; there was no longer any great magic there.

"At that time," Olympia went on, looking dully before her and becoming more and more absorbed in her own thoughts, "an awful man came to Santo Domingo. He had been a slave-trader, and he was a very rich man. But he built only a small house for himself, far away from other white people. He did not keep company with any of the big families in the place, and all his money he buried in the sand. He was an awful man. He was a white man all right, but he was gray to look at, his face was gray, and so were his hands. He was now too old to sail in the slave traffic, and he dared not return to the place in England from which he had come, after the things he had done.

"Aye, he was an awful man! He was after human flesh, like the leopards in Africa at night. Some people said that once on a journey his ship had sunk, and he had saved himself in a boat together with another white man and a black slave, and when they were starving in the boat, the two white men first killed the Negro and ate his flesh, and then they drew lots to decide who was to die next, and our old man won, and ate his friend before he himself was taken up by a ship. From that time he had acquired a taste for human flesh, and his mouth was ever watering for it. But other people said of him that he had learned to eat it in Africa with our own old tribes. Now is it fit for a white man to eat human flesh? There were also people who told that he had sold himself to that Devil of whom the white people speak, and of whom they read in the Bible. But of those things I know nothing.

"He now said to us, 'I have been to Africa, to the very places where your own fathers lived. I have known your own tribe, as it is before kind white people help it to get to America. I have learned your old magic, and have seen bigger snakes there than you have ever set eyes on. Now I am Papa le Roi.'

"That was a bad thing, an ugly thing, my children," said Olympia. "That black people make magic in the black night, that is as it should be. But what has a white man got to do there? This old man could not sing, he could speak but low, for his voice was weak and hoarse. But all the same, he was a man with great power in him. Soon we could not live without him, and people who had never been to the wood before now came there from all parts of the island. Oh, oh, great was our joy then. We shouted, we cried with joy. We fell down with joy and bliss.

"And now the gray man said, 'The snake wills that we sacrifice the goat without horns.' And soon one child disappeared, and soon again another. Oh, oh! But these children always belonged to the Negroes of the plantation, and never to those of the houses.

"I myself by this time had got a baby," the old black woman continued. "But I did not care much about it, for had I not meant to have a white child, the child of Master Ambrose? My old master and missus had the child christened, and then the Negro to whom I was married, and whose name I have forgotten, said, 'We have now got a christened baby. It is better that we should no longer go to the night dances.' But this, my children, our Papa le Roi did not like, for he wanted me to come, because I sang and danced better than the other women. Also, he never cared to let go his hold on anybody, but meant to keep all people in his own hand. And this small gray man who was never invited into any decent house, who had no carriage or pair, but walked on the road, like a Negro, passed me there in the dust, which rose behind him, as if he had really been a devil, trailing his long tail, and in passing me whispered in his hoarse voice: 'He is waiting for you. Is he to wait in vain?' And I kept on coming to the woods.

"When Miss Eulalia, my fifth lady, was to be married, then you may be sure, we had a fine feast at the house. Twenty courses at dinner, and a band of fifty fiddlers and drummers in the ballroom. Master Ambrose by this time had come home again, together with the young lady to whom he was now engaged to be married. And in the evening, while the music was playing sweetly, he said to me, 'Come, Olympia, my little black darling, and stay with me tonight for the very last time.' Alas, it was more than I could resist, to have him looking at me and touching me in that way. The Negro to whom I was married was drunk and lying in the garden. We spent that night together as blissfully as two angels in heaven, Miss Zosine and Master Ambrose. He said to me, 'I shall never forget your kisses, Olympia.'

"But when, early in the morning," Olympia cried out in a dreadful voice, "I came back to my own house, my child was not there.

"I then remembered that it was my own baby, which I had borne from my body, and it seemed to me only the more lovely because it was black. Then the old white priest's words of the goat without horns rang awful in my ears. I wept and wailed in that hour of dawn, so loud that all the black men and women from the house came and stood round me. They wept and wailed with me, but they said: 'Do not speak of this, or the master and missus will want to know what has become of the other children who have been lost, and find out that we have known about them.' I myself thought of what Master Ambrose's young lady would say to him, if she got to know that he had been with me all night. I then made up my mind to tell the white people that I had lost my baby, and had already had it buried, and all the others told that they had assisted at the funeral.

"But all the same I could not stop screaming." Olympia continued her tale in a fainter voice. "I heard my own shrieks, and I thought, 'I must go on shrieking in this way, until I have got the gray Papa le Roi killed.' The family came down, and said: 'Olympia is off her head.' The bride and the bridegroom came down, all drowsy. The bride said: 'Nobody can stand that howling of yours, Olympia.' But all the same the dear lamb wept with me. But Miss Clara, who had been married the year before, declared, 'It is her milk worrying her. I shall take her on as a nurse to my own baby. Then she will get something else to think of.' The missus said, 'No, not as long as she keeps shrieking like this. It may get into the milk.' But Miss Clara had always been like her son, your Papa, Zosine. She answered, 'Nonsense, Mama.' I cried out, 'I will not be nurse to a white child. I see the head of a devil at my breast. I see the head of a big snake that sucks my milk.' But they insisted, and laid the baby in my arms.

"Oh, Zosine," cried out Olympia, "your Papa was a great man with more power in him even than that devil of the woods. There was such strength in his little mouth that it sucked the fury and the despair from my heart as you suck the poison from the flesh of someone who has been bitten by a snake. My fear was sucked out of me. My great sins were sucked away. I had paid for them; now I was a good woman again. When he had drunk his fill, and slept, then I myself could sleep. You will remember, all of you, how he could smile at a person? In that way he first of all smiled at me. He knew me, he looked into my eyes, the same as he did yesterday, when he said good-bye to me. No other human being in the world could then have helped me, but he was not like other human beings. When the time came that he could speak, he said, 'Olympia is my lump of black sugar.' Ought I not then to cry out his praise loudly now to all the world? Ought not the court and all his creditors to understand that they must let him off, for the sake of his nurse?"

Olympia once more drew her breath deeply, and gravely and proudly looked round on all sides, as if defying unseen enemies. "Ought I not," she said slowly, "if I was able to do so, keep them from him as long as I am alive myself?" She dipped her hand into the deep pocket of her folded skirt, and pulled out a heavy old pistol. "They would not," she declared, "have dared to come near him, as long as my master's old Olympia could stand on her two legs." With her free hand, she lifted her skirt a little, as if to show her audience how solid these two legs still were, and pointing at the floor with its muzzle, she drew a circle around her with the pistol, nodded her head to Zosine and Ambrose, and again pocketed the weapon. "We should," she said, "in any case have gone together, Master Theodore and I."

She was silent, folded both her arms on her breast, and laid her face upon them.

Zosine had listened to her story only with half an ear. Lucan was too amazed by it to utter a word. Ambrose said, "And have you not heard then what happened to your old devil of a priest?"

"Aye," said Olympia, and looked up dully, "I have heard it. He was hanging by a rope from his ceiling one morning."

12. upon the ruins

LUCAN had declared that she was used to being poor and had thought that Zosine might benefit from her own sad experiences. But already on the first day she realized that the catastrophe which she met here was totally different from the kind of distress with which she was acquainted. She thought, or vaguely felt, that till now she had been like a bird in winter, working for the humble nest which was to give shelter to her father and her brother. But here she stood in the midst of a gigantic building that an earthquake had overthrown. At every hour new masses of stone and timber were falling in upon her, so that she was overcome with dismay, and her first instinct was to run away.

Zosine spoke but little, and left all decisions to her friend. In this way it fell to the young girl, who had only been in the house for twenty-four hours, to take charge of its daily life and to give orders to its big staff of servants. She had come to a radiant palace as a stranger and a fugitive. The very next day she was, so to say, mistress of the place. But meanwhile the palace itself seemed to sink and vanish around her.

She dared not let Zosine see the letters that arrived for Mr. Tabbernor, and she herself interviewed the strange official men who seemed to possess the house, and tried to keep them away from her friend.

Lucan had copied out her father's accounts for him, and in a modest way knew something of business. Zosine talked of her father's speculations as she would of the weather, and in reality knew but very little about them.

But from her explanations, and from what she heard round her, Lucan gathered that Zosine's Papa had embarked upon some gigantic and extravagant speculation. It concerned, she thought, tobacco in Cuba, where Mr. Tabbernor had reckoned on conquering the entire trade of certain sorts, but it had not been undertaken in his own name, and in England nothing was known of it. Great misfortunes, fire and shipwreck, had hit him. He had spent his ready capital and encumbered his papers and property, and in the end Tortuga itself and all that it contained. And when his creditors threatened to take possession, he had, whether altogether legally or not, Lucan did not know and did not try to find out, laid hand on various deposits, all the while hoping or expecting that his successful speculations would soon bring in the money again. On his flight he had taken all his papers with him.

Lucan wondered that people, who possessed all that they could wish for in this world, should still risk their all in order to gain more. But she would not, even in her heart, take Zosine's father to task, and in the daily concerns there was enough to occupy her mind.

The day after Mr. Tabbernor's flight, the people of the bankruptcy court presented themselves at Tortuga and sealed up, or made out lists of all valuables in the house. Lucan was amazed and almost shocked at the sight of the sumptuous plate, the lovely china, the unique treasures and collections which were brought forth and counted up. The very figures written down appeared fantastic and incomprehensible to her, until she became somehow familiar with them, almost as the pupil of an astronomer, copying his researches, may become familiar with the incomprehensible figures of the distances within the universe. "Can people really live in this way?" she thought. And she sighed as she realized the vanity of beautiful dreams and of all worldly glory.

Even the dry and pedantic servants of the court, who were used to seeing ruins around them, felt compassion for the two forsaken girls in the big house. Zosine got permission to stay on in her rooms and to keep what she wished of her own belongings.

She might have obtained a great deal more, if she had not from the very beginning stubbornly refused to accept anything that might be considered a favor. She appeared determined as far as possible to share her father's circumstances. Her old lawyer, who tried to discuss the case with her, was met by a childish, passionate, almost hostile opposition. The only things which the Nabob's daughter consented to keep were the clothes which, upon the evening of the ball, she had given to Lucan. At that Lucan asked the old gentleman's advice, and took out such garments and articles as she thought most useful to her friend.

The following days, from morning to night, were taken up with visits from Mr. Tabbernor's family, who appeared with great haste and alarm at Tortuga.

Heavy, pompous carriages rolled up in front of the door, as on the evening of the ball. Dignified old gentlemen in stiff stocks and ladies in silken pelisses and velvet bonnets descended from them, anxiety or indignation written in their faces. Zosine herself received the first two or three of them, and Lucan did not overhear the conversations which took place between her and her uncles and aunts. But Zosine, with flaming cheeks, when the carriages had again rolled off, recounted to her friend all that had been said, and Lucan listened to her reports with distress, for it appeared to her that with each visit her friend's position became more uncertain. She realized that the difficulty here, as with the people of the court, arose from the fact that Zosine would not tolerate any censorious words about her father. Even the mildest reproach was likely to throw her into violent revolt, and at the very first meeting this circumstance had brought on a definite breach between her and those of her relations who had come to assist her. She was so indignant and so much hurt that after a few days she downright refused to see any of her own family. It was now Lucan who must receive the angered old ladies and gentlemen and, embarrassed, explain to them her presence in the house and her friend's attitude. An old uncle, who had rushed from far away to the assistance of his niece, waited in the house for a whole day, and in the end had to go away without having seen her.

When the young girls were again left to themselves, Lucan at times tried to reason with her friend, but Zosine would not listen to her. All the same, it was obvious that with every day she confided more in her old school friend. She often held her hand, kissed her and talked to her of her father. "Now Papa has got Ireland behind him," she said. Her thoughts were on the sea, and Tortuga and the happenings there hardly seemed to exist for her. It was as if she closed her eyes, and in the darkness that surrounded her clung to the arm of the other girl, and Lucan with a heavy heart remembered the blind boy whom she had likewise guided. While Zosine slept at night, she lay awake and pondered on the future of her friend and herself. She had written to the aunt, who was her nearest relation, that she had given up her former situation, and was now, in the house of a friend, looking round for another. She would indeed have done so, if Zosine's dependence on her had not made it impossible. After a short time she ceased to think about herself and gave all her time and all her mind to Zosine.

Zosine's cousin Ambrose frequently came to Tortuga. He still had a fine riding horse stabled there, which his uncle had given him, and when he was not galloping about in the neighborhood, he was trying to get Lucan's advice as to whether he ought to keep it or sell it. Ambrose was the only one of her family who was really and heartily welcome to Zosine. They never talked of the future together, but recalled their childhood, and the games and tricks of the happy time. In his company Zosine still laughed and jested. It seemed as if, apart from Lucan, Ambrose was her only friend in life, and as if the three were now to hold together against all the world. Ambrose from time to time asked if Zosine had heard from Aunt Arabella. It was obvious that Zosine too was looking forward to hear from her aunt, or expecting to see her arriving at the house. With the passing of every day, the unknown old lady became a more important figure in Lucan's thoughts. "She is different from all the others," Zosine declared. "She has loved Papa."

One day Ambrose, somewhat downhearted, questioned his cousin for a long time about one of her friends, a Scotch heiress.

He was evidently planning to demand the hand of this young lady and was building up his future on the prospect. When he had gone, Zosine said to Lucan, "Poor Ambrose. It is indeed hard on him. He is good for nothing at all." All the same, for the first and last time of their friendship, she became very angry with Lucan, when she ventured to suggest that the young lady might refuse her suitor.

Only once did Lucan see her friend deeply depressed. It was on the day she was taking leave of her riding horses. All the evening she could not stop weeping. She talked for a long time about each of her horses, the while referring to herself as a good horsewoman in a peculiar, childlike and moving manner, as if she were talking of a dead girl.

Among the large staff of Tortuga a sad silence reigned. Lucan gathered that they must all have been highly devoted to their master. At the end of the month most of them left the house, and it was strange to watch the big house thus slowly emptied of life and movement. When the plate of the house was taken out and recorded, it was as if old John was collecting all his own existence and silently laying it down in the tomb.

Olympia was far more energetic, but her energy often embarrassed Lucan. The old Negress was jealous of Zosine's new friend, and found fault with everything she did. When Zosine retired to her room and locked the door, Olympia would place herself in a chair outside, and sit there for hours in gloom and wrath, as if petrified with grief. Lucan sometimes wondered whether the catastrophe had not deranged the mind of the old black woman. She now frequently mistook Zosine for her father, and talked of the girl as of her little boy or as of Master Theodore. When, during the investigations of the court, a big box with toys, which appeared to have belonged to a small boy, was carried in, Olympia at once worked herself into a fury, shrieking out horrible threats, and tearing the box from the people carrying it, until a good-natured old gentleman of the court shrugged and let her take it away. Olympia at once disappeared with the box, and probably hid it in a place known to herself only, for Lucan never again set eyes on it.

To divert her friend, Lucan told her of the old black woman's gallant fight and victory. Zosine listened to her, grave and dumb. "You old fool," she said to Olympia, "why must you interfere with the business of Tortuga? Those gentlemen are laughing at you. They are well aware that there is no strength inside all your fat. If they cared to, they could set you down in a chair like a doll, and there you would have to remain. You are making a show of yourself and of Papa." Olympia did not move a muscle of her face, but quietly held on to her triumph.

"What?" she said. "Master Theodore's little axe and toy pistol. Would I let them go? I have more sense than that, and know well enough what may be useful to us! An axe is a good thing to hold in one's hand."

At this time Lucan began to worry about the balance of Zosine's own mind. She kept to her rooms as strictly as if she held herself to be a prisoner there in her father's place. Only after continued persuasions did Lucan succeed in making her go out into the garden and the park. Here the two girls walked together in the lovely May evenings, and here Zosine at times would refer to the happenings of the day.

On such an evening she said to Lucan, "You have gone through much, and you are not older than I. I wonder if it is your sorrows which have made you so strangely wise and good? I have had no sorrows. My mother died when I was born, and they did not talk of her to me till I was nine years old. Then they showed me her picture. And it was only as if I had found one more happiness in the world. A sweet beautiful angel loved me, followed me everywhere and took care of me. Can there really be any truth in what old people tell you, that human beings are improved by misfortune? I have always believed that they were talking nonsense on purpose, in order to appear brilliant."

13. aunt arabella's letter

ONE day Ambrose brought Lucan a small parcel of papers, tied together with a silk ribbon.

"These are poems that I wrote to Zosine at school and at the University," he told her, "at the time I somehow felt it my duty. When now I look back upon that period of my existence, I can see that I lived in a pretty rosy state of bliss, as Uncle Theodore's future heir and Zosine's future husband. She was not in love with me, and altogether did not think much of me, but in the end she might have done what my old uncle desired. They are highly melancholic poems, Miss Lucan. They made me laugh in the midst of our misery. Perhaps they will make Zosine laugh as well—or even you, sweet miss. You were already laughing at me, I bet, by the time we were sitting in the winter garden. But hang it all, it was not easy to keep up conversation, when every word might mean life or death to Uncle Theodore."

Lucan could not resist throwing a glance at the poems. They did indeed make her laugh, and she took them along with her in the hope that they might cheer up Zosine. She found her friend by the window of the morning-room. Zosine too was holding a paper and gazing at it. She was very pale, and looked up with clear, dark eyes.

"Now I have heard from Aunt Arabella," she exclaimed, and handed Lucan the letter. "No, wait," she said, and took it back again. "I will read it aloud to you. I want to hear how the words sound, when you hear them spoken."

The letter had no heading, or Zosine did not read it out, but began straightaway.

"Ever since your Papa's flight"—Zosine's voice trembled, and she stopped a moment at the word "flight"—"I have been waiting to hear from him. But my letter is, in reality, the reply to another, which your Papa ought to have sent me before he fled from the country. And it is not my fault that now you get it in his place. It would not have happened, if he had remembered to give me his address.

"When I was a young woman, I loved your Papa. But he despised me, because I was ugly, although I knew myself that I was not as ugly as he thought. My love for your Papa and his contempt of me, these two things have been the great adventure of my youth; yes, they were my youth itself. The view of life, out of which I now write, in this way is the work of your Papa. I state this without bitterness, for it is surely good and useful to learn to know life. For this reason you too must read my letter without bitterness.

"Even after your Papa had married your Mama, who was a beauty, I would have become his without hesitation if for a moment he had given me to understand that he wanted me. But that moment never came, and I can thank your Papa—yes, I do indeed today thank him—because I shall go as a maid into my grave.

"Now we were both old, and the face no longer decides our destinies. (And I myself, who have kept my figure, in any case may today be said to be as good-looking as Theodore.) Now there came a moment when, to save his happiness and his honor, it was money that he needed. That money I had got. He knew it well enough; he was aware that I was a rich old woman, one of the richest in England. Now, also, I would have given him all that I owned in the world, if for a moment he had given me to understand that he wanted it. The happiness of my youth I have lost through him, the greatest happiness of which, in my old age, I could have dreamt, would be to have sacrificed my wealth to him, and to have become as destitute and outcast as he is himself today, in order to save him and the child who resembles him from ruin.

"But it was not to be so, and once more he has despised me. I *did not even know that he was in danger until, by the mouth of strangers, I learned that he was already lost. Today, according to his wish and his resolution, I sit here, an old, cold maid, on a heap of old, cold gold, which to me is worth no more than a heap of old rags. It is his choice, and I will not complain of it, or feel sorry for myself, any more than I will feel sorry for him or for you. And this assurance is the best thing that, in the present situation, I can give you.*

"We two are not likely to meet again in life. Why should I wish to see you again? It is enough that every single possession of mine will recall to me every day the picture of your Papa in his misery and disgrace, and that my wealth at every hour will confirm the fact that I have never really existed for him, neither as friend in the hour of need nor as a woman in the days of youth. This knowledge I shall carry with me into my grave.

"You will notice that, as I write this down, my hand trembles. It has surprised me, for I did not know that I was still capable of suffering so deeply. But do not take it to heart. I know that your Papa is at this moment carrying burdens as heavy as my own, the heaviest among them being the anxiety for you and your future. I know too that you will have to suffer in life. It gives me no pleasure to think of these things, but they are there, whether I choose to think of them or not.

"Nay, your Papa has never really been aware of my existence. You, who are like him, will soon forget it. I myself, only, will have to remember from hour to hour that I do still exist, and that my life is what it is. In this way we will, each of us, fulfill the destiny of our nature, and preserve that dignity which consists in accepting our destiny.

"For the last time I here sign myself,

"Your Aunt Arabella."

Zosine put down the letter, and for a few moments remained standing by the window erect and pale, absorbed in her own thoughts.

"Yes," she said, "it does sound different when read aloud. But it is just as terrible. Here indeed is a person whom Papa has wronged. I have never reckoned with the charges that other people have brought against him. They talk of his debts, of what he owes them. I have no knowledge of such things. But to Aunt Arabella, Papa owes a debt which it will be hard for him to repay." She put her hand to her heart. "I cannot," she said, "where Papa's creditors are concerned, accept, as they say, assets and liabilities. I am an ignorant, frivolous girl. Nobody can believe that I shall ever earn the money to pay them back. But with Aunt Arabella I do accept assets and liabilities."

"Oh, Zosine," said Lucan sadly, "how little you understand your aunt. It would be the greatest happiness to her, and the best comfort in her distress, if you would now turn to her for help. You forget that she still loves you and your Papa."

"No," said Zosine, "I shall never forget that. But I do not forget either that she is a proud woman. And Papa and I, who have wronged her so deeply, we too have got our pride. She shall never set eyes on us again." She pressed the letter to her breast. "I swear," she declared slowly and solemnly, "that never again, no, not to save my life, will I mention Aunt Arabella, or this letter of hers."

Lucan stood aghast. It seemed to her that Zosine was here, in childish obstinacy, throwing away her one hope of salvation. What would now become of her? "It is wrong of you to speak like this," she exclaimed. "You talk as if you and your father were on the stage, where the great thing is to make an impression by words and gestures. But you are not on the stage. You have your whole life to think of. Such vows as you were just now making are unworthy of you and of any sensible human being."

Zosine looked at her. "Nay, Lucan," she said, "Papa and I must stand and fall together. But since you also have stood by us—although you are so different from him or to me—I will not distress you. In return for your sympathy and loyalty I promise you that, if it can save my life, I will mention Aunt Arabella and her letter." She drew in her breath deeply. "But never till then," she cried. After a pause, she took Lucan's hand, drew her toward her and kissed her. "Come, let us burn the letter, then," she said.

She threw a last glance at it. "I have forgotten to read the postscript to you," she said, and read aloud:

"P.S. What are you going to do with Olympia? The crack-brained woman will never be tolerated in any decent house. Send her to me. I will look after her for the time she has still got to live."

On the same evening Zosine recounted to Lucan that in the course of the week she had received three proposals. "The one," she said, "came from a young gentleman who has already once asked Papa for my hand. At that time we refused him. Why, do you think, does he believe that I will accept him now? The two other young men have never proposed to me before. What on earth makes them do so now?"

14. against all the World

ZOSINE had reckoned that her father's journey would take six weeks. At the end of this time she said to Lucan, "Now I can think of the future."

Lucan had been almost angry with her friend, because she appeared to live only in the moment and to shun all thought of tomorrow. Now she collected all her experience and imagination in the task of advising and helping Zosine. But at the same moment, with a heavy heart, she felt her own deficiency and the difficulty of their position.

"Do not think," said Zosine, "that I am afraid of the future. I know that I shall have to serve my apprenticeship, before I am good for anything in this world. But perhaps, I have reflected, it will turn out almost amusing to be, for a while, as wise and prudent as yourself. There is only one thought which now frightens me. We two are not to part, Lucan?"

"I will not leave you as long as I can be of any use to you," said Lucan. "I myself have come to you as a fugitive without a home."

"Yes, thank God," said Zosine, "that you came to me as a fugitive. If you had had a home, I must have let you return to it. But as it is, we two can now vow alliance and brotherhood, like the knights of old, and hold together in life and death." They clasped hands and smiled to each other, but their lips trembled.

"To be sure, it is an imposing alliance," said Lucan. "We are two girls of eighteen years and six weeks each. There is hardly any human being against whom we could hold our own, if it came to a trial of strength. And we intend to stand up against all the world."

"There you have hit the nail on the head," cried Zosine. "It is exactly here that we score. We are only two frail girls, and it is evident that, in spite of our charm and our talents, any man may give us a black eye. But it is as evident that even the strongest man on earth, Hercules himself, will fail, and will be in the same position, if he is to stand up against all the world. The strength by which he exceeds you and me in that case will be of no significance whatever. Which goes to prove that in our case the point is always to fight the whole of humanity, and to avoid fighting any particular human being. Throw the gauntlet to the whole world, Lucan. Then we shall be as strong as Hercules."

"The whole world," Lucan repeated thoughtfully, "in our case will be most appropriately represented by an employment office. I do not want to go back to the office where I was before, for there they will ask questions about my former situation. But these offices usually advertise in the paper. Let us look them up there." The young girls put a dark and a fair head together over the day's paper, and gravely went through the list of employment offices in London.

"It is not a pleasant thing to be a lady companion," Lucan said, "and yet, if my old mistress had not died, I should probably have been in her service today. But as I told you, I was for a time very happy as a governess."

"But I cannot become a governess," Zosine replied dejectedly. "I have not been taught anything that I could teach to other girls."

"You know French and Italian," said Lucan. "You can recite poetry and play the guitar. Perhaps we could get situations as governesses."

"From which we should have to run away in the middle of the night, because we were all too charming. No, you are right," she interrupted herself at the sight of Lucan's sad and puzzled face, "we must have faith in our fortune, or we shall never get anywhere. We must strike home. Now you will count the buttons of your bodice, while I count the advertisements, and may your buttons bring us luck. And when we have made our choice in this way, nothing shall make us alter it. The worst thing that could happen to us would be to lose confidence, and run about from one office to the other. Whatever comes, we will believe that an angel is leading us on. How many buttons have you got?"

"Eleven," Lucan answered.

In this way it happened that the girls, two months after their birthday, in a small boarding-house in London, the name of which Lucan knew through her aunt, tied on their bonnets to begin a long pilgrimage.

It was July. Lucan noticed that Zosine, who had always lived in luxury when in London, was pale and worn with the heat. She herself, at the sight of their poor and joyless surroundings, felt strangely guilty toward her friend, as if she had deliberately lured her among them.

Tortuga already seemed far away. Zosine had declared that the parting with the house and park would not grieve her, so sure was she of returning to it all within a short time, by the side of her father, when he should have triumphed over his enemies. She had taken but a hasty leave of old John and Olympia, who, out of the big staff, were now the only two servants left at Tortuga. Lucan for a moment thought that the farewell to Tortuga was more heart-piercing to her than to Zosine. But on the journey to London Zosine fainted in her arms, lay unconscious for an hour and gave her friend the fright of her life. Lucan felt the hard, merciless world close around them.

But as soon as Zosine regained her strength, she did, however, reject Lucan's sad forebodings. Poverty itself, with which she here became acquainted for the first time, seemed to her almost fascinating, like a tragic or comic exhibition on the stage. She was amazed at the sight of the napkin-rings of the boarding-house, asked Lucan to explain their use to her, and on no account would believe her explanation. The sight of them invariably made her burst into laughter. To walk afoot in the streets, to dress as unassumingly as possible, so that nobody should pay any attention to her, to sit down on the humble seats in the parks—all this to the rich, spoiled and capricious girl seemed like a kind of fairy tale. One day the girls passed a fine big house close to a park. "That is Papa's London house," Zosine told her friend.

Ambrose was the only person who knew their address, and came to see them there. The first time he was struck dumb at the sight of the boarding-house, but later on he seemed to feel at his ease there, and brought the girls big boxes of chocolates, fruit and large bouquets. He also invited them to the opera, and Zosine accepted the invitation, on the condition that they were to sit in a back row of the gallery, well out of sight of her old friends in their boxes. But, on their return from the theater, she was graver and more silent than usual, and she would not repeat the experiment.

The night before their first visit to the employment office, Zosine dreamed that the people there, as she gave her name, mockd her father, and repeated the slander about him. She always lived in fear of such a thing happening, and in the morning, in great agitation of mind, asked Lucan if in the future she might call herself by her name, and pass herself off as her sister. "I am afraid we are too different to pretend to be twins," she said, "but with my silly short hair, I probably look younger than you. We will tell people that there is a difference of ten months between us." In her character of a sister, she now became particularly affectionate and compliant toward Lucan.

The office at which the young girls had applied, and at which, within the following weeks, they were to spend a great deal of their day, lay in a narrow street, and looked out upon a small, dark court. The furniture was all polished with use, and the wall-paper was faint and greasy. The place was owned by a married couple, a long, thin and bald gentleman with a pair of strong spectacles, and a small, rotund, colorless lady. It was Mrs. Quincy who attended to most of the business, and she worked hard from morning till night. She did her best to help her clients and endeavored to keep up the courage of the young girls, when the first weeks passed without any result. But in her own manner there was so much resignation, so much familiarity with the hardships of life, and so little genuine faith in any kind of miracle, that her comforting was disheartening to the girls.

Her husband, who took but little part in the affairs of the establishment, was a person of romantic temperament. He furnished the two girls with surprisingly precise and detailed information about each of the ladies and gentlemen who came to look for a companion or a governess. The young girls at first feared that he should direct his scrutinizing glasses toward themselves, but they probably looked so young and simple that it never occurred to him to distrust them. He only felt convinced of their interest in his gossip, and when they had to wait in the office, he entertained them with a series of fantastic tales about his other customers. When afterwards they undressed at night, the girls discussed these tales between themselves. Lucan generally only smiled at them. Zosine sometimes took them in dead earnest, while at other times they made her burst out laughing.

Meanwhile their search for a mission in this world advanced but slowly. All day they were the object of inquisitorial glances and questions, but in the evening they found themselves no further on the road to success. A number of elderly married or unmarried ladies who were looking for a companion, and several dignified and tender mothers, who wanted to have their daughters trained in deportment and in French and Italian, had come into their existence, and had gone out of it again. A young dandy, who was charged with finding a *liseuse* for his mama, directed such ardent and admiring glances at Lucan's pretty face that Zosine was tempted to box his ears, but when his mother appeared at the office to inspect the girl, she obviously made up her mind at once to put an end to her son's tender inclinations.

The girls soon found out that their greatest difficulty lay in their resolution to remain together. A couple of times Lucan could have obtained a satisfactory situation, but she rejected it, when she saw how terrified Zosine was at the idea of being left alone. She herself viewed a possible separation from her friend in the light of a catastrophe. Their sorrows had merged her and Zosine together; their old school friendship within these weeks had grown into a passion. They called one another sister even when they were alone. They were happy in each other's company.

All the same, things could not go on in this way. Their small capital was quickly ebbing. Even Lucan's most thoughtful economy could not keep it going for ever. Lucan bethought herself of the old lady in the inn, who had hinted at the prospect of a good situation. Now she might perhaps have become the saving angel of the distressed girls. But Lucan did not have her address.

"Ought we not," Zosine exclaimed, "to try to be taken on at the ballet? And yet, there our relations would spot us, and put a quick end to our careers." Her childish thoughtlessness made Lucan's heart sink. She wondered whether, after all, if it would not be better for Zosine to make it up with her uncles and aunts and return to her own sphere of life.

But at the same time Zosine's dependence on her strengthened her. She cheered and comforted her friend. "Do not lose courage," she said. "If we can hold out, everything will be all right in the end. It is better to cut down our pretensions, and to go through a short hard time. If only we can keep our self-respect, we shall win the respect of others as well."

To both the girls there was something hideous and almost unnatural in having to occupy themselves with practical matters and business without the aid of a man. They often felt like a pair of coarse, mannish women, and at times, as they walked in the streets without the escort of a gentleman, they felt as if they had come down there only half dressed or in their nightgowns. It frequently happened that young men addressed them in the street. This set them both in great fright, and they took care to put down the veils of their bonnets whenever they walked out. But at the same time their talk in the evening now invariably turned to Ambrose, Mr. Tabbernor, to old John, to Zosine's father or to Mr. Armworthy himself, as if they felt the necessity of keeping a masculine element in their existence.

Thus sadly did matters stand with them, when one day Mrs. Quincy wrote and told them to come to the office as quickly as possible, for she had good news for them.

15. the reverend mr. pennhallow

"YOU have been most wonderfully lucky, my dears," cried Mrs. Quincy, when the girls, filled with expectation, had sat down in her small office. "A worthy, pious and learned gentleman, the Reverend Mr. Pennhallow, and his lady, to do a good deed, will receive, free of charge, two well-bred girls of limited means into their own house, and will teach and perfect them there. Mr. Pennhallow for the sake of his health lives in France —surely a most interesting country. I am expecting the reverend gentleman here in half an hour."

Lucan and Zosine looked at each other. In their minds they already saw themselves in France, in the country, far away from all their worries.

Mr. Quincy, from the other side of an old ink-stained desk, here interposed. "I am in the fortunate position," he said, "to be able to give particular information in this matter. The family of Pennhallow is well known in the northern parts of our country, where for many generations they have done noble work, and held great influence. They belong to a severe and ascetic religious sect, the name of which I have forgotten, which holds the second coming of Christ, and the end of the world, to be near at hand. They have all been highly admired preachers. But they have been even more looked up to on account of their pure and elevated morals. The grandfather of our—I take the liberty of using the word 'our'—Reverend Mr. Pennhallow was regarded almost as a prophet and an oracle in his own country, and many wonderful legends are still told about him. There are, indeed, other tales of black sheep in the family. But such tales often arise from envy, or from lack of understanding of the great and unusual. The Reverend Pennhallow in his early youth had been a tutor to some of the greatest names of the country. Seven years ago he suffered the misfortune to lose his voice—a weakness which seems to lie in the family—and to have to retire from his office. Since that time he has lived in France, without doubt occupied with his learned studies, and has but rarely come back to England. It would be a privilege to live in the nearness and under the eye of such a man. I congratulate you, my young ladies."

At that moment the handle of the door was gently turned, and a little old gentleman noiselessly stepped into the room.

He was dressed in such a queer, old-fashioned style, in a long, worn, black coat, a pair of heavy shoes, and an absurd old tall hat, with a faded umbrella in his hand, that he looked more like a village verger than a clergyman, and Zosine put her handkerchief to her mouth to hide her laughter. But he carried himself, in these old clothes, with a surprising, almost solemn, dignity, as he now greeted, first Mr. and Mrs. Quincy, and then the two girls. He spoke very quietly, but all the same he did not seem to suffer from any ailment of his voice or throat. He rather gave the impression of deliberately subduing his voice, out of some particular consideration for the person to whom he talked.

"So I am here, then," he said, looking at Lucan and Zosine, "in the presence of my daughters-to-be? It is a privilege and happiness to be allowed to guard and guide the young women of this world upon their perilous road in life. But the lambs, too, should feel confident and happy in their shepherd's charge. I am an old man, and may be ignorant of the wishes and dreams of a couple of young maids, but what I can give, I offer you. If you, my dear young women, wish to extend your knowledge and to enrich your minds, I may still be of use to you. I shall endeavor to instruct you in the history of mankind, and in the languages of other countries. Yes, if you should want it, also in the classical tongues, although there are people who think such studies not quite womanly. Those boys and young men who have, in old days been my pupils, succeeded in making teaching a pleasure to me. I foresee that the same thing will happen to you and me."

Mr. Pennhallow was between fifty and sixty years old, short and slight of stature, but erect and collected. His thin hair was almost white, and beneath it his long face was of a singular dark-gray tint, as in a person who has lived much indoors. He had coarse and flat features, as if roughly cut in wood, and from his nose to the corners of his mouth two deep furrows ran, broad nose, a long upper lip and a long, tightly closed mouth. But it was his eyes which made the deepest impression on those he looked at. They were very light, clear, watchful and piercing, and at the same time they seemed to gaze at faraway objects, as if they had a double bottom to them. At the moment, as he took a view of the two young girls, a faint blush, as if of pleasure, mounted into his long gray cheeks.

Lucan looked back at him, and reflected that he was like somebody she had seen before, but she could not remember who it was.

After Mr. Pennhallow had sat down, he kindly and slowly, with his hands folded upon the handle of his old umbrella, asked the girls a few questions about their lives, circumstances and tastes. In the course of the talk he smiled mildly at them a couple of times, and his smile was as remarkable as his eyes. It was as if he might have smiled deeper than other people, but was subduing his mirth, out of some particular leniency toward the people at whom he smiled. Zosine at first had reflected that the deep furrows around his mouth must have been drawn by pondering and vigils, perhaps also by care, hard work and poverty. Now she thought that they had grown so deep because, in the course of his long life, the little old man had smiled so often.

Carefully and without haste he described to the girls the kind of life that would await them in France. He and his wife led a quiet existence in a lonely, peaceful house, in a fine and romantic neighborhood. Here their foster-daughters, like themselves, would pass their days among books and studies, or at work in the house and the garden. From time to time he paused, and seemed lost in his own thoughts. While he sat thus, silent and immovable, he gently ran the tip of his tongue over his lips.

After such a long silence he mildly, and as if casually, asked the girls whether they were all alone in the world. When they told him that they were, and that they had no family or friends, he sighed deeply. He doubted, he humbly said, that there were many human beings who felt a deeper sympathy with the lot of lonely young women than, for certain reasons, he did. It was a sorrowful subject; it was painful to know that gentle, pure defenseless creatures should so often be forlorn and without aid or guidance in life. He had given much time and thought to the problem. It should be possible to provide a home and a shelter and employment in life to such young women, and at the same time to let the world benefit by the sweetness and the strange vigor of their nature.

Mrs. Quincy was deeply moved by his discourse, and from time to time threw a quick glance at her young clients, to see if they too were appreciating it. At the end of his speech she deferentially asked him whether he was taking on this task from sheer philanthropy. Mr. Pennhallow for a moment thought her question over, and then, with a still face, answered that he and his wife had lost a child, a young daughter. It was in memory of his child that he now wished to open his home for the two homeless young women. In his house his adopted daughters would take the place of his dead child. Still, it was not his intention to tie the girls down before they knew what they were doing. He proposed that their agreement should be made up for the period of one year.

It was, he went on a little later, because this subject meant so much to his wife that he had come to see the two young women alone, before bringing her. She must not be disappointed. But, he added, he was thankful to feel that there was, in this case, no danger of disappointment. It was Providence itself who had brought the four together.

He became so absorbed in his thoughts that Mrs. Quincy, to break the silence, asked him if he had never before thought of taking a homeless girl into his house in his daughter's place. Mr. Pennhallow looked up. As before, he seemed to fix his clear eyes straight on the person to whom he talked, and at the same time to be lost in the view of strange and wonderful things, far away and invisible to others. Yes, he said, he and his wife had before made the experiment. He once more sighed deeply, and his audience understood that a melancholy experience lay behind his silence.

He informed Mrs. Quincy that he would return to the office within a day or two, and bring his dear wife with him, to make the final arrangements in the matter. A moment later he was gone. In spite of his slowness and dignity he moved, in his heavy shoes, almost noiselessly. He had slipped from the room without a sound.

The two girls, till this moment, had not made up their minds whether to accept the Reverend Mr. Pennhallow's offer or not. But it now became difficult for them to resist the genuine, kind triumph of Mr. and Mrs. Quincy, or their joyous congratulations. More than these, even, something in the manner of the old man himself seemed to render a refusal impossible. This small, still, humble gentleman would surely have ruled his congregation with the authority and the power of a prophet.

Lucan was used to be met by Zosine's laughing or indignant remarks about the ladies and gentlemen in the office as soon as the door had closed behind them. Today she was looking forward to them. But today Zosine was silent. Only when they were in sight of their own front door, she exclaimed, "How strangely content and happy that old man was. I should like to know how he works it. For he seems to be poor and lonely, and he is, in any case, both old and ugly. And yet I do not know if in all my life I have met any human being as contented and pleased with the world as he is. Can he teach us that art too?"

"Within a year," she said again, when they had taken off their bonnets and sat down in their own small room, "everything will be all right once more. Papa will have come back by then. And he will find me much more clever and accomplished than when he went away. He will be proud of me. For I mean to profit by Mr. Pennhallow's wisdom. I mean to learn much from him in France."

The next morning she again talked about the old clergyman,

and asked Lucan if she had dreamed of him. "No, I did not dream at all," Lucan said. Zosine looked very thoughtful. "I dreamed of him," she said. But she would not tell what her dream had been.

Two days later they once more walked to Mrs. Quincy's office, to meet Mr. and Mrs. Pennhallow.

Lucan felt a slight shock, and grew quite pale, when in Mrs. Pennhallow she recognized the little old woman who, on the night of her flight, had spoken to her outside the inn, and whom she had taken to be an old maid, and, in jest, a fairy godmother. The old lady was dressed as she had been then, with a small gray veil to her bonnet, and did in the same way, when she was not speaking, gently grind her big teeth against each other. But at the inn she had approached the girl, had opened the conversation, and had seemed to have much to say. Here, in her husband's presence, she was dumb. Only a couple of times she fixed her eyes on Lucan's face so searchingly that the girl became embarrassed. Lucan also noticed that the old lady exchanged a few words, in a low voice, with her husband, and that they were then both looking at her. The Reverend Mr. Pennhallow for a moment was thoughtful. Then he gently shook his head, and went on talking as quietly as before. But later, Mrs. Pennhallow, when her husband was engaged with Mrs. Quincy, came half sideways up to Lucan and remarked curtly, "I think that we have met before."

Her manner made Lucan slightly uneasy, and nothing more was said.

The interview this time did not last long. The agreement between the old couple and the girls was made up verbally and informally. Mrs. Quincy had her salary paid out to her, and took a heartfelt leave of her young clients. The small party of four was to travel to France the following week.

Since their meeting with the old clergyman a peculiar silence or shyness had come upon the two girls. They no longer, in the evening, laughingly drew up pictures of the future. They felt the dice to be thrown. And in a strange way it seemed to them that they themselves had had nothing to do with the event. They had got into the power of another person, of an old and almost ridiculous country clergyman—and such a thing had been very far from the programme of the two young conquistadores!

Lucan did not tell Zosine that she had already met Mrs. Pennhallow. But one day she asked her friend what she thought of the little old lady. Zosine for some time thought her question over. "Do you know," she said, "I feel sorry for her. She seems to me to be so unhappy."

In the course of the week Zosine said, "We shall let nobody know where we are going! I shall write to old Uncle Archibald, who is my guardian, that I am going to stay with my Mama's relations for a while. That will aggravate him, and all my uncles and aunts, for Papa's family have always looked down on Mama, because she did not have as much money as they. And indeed Mama did come from France, and surely must have some kind of people there, so that after all I may be speaking the truth."

"I should have liked to say good-bye to Ambrose," she said another day. "He has promised to let me know at once when he gets news of Papa. But he is away in Scotland with his future wife's family. Now I cannot even give him my address. But then I shall be proud to have stood on my own legs, without the advice or assistance of anybody."

As they were packing up their modest belongings, Zosine suddenly put down what she had in her hands. "Stop," she cried. "I will have a pretty frock to travel in, whatever else is going to happen to me. And you, Lucan, must take out another just as nice. Even if in France, to begin with—for nobody can tell what wonderful adventures we will meet there later on—we shall be nothing but the adopted daughters of an old country parson and his wife, we will still look lovely as we leave England."

At this she selected two elegant frocks for her friend and herself, and added shawls, bonnets, shoes and gloves to match. "We will sail across the Channel," she cried, and kissed Lucan, "like two great and charming young ladies without a care in the world."

PART TWO

the canary birds

*

1. the french farm

SIX miles from the small town of Lunel, and about a mile and a half from the village of Peyriac, in a garden surrounded by a low stone wall, there stood a long, pink house. It was called "Sainte-Barbe," and it had once been the main building of a farm.

The house had a strange history, and still held an exceptional position among the farm houses of the neighborhood. While all land around it belonged to the feudal estate of "Joliet," Sainte-Barbe was a freehold property, and had been so for fifty years, ever since the days of the Revolution. At that time a tragedy had taken place there. A commissary of the Convention had suddenly arrived in the district, and had taken up lodgings at Sainte-Barbe. In the night he had the lord of the chateau arrested, on the charge of having assisted a Royal Prince, a relation of King Louis, on his flight through France. The prisoner was brought to Sainte-Barbe and shot. A few days later the chateau of Joliet was partly burned down, but the lady of the manor and her children were spared. They stayed on in the remnants of their home until such time as King Louis XVIII returned to France, when they were restored into their full rights and had the chateau rebuilt.

But the widow of the murdered man, after the bloody night, would have nothing of Sainte-Barbe. There was, she said, a curse on the house. She no longer wished the farm to belong to the estate of Joliet, and she would not accept any selling price for it. She laid the fields, which had formerly belonged to Sainte-Barbe, to the neighboring lease-hold farms, and left the house and garden, where the murder had taken place, to the farmer, who lived there and, although nothing could be proved against him, was suspected of having betrayed his master.

Sainte-Barbe could now no longer subsist as a farm. The proprietor for some time kept an inn there, but he was shunned by his neighbors, and had to give it up. His daughter inherited the house and with it the bad name of its owner, but she had long known that she was an outcast. She kept to herself and worked hard, hoping to buy back, some day, Sainte-Barbe's fields and vineyards. She married a farm-hand, to get cheap labor for her purpose, but he could not stand the isolation, the toil or the avarice of his wife. He ran away and enlisted as a soldier, and nothing was since heard of him. His wife was now once more alone, kept to herself as before, worked hard and laid by money. Her name was Baptistine Labarre. When she was already an elderly woman, she hired out the house, and herself took service as housekeeper and cook with its tenants. Her new master was an old English clergyman and his wife.

The peasants in the neighborhood had at first been scandalized by the unusual kind of household, until they were informed by their own priest that in England the clergy were free to marry. But they still thought the new occupants of Sainte-Barbe peculiar, like the place, and saw but little of them. The English clergyman and his wife were themselves reserved people, and obviously had no wish to associate with their neighbors. They had lived at Sainte-Barbe for five years without making an acquaintance.

It was already dark when the small cart, which had carried the travelers from the village, stopped outside the door in the garden wall. As Mr. Pennhallow pulled the rope of the bell on the doorpost, a star fell. Zosine, in a loud exclamation, drew the attention of her traveling companions to it, and their eyes followed the delicate, luminous track across the dark sky. When it expired, she said, "Now I have wished."

"And I too," said Lucan.

"And I," said Mr. Pennhallow, and laughed a little.

A light appeared behind the shutters of the house. Soon after a young man with a lantern came out and opened the door. Mr. Pennhallow spoke to him in French, with a strong English accent, and called him "Clon."

At the door of the house itself they were received by a stout peasant woman in a white cap. In the lamplight the girls saw that the person who had opened the door to them was a very young man, or a big boy, tall and strong-limbed, with a heavy head and a pale, sullen face.

From a whitewashed corridor with a stone floor they came into a long, low room with green walls, a shining floor and a fireplace. Here a neat supper table was laid for the travelers.

"This house," Mr. Pennhallow said, as they sat down to it, "was once the center of fields and vineyards, and no small place. The farmer and his laborers, according to the custom of the province, had their meals together in this room, and one can tell what a prosperous man he was, and how many people he employed, from the fact that there are no less than two solid map-hooks to the ceiling."

The old man was obviously pleased to have reached his destination. When he folded his hands on the table to say grace, it almost sounded like a thanksgiving. "The two people," Zosine later said to Lucan, "have lived in terror of being seasick on the water, or kidnapped by robbers on their way through France. They now thank God for having got off so easily."

"They have been very careful of us as well, on the whole journey," said Lucan.

"Oh, they were proud of us," Zosine exclaimed. "They almost showed us off to the other passengers on board, and in the diligences. It is because you are so pretty," she added. "They were proud to have such a lovely girl with them."

The old house was irregularly built, with many steps and nooks, a very large kitchen and a long corridor. It was simply furnished, but clean and neat. It could be seen that Mr. Pennhallow had lived here for several years, for the old French farmhouse had taken on a pretty English look. There were biblical pictures on the walls, and upon the shelves rows of classical English books, in old leather bindings. The bedroom of the two young girls, next to that of their hosts, had a door opening on the corridor. This room also was but sparsely furnished, but all the same pretty and homelike, with white bed curtains, and a work-table and two old wooden chairs by the window. The air in here was a little musty and stale, as in a place where nobody has lived for some time. Lucan opened the window and looked out. In the dark she dimly saw a couple of tall poplars inside the garden wall, and behind them the outline of a long, low hill-crest. Zosine came up to her, and put her arm round her waist.

"God knows," she said, when for a while they had stood like this, close to each other, "how our Reverend Mr. Pennhallow struck upon this house of all houses in France. If I had not been taken straight to it by a boat and a diligence, I should never have imagined that it existed. And still, all the way I have felt that we were making for one single goal—yes, that we were drawn toward it, and could not possibly swerve off our course toward any other place in the world. And the place waiting for us, as we have now seen, was Sainte-Barbe. What is the magic attraction of Sainte-Barbe, Lucan? Do you think that a treasure is buried in the garden, and that one day Mr. Pennhallow will tell us to dig it out? And do you think that happiness is waiting for us here, in the long room where we had supper?"

"Father," Lucan answered after a short pause, "always held that when we question others upon our own affairs, we should be able to answer the question far better ourselves, if we only dared to put it earnestly enough. You may ask your own heart."

"I believe that we will be happy here then," Zosine said thoughtfully. "I am sure that we mean much to Mr. Pennhallow, and that he could hardly do without us. And I believe that he will teach us many things, of which we know nothing now. We shall leave Sainte-Barbe different girls from what we are now. I also really believe that a treasure is indeed buried in the garden, and that we have only to find its exact place. Listen," she added, as in the same moment a night-bird in a tree gave a short, hollow cry. "That is an echo coming from the future, of our spade-strokes, as we dig out the treasure.

"But tonight," she continued, as she closed the window and

turned toward the candle on the table, "I have reflected that, just as we have gone a good long way from England, we have got away from our ideas there. We then thought that we would become free and independent, once we got out into the great world. But here at Sainte-Barbe I feel as if that old clergyman was surrounding us on all sides, much more than the wall which we see down there. I could easily climb over the wall. But can I climb over the old man? And how shall we now be able to fight the whole world, as we resolved to do?"

The landscape around Sainte-Barbe was open and stony. At first its lack of color disappointed the young English girls. But it was still so different from all they had seen till now that soon it made a deep impression on their minds. Its vineyards and olive woods, and the long rows of poplars which protected the fields against the cold north wind, the "mistral," looked to them romantic and mysterious. The houses of the village were built closely together in one long street and a kind of market place, of gray stone and flat tile. Most of them had shutters at their street windows, which gave a secretive look to the little town.

It was a dry summer. From time to time big clouds gathered, and the dust rose in tall spirals on the roads, but no rain came. At night Baptistine opened the front door, and solemnly sniffed the night air, to scent out any sign of rain, then shook her head and remarked that this was a strange year. Remarkable things might happen before the end of it.

Baptistine was an unaccountable, close woman, who had an eye on everything in the house and in the garden, but might herself be dumb for days. Still she had a rich stock of information concerning her neighbors of the district, and at times suddenly and sullenly would open up to the girls. On such occasions it was not the virtues of the people of Peyriac upon which she dwelt; she talked of them all in a biting, malicious manner, as if she found a hidden happiness and triumph in her knowledge of the frailty and foolishness of human beings.

A couple of days after their arrival the Reverend Mr. Pennhallow talked to the girls of Baptistine's assistant, Clon. "That unfortunate boy," he said, "young as he is, has already been in jail.

He is but a child in mind, a foundling, who has never known his father and mother, and has not been taught in time the difference between good and evil. I have taken him into my house from charity, and I have promised myself never to tell anyone what brought him to prison."

2. daily life

IF, six months earlier, Lucan and Zosine had been told that they would come to pass their days among dry and dusty books, in the company of a little, old, dusty man, they would have been seized by panic, or they would have laughed. But Mr. Pennhallow was a schoolmaster by the grace of God, and at his hand they wonderingly, almost devoutly, entered the temple of learning.

He had informed them that he was, in the solitude at Sainte-Barbe, finishing a great philosophical and religious work of many years. They often saw him absorbed in his manuscript, and heard him rustling it late at night, and during the first week his school lessons with the girls seemed more of a pastime than a real task. But he was carried away by his own genius, and after a while became so thoroughly lost in his teacher's work that he forgot the time, as he made his pupils forget it, and kept them at their books until it grew too dark to read. It was as if he had been, for a long time, starved in his craving for displaying the power of his mind, and now, in a kind of intoxication, was giving himself up to it.

Within his heavy and coarsely shaped head a fund of knowledge was stored, which almost seemed to be too rich for one single person, and must have been accumulated there through many generations. When he said, "My grandfather gave much time to these studies," or, "My great-grandfather published a book upon this subject," Lucan and Zosine felt that his ancestors, by a particular magic process, had passed on their learning to their descendant. And yet the real charm of the school did not lie in the omniscience of the teacher. What fascinated and held the girls was his strange power to call forth, lightly and as in play, long-past ages and long-forgotten events and figures. Moses and Pharaoh lived to his pupils, in gigantic, shadowy forms, just as well as King Richard III, Tamerlane or Dr. Faustus. They felt that they themselves had been present when Nero played on his fiddle, with Rome aflame at his feet. With horror and grief they followed the Maid of Orleans from the Court and the stony faces of her judges to the prison and the stake. And all their life they remembered—although they never spoke of it—how, at the return of Odysseus, the unfaithful servant-maidens had been hanged on a rope like thrushes, and there "had writhed with their feet for a little space, but not for long."

Lucan had studied history with her father, but to Zosine the world of learning was almost unknown. At school she had eschewed her lessons as much as possible, and later on, in her gay home and on her travels, she had given little time to studies. Now that her whole nature was moved by the happenings of the last months, she sought refuge in this new world. Soon she was worshipping the old teacher, whose appearance a short time ago had made her burst into laughter, with the romantic infatuation of a schoolgirl. She no longer thought him ugly, but gravely confided to Lucan that Socrates must have looked like that.

"How much time and hard work it must have cost Mr. Pennhallow to learn all that he knows," Lucan one day said to Zosine.

"He has not learned it," Zosine replied. "He has really seen, or lived through, it all. I feel quite sure that he has gone through a number of successive existences, and that he knows things hidden to all other people."

She took her Latin readers to bed with her, and, each by her own candle, the girls read on, and read aloud to each other until long past midnight. They never reflected how, in the company of other girls, they might have feared to be mocked as bluestockings. They began to talk to each other in Latin, and, with inky fingers, discussed science or theology as eagerly as if they had really been a pair of zealous young doctors.

Zosine at times felt guilty because she was hiding part of the truth about herself to that old man who had opened such rich new horizons to her. Once or twice she came near to a confession of her real name and her history to him. But she had promised herself, for the sake of her father, not to mention the past. "And perhaps," she excused herself to Lucan, "even if I told him all, it would mean nothing to him. Such matters are all too worldly to interest him." At another time she solemnly declared to her friend, "He already knows it all. He knows more about us than we do ourselves."

The old man was also something of an artist, and did little pencil sketches of landscapes or flowers. At rare intervals, late at night, in the long dining-room, he took out a queer, old-fashioned flute, and played on it. There were ancient, sweet melodies on his programme, and some strange exotic tunes as well. He was no virtuoso, but his playing had a peculiar, unaccountable charm, which made the girls listen in breathless silence and sigh deeply when it ceased.

"What an eminent career," they said, "this old man must have had before him until his voice got cracked and hoarse. And what great strength of mind he must possess never to show any regret for it, but to be ever happy and at ease in his lonely little house, in his plain and blunt wife's company."

Mrs. Pennhallow had none of her husband's magnetic and inspiring power, nor his deep, thoughtful equanimity. Everything she undertook was done in fits and starts, "like a cart on a bad road," said Zosine. All the same the books would strike sparks from the flat-breasted, awkward figure, too, and she would teach in a kind of passion or ecstasy, like the man, and, like him, lose herself in her occupation and forget the hours.

"Do you know," Zosine one day said to Lucan, quite thoughtfully, "they both teach like people who, after having been brought almost to death by thirst, at last are able to drink their fill from the well? Or like drunkards who, after a long abstinence, come upon a cask of wine! And you and I!" she added. "Do you remember how, in London, we talked of conquering the world?

We have, in a way, conquered a new world. Or it has been laid open to us, by the two mighty old magicians! We owe much to them, Lucan. I wish I might be able to repay them, some time."

Only when the lessons were finished and the books put aside did Mrs. Pennhallow fall back into her old, abrupt, peevish manner. She could then, at times, while sitting quite immovable, keep her eyes so long and so sharply fixed upon the girls' faces, just as if in her mind she was making up some kind of account, that they became quite embarrassed.

"It is you she is staring at," said Zosine to Lucan. "Her eyes are quite glassy. She has been at the corner cupboard." To amuse herself, and without really believing in her own theory, Zosine would declare to her friend that the good old lady was fond of a drop of liquor, and was at times bracing herself with a glass of rum. "Or otherwise," she went on, "she is envious of your looks. You are getting prettier with every day, and perhaps, when our old foster-mother cannot take her eyes off you, she is trying to draw the beauty from your face into her own."

"I have read, or heard," she said, a few days later, "that a married couple, who are very happy together, will in time become like each other. This is what has happened to Mr. Pennhallow and his wife. One cannot exactly congratulate any of the two on the fact."

It was, however, only rarely that the girls would thus make fun of their adoptive parents. For apart from the strong, spiritual atmosphere there was, at Sainte-Barbe, an influence which moved and touched its two youngest inhabitants and filled them with a new devotion for their teacher and with a kind of laughing gratitude toward his old woman.

It had soon become obvious to the girls that they were indispensable to the old people, yes, that they were indeed their most precious belonging and the apple of their eyes. Mr. Pennhallow and his wife were loath to let them out of their sight. If they went for a walk, and came back later than they had meant to, they would find the old man or woman at the door, all upset with affectionate anxiety. It happened, when they were going to bed, that the door gently slid ajar, and Mrs. Pennhallow's gray face peeped in, as if to make sure that they were still there, and that, late at night, they heard her steps in the corridor outside their room. Mr. Pennhallow never spoke to them without a little, kind smile, and his wife, when she addressed them, softened her raucous voice. To Zosine, who had been looked after and spoilt all her life, this omnipresent, watchful tenderness was not always welcome. She would even become impatient with it, and complain that she was being treated as a baby. But Lucan, who had so long been left to look after herself, was deeply impressed by it. She often thought of that lost daughter, of whom the old people had talked, and felt grateful to the dead child for the kindness that now surrounded her.

The foster-parents, a short time after the arrival at Sainte-Barbe, had begged their adopted daughters to address them by the names of "Father" and "Mother." The girls did indeed at times, in a kind of gratitude, when speaking to Mrs. Pennhallow, make use of the word "Mother"—although they did so somewhat shyly or reluctantly, for there was in the dry and spare figure of the old woman but little of the attributes which one generally attaches to that sweet and sacred name. But Zosine, in her great admiration and devotion, almost from the first day of their lessons, had found a name of her own for her old teacher. She would call him "Master," and would hardly ever speak of him but as "our Master."

The solicitude of the old people was the more touching or pathetic because they were obviously quite unused to the company of young girls, and seemed to have no real idea of how to express their feelings for them. When they were not actually teaching, they had but little to say to them, and they would indeed very often talk to them as if they were babies or as if the old people themselves were somewhat in their second childhood. But they would also order Baptistine to make a sweet cake for them, or they would make them a present of a kitten or a bird in a cage. As Zosine had said, they were proud of their adopted daughters; they sent them to Peyriac to fetch their letters at the post-office, and on their return asked them if they had met many people on the way, as if they were keen to show them off. They many times expressed their regret at the fact that they did not know the people of the neighborhood, so that they might have introduced the girls to them.

One night, when the two girls were reading through their lessons for the morrow, the old clergyman, sitting by the lamp, gazed at them for a long time with a gently beaming face. He folded his hands on the table, and in his low, husky voice said to his wife, "So we have, my dear, in the end become a couple of real shepherds to our little white lambs." His wife joined him in a little heartfelt chuckle, which had a strange sound with her, as if she was not in the habit of laughing.

It seemed to Lucan and Zosine that the old people spoke but little to each other. It happened, though, that they would, between themselves, discuss matters of which the girls had never heard, and understood nothing, and would, herein, use words and turns unknown to them. But if they noticed that their pupils were listening, they at once broke off their conversation.

"It is probably," Lucan said, "some learned, theological theme that they are discussing, and they know that it is too complicated for us." At night, when they were in bed, the girls for a long time heard their low voices in the dining-room. "Now they are talking of the Master's book," they said.

At times the old people took down heavy books of account, and sat absorbed in them for hours. "Mr. Pennhallow," Lucan said, "will, surely, be keeping the accounts of many charitable institutions."

"When they are sitting like that," said Zosine, "their old heads close together, one clearly feels that they belong to a religious sect which is waiting for something. The second coming of Christ? The end of the world? I know nothing of theology. But I see in their faces that they are keeping a watch. They are, both of them, waiting for something, quite quietly."

3. Clon

THE Reverend Mr. Pennhallow was an ascetic by nature; he took no meat, drank nothing but water and, like the hermits of old, lived chiefly on dry bread and herbs. Mrs. Pennhallow took no interest in housekeeping; her mind was altogether absorbed in her husband and her books. But Madame Baptistine, like most Frenchwomen, was an able housekeeper, and the fare at Sainte-Barbe was plenty and pleasant.

Baptistine likewise had good knowledge of gardening. She sold vegetables and fruit to Peyriac, and on fair days made the boy Clon drive her goods in a small donkey-cart as far as Lunel, where she was well known for her crisp lettuce, sweet melons and juicy peaches.

In the early hours of the morning and when, after a burning hot day, the afternoons were cool and fresh, the two English girls worked with Clon in the garden. To Lucan and Zosine it was a welcome change from the lessons in the house to plant and sow, to tie up the melons and to carry clear water from the well to the herb beds. The little gray donkey soon became Zosine's favorite and pet. She curried it, fed it with sugar and led it by a rope to graze at the road-borders outside the garden wall. Lucan had a deep, instinctive love of all plants and flowers. She carefully weeded and watered the long rows of beans and cucumbers. She followed Clon's instructions about digging and hilling, but was also many times able to teach the boy new ways of treating the soil and the young plants.

During these peaceful hours in the garden the girls talked of their studies and of the past, and after some time they also began to discuss the future and to wonder what would happen to them when, in course of time, they were to take leave of Sainte-Barbe and to go forth into the world. Zosine expected great things of life. When her Papa came back, she said, the two would travel to China together, and she would, she declared, never marry and settle down before she had had suitors in every single country of the world. Lucan listened to her fantasies; she could not herself invent such gaudy and daring pictures of the future. To her it seemed to lie behind a veil, sometimes colorless, sometimes irradiated by a mysterious, enchanted light. She waited for it, silent and obedient. "Perhaps," she thought, and smiled as she carried a load of green peas to the house in her apron, "perhaps I am really an Adventist, just like Mr. and Mrs. Pennhallow themselves."

Clon was a taciturn boy. He was very proud of his great strength, and haughtily confided to the girls that he could make a grave quicker than the grave-digger of Peyriac himself. But he was shy and distrustful, and at times almost seemed to be afraid of the young girls, following them with dark, frightened eyes as they went to and fro in the garden. Zosine, who had little experience of timidity or of timid people, declared to her friend that the boy was not right in the head. But Lucan felt his sulky, diffident manner to be due to his imprisonment. She thought of her own small brothers and pitied the lonely boy. "It is unjust, it is a shame," she said to Zosine, "that a poor child, who may once, when he was hungry, have stolen a loaf of bread in a baker's shop, should be shut up with evil men, and ever after come to fear and shun all human beings." The quiet, sweet gentleness with which their Master treated the boy, the unfailing patience which he showed him, also impressed the girls, and made even Zosine promise herself to forbear with his strange, rude and clumsy manners. As one day Clon, in splitting firewood, cut his finger badly, she washed and dressed it for him. Her kindness and sympathy seemed to surprise, even somehow to offend him. Still from that time he would follow her about as she worked in the garden and carry the heavy pails from the well for her.

Clon had been taught by his master to fecundate melon plants by carrying the pollen of one plant to another on a small stick. Mr. Pennhallow at first had hesitated to let his young girls take part in a work so closely related to the mysteries of life, but he found that Lucan did already have good knowledge of the practice, and that in her innocence and her love of nature she connected no secret thought with it.

On a beautiful, cloudless day she and Clon were alone and at work in the melon beds. A little bashfully, because she felt that she could not express herself in French as well as she wished to, the girl tried to make the boy open his mind toward her. She avoided any talk of his own past, because she felt that it contained too much darkness and pain, but she spoke to him of her old home in England, and of how everyone there had done his best to be kind and helpful to the others.

Clon listened to her with a closed, set face, and with a faint, almost scornful smile. But as they rose from their knees among the melon rows, he stood for some time in deep thought. "I also," he suddenly broke out, "I also once tried to do something good. I too tried to help someone. Someone," he continued, with an odd movement in his sullen face, "who had hair like yours. And who spoke in the same way." He was silent and immovable for a minute. "But no one knows of it," he added, in a low, harsh voice.

Lucan looked into his face with her clear blue eyes. "Oh, yes, Clon," she said, gently and gravely, "He, who sees and knows all, knows of that too."

The boy stared at her, quickly glanced toward the house, and grew very pale. "No, no," he exclaimed, and would speak no more.

The next morning he came up to the girl with a queer, secretive excitement on his face, and proudly showed her a small squirrel which he had caught and was holding in his large, ill-shaped and spotted hands. Now, he told her, he would show her something; now they were to have some fun. As, with a little smile, Lucan asked him what he meant to do with the small, scared animal, he explained his plan to her, and it was so cruel and so mad that at first, in horror and dismay, she held her ears, and then, quite pale, ordered him to set the squirrel free and let it run away. Clon did not understand her, or he would not obey her; he only squeezed the squirrel tighter to his chest.

"Clon," she cried, endeavoring to steady her trembling voice, "do you not remember what I told you yesterday of Him, who sees all? What would He say to you, do you think, if He saw you torturing a meek creature which has done you no harm?"

Clon for a moment stared at her, as if her words were incomprehensible to him. Then slowly a hard, wild smile spread over his face. "He," he exclaimed, "would He not just like it? Would He not just think it a fine thing?"

Lucan reflected that, after all, Zosine had been right, and that the boy was demented. Alarmed and revolted she forced the small animal from him, and let it skip away. Clon had grown as pale as she, and he scowled angrily at her.

"When are you two going away?" he suddenly cried out, in a threatening, savage voice.

"Away?" Lucan asked.

"Aye, away," he repeated.

"Where do you want us to go, Clon?" she asked him gravely.

"Away! Off!" he cried. "Away from here! Like the other mesdemoiselles, who were here before."

At supper Mr. Pennhallow, who, on the way home from his daily work, at a distance had observed the young girl and the boy talking together, smilingly asked Lucan what she could have been discussing with the shy, dull village lad. Lucan would or could not mention the boy's ferocity. She answered, a little embarrassed, "He told me of some young ladies who had been here before us. I do not know what he meant."

She was so much upset at the boy's heartlessness, and at the idea of the small, defenseless creature in his hands, that at night she could not fall asleep. While she lay awake she remembered that she had left her watering can in the garden-path. It had happened before that Clon had been scolded for some forgetfulness of hers or Zosine's. She did not wish it to happen again. Very quietly, so as not to disturb her friend or anyone else in the house, she put on her shawl and slid out, to return the can to the small, low shed at the corner of the garden wall, where all garden tools were kept. It was still sufficiently light for her to find her way. She picked up the can in the path, where she had left it.

As she was about to open the door of the shed, she stopped, terrified at hearing a long, low wail from inside it. It sounded as if a human being had been shut up there and was lamenting in the loneliness of the night.

She tarried upon the path, called out in a low voice a couple of times, and at last lifted the latch and opened the door. Clon came tumbling out on all fours, and fell upon his face on the ground in front of her. He seemed to be beside himself with terror, and unable to rise. He trembled from head to foot, and kept on crying hoarsely and miserably. Lucan reflected that he must have fallen asleep in the shed, and that someone, unaware of his presence there, had locked the door on him. She stood and looked at him for a while, without speaking to him, for she could not forget or forgive his wicked, greedy eyes when he had been pressing the squirrel to him. But in the end she conquered her repugnance, bent down and laid her hand on his shoulder. "Clon," she called, and tried to raise him up.

"I cannot get out," the boy groaned. "I cannot get out." He shivered so violently that his teeth chattered, and she only grasped his wild, desperate words after he had repeated them many times. Lucan gently shook his shoulder, and at last got him on his feet. He clung to her hand, and stared at her in the half-light, as if he did not believe his own eyes. In the end, when he recognized her, he suddenly dropped upon his knees once more, pressing his body against her clothes.

"You see!" he cried out. "You see! He knows everything! He gets to know everything!" His voice was changed, so hoarse, broken and terrified that Lucan herself was frightened at the sound of it.

"I will never again speak of the demoiselles who have gone," he cried. "Is it not the same to me what has become of them? I will never again speak of any of them."

4. ~ mazeppa

WHEN at times Baptistine broke her sulky silence and entertained the English girls about people and events in the neighborhood, there were two names which constantly appeared in her reports. The first of the names was Joliet, the estate to which Sainte-Barbe had belonged, and which surrounded it on all sides; the other de Valfonds, the family who owned the land and resided at the chateau. Of this place and of these people the hard, sneering woman, contrary to her usual practice, spoke with respect. It might seem a strange thing that she, an outcast from Joliet, who must lay the blame for her isolated position on the de Valfonds family, should still feel so strongly attached to both. But Lucan and Zosine understood that the estate and the family which the peasant woman's own fathers had served for so many hundred years, in her eyes still had the splendor of a kingdom and of a royal family.

No estate in France, Baptistine proudly declared, was as well worked as Joliet; no soil produced a better wine, nowhere were the farmers, tenants and day-laborers so prosperous or so contented. The old lord of the land himself, who was murdered in the garden of Sainte-Barbe, had been a just and gracious master, at a time when other great landowners suppressed and ill-treated their peasants. His widow, who at the time of his death was but twenty years old, and who remained on the estate when other great families emigrated from France, had carried on the work in his own spirit, but had added a new feature to the tradition of the family. No Valfonds, after the time of the murder, had left the province. They lived and died in Languedoc. This peculiarity, too, Baptistine pointed out with pride, as if the family had thereby appropriated the province. It was the widow of the murdered Baron de Valfonds who still lived at the manor. Her only son and his wife had died; her grandson was now possessor and lived with his grandmother. This young nobleman had never been out of the country either, or even as far as Paris. He remained inside the borders of Languedoc, and was to be found on his own land.

All this strongly moved the imagination of the young English girls. Joliet to them became the castle of fairy tales, and part of the history of France, which they were just then studying. When they read of the crusades, it was now a Valfonds who set out for the Holy Land, while his lady waved her long veil from the battlement of Joliet. But a day came when they turned from their books to the real world. After the course of a month or two they often took the road through the pretty woods of Joliet on their walks. From a bench they could see the white building between the trees.

At the foot of the long hill upon which the castle stood there was a big grassy inclosure in which many fine horses were grazing. They were the riding horses of the young Baron de Valfonds. His family had always been able horse breeders and horsemen. Zosine, who till now during her sojourn in France had had to content herself with a donkey, was enchanted by the sight of the horses. She soon knew them all, and found a name for each of them. She made Baptistine give her baskets of stale bread, and carried it to her friends, who in their turn learned to recognize the girl, and came up to her, when she called them in her clear voice. Baptistine was quite pleased at the idea of Joliet's horses being fed on bread from Sainte-Barbe, and she was always less sulky with Zosine than with her other housemates. While Mrs. Pennhallow had got into the habit of staring at Lucan's pretty face, it happened that Baptistine fixed her eyes searchingly on Zosine, as if, to the peasant woman, her features recalled others that she had seen long ago.

Zosine had never spoken of Tortuga since they came to France. But when she sat on the gate of the fence, she talked freely of her home, as if she felt that she had here in some way come back to it. A big beautiful white horse in the inclosure reminded her, she said, of the riding horse that had been her Papa's favorite when she was a child. She named it "Mazeppa" after this horse, climbed the fence to pat it, and walked about with it on the grass, holding it by the mane.

One late summer day the young girls were down by the inclosure. It looked like thunder; the sky was a dim dark blue, with big clouds gathering up from the horizon; the big old oak trees round the field were almost black, and the white horse looked beautiful in the somber landscape, as with lifted head and tail he came trotting up to the gate.

Zosine turned toward Lucan. "I could easily ride on Mazeppa," she said. "I have often ridden a horse barebacked. When I was a child, a traveling circus came to the village at Tortuga. There I saw ladies both sitting and standing on unsaddled horses, and I was so keen to imitate them that Papa made one of the men come up to the house to give me lessons. If you will feed Mazeppa with bread to keep him quiet, I can mount him from the gate."

Lucan tried to make Zosine give up her whim. What, she admonished her, would the Master or Mistress of Joliet think, if they happened to pass, and saw her riding their horse? Zosine objected that they had never passed till now, but Lucan saw that her face shone at the idea that they might really come by in time to admire her horsemanship. She persuaded her timid friend to hold the white horse by the forelock, while she herself at the gate gathered her clothes together. "Now let go," she cried, happy as a child, as, holding on to the mane, and patting the horse on the neck, she set off past Lucan at a walking pace.

Lucan followed her with her eyes, and reflected that Zosine must always have looked well on horseback. At first it went slowly, but soon the girl made her horse trot. She had been sitting as in a sidesaddle, but as the movements of the horse became livelier, she dauntlessly, like a boy, flung her leg across the horse's neck, turned round and laughed at Lucan. She made the tour of the whole field, and then set her horse into a canter. For a time all went well, but then Lucan saw that she was sliding and losing her seat, and a moment after was thrown to the turf. For a second Lucan's heart stood still with fright, but Zosine sat up, shook her curls and once more turned a radiant face on her friend. Just then Lucan noticed that a young man had come out from among the trees on the other side of the inclosure, and stood looking at Zosine.

Lucan blushed. Zosine had the sun in her eyes, and did not see that her frock had slid up above her knees. Lucan would go up to her, but the young man had already swung himself over the fence, and had come to the assistance of the fallen Amazon. Zosine was still wild with joy. She kept sitting in the grass and laughed in the face of the stranger.

"You have not been hurt, Mademoiselle?" he asked her.

"God," Zosine cried, without answering his question, "what a sweet, wonderful horse Mazeppa is to ride!" She here caught sight of her own legs in the grass. Zosine had a pair of delicate, straight legs, but she thought that they were too thin. She rose up quickly.

The stranger was dressed in a blouse like a peasant's, but was gentle and graceful in his carriage and his movements. His fair hair, uncommon here in the South, was thrown back from a white forehead; his clear eyes laughed toward the girl. "So you are in the habit of riding barebacked, Mademoiselle?" he asked.

"I have ridden like that when I was a little girl," said Zosine. "But this time it was not exactly a success." She suddenly realized that the young man must have seen her falling off the horse, and now she would have liked to run away. But he was so respectful that she got back her pluck. "It is probably," she thought, "one of the grooms of Joliet. Perhaps he will not give me away to his master."

"Are you taking care of the white horse?" she asked.

"Yes, Mademoiselle, and he knows me well," he answered. Zosine gazed at him, the sun was still in her eyes. She was a little dizzy after her fall, and at the moment could not quite distinguish between the man and the horse. Was it a young groom of Joliet, or Mazeppa himself, with the beautiful, limpid eyes and the vibrating nostrils who stood and talked to her?

"I have once," she said, "seen pictures of centaurs, creatures half man and half horse. How glorious it must be to be a centaur."

"Aye, there may still be a few of them left in the woods of Joliet," said the young man, "and they would certainly welcome you in their brotherhood."

The young girls walked home all excited by their adventure. It was such a long time since they had talked with anyone but the people of Sainte-Barbe. Lucan was still embarrassed at having been caught trespassing. She gently scolded Zosine, and told her that she would not go with her to the paddock at Joliet again.

Zosine listened patiently to her for some time, and did not retort with a word. But as, at a turn of the road, they caught sight of Sainte-Barbe, she suddenly stood still, and turned on Lucan. At this moment she was not the docile and ambitious disciple of Mr. Pennhallow, but the old Zosine from Tortuga and the night of the ball, the spoiled, radiant girl, to whom life had been a rose garden, and its combats but a game. Her face was still aflame with the daring ride and the adventure.

"Do not scold, Sister Lucan," she begged, very sweetly and insinuatingly. "You serious people must not be too hard on human beings for what they choose to amuse themselves with when they are shut up as in a prison, and are not even allowed to say that they are prisoners. If I do not soon get a little bit of fun, I shall die."

5. mrs. pennhallow's admonitions

IN the whole district of Peyriac, where the famous dessert wine Muscat de Lunel is grown, the vintaging is the great event of the year. It is initiated by the priest, at first by a Mass in the small church of the market place, and later by a blessing of the vineyards themselves. All the dignitaries of the neighborhood are present; they join the procession on foot and kneel in the fields like the laborers of the vineyards, while their elegant carriages follow them at a distance and wait for them in the shade of the big trees.

Lucan and Zosine got permission to go down to the village with Baptistine to watch the ceremony. Baptistine had attended it every year, but had held herself back from the villagers. Now she became talkative in her usual malicious way.

As a fine carriage drove past, she told the girls that it came from Joliet, and that it was the old Baroness herself and her companion who sat in it. Her grandson, according to the old custom, would later meet the procession at the head of his laborers in the vineyard. The delicate, waxy and grave face of the old lady was framed by a bonnet of black lace; she was greeted with respect by everybody and graciously bowed her head in return.

"It is time for Baron Thésée to marry," Baptistine remarked, "but his grandmother will want a wife for him who comes from our own province and who will remain here. And the young ladies of the neighborhood are flighty misses. They are keen enough to become Baroness de Valfonds, but they are as eager to go to Paris to see our good King and Queen Amélie. The Baron himself will not leave the place, and will not be likely either to let his lady travel to Paris on her own."

"Is Baron Thésée like his grandmother?" asked Lucan, who could not forget the old lady's beautiful and noble face.

"No," said Baptistine, "he is like his grandfather, our old lord of Joliet, who came by his death when there was a revolution in France. But his father, Baron Sigisbert, the old lady's own son, who is now dead, was the living picture of his mother. He was the handsomest young man in France, they said. When King Louis came back, he sent for him, and would have given him a mighty position at his court in Paris. Yes, it is said that he would have married him to a Princess of the blood royal, because his family had been so loyal to the King of France. But Baron Sigisbert would not leave our province of Languedoc."

A young man in black, with a pretty white-and-pink complexion, passed them, and the peasant woman laughed to herself.

"There goes Monsieur Emmanuel Tinchebrai," she said. "He is head clerk to our old judge of Lunel. What do you say, my young mesdemoiselles; is he red-haired or not? Aye," she went on, laughing at the amazed faces of the girls, "the fact is that Monsieur Tinchebrai's father was a respectable flour merchant of Lunel, and had a pretty wife. His house lay opposite to the Bishop's palace, and when that was burnt down twenty-five years ago, Monseigneur the Bishop of Nîmes on his next visit to the town took up his residence in the flour merchant's house. His Excellency is out of a fine old family who are all handsome and generous people, but who are also all of them red-haired! Now when Master Emmanuel was born, all people were curious to have a look at the child's hair. If he was red-haired, he would be sure to get on in the world. But then too, one might find nasty names for old Father Tinchebrai and his young lady. What, now, did little Emmanuel himself hope for, when he was gazing at his picture in the looking-glass?" Baptistine finished with a little chuckle. "He never played much with other children. But he has been to a fashionable school, and he will certainly become a judge himself, in time. Once he used to come and visit my old master at Sainte-Barbe, in order, perhaps, to find out what a priest, who has got a wife, looks like. But they must have fallen out in some way, for he has not been to see him within the last six months."

The girls followed the procession part of the way, but then turned back, because, as they were both good Protestants, they could not kneel down with the others.

A few days later they met the priest of the village, Father Vadier, on the road. He addressed them kindly, and questioned them upon their life at Sainte-Barbe, but he became silent when he gathered that they were heretics. In the course of their talk he mentioned that he was Father Confessor to the old Baroness and her grandson. This made Lucan and Zosine regard him with reverence. The chateau of Joliet had lately played a big part in their talk and thoughts. They had wondered what people were doing or feeling there. And this kind, quiet man knew it all.

Against his habit, Mr. Pennhallow was out when they returned to Sainte-Barbe, Mrs. Pennhallow was restless and silent during supper, but later on she seemed to remember her duties toward her adopted daughters. She sat down at the table, opposite to them, and began to talk to them more animatedly than usual. But when they told her of their meeting with the priest, and how he had inquired about their life and studies, her face darkened.

"The Roman Catholic priests," she said with a little arrogant smile, "are ignorant and uneducated people. They want to poke their nose into everything, and would have us all go to confession with them. It is not the first time that the priest of Peyriac has come prying into our affairs at Sainte-Barbe. He would do better to keep out of them.

"Never," she said after a pause, with a slightly trembling voice, "listen to any papist. In this benighted religion, the priest himself drinks the communion wine, without giving the congregation part of it. Their priests must not marry! And the Roman Catholic Church worships a woman. In their churches you see a woman's image on the high altar. This is blasphemy."

The old woman's hands were trembling as she talked. She took hold of the lamp on the table to move it, but had to put it down again.

"Man," she said, "is made in the image of God, so it is written in the Scriptures. But woman is the most hideous of all creatures. The naked woman is so loathsome that thought shrinks from her. Never have I dared really to put up before myself the picture of a naked woman. If it had happened to me to view myself naked in a looking-glass, I should have had to stay in a dark room for the rest of my life. The particular functions of women are so abominable that even among themselves women will only mention them in a low voice. It is a terrible lot for a human being thus to despise and shrink from itself, and to know that there is no escape from the horror and debasement. A few of us, perhaps, have lived in the hope that man, as the higher being, would show forbearance with our misery. But these too have finished by telling themselves, 'It is impossible.' "

Her face twisted and quivered, as if she was smelling something disgusting, or was about to burst into tears.

"But then," she continued after a pause, with a strange, sudden light upon her features, "a miracle happens. Yes, those who have experienced it will know it to be nothing less than a miracle.

"Man, from whom we could not hope for forgiveness—see, he does not forgive us, he worships us. He does not bear with our hideousness, but he adores it. He does not mercifully close his eyes to our disgrace, but he cannot satiate his eyes upon it."

She once more made a short pause, and then cried, "This is grace. This is the rehabilitation and sanctification of woman by man. This is the great miracle of our existence. Those who ought to have been punished are honored. That from which men ought to have turned in disgust is celebrated in song. Yes, in the Song of Songs."

The old woman kept standing upright by the table. Her chin, which was adorned with a few gray bristles, quivered. She pressed her hand to her flat breast. The two girls had laid down their needlework in amazement. They stared at the awkward figure in its outburst of passion. But Mrs. Pennhallow did not look back at them. She almost seemed to speak to herself.

"It is a dreadful time," she said slowly and heavily, "the time in which we still doubt that a man shall wish or shall be able to save us. What horrible efforts are we not forced to make, in order to become a reality in his life. We are torn asunder between our hope of glorification and our dire remorse, as we feel, that while we are making him lift us from the mire, we are ourselves dragging him down into it. That time may last long, it may look as if it might be all too late, and still we must hold on. We must use force, even toward him who is going to save us. Oh, we ourselves suffer by it." She shuddered and for a moment held her hand to her mouth.

"But once it has happened," she said very slowly, "then we have reached beatitude. This is beatification of woman by man.

"And must we not," she continued, her pale eyes turned toward the ceiling, where two heavy sooted hooks showed against the old dark beams, "after that moment forever thank and serve him? We must submit to him, and toil for him; his wish must be law to us. Through him we have become beautiful, and if, once more, he were to turn his eyes away from us, we would sink back into our misery, and be lost for ever. Must we not, then, do all that he demands of us? We must never forget what we owe to him, and must ever be ready to give our life, yes, our soul itself, for that glance which has saved us."

She stood for some time, lost in her own thoughts. Slowly her face became tranquil, and altogether void of expression. The young girls once more ventured to look at each other. Zosine, to whom the irresistibility of her own beauty and of that of every young girl was an article of faith, laughingly threw a secret glance at the corner cupboard, wherein Baptistine kept her excellent, home-made cherry brandy.

At this moment they heard footsteps on the gravel of the garden path. The old woman's gray face slowly colored; the rigidness of her body dissolved; she still made a few little spasmodic movements with her hands and sunk down on her chair by the table.

"It is Mr. Pennhallow coming home," she whispered. "Thank God he is home safely. Be quiet now, girls. We will not speak to him of these things."

6. mr. pennhallow's old pupil

LUCAN these days was often troubled and heavy at heart. She had come to love Zosine as a sister, and the girl's trust and confidence every day meant more to her. But she could no longer be altogether frank with her friend. The rich, spoiled child of Tortuga knew but little of the world in which she was now living. It might surprise or amuse her, but she did not, on her own, attempt to understand it or explain it to herself. In her new circumstances Zosine relied on Lucan as on the person who had brought her there and who was already familiar with them.

And yet there was at Sainte-Barbe something that Lucan could not explain to herself. At times it seemed to her as if the house had a secret inhabitant on whom she had never set eyes. She told herself that it was nothing but a fancy, and still her strange suspicions would come back. Whereto, she thought, had she brought her light-hearted young sister who had such faith in her? She herself had before now learned something of the treacherousness of the world and ought to be able to see into it and judge their position.

Zosine seemed happier than before and more affectionate to her friend. A couple of times she asked Lucan if she was ill or worried by anything. Lucan shook her head, she would not let a fancy disturb Zosine's balance of mind. But it happened that she would walk off on her own, and in her solitude would, as it were, look about and listen.

One afternoon, when big rain clouds were gathering in the sky, Lucan was plucking apples in the garden when she saw a young man coming down the road by the garden wall, stop to take a view of the house, and in the end pull the bell-rope at the gate. She left her basket and went down to open it to him. The stranger gazed at her with deep surprise and admiration for a second, tore off his hat, and inquired whether the Reverend Mr. Pennhallow lived in this house. As Lucan said yes, he took out a card, handed it to her, and begged her, if convenient, to inform the old clergyman of his presence. He was a fine, vigorous young man, with thick dark eyebrows and blue eyes; his carriage was free and natural, as in a person who has lived much in the open air. His voice was strong and sonorous, but he spoke with an accent.

"But you are not French," exclaimed the girl. "You are English."

"And you," the young man cried, as pleasantly surprised as herself.

Lucan told him who she was and that she and her sister were staying with Mr. Pennhallow and his wife.

"Is he married?" he cried out in amazement, and at the next moment went on happily. "But then you must bring me to him, and tell him that I am an old pupil of his who has looked him up in his hiding-place."

While they were talking, Mr. Pennhallow himself, who had heard the ring of the doorbell, opened the door of the house, and shaded his eyes to take a view of the visitor.

The young man had kept his hat in his hand. He now took a step forward, and asked, "Do you recognize me, my old tutor?"

Mr. Pennhallow for a moment stared at him, and then smilingly replied, "So this is really you, Noël? No, I beg your pardon," he corrected himself. "Sir Noël. I am already aware of the change of your fortunes. Your cousin has died from a fall from his horse, and you are now Sir Noël Hartranft. But what brings you to France, Noël?"

"Let me come in, my venerable master," said Sir Noël, "and rest myself by your hearth. I am in sorry need of your wisdom and your friendship. But first we will recall old times together."

Mr. Pennhallow never appeared surprised or put out. All the same he gave the young man a long, gentle, attentive glance before he led him into the house. Here he introduced him to his wife, and to Zosine, who came running along at the sound of a strange voice, as Sir Noël Hartranft, one of his dearest disciples from the old days.

"You were an unsteady disciple," he said with a smile, "and caused your tutor some moments of perplexity. But I must grant you that you never knew fear, and never told a lie. I was informed that you had gone to sea, and I thought that the sea might have knocked you into shape."

"I have had a few things happen to me," said Sir Noël, and passed his hand across his forehead. "I have been to sea five years, and have sailed round the world more than once. But now I am, as you said, a respectable landlubber in England. 'Nihil est agricultura melior.' You yourself taught me that, so it is sure to be true. Today, in your presence, I once more feel a boy of fifteen."

Mrs. Pennhallow seemed to be uneasy at the arrival of her guest. A couple of times her eyes sought those of her husband. But the old man genially placed the visitor and himself in two chairs in front of the fire, invited him to take a glass of port, and talked to him kindly and artlessly. The old teacher questioned his former pupil on his career and adventures in the world, and on late friends and acquaintances. He recalled events of ten years ago, and in jest catechised his disciple on the doctrines he had once imparted to him. Sir Noël explained that his ship was at anchor in Marseilles, and that he himself was staying at a hotel in Lunel, and was going back there that same evening. The girls looked with big eyes at the handsome sailor.

When the teapot was set on the table, the young man became silent for a while, and then declared that he might as well straightaway confess what had brought him to Sainte-Barbe.

"Although," he said, "it will probably appear to you as fantastic and unreasonable as the frenzies with which I distressed you in the old days. No," he added, as Mr. Pennhallow signified to his wife and the girls that he wanted them to leave him alone with his guest. "No, I do not mean this tale for your private ear. The whole matter would look too confoundedly solemn to me myself, were I to confess it to you alone. Please beg your good lady and the girls to listen, and to laugh at me. After all, the ladies are the true arbiters of our activities."

He obviously did not want to take his own business seriously, but all the same his voice had changed.

"You will remember, my good old teacher," he said, "how many lectures and admonishments you had to administer to me, to keep me in the right path. Many times you must have thought that they were lost upon a hardened young sinner. But I swear that there has been no human being, whose words have stamped themselves so deeply upon my unruly mind.

"It is true that your principles seemed to me all too lofty for those who realized that they were just very ordinary Englishmen, and your rules of conduct far too heaven-aspiring for a boy who had no ambition of becoming a saint. But at the same time it seemed to me that no one but you did understand my nature and everything in it, even the feelings that I could not explain, and which were hardly clear to myself. Yes, it appeared to me, when you interpreted the Scriptures or history to me, that you thoroughly understood the nature of all people, both dead and alive. Do you remember how severely my uncle once punished me, because, at night and in a storm, I had sailed out in my small boat? I thought his verdict unfair, and was furious with him, and with everybody in the world. Then you came, and spoke to me, just as if you yourself had been with me in the boat. Yes, as if you had been out on darker nights and in fiercer storms. I was silenced and brought to heel at once. I no longer raged against my uncle.

"And do you also remember," Noël continued, "that in your untiring fight against the powers of darkness, on behalf of our precious little souls, you recounted to us of people who had made a compact with the Devil himself and had sold their souls to him? You were well versed in these dark matters, and must have studied them with zeal."

Once more Mr. Pennhallow gave the young man a long, mild, intense glance. "So you still remember those old grandmother's tales?" he inquired.

"Yes, I remember them," Noël said, "or they have been brought back to me later in life by the things that have happened to me. I have pondered so much upon them that in the end it became necessary to me to look you up, and to talk with you about them. You were, it seemed to me, the only person in the world who could enlighten or advise me."

"It is," Mr. Pennhallow said thoughtfully, "such a long time since I have occupied myself with these matters. And I am not, I am afraid," he added playfully, "the right person to set up such a contract on your behalf, if that is what you have in your mind. But I promise you to give your tale my full attention and, when you have finished it, to enlighten and advise you as far as my insight and experience go."

Noël was silent for a while, then he drew his breath deeply and began:

7. a soul was given away

"FATE," he said, "has played with me in her own manner. A year ago I was very well pleased with the world and with myself. Six months ago I was in hell. I beg your pardon! I mean that six months ago I was a desperate and desolate person. Today, today I do not know," he repeated with a grim smile, "whether, in the most solemn and eternal sense of the word, I may call my soul my own.

"As you know," he went on, "I was brought up in my uncle's house, Wanlock Hall, with his son, my cousin, who was of my own age. I went to sea, as you said. I became a captain on Her Majesty's ship *Lion*. A beautiful girl, who was courted by all my friends, told me that she liked me best. Everything looked pretty rosy for your obedient servant. But all of a sudden the whole business went to—I mean that all at once the whole thing took a most confounded turn for me.

"I happened to be ashore one night, and up in London, playing cards with my cousin and his fine friends, in his own club there. I won from him the whole night, and he, who was a bad loser, grew sore and sulky over it, and suddenly accused me of not playing fairly. A violent quarrel followed. I insisted upon an apology, and he would not give it. He was popular in the circle into which I had dropped, but none of them knew me well, and I went away in a rage. The very next day my uncle sent for me, and had, I suppose, already had the matter well dinned into him beforehand. I let the old gentleman know what I thought of his son, and, in short, I sailed from England on extremely bad terms with all my relations, and with a mad suspicion upon me. My girl wept, but she promised to wait for me, and that was my consolation.

"But as my ship came to Cadiz," said Sir Noël, "they handed me two letters. The first was from my uncle, who had by now made up his mind about his worthless nephew. He would, he said, never again set eyes on me, and he cut me off with a shilling. The second letter was from my young lady, and it was, she vowed, written with streaming tears. As if that was likely to cheer me up! Her people had worried and bullied the poor pretty child beyond her endurance. She gave me my word back, and wanted her own in return, for within a month from the day on which her letter was written, she was to marry my cousin.

"One feels fairly faint at such a double rejection. I could not stand to be alone, but wandered about in town. First, to distract and amuse myself, I went to see a bull fight. But it did not amuse or distract me. It seemed to me that I was the bull myself and was being teased, stabbed and pricked at from all sides, and I reflected that this was an unfair way to treat a beast or a man.

"Late in the night I once more found myself playing cards at a gambling house. I cannot remember that I had drunk anything. I lost, and went on losing, and in the end I had only a single coin left to me. I do not, in general, take my losses at cards to heart, but on this night it was as if the queen of diamonds and the knave of clubs were real little devils teasing and pricking me. And I do not know how it came to happen," Sir Noël continued, drawing in his breath deeply, "but as I sat there, and a lot of old reminiscences from England ran through my head, I did, all of a sudden, strike upon your tales of people who had sold their soul to the devil and made good on it.

"As now the cards were again dealt round," he went on, "I said to myself, 'We Hartranfts have never been particularly clever at selling things, and God knows that I do not know, either, in what price I should hold my soul, were I to display it for sale on the market. But I could do, tonight, with the support of His infernal Majesty. I will make him a present. I will hand him this soul of mine, of which people speak, as a gift. If he be, as Shakespeare tells us, a gentleman, he will possibly pay me some kind of compliment in return.' Yes, my good old tutor, it will surely be incomprehensible to you that a human being should reason in this way. But on that hot night in Cadiz it seemed to me a perfectly natural and commonplace arrangement. 'Please, Sir Beelzebub!' I said, and I was, I assure you, as much in earnest as I have ever been in all my life.

"The next moment I took up my hand, and saw nothing but trumps. I won, and went on winning all through the night. As I came aboard early in the morning, my pockets were filled with gold, silver and notes."

Here he looked up, as if to watch the effect of his story on the audience. Lucan had been listening with awe, but at the same time with deep sympathy and compassion. Her sweet blue eyes were fixed on the face of the narrator. He stared back at her, and was silent for a minute, as if collecting his thoughts.

"The day after," he said, "I did not give the matter a thought. I made up my mind to go on living, in spite of my uncle's illnature and my sweetheart's fickleness. I thought of my career at sea, and of my country, and I was longing to get out on the open sea once more. But in the first harbor in which we laid to, I had news that my uncle was dead, and, immediately after, that my cousin had been thrown hunting, and had died from the fall, and that in his last moments he had withdrawn his charge against me. I was now Sir Noël Hartranft, as you were just now saying, and Wanlock Hall was my own house. Not a month hereafter my own true love wrote me that I must forgive her her weakness, and that she was once more mine own forever."

The young man sat for a while silent and in deep thought. "And in this same way," he said, "things have gone on for me ever since. Whatever I do falls out luckily. A horse, which I bought in May, just as a whim, in that same month, won a race. If I am out fishing, I make a catch every time I throw my line. And I cannot, when I shoot, miss a bird. My wedding is to be celebrated next month.

"But the queer thing about it all is this," he continued, and his voice suddenly changed, "that I do not get any real pleasure out of this good luck of mine. My money disgusts me. It is, as

Scripture tells us, dust and ashes in my mouth. My friends now seem to me friendly only because they know that I am a rich man. My fiancée herself is no longer the same as before. Indeed, I am almost frightened of her. I have no longer, it appears to me, anything to wish for or to look forward to in life. Indeed, life itself looks to me the devil of a business. I went for a last trip with my ship to get away from my splendor and my wretchedness in England, but even a ship could not help me.

"And now I have come to you," he said, "and I beg you: do answer me, you who have taught me when I was a small boy, and about whom I have always held that you had more knowledge of secret things than any other man. Am I mad? Or can it really be that the Devil, whom you and all our Holy Church proclaims, has accepted my gift, and that I am now forever bound to him? It is not that I worry a lot about the fate of my soul after death. But may I never again, in this life upon earth, feel like a free man and a gentleman?"

He had spoken so earnestly and with so much weight that the strange tale of his had almost become real to the small party in the dining-room of Sainte-Barbe. Mr. Pennhallow sat for a long time without a word. Then, from his deep grandfather's chair, he smiled to the young man.

"You may set your mind at rest, Sir Noël," he said very slowly. "You have made no compact with the Devil. When you tell me that you are uneasy in your heart, and that you are getting no pleasure from the good fortune which has fallen to you, you two have nothing to do with each other. The Prince of Darkness has allowed himself a small jest on your behalf. He is, indeed, as our immortal bard tells us, a gentleman, and as a gentleman, he has shown his appreciation of your own fine and rare gesture toward him. But he has not closed with your offer; he has not accepted your soul. Possibly he does not ever accept any gift at all.

"No," he continued in the same manner, "that which, according to our old tales, and as far as I can now recall it, one gains in making a compact with that high power to which you have addressed yourself is neither gold nor honors. No more is it a lovely bride. He, of whom you speak, has more esprit than that! He does not bestow upon us such things as one human being might give another. The reward which his servants do receive from him is not to be described in words. It is an inner happiness, a deep and quiet beatitude, a peace of heart which cannot be shaken by outward circumstances. It is the certainty, the confidence of knowing that you are, now and forever, within his hands.

"Wealth?" the old man continued with the same mild and ironical face. "The esteem or admiration of people? All this is as play-money to pure gold, in comparison with the values of which we are now talking. His true and faithful servant is blessed and secure wherever he moves. He may be sitting within a hut, and under conditions of which other people—" He slowly moved his clear glance round the circle, and for a moment let it rest upon the face of his wife, "—would bitterly complain, and still in his heart, with untroubled firmness, know that he has received full value for that which he has transferred to him."

The young man looked at him, once more drew his breath deeply, and then smiled back. "Do you assure me of this, my old tutor?" he asked.

"Yes," said Mr. Pennhallow.

Once more Lucan, who, like the others, had been listening in keen suspense, wondered at the strange authority with which the small, plain man did speak. It was as if, in a moment like this, no human being could possibly doubt his words. Sir Noël let his hand pass over his eyes.

"Well," he said, "if you tell me that it be so, I will believe you. I see that I have been right in coming to you, and, however foolish it may have sounded, in speaking freely and openly to you. Maybe no one but you yourself would have had the patience to listen to me. And surely no one but yourself would have been able to lighten my mind of its burden."

"But there is one thing," Mr. Pennhallow said after a long pause, "I would like to ask you. How did you come to know where to find me? In Scotland, as far as I remember, I did not leave any address."

"It did indeed happen in rather a strange way," Sir Noël exclaimed. "On this last journey the *Lion* lay to in Buenos Aires.

And there, one evening, in a somewhat questionable place, I ran into a countryman who had not been in England for many years. He made a few corks pop to celebrate our meeting, and to drink to the old country and to friends at home. As I mentioned my own birthplace, he cried out that this was the very home of his own best friend in life, and he named you. I asked him in surprise if he was an acquaintance of my old teacher. 'My God!' he cried. 'An acquaintance! I am the servant and slave, until my death, of the Reverend Mr. Pennhallow.' 'And do you know where he may be found now?' I asked him. 'Indeed I do,' he answered again. 'Did I not receive one of his dear epistles only yesterday?' At this he pulled a letter out of his pocket, and he let me copy your address from it. But it is true," the young man added, "that soon after he became very taciturn, when I questioned him about his acquaintance with you. For indeed, he was the last man in the world with whom I should ever have connected you. He even followed me down the street, and a couple of times suggested that I should return him the address which he had given me. I reflected that he would be some sad wreck whom, out of charity and philanthropy, you had supported, and whom you were still trying to keep upon the right way. But I have forgotten his name."

"Is that so?" said Mr. Pennhallow.

8. in the moonlight

WHILE they were talking, the wind had begun to blow, and in the short silence which followed Mr. Pennhallow's last word, they now heard the loud sound of streaming rain. The old clergyman would not allow his guest to go away in such weather, but told Baptistine to put the gable-room in order for him. The small party thus kept sitting round the fire, and the girls wished that the conversation would last all night.

As if Sir Noël found his confession too fantastic or extravagant, and wanted to wipe it off the mind of his audience, he now entertained them freely and gaily with accounts of his travels and experiences. He had been through a shipwreck and a fire at sea, and had witnessed a mutiny in the Indian Ocean. He had visited Santo Domingo, and described the very neighborhood wherein Zosine had lived as a child, and the girl, who dared not betray her own familiarity with the place, listened with clear, wistful eyes. As the night advanced, the guest obviously felt more and more at ease in the circle, and he looked with delight from the one pretty face to the other.

In their bedroom Lucan and Zosine discussed the handsome, fascinating stranger for a long time. Zosine told Lucan that she had already known him by name, and that his cousin had been one of her beaux, and she radiantly confided to her friend that Sir Noël admired both her and herself madly. "And have you not noticed," she exclaimed, "that he is the very picture of Lord Byron?" Lucan had indeed already, in front of the fire, thought of the same thing, but to her it was a sacred matter. The first memory of her childhood had been her mother's tears at the tidings from Missolonghi, and in her home the portrait of the poet had held a place of honor. It was a wonderful thing for her to have met and talked with a human being who might at all be compared to him. But would she, she thought, if it had indeed been Lord Byron himself whom she had lighted up the narrow stair, have had that same strange feeling of safety at the idea of his presence in the house? It was to her as if a friend and protector now slept under the roof of Sainte-Barbe, and as if she might have unburdened her heart of all depression and anxiety to this stranger, who had himself come here to find comfort for his restless mind.

The following day was clear and quiet. Old Mr. Pennhallow jocularly explained to his old pupil how he, who had formerly taught wild boys, was now a mentor to tender and timid maidens, and he made them show off their knowledge in Latin and history to his guest. As at last the young man was about to take leave, he gave the girls permission to see him off part of the way. The air was chilly after the rain. Zosine threw a white shawl over her dress, and Lucan a tartan cape. Mr. Pennhallow took a hearty leave of his young friend. His wife too smiled at him as kindly as she had done when Lucan first met her at the inn, which made the girl reflect that perhaps the old woman's amiability was particularly displayed toward travelers.

The three young people were alone and soon talked gaily together. They walked on quickly in the clear air. Zosine was accustomed to having young men at her pretty little feet. She laughed and jested with Noël, and even teased him a little about his own romantic tale of last night. She sang to him, and made him join her with his fine voice in some of the songs of their home country. In her father's house Lucan had mostly known men a great deal older than herself. She wondered at the gay and frank familiarity of her two companions. Could one really, she thought, talk to a man, to a member of the graver, superior sex, as one did to another girl—and make him join, and take pleasure in, the same debonair, capricious kind of chat?

Once during their walk she happened to be left a little behind them. She watched their two happy and graceful figures so close together against the sky and the field. Zosine, as ever, carried herself lightly and erectly. "They are the same kind of people," she thought. "If Sir Noël was not, as he told us, already engaged in England, he would surely fall in love with Zosine, and she with him. In that case, I should no longer need to feel any anxiety about her future, or about having brought her here."

A little later Zosine, in picking blackberries in a hedge, had got behind the others. At that moment Lucan found Noël's eyes fixed upon her face with a strange, deep gentleness. He smiled at her, but all the same seemed grave.

"You probably cannot understand," he said, "for I hardly understand it myself, with how much sadness I am leaving a place that I have only known for a day, to go back to my own home. You, who are so young, would not understand that one may, within twenty-four hours, live more intensely than, at other times, within a whole year."

"Perhaps," Lucan thought, "he would now have liked to talk to me of Zosine."

They parted on the top of a hill, and the traveler deferentially kissed the hands of the young ladies. He turned round many times and waved his arm to them, and they waved back. When they had seen his straight lithe figure disappear at a bend of the road, Zosine suddenly put her arms round Lucan's neck. "Do you know," she exclaimed, "I believe that things will happen to him altogether differently from what he now imagines."

In the evening Zosine went to bed early, in order, she said, to dream of their guest, who was already so far away. Lucan saw that the moon was up, and longed to get out in the open air. She could not find her own cape, so put on Zosine's white shawl.

The moon stood high in the sky, but there were big clouds, and the garden and all the landscape were dim. The girl sat down on a bench under a tree. She thought that she saw something move by the door in the wall, and the moment after she heard a low whistle. It was the tune that Noël had sung on the road. Her heart beat strongly as she walked down to the door, and in the moonlight saw himself standing outside it. He held his hat in his hand, as he had done the day before, when she had first opened the door to him, and he did not come any nearer to her.

"Yes, it is I," he said in a low voice. "Forgive me that I have come back from Lunel. I only wanted to see the light in your window. I dared not even wish that you should come out! All the same it will be my thoughts which have drawn you from the house." The moonlight fell straight on his face, but Lucan knew that she herself stood in the shade of the trees. He was very pale, as he took a step forward, and crossed the threshold to the garden.

"But as I have now been blessed with the happiness of seeing you once more," he exclaimed, deeply moved, "a happiness that I dared but hope for—nay, that frightened me, when I recognized your shawl in the moonlight—I must also be allowed to speak to you."

She was going to speak, but he stopped her. "No, speak not," he cried. "It is not fit that you should speak to me, or you will only do so to forbid me to go on. I beseech you, do not speak. But you must listen to me these few minutes before I go away. These minutes I will remember all my life. Let them, then, also contain all my life to me."

Lucan's heart seemed to stop beating, and the moment after throbbed violently. Her strange and terrible position almost seemed to kill her. For the second time a man declared his love to her, and begged her not to speak herself; for the second time, bewildered, horrified and dumb, she listened to him. At this moment it seemed to her that no time had passed since, in the dimly lit drawing-room, she had been listening to Mr. Armworthy. But then she had been kept back from throwing her refusal and disdain into his face. Here in the moonlit garden, Noël's entreaty prevented her from informing him that he was wrong and that she was not the person whom he took her to be. She trembled from head to foot. And at the same time, something in herself kept her from speaking. Even if she knew his words to be addressed to another woman, there was an infinite sweetness and bliss—such bliss as till now she had only experienced in her dreams—in listening to them. Time and space ceased to exist; only his voice in the night air was real.

"I have thought of many things since I left you," he said. "When I sat in the hotel at Lunel, waiting for it to be dark enough to drive back here, I came to understand all that has happened to me, and all that I am myself. It is not, as my old teacher explained to me, from any mystic or fantastic reason that the gifts of fortune have failed to make me happy. No, my discontent and my restlessness arise from the fact that all that, which till now I have coveted, and all that which I have won, is but vanity and emptiness. I have not deserved better. But then, until yesterday, I have never known the real gold of existence. I have been but a careless thoughtless boy. You yourself have met me at a moment when I confessed a foolish aberration. If, since then, I am changed, it is not due to my own merits.

"What," he went on, in a deeper, trembling voice, "is wealth that we should thus run after it all our life? To me it no longer means anything. The girl who awaits me in England is not in love with me, and is probably not capable of loving any human being. She rejected me, and took me back, all according to the wealth and position I could offer her. And I do not blame her, for I am now aware that I have never really loved her myself. I wanted to win her from my rivals, as I wanted to win a race or a game. How is it," he went on in violent agitation, "that the eyes of a man are suddenly opened, in a single moment, and that then for the first time he realizes the worth of a woman, of a sweet, innocent girl? How is it that he will only then understand that it would be the highest imaginable happiness to him to serve her all his life? Yes, that in this one moment, trembling and transported, he realizes that her own love, could he win it, would mean heaven itself to him." He was silent for a while, his voice failed him.

"A boy," he added after a silence, "is a weak and wild creature —how weak and wild, in your own innocence you do not guess. He does not become a man before the heavenly purity of woman is revealed to him. I felt it last night when I was talking to my old tutor. Something had been brought into the atmosphere that should not be there, something dangerous or vile, I know not what, which ought never to thrive in your nearness. I could not explain it to myself. I only, with a kind of horror, felt it to be disturbing the harmony round you, to be in some way threatening you. And it must have been my own unworthiness and wantonness. What else could it be beneath the roof of that good old man?

"Alas, I have looked on woman as on a toy for my own turbulent nature. I have scorned the highest which this life has to give. But from this moment I shall never again regard any woman, not even those deepest sunk, without reverence. She will be of your sex, and will be high above me, in the light of your innocence! I shall, from today, be the knight of every woman because you will forever be in my mind.

"I speak of what I will do," he said, with a little short laughter, "as if I still had a free will. But my position is terrible and ludicrous. I am Fortune's fool. I am bound to return to England. You yourself, I know, will hold me to my given word. But all the same, from now, in every place and at every time, I am at your service. I will honor my wife and make her happy because she is a woman like yourself."

Lucan felt the tears mount to her eyes. "My God," she thought, "you call your position terrible and ludicrous. What, then, is my own?"

"And since I can swear this to you," said Noël, and took a step toward her, "since from now until my last hour I am your servant, I may give expression to the words which burn in my heart and upon my lips. You know in what deep reverence I pronounce them. My words are not changeable, like that moon that looks down upon us. They are firmer and more eternal than anything else in me. Let them become sacred to myself because you have listened to them! I love you."

Lucan, at this moment in such great and overwhelming emotion as she had never in her life experienced, lifted her heart in a prayer to God. She would afterwards remember that she had prayed in this way, as with her whole being. But she could never recall what she had prayed for—or indeed whether she had prayed for anything at all.

Before she could prevent it, he had bent his knee before her, seized her hand, and carried it to his lips. She stood immovable. Her beatitude and her despair became one to her. She felt that she smiled in the deep shadow which lay over her face. For a moment she laid her trembling hand upon the dark head so deeply bent before her. Within the next moment he had risen, had drawn back a step, and once more had closed the door between them.

She listened to his hasty steps for a long time. As the sound died away, she slowly lifted her face toward the moon and the clouds, and the hand that he had kissed to her own lips. Although she was as silent as the night itself, in her ears and her heart his words re-echoed in a deep, immortal ring: "I love you."

9. are we rivals?

UNTIL this day Lucan had given but little thought to herself or to her own concerns. When she was a child her mother and her small brothers had taken all her time and her thoughts; later on they had been her father's, and, for these last months, Zosine's. Now all this was suddenly changed, and the new, strange state of things in itself alarmed and confused the girl.

It seemed to her that all the world had turned against her, and that no girl could ever have found herself in such a cruel situation as she. Noël's words about the fighting bull that is attacked and stabbed from all sides came back to her. As a child she had heard her father talk with abhorrence of bull fights, and the ferocious picture had stuck in her mind. But was it not even more cruel when the stabs were aimed at a timid girl who had never harmed anybody? She would have fled, if it had been possible. But where would she fly this time? No flight could take her away from her misery.

Was it not, she asked herself with pale, quivering lips, hard enough that she should love a man who loved another woman, and that this woman should be her own best friend? Must she also be forced, by strange, unhappy circumstances, to listen to the burning declaration of his love, to the sweet words and vows, that were not meant for her? And must she know, in the midst of her own distress, that he too was unhappy and lonely, and that she could give him no help or comfort?

There was no one in the world to whom she could confide her misfortune. She must hide from Zosine what had passed between Noël and herself in the moonlit garden, for she felt as if she would die if she repeated it. No feeling of loyalty to her friend could compel her to do so either, for Noël was bound by his word and honor to a bride in England, and had gone back there to marry her.

And if it had not been so, she thought, could she have found any consolation, any faint reflection of content, in the sight of the happiness of her friend? For some time Zosine had spoken much of the handsome, fascinating stranger. It was probably Lucan's own silence on the subject which had gradually stopped her gay, fanciful talk. Lucan loved Zosine as a sister. She had always admired her without envy or bitterness, and she saw that she and Noël were like each other, so beautiful to look at, so gay, gallant and generous. She had worried about the fate of her friend, and had felt her own responsibility toward her deeply. She would not grudge Zosine any luck or triumph in life. Still sometimes, at night, in her dreams, for a moment of infinite sweetness, it happened that the white shawl was hers, and that Noël's words were indeed meant for her. Then she would wake up to find herself in a bleak and empty world. She would look at her sleeping friend, wring her hands and reflect that she had never known unhappiness till now.

All the same she felt that now she lived more fully than ever before. Each hour of the day had in it a significance which strained her whole nature to its utmost capacity, but which also gave weight and richness to her existence. She now remembered, with a strange thrill, how, as she was considering Mr. Armworthy's offer to her, she asked herself, "What is it that I demand of life and have always longed and hoped for?" And how her own heart had answered her clearly and loudly, "It is love."

It was true that she had then dreamed of a happy love, and that the idea of an unrequited passion would have horrified and distressed her. But her vague presentiment of that spring night had been confirmed to her. The beauty of nature, music, poetry and art are all inextricably bound up with the idea of love. The woman who has denied love, she had then dimly guessed, will no longer dare to learn a poem by heart, to listen to a song, to pick the wild flowers of the woods, or the roses of her garden. Now, in pain and ecstasy, she knew for certain that the magic kingdom of beauty, sweetness and poetry in this world is open to the lovers as to its lawful heirs.

Could it be, then, that it was in itself a happiness to love, even when one loved without hope? She wondered, doubted and despaired, and again felt a strength and a bliss she had never known before. Time after time she went through the hours she had passed in Noël's company, and in her heart knew that she would not exchange her sadness for any secure and prosperous everyday existence, nor the picture of a young man, whom she had known for a day and a night, and would never meet again, for the whole world.

She so thoroughly lost herself in her own thoughts that she hardly saw what was going on round her. Some time ago she had wondered and worried at the idea of some sinister secret at Sainte-Barbe; now her anxiety vanished before her own secret. She sought refuge in her books because there she could get away from the world of reality, and in her daily life she was happiest in Clon's company, because there she could be silent when she wanted it. Since the evening when she had freed the boy of his prison in the shed, he had for some time kept away from her, and had looked at her almost with fear, but lately he had come back to her, slowly and shyly, and was now following her about everywhere. His odd, wild manner no longer alarmed her. She sometimes tore herself away from her dreams to talk to him, and gently tried to enlighten and guide him. The thoughtful girl and the dull boy worked together in the garden, carried baskets and vegetables and fruit to the house, and fed Baptistine's hens and pigeons.

Lucan did not know that under her great agitations of mind she grew lovelier day by day, nor that Mrs. Pennhallow's round gray eyes were now resting on her face more constantly than before.

On one of the last fine days of September Lucan and Zosine walked in the woods, and sat down on a fallen tree at the edge of them to gaze over the fields toward the distant blue hills. Zosine was playing with a broken-off branch. "Lucan," she suddenly and softly asked her friend, "do you believe that love can work miracles?" The question hit Lucan in the heart. She could not answer.

"You are so very pretty," Zosine went on after a while. "Many men must have been in love with you. But have you ever, yourself, in your heart believed that they loved you?"

Lucan felt that she blushed, and the moment after grew pale. But she could not deny the power that ruled her whole life. "Yes, surely love can work miracles," she said.

"I have had a lot of suitors," said Zosine, "but I have never for a moment believed that any of them loved me. I used to laugh at them, and to make Papa laugh too. But here in France many things have become different. Is it, do you think, because France was my Mama's country, that it is now so very dear to me? Sometimes I wonder whether I have not, a hundred years ago and in a former existence, lived in France. And here, too, I think I should believe him, if somebody told me that he loved me."

"Whom are you thinking of?" Lucan asked.

"I am thinking of no one," Zosine answered, tossing her head. "I am making a fairy tale to amuse myself, and I thought it might amuse you as well, for a moment."

"And what happens in your fairy tale?" Lucan asked, and smiled at her.

Zosine was silent for a while, and laid down her branch. "Listen," she said. "You will have read of that white doe which was really a maiden and which would get back her own form only if a young knight told her that he loved her? In my fairy tale the doe is a spoiled, frivolous and selfish little thing, which is used to getting everything she wants. As it happens, she meets a beautiful young knight in the wood, a knight like—like those of whom we have read. She thinks, 'If now he would only tell me that he loved me, I should become a real human being.' But at the same time she clearly sees that he can never love a little silly doe that only plays and prances in the wood."

"But does the doe herself love the knight?" Lucan asked.

Zosine slowly shook her head. "Do you think," she asked, "that a doe can really love anybody at all before she has become a human being? All the same," she added, took up the branch, and fanned her face with it, "she can never forget him."

"But a fairy tale," Lucan said lowly, "ought to end up with a happy marriage."

"Perhaps it ought to," said Zosine, "but there are so many difficulties and obstacles between the two—as always in fairy tales—that I do not know what to think about it. And I have not quite finished my tale yet."

"Alas," thought Lucan, gazing into the green shade of the wood, "are we two rivals in a love that can never be fulfilled, in a dream? Are we standing hand in hand, gazing into a promised land, the threshold of which we shall never cross?" She had felt a kind of reluctance at the idea of anyone entering her own world of dreams; for a moment she had almost shrunk from her friend's confidence.

"Nay," she thought, as they walked home, "it could not be otherwise. Who could help loving him? Surely I must allow my sister to dream of him, as I do myself."

After a while she took Zosine's hand.

10. mr. pennhallow preaches a sermon

THE cold north wind that people of the province called the mistral blew across the empty, faded vineyards. It did not agree with old Mr. Pennhallow; his voice, always faint, vanished under it, and for a whole month he was dumb.

The girls were surprised to feel how much this low, hoarse voice had filled the house. Sainte-Barbe now seemed silent as death. The old man himself was changed. He, who before had always been busy at his teaching or at his books and accounts, now for a long time did nothing at all. From the early hours of the morning until late at night, he sat quietly in his big grandfather's chair and hardly noticed who entered the room or moved and talked around him. To his pupils it seemed as if his body itself, while he sat so still, was growing with his thoughts and made heavier by the weight of them. He never complained of his trial; it was as if by his own free will he had renounced the use of speech, so as to give himself up wholly to the world of thought. From time to time a delicate light passed over his immovable gray face.

The old man's wife was worried about his condition; she was loath to leave him, and was continually ordering Baptistine to prepare new decoctions for the sufferer, who drank them patiently, although they never seemed to help him. She also, almost in distress, told the girls to read aloud to him, to chase away his melancholy.

Lucan was wont to read aloud to her father, and she had a clear and sweet voice. It soon became her task to while away the time for her silent old teacher. At such hours she sat on a stool close to his chair. At first she read the pious books which Mrs. Pennhallow gave her. She found no consolation for her own grief in them. They renounced all beauty and pleasure of the earth, and seemed to distrust and denounce even its most innocent joys in their everlasting striving toward heaven. But Lucan's heaven was on earth.

Later on she read a number of scientific works, which Mr. Pennhallow pointed out to her on his shelves, and which to begin with caused her much trouble and embarrassment because there were so many words unknown to her in them. And yet she would often feel, when she put them back again, as if, in a strange way, and without any effort of her own, she had acquired new, surprising knowledge. Could it, she thought, be the old scholar's presence, and the clear eyes resting on her face during the lecture, which in themselves, and by roads unknown to her, conducted the wisdom of his books into her mind?

During these weeks she did not see as much of Zosine as usual, and it was as if, day by day, the old man took up more room in her thoughts. She wondered how it felt to be old and to have but little more to hope or fear from life.

After a month Mr. Pennhallow was again able to whisper a few words. One night he took down a book and handed it to her. "My good child," he said in a hoarse and broken voice, but with a little mild, fatherly smile, "you have now read many learned works to me. Here is a book that goes better with your age." Lucan was delighted when she saw on the title page the name of Daniel Defoe. She had read *Robinson Crusoe* to her father, and they had often discussed it. This book was different. She did not understand everything in it, and a good many pages, while she read, made her face burn. All the same, it fascinated her, and she followed the heroine's destiny, from page to page, in breathless suspense.

As she closed the book, Mr. Pennhallow sat for a long time silent and immovable.

"Such books," he said slowly, "describe life delightfully, as if it were a dance, or a sweet tune. But awful, awful is in reality the lot of the wanton woman." Lucan looked away. "Awful it is, too," the old man went on, slowly and raucously, "to know that every year a hundred innocent English maidens, radiant, with golden hair and pious and childlike minds, are setting out on a road beckoning with pleasure, but ending in horror and in the abyss."

He sat in his own thoughts for a while. "Yes," he went on, "in a horror to which life has no equal. The world of dire penury itself, eaten up by rats and vermin, hides its face at the sight of such women. Any other misery may find compassion in some human breast. But from her anguish the thief turns away with loathing; in her face the murderer spits. The deepest sunk creature refuses to drink from the cup out of which she has drunk. The perjurer regains his self-esteem when he kicks her from his doorstep. Wasted by fever, homeless and disfigured, she meets but contemptuous and spiteful eyes. It is a sin even to think of her with anything but aversion, or to wish her anything but ruin."

He slowly rubbed his large, dark and bony hands against each other.

"And we are acting so," he said, in a voice that trembled and at times became inaudible, "in the service of an ideal, of pure and guiltless womanhood. An old French philosopher has said, 'If God does not exist, we must invent him.' It is the same thing in the matter of which we speak. If pure and guiltless womanhood does not exist, we must create it. To this end we thrust one group of women into the abyss, and keep the others in ignorance thereof, so that they shall not become defiled by compassion.

"It is not our own weakness nor our own degradation which we keep from the knowledge of woman. It is the weakness, it is the degradation of her own sex. A young man may confide to his sister that he has committed a murder. But he will bite off his tongue before he will confide to her that he has frequented a wanton woman. For he will not allow the knowledge of a woman's disgrace to upset or overthrow the balance of the pure maiden's mind.

"A man," he said, "honors the woman who visits the convicted sinner in his prison, and her who, out of mercifulness, accompanies the murderer to the gallows. But no man would tolerate the nearness of a woman of whom he knew that she had endeavored to bring comfort or consolation to one of the fallen creatures of whom I speak in her dark and wretched haunt. Even when these creatures, contrite and penitent at the threshold of death, cry out for a word of commiseration, no innocent girl may pronounce it, without exposing her own soul to the gravest of dangers. A man may do so, because his moral nature is conscious and controlled by his will. A woman must flee with averted face, and must not venture to shed a tear of pity.

"The Church," he said after a pause, "long ago realized how the terrible contagion of perdition would leap from woman to woman. She approved of pious women's visits to prisoners and criminals, even to the most brutish and depraved of them. But in her wisdom she allowed no woman, not even the purest and firmest among her daughters, to enter, in pity and charity, that dark cell wherein a witch was waiting for the stake.

"And this," he went on, "is as it must be, and forever will be. For without the darkness behind it, the white lily would not be so white."

The old man fell into deep thought, and after his habit slowly passed the tip of his tongue across his dry lips. "And without that," he suddenly exclaimed, in a louder, clearer voice, "without our white lilies, what satisfaction would we find in our struggle and perseverance? It might happen, my child, it might then happen that we could never obtain the smile with which the high powers that we serve now reward our zeal. Oh, we must have our lilies, the whitest—I have seen it, I know it—the whitest that this world has to offer."

Lucan was alone in the room with the old man. At first his words had terrified her, although she did not understand all that he said. For, even before this moment, talks of men she had happened to overhear, and passages in books that had not been meant for her to read, had convinced her that there were abysses in life from which her very thought must recoil. She vaguely recalled Mr. Armworthy's proposal to her, and as if she realized that she herself had once stood upon the verge of the precipice, she shuddered and grew pale.

But Noël's voice in the garden, which forever resounded in her heart, again came back to her. For the sake of the one woman whom he loved, he had declared, he would forgive, aye, he would honor all women, even the deepest fallen. Thus love was mightier indeed than the power of evil; its light penetrated the blackness of horrors. In the silence that filled the room when the old man ceased to talk, she gently shook her head without being aware of it herself.

"Why do you shake your head?" he asked in his hoarse voice.

"Because," she said slowly and softly, "it cannot be as you say. There is, I think, forgiveness for all people on earth. There is an infinite grace in the world."

Her words had a strange effect on Mr. Pennhallow. His face slowly became ash-gray. "Grace?" he whispered. "For all people?" He was silent a long time, the while faintly gasping for breath, until his voice was once more strong enough to be heard. "You do not know what you are saying," he said slowly. A strange, an unfathomable smile spread over his face, and he sat still as before.

11. two gentlemen of the police

"I WILL tell you something," Zosine said to Lucan, "which you might have told yourself, if you have not become so absent-minded that you neither see nor hear what goes on round you. Young Monsieur Tinchebrai with the sweet pink and white face, whom we saw in Peyriac, is in love with you. You will surely remember how he stared at you on the Friday when we were in Peyriac to fetch the master's mail, as if you had been an angel straight out of heaven. And also how, upon the next Friday, he took care to be outside that shabby little shop that deals out the mail, and to pick up your pocket-handkerchief when you happened to drop it.

"But what you do not know," she went on, "is that he has come to Sainte-Barbe as well, and that he was walking slowly down the road past the house, staring up here, in the hope of getting a glimpse of you. I was in the garden with Baptistine to pick up chestnuts, and he could not see me from where he stood. You sat and sewed by the window, and did not look up at all. But he stood still outside the gate, like a really dainty wax figure, and three times slowly lifted his hand to his lips, as if he would blow you a kiss. It is three days ago today. Poor old Mr. Pennhallow himself was reading by the other window. He saw it all, and became quite petrified by the impudence of the young gentleman. I believe that he was really magnetized by it, for I swear that he quite slowly, as if under a spell, repeated Monsieur Tinchebrai's movement three times. But he has got over it, as he gets over everything; he is as quiet and content as ever.

"But what do you think of Monsieur Emmanuel yourself?"

she asked. "And now that he is going to propose to you, will you answer yes or no?"

The two girls sat together in the room next to the dining-room, and were busy making little smelling-cushions filled with the lavender that was spread all over the table. Lucan, from her old home, was used to making such pretty cushions or bottles from the lavender in the garden. Outside the wind was still blowing, but in here the air was sweet and summer-like with the scent of the dried flowers. The girls talked together softly, for the door to the dining-room was ajar. Mr. Pennhallow was working in there, and they must not disturb him.

"Take him!" Zosine exclaimed, without giving her friend time to answer. "Baptistine has told us that he is a young man who will get on in the world, and I should like to see you as Madame la Préfète of Lunel."

"Why would you like that?" Lucan asked in surprise. Zosine left her own seat by the table to come and sit down on the arm of Lucan's chair. "Now already a third of our year here has passed," she said, "and when it is finished we shall never come back here. But if you were married to the Prefect of Lunel, I would visit you here, and see the country and everything again."

"Would you be pleased to see the country again?" Lucan asked.

"Nay, but it is strange," said Zosine, "to leave a place that one knows so well. Will not the road through the forest miss me, if I never again set my foot on it?"

For a moment it dawned on Lucan that Zosine might have had experiences of her own at Sainte-Barbe, while she herself had read aloud to the old clergyman and gone through the events of a moonlight night in her thoughts time after time. She put down her sewing.

"You surely are not in love with Monsieur Tinchebrai yourself?" she exclaimed. "Do you not remember what Baptistine told us about him?"

"It was no fault of his," said Zosine and colored lightly. "It seems to me that it was all a kind of romance. I believe that every single person, when you really think about it, has got a romance in his life. And only fancy what it must be like not to know for certain whose blood it is that runs in our veins. He has gone through much, you may be sure. A small town like Lunel has got sharp, cruel eyes, and it must be hard to have them all turned upon you. Now he has seen you, and the real worth of a sweet, innocent girl has been revealed to him. He is dreaming of taking refuge from his hard fate in your long golden ringlets." The unintentional parody of Noël's words in the moonlight made Lucan silent.

"Yes," Zosine continued thoughtfully. "I believe that even our old foster-parents have got a romance in their life, if only we knew about it. What is it that happened to them, once upon a time, I wonder, and now makes them sit here at Sainte-Barbe as quiet as a pair of mice? Is it something that they want to think of forever? Or is it something that they want to forget?"

She rose from the arm of the chair, went to the window, and looked up toward the sky and the drifting clouds. "Is it good, or is it intolerable," she said, "that we cannot look into the future and know what is going to happen to us? Now if this was a book that told of you and me, the reader could skip a few pages, when it became too slow or too exciting, and would be diverted or set at rest. At times I feel it to be the same in life, only we do not understand how to skip the pages. My governess scolded me when I was too impatient to read my books of fairy tales page by page. If today we could skip two or three pages of our own life, would it not be pleasant? Should we not with content turn back to the page on which we now find ourselves and go on from there?"

While she spoke, they heard the din of a carriage on the road. They listened, and it came nearer. It was rare that a carriage passed Sainte-Barbe, and Zosine pressed her face to the windowpane to see who drove past the house.

"It stops here," she cried out, surprised, and a moment after, "It is he!"

"He? Who?" Lucan exclaimed and rose.

"He of whom we were talking," Zosine answered, delighted. "Monsieur Emmanuel. He is coming here in a fine carriage, together with a fine old gentleman. Now will you believe me another time? It is the judge of Lunel himself who will help him to apply for your hand with our master! Only, why have they not brought a bouquet for the occasion instead of their big portfolios?"

Lucan now went to the window herself, and really saw a fine, old-fashioned carriage outside the gate. A footman leaped from the box, helped the old and the young gentleman to descend, and thereupon pulled the bell. When Lucan recognized Monsieur Emmanuel Tinchebrai, she withdrew behind the curtain. She had indeed, although she did not want to own it to Zosine, observed his ardent admiration of her.

It took some time before Clon came from the garden to open the door, and when he caught sight of the footman outside it, he behaved in a very strange manner. He stopped short, and thereupon slowly drew back, like a rabbit which retires backwards into its hole. He vanished from the picture altogether, and did not show himself again.

After another minute or two, the old gentleman himself authoritatively gave the bell-rope another pull. This time the ring called Baptistine out of the house. She came down the garden path in her white cap and her apron, as solid and unaffected, Zosine whispered, as the stack of wood by the house, but all the same received the visitors with more politeness than she was wont to display.

"Now they first inquire if the Reverend Mr. Pennhallow is at home," Zosine whispered, "and then they ask about you. Monsieur Emmanuel's heart is beating strongly. His nice pink cheeks are almost pale today. It is not to be wondered at, when this conversation is to decide whether he is to live or die. You must take pity on him, for how would we look ourselves at this moment if this same conversation were to decide whether we should live or die? The old judge's footman himself looks quite solemn. My God," she suddenly interrupted herself, "it is not a footman. It is a gendarme."

For a moment the two girls stared at each other in silence and amazement. Then Zosine pointed to the door of the dining-room, which was ajar, and laid her finger on her lip. They would be able to hear every word pronounced in the adjoining room.

In there Mr. Pennhallow rose, and immediately afterwards the door to the corridor was opened. The visitors had come into the room. A few seconds went with slight scraping of feet in formal mutual greeting. Then the old gentleman from the carriage spoke.

"I take the liberty," he said, expressing himself slowly and precisely, as in the feeling of his own importance, "to introduce myself as Monsieur Belabres, Judge of Lunel, and my companion as my inspector, Monsieur Emmanuel Tinchebrai. I am not wrong in presuming that I speak to the Reverend Mr. Pennhallow, from England?"

"No, you are quite right, Monsieur le Préfèt," said Mr. Pennhallow. He too, according to his habit, spoke slowly and softly, but in contrast to the Frenchman's pretentious voice, his own voice was meek and complaisant. By the sound of it the girls almost guessed a little mild smile at the solemnity of the high official. "You are welcome under my roof, gentlemen. Be seated, if you please. To what do I owe the honor of your visit?"

Zosine could no longer remain in her chair by the table. She got up from it without a sound, slipped to the door and peeped in.

12. the accusation

THE judge from Lunel was a handsome old gentleman with silvery hair. He carried himself with grace and dignity, but he appeared alarmed and revolted.

"It is highly painful to me," he said slowly, "to present myself on an errand of this nature in the house of a learned and reverend gentleman of a nation, the royal house of which is bound with ties of amity to our own country, and no less than that gives its subjects a noble example of high human and domestic virtues. But I come here today, not by my own wish or on my own behalf, but in the name of law and justice."

"In that case," answered Mr. Pennhallow gently, "I once more bid you welcome."

The judge placed his tall hat on the floor by the chair and his portfolio on the table before him. "And in these names," he gravely announced, "I must now put a series of questions to you, and I adjure you to answer them with the severest conscientiousness."

"Is there any event in the neighborhood," Mr. Pennhallow asked, "on which you seek information from me? I do not often get outside the walls of my quiet study. But as far as my ability goes, I am at your service."

"No," said Monsieur Belabres with weight, "this is no local affair of the district. It is an order to assert justice in France, yes, in two continents, that I have crossed your threshold today."

"Good God," said Mr. Pennhallow.

Monsieur Belabres now seated himself in the armchair by the table, and without a word the young inspector sat down on a chair by the window. Mrs. Pennhallow had grown very pale, and her hands trembled, but the old clergyman remained as quiet and attentive as if he was really listening to an instructive and edifying lecture.

"I understand," said the judge, "that you have, for many years, been a servant of the Church in your own country."

"Yes, I have been so highly favored by fortune," said Mr. Pennhallow.

"But you have," the judge continued, "on account of your health, had to give up that vocation?"

"Yes, that cross was laid upon me," said Mr. Pennhallow.

"And you have then," said Monsieur Belabres, "for seven years been a resident at Sainte-Barbe, in our country of France?"

"It is as you say," said the old clergyman.

Monsieur Belabres was silent for a minute. "People of Peyriac," he then said, "have reported that in these seven years a number of young women from your own country have stayed in your house. It has been noticed that they were all very young and of uncommonly good looks, most of them very fair." Mr. Pennhallow here made a movement as if to interrupt him, but Monsieur Belabres likewise with a movement of his hand bade him hear him out. "These young women," he said, "have succeeded one another, so that when one of them left Sainte-Barbe, another soon after was received here. Answer me, Mr. Pennhallow, upon your conscience, do you know what has become of them?"

Mr. Pennhallow slowly folded his big hands, drew a deep sigh and looked down. "You are," he said, "touching on a painful subject. I will answer you. But I beg you first to finish your speech, and to tell me why you put these questions to me."

The judge kept his eyes on his face. "Yes, I shall do so," he said. "In case you are not already aware of it, I shall let you know why I am putting these questions to you.

"The humane feelings of our century," he said, "have abolished the trade with Negro slaves. But there are still, in our community, human beings so avaricious, so merciless and unscrupulous as not to shrink from selling and buying its most defenseless members, the innocent young girls. They enrich themselves in trading our sisters and daughters to a fate more appalling than of the black slaves themselves in foreign countries or continents."

"Alas, what are you saying?" said Mr. Pennhallow.

"You will surely have read or heard of these things, Reverend Sir?" said the judge.

"Who has not read or heard of the abysses of this world?" Mr. Pennhallow answered. "My own father's brother sacrificed his life to the fight against the old slave traffic. He went away to the west coast of Africa, to acquire a thorough knowledge of it. And he died in his vocation, I believe, for he never came back. But alas I have not his spiritual strength, and, in my still, studious existence, I have tried to keep these horrors of life from my consciousness, as from my house."

"Some of these unnatural transactions," said the judge, "in likeness to those of the African slave traffic, have been stained with blood. The criminals, when they have seen themselves pursued, have got rid of their victims. The guillotine has had the last word in these matters. It has happened here in France not a long time ago."

Mr. Pennhallow ran his hand over his forehead.

"It happened less than a year ago," said the judge in a stronger voice, "at Marseilles. Two of the miserable scoundrels of whom I have talked had to pay for their crimes with their lives. An old woman was sentenced to prison for life. But from papers later on found in the haunts of the dead men, it was proved that the principal malefactor, who was only referred to under a fictitious and dreadful name, had escaped retribution. The old woman was examined in prison, but revealed nothing. It was as if, even there, she stood in awe of the nameless man, or as if she were under a spell, and was really incapable of speaking. A short time afterwards she died in prison."

"Can I, perhaps," Mr. Pennhallow said, "be of assistance to you in the search of this man? I am at your service."

The judge hesitated to answer his question. "While the investigation took place," he said very slowly, "evidence was produced that seemed to concern you."

"To concern me?" Mr. Pennhallow asked in surprise.

"Yes," Monsieur Belabres answered, "that concerned you.

"There was a village girl from this district," he went on, slowly as before, "who had married a dock laborer of Marseilles. One evening, when her husband was working overtime for a ship already under sail to leave the harbor, she took her husband's supper down there for him. Just at that moment a young woman was brought down in the boat that carried goods and passengers to the ship, between two men, and so dead drunk that they had to support her. In this woman my witness recognized, with amazement, a fair young girl, who had been staying in your house, with whom a couple of times she had talked on the road, and who had then told her that her name was Rosa." He stopped, as if to give Mr. Pennhallow time to answer. But the old man leaned his elbow on the table, his forehead in his hand, and did not say a word.

"And while we were going through the young woman's statement," the judge said, as if he was now approaching the end of his speech, "one of our own policemen brought us a new piece of information.

"During the week in which the ship sailed, on his chase of a gang of thieves, he had been watching a small street of ill repute near the harbor. There, one evening, he saw an English gentleman, answering the description of the reverend gentleman to whom I now address myself, come out from a small disreputable hotel in the company of its proprietress, that same old woman who later on died in her prison cell. The Englishman talked with her by a street lamp, and our inspector, in passing, chanced to overhear the conversation. Although it happened a long time ago, he still, he said, remembered the voice of the old gentleman, he even imitated it to us. And it was like your own voice."

"He imitated my voice?" Mr. Pennhallow repeated, and looked up with a faint, almost bashful smile. "Well, it is probably an easy voice to imitate and to make fun of. And still," he added gravely, "perhaps the utterance of this weak voice made an impression upon him. Was it so?"

"Wait," said the judge, who, as the fatal conversation was

advancing, spoke with growing authority, but also with growing repulsion, or horror, of the man to whom he spoke. "There is still one circumstance with which you ought to be acquainted. After the death of the old woman, a piece of paper came into our possession in a strange way. It is a letter from you to her. It is a receipt for an amount of money which you had duly received. It is dated Sainte-Barbe."

"Yes," said Mr. Pennhallow slowly, searching his memory. "Sainte-Barbe, March 15th."

Monsieur Belabres sat back in his chair, almost as if he receded, in order to lay a few feet more between himself and the old Englishman. After a moment's silence he spoke again. His voice was changed and almost as low and dull-toned as Mr. Pennhallow's own voice. "You remember and admit that you have written this letter?" he asked.

"Yes, I remember it quite clearly," Mr. Pennhallow answered. "I have, I believe, still got the account to which it refers in my writing table. The date stamped itself on my memory. You know," he added smilingly, "beware the Ides of March. If you wish, I will show the accounts to you. But I beg you, before that, to finish your tale of the unknown criminal in Marseilles. It has captivated me, Monsieur Belabres. It will be difficult for me to turn my mind to other things until I have heard it to the end."

13. the defense

IN the silence that followed, the people in the room and the girls listening by the door, all heard the measured, creaking tick of the old clock on the wall, imperturbably dividing up time in minutes and seconds. There was no other sound or movement. Monsieur Belabres' handsome face changed its expression a couple of times. At last he spoke, stressing each word, as if he sat in a judgment seat.

"It is you, Mr. Pennhallow," he said, "who are to speak. I have asked for your evidence concerning three points in what you yourself call my tale of an unknown criminal."

"If that is so," said Mr. Pennhallow, "I beg you to name these three points to me once more."

"As you wish it," the judge said. "Then first of all answer my first question: Where are the young women who were living in your house?"

"Indeed, that was the first question," said Mr. Pennhallow, and for a while remained sunk in his own thoughts.

"The people of the neighborhood," said Mr. Pennhallow, "are mistaken when they believe that a series of young women have been staying at Sainte-Barbe. We have sheltered three young English maidens in our home. To be sure, they have at times traveled to England and have come back here again. To be sure, again, one of them, in the unreasonableness of youth, had had her hair dyed, so that only here, where we could not allow such folly, it regained its natural color. These circumstances may have misled the people of Peyriac. But for these three of whom I speak we have tried to create a home at Sainte-Barbe.

"The first of them," he said, "was my wife's niece. She was engaged to be married in England, but the family of her future husband opposed the marriage. To comfort her in her grief, we took her into our house, and it did indeed happen that the proud family gave up its prejudice. She is now married.

"But of the two others," he went on after a long silence, "I can only speak with bitter distress. The one was the daughter of an actor and juggler, whom I had tried to drag from a degraded and poverty-stricken home, but who, by her own choice, turned back to it, and to the stage. The last of the three," he said, suddenly looking the judge in the face with his clear and quiet eyes, "fled from our roof in the night, with the help of a poor, imbecile boy, who is in our service. For a time we tried hard to find her, but it was all in vain. We never saw her again.

"I have thought this matter over many times," he said, and looked down, "I have reflected that I may have known too little about the nature and inclinations of young women. Life at Sainte-Barbe is lonely and monotonous. What I have been able to offer them has not made up for the allurements of the great world. It is sad to an old man to feel how little his best efforts will avail against the bad and corrupting powers of life.

"We have a housekeeper," he added after a moment, "the real owner of Sainte-Barbe. If you wish it, she will confirm my statement."

Baptistine remained standing up straight, just inside the door, and curtly answered the questions put to her. As Monsieur Belabres asked her how many young girls from England her master had housed during his seven years at Sainte-Barbe, she answered, "Two."

Mr. Pennhallow mildly corrected her, but for a while she stuck to her opinion, and when at last she realized that she had been wrong, she only remarked that these girls were no business of hers. As soon as the judge granted his permission, she walked back to the kitchen in her old slippers.

"Was it," the judge asked, a little less sternly than before, "to make a profit or from pure philanthropy that you took on these young girls?"

"It was not with the idea of any profit," Mr. Pennhallow answered slowly and, as it were, reluctantly. "Neither was it out of philanthropy alone. We took on these young girls in memory of our dead daughter, Evangeline.

"We lost our child," he continued after a minute of deep thought, "in a terrible and tragic manner. The lonely place in which we then lived was visited at times by gypsies. The beauty of the child attracted the vagrant tribes. As one day a gang of them left the neighborhood, our child was gone with them."

"My God," Monsieur Belabres exclaimed, "and did you never find her again?"

"Yes," the old man answered quietly, "after a long search we found her again. It happened at one of the great markets in a town far from our own house. The itinerant existence and the hard conditions had broken down the health of the child. She died a month later."

The judge remained silent for a minute, as if to show his sympathy with so deep a grief. Mrs. Pennhallow till now had been dumb, and had only let her watchful glance run from the face of her husband to that of Monsieur Belabres and back again. Now in a little hard voice, which all the same had in it a kind of triumph, she remarked, "We have, even today, two young girls from England in our house. You might have them in and have them examined as well."

Her husband made a slight deprecating gesture and turned to the judge. "And what was," he asked, "your last question to me?"

Monsieur Belabres looked down into his portfolio. "I wish to hear by your own mouth, Mr. Pennhallow," he said, "what brought you to the boarding-house in the harbor street of Marseilles."

Mr. Pennhallow slowly turned his thoughts from the past to the present. "Is it possible," he exclaimed, bewildered and almost frightened, "that the dead man in Marseilles can have been the man for whom you are looking? Can it have been he who— No, no, I cannot believe it. And still," he added solemnly, "if that is the case, the criminal has repented in his last hour, and has turned back from his wickedness. And maybe his crimes have been forgiven him."

"I do not know of what you are speaking," said the judge, "but I ask you to account for the true facts of the case."

"It is not difficult," said Mr. Pennhallow, and began: "In the first days of March, I had to go to Marseilles on an errand important to myself. An old friend of mine had died in Calcutta, and had left me a case of rare books. I fetched them myself on board the ship, and a boy from the harbor was carrying the case to my lodgings for me.

"When I had paid him and would send him away, he looked at me and asked me if I were not an English priest. And as I answered him in the affirmative, he told me that in a small hotel in the street where he worked, an English mate or master was on his deathbed, and that he had many times begged to have a priest from his own country brought to him. I immediately followed the boy to this hotel, an evil place in a dark street, which almost struck terror into my own heart. There I found an English carpenter who was dying from consumption. I stayed with him for an hour or two. He confessed himself to me, Your Honor. But the confession of a dying man is sacred to us, as well as to the priests of your own Church. This is my whole story. In itself it is simple, and yet to me it is beautiful and momentous."

"Do you recollect," the judge asked, "whether the hostess of the boarding-house came out into the street with you as you left it?"

"I think that she did so," Mr. Pennhallow answered.

"What did you say to her before you parted?" the judge again asked.

"It is not easy for me to recall our conversation word for word today," said Mr. Pennhallow. "And yet I seem to remember a little of it. You will keep in mind that we came from a deathbed. I talked of death as of a long journey across a dark and stormy sea, and emphasized our trust, also, in the resurrection of the flesh upon the other shore.

"And as now I remember your third question," he said, "I

shall answer it without delay. For it hangs together with what I have just told you.

"About a week later, to my surprise, I received a letter and a small amount of money from the very same old woman at Marseilles. Her lodger had died, and, before he died, had enjoined her, after having deducted what was due herself, to send me this money, the savings of his whole life, for the benefit of the poor of my parish. It seemed to me very remarkable that this woman, who could so easily have kept the small sum to herself, should thus have carried out the wish of the dead man. May one not believe that a word from me, in a solemn hour, had reached her heart? I, as you know, sent her a receipt for the money. I added, I believe," he finished, as Monsieur Belabres was turning over the papers on the table in front of him, "that the idea of the constant, hard and faithful labor by which this amount, coin by coin, had been put together, had moved and touched me."

The judge pushed his portfolio away from him.

"You almost seem, Mr. Pennhallow," he said, "to have your defense on every point firmly consolidated."

"Defense?" Mr. Pennhallow exclaimed.

He sat for a moment with his eyes on the judge's face, speechless. His own face during this short space of time changed and took on an expression of perfect calm, almost of mirth.

"I see," he said slowly, "I have sat here as the defendant in the case. I have been very slow to comprehend your meaning. Believe me, had I understood it before, I should not even have tried to refute your charge!"

He rose very quietly, and kept standing by the table. He was a small man with short legs, not much taller when he stood up than in his chair, but there was a strange dignity about his humble figure, and his face was alight with gentle, triumphant scorn.

"Do you really believe," he said, "that I hold my own life, and the fate which may befall me, to be of any moment whatever against the certain knowledge that evil, misery and horror exist in the world? For the evil of this world is mighty, an abyss, a deep sea that cannot be emptied with a spoon, or by any human acts or measures. I, who know, who may proclaim the power of evil, should I ever on my own behalf take fear or lose heart?

"I will not try to refute your accusation. The righteous are doomed, the innocent are degraded, the weak trampled into the mire. That is enough. I beg you to let the law take its course. It cannot harm me. I am in safety here, as wherever I am."

He seemed to grow and to broaden while he spoke. Mrs. Pennhallow's face, darkening under the last part of the examination, now became almost as calm as that of the old man himself. The judge could not take his eyes off the face of the accused.

The young inspector in the chair by the window for the first time joined in the conversation. "Would it not, Your Honor," he said, "be a good plan to examine the two young English girls who at this moment find themselves in the house?"

14. the acquittal

LUCAN and Zosine, from their own room and through the chink of the door, had followed the discussion in the long dining-room. They could hear all that was said, and much of what they heard was incomprehensible to them. They changed color and gazed in amazement at each other while they were listening. Here great things were at stake. A stranger had come to Sainte-Barbe, a French judge had addressed unheard-of, incredible accusations to the English clergyman.

Lucan now remembered how she herself, not a long time ago, had felt a vague, dreamlike mistrust of the house of Sainte-Barbe. She was almost struck with terror as she recalled her own thoughts. It was as if she had drawn down a suspicion upon the house that had given friendly shelter to her and Zosine, and upon the garden, where in the moonlight she had talked with Noël. It was as if her thoughts, without her own knowledge or wish, had called forth the hidden secret inmate of Sainte-Barbe.

Zosine, who had returned to her own place at the table, was leaning across it, with shining eyes, much as, in former days she had leaned over the edge of her box in the theatre and had followed the struggle of virtue and villainy on the stage. She remembered events in the history of the world which Mr. Pennhallow himself had made vivid to her. Great images ran through her mind. The old man's tale of his lost daughter deeply moved both the young girls. They too had lost and searched, and for a moment their eyes filled with tears.

In the pause that followed upon Monsieur Tinchebrai's words they realized that they themselves were now to be flung into the center of events. They trembled, as they collected their strength for the task which lay before them and which they themselves did not fully comprehend. When they heard Mrs. Pennhallow push back her chair, they mechanically resumed their work in great haste. But their hands only faintly grasped at the lavender on the table.

"Girls, are you there?" said Mrs. Pennhallow from the doorway. Her voice was strange, milder and blander than they had ever heard it. "You must come with me into the dining-room. Here are two good gentlemen from Lunel who want to see you." The two girls stood up at once. Lucan was pale, but Zosine's cheeks flamed. Without looking at each other, they followed the angular, grave figure across the threshold.

The two French gentlemen rose as they entered the room. The judge himself, who had been absorbed in his documents, gazed at them with surprise and admiration. It was as if Mrs. Pennhallow had come back to the fatal meeting with a bunch of roses in each hand.

During all the following interview Lucan felt the young inspector's eyes upon her face. She herself only once swiftly gazed at him, and then he immediately looked away. Mrs. Pennhallow was staring down into her lap. Mr. Pennhallow was the only person in the room who did not appear to be held in strain and suspense by the situation. From the time when, a moment ago, he had finished speaking, he had stood immovable, as if he were looking at things far away. As his glance swept over the figures of the girls, a faint shade of pity or tenderness ran over his face, but immediately afterwards his eyes were as distant as before.

Lucan and Zosine sat down. And hereby the circle, round the table, of three old and three young people, each one in a highly unusual state of mind, was closed.

Monsieur Belabres begged the young girls to forgive him, in case he had disturbed or possibly even alarmed them. He further prayed them to be without fear or anxiety. He was only going to ask them for trivial information. They themselves knew better, and Zosine gave him a direct, challenging, almost contemptuous glance in return. The very carriage and voice of the judge revolted her, and she remembered how her own father had been accused. At this moment Mr. Pennhallow's humble and awkward figure in her eyes recalled the mighty, genial form of Mr. Tabbernor.

The judge briefly questioned the girls on their age and circumstances. Here Lucan had to answer for Zosine. She made her friend exactly a year her junior, in order not to have to tell lies, as far as the month and the day of her birth went. But she blushed as she spoke, and became the more embarrassed because Monsieur Tinchebrai seemed to notice her blush and to be watching her with admiration.

The judge was silent for some time, his face deeply stamped with distress and irresolution.

"It has become indispensable," he said at last, "in a matter which otherwise will cause you, my young ladies, no inconvenience, to obtain a clear account of how you have come to France. I beg you to inform me how you first came in touch with Mr. Pennhallow."

Lucan thought, "It was a good thing that the judge did not name Mrs. Pennhallow as well, for in that case I should have had to tell him of my meeting with her in the inn. And that meeting to me now seems quite blurred and almost unreal."

"My sister and I," she said, "were looking for a situation in London, and there we met our master—Mr. Pennhallow—at an employment office. The lady who owned the office was called Mrs. Quincy."

The judge regarded the two pretty girls with sympathy and compassion. "Since you were looking for a situation through an employment office," he said, "I must presume that you were alone in the world, without any near relations or friends. Was Mr. Pennhallow acquainted with this fact?"

"Yes," said Lucan, "we told Mr. Pennhallow so, the first time we met him. He then said it was sad and unjust, and that young girls ought to be guided and protected by kind, honest people, with knowledge of the world."

"But when you accepted Mr. Pennhallow's offer," the judge said, "were not prospects of happier, freer and more prosperous conditions held out to you? Perhaps a later radiant future, in a foreign country or continent? You may," he gravely added, "speak openly and without being afraid that your evidence will cause you any harm in your relations with Mr. Pennhallow and his wife. I myself will vouch," he finished with great dignity, "that such a thing will not happen."

This time it was Zosine who answered, instead of her friend. "We speak as openly now," she said, "as we have always done in this house. We are not afraid of Mr. or Mrs. Pennhallow, and we have no reason to be so. There was nobody but them in all London who would have us. We had been looking for a situation for a long time, and were afraid never to find any at all, when we first met Mr. Pennhallow."

"Have you never, here," the judge asked, "been promised such pretty frocks, bonnets, and shawls which must be the natural craving of your age?"

"No, indeed. You do not know what you are talking about," Zosine exclaimed scornfully. "Look round the house yourself. There is hardly a looking-glass in the whole place. We have had other things to think of here at Sainte-Barbe."

"Did not," the judge again inquired, "Mr. Pennhallow bring people into your existence who may have appeared to you strange or remarkable?"

"Yes, he did indeed," cried Zosine. "He gave us lessons in history and Latin every day. He talked to us of the great heroes who lived long ago, and who might serve as examples to pretentious persons of our own unheroic, matter-of-fact age."

She looked at her old teacher, who without a word or a movement was facing the attack of the relentless law. She bethought herself of Socrates before the tribunal of Athens, and was deeply moved. "Was it," she thought, "ever the fate of great and noble people to be slandered and brought down by the law and trivial natures?"

"Nay, set your mind at rest," she said, very solemnly, with trembling lips. "Mr. Pennhallow has never meant to betray or to harm any human being. But he has always wanted to lift up, and to inspire everyone near him. When you now enjoin us to tell you the whole truth, I have to let you know that it is I who have been deceiving our master. I did not, at the beginning, tell him all. And here, at Sainte-Barbe, too, I have done things of which he has known nothing. Until this moment I have wished to keep them to myself. But now, when I see that you dare to distrust him and his words, I no longer mind confessing everything." She spoke with great energy; her face was aflame and her eyes filled with tears.

A little smile flickered on the face of the judge. "No, Mademoiselle," he said, "we are not so barbarous. We are quite ready to let young ladies like you and your sister keep the secrets of their hearts to themselves." He let his eyes run from the childlike, blushing face of the witness to the gray and furrowed features of the accused. In the light of the girl's firm confidence, the old man's expression changed from what it had been a moment ago.

Monsieur Belabres sat for a long time in silence. "Only one more question," he said with great weight. "Have you, in this house, heard immorality judged with leniency? Has the conduct of the unchaste woman here been treated with indulgence? And have you been encouraged to believe that human beings may possibly find happiness outside the narrow road of duty and law-abidingness?"

He spoke with embarrassment and looked down. He had not imagined the young English girls at Sainte-Barbe so pretty and gentle. He had daughters of his own, innocent maidens ignorant of the evil of the world, and he only reluctantly brought a subject like the present one into the pure atmosphere that surrounded these young creatures.

Zosine did not understand what he said, and was still all absorbed in her own violent emotions. She kept gazing at him with knitted brows. But Lucan cried out, almost against her own will, "Oh, no!" and grew red, and once more very pale at her own words.

Both the judge and his inspector turned toward her. "You have got something to tell us, Mademoiselle?" the judge asked.

"I do not," Lucan said, as calmly as she could, "quite understand what you mean by your question to my sister. And yet I somehow feel sure that you are wrong. Mr. Pennhallow has once spoken to me of the very same subject to which you were referring. He described the punishment of immorality, and the fate of the unvirtuous woman, in such terrible words that I almost wished to stop my ears to them. I have not heard him talk like that on any other subject. I shall never forget it."

The judge looked from Lucan to Zosine and drew his breath deeply.

"Both the young ladies," he said, once more turning to Mr. Pennhallow, "have spoken as openly and candidly as I begged them to do. There is no doubt that their words have come from their hearts. Their evidence has mightily strengthened and confirmed your own defense. I can leave Sainte-Barbe assured of the gratuitousness of the suspicion which I have been forced to advance.

"I cannot ask for your forgiveness, my Reverend Sir," he addressed himself to the old Englishman, "for I came here, not by my own wish, but compelled by my sense of duty of right and wrong. I congratulate you—and myself—on this hour. It is a bitter thing that innocence may be accused. But it is a fine and beautiful thing to see the accusation repudiated. And it is great and elevating to find righteousness, where, for a moment, we had dreaded to meet with depravity or baseness."

"There is no need to ask for forgiveness," said Mr. Pennhallow very slowly. "I am an old man; I need rest. And as long as I may follow my own path in life, I do not wish to judge my neighbor. In my thoughts I shall keep close to those, younger and stronger than myself, who take up the fight against the evil of this world, with admiration, and, I give you my word, in particular to you."

15. When danger is over

FOR a whole week after the judge's visit to Sainte-Barbe the two girls felt like old grenadiers after a battle. They had been sent under fire and had stood their ground.

They now wondered that they had ever thought their old teacher ugly or awkward, or that they had been lightheaded and silly enough to laugh at him. His figure seemed to have grown and to shed light on all sides, and they themselves looked very small beside it. They resolved to become more worthy of the man whom they had defended. Zosine promised herself to keep a grave face during grace, and they both set to work to learn long Latin poems by heart, with which some day they would surprise and please him.

The old man and his wife, on their side, were kinder to them than ever before. Mr. Pennhallow did not speak of the sinister incident, and enjoined his pupils too to forget it. It was sweet to forget and forgive, he said, and as he spoke he looked as if he was really tasting something sweet. He had forgiven the slanderers and the obdurate men of law who had attacked him without knowing what they did. If he found it harder to forgive them that, through him, innocent girls had been brought into contact with the horrors of life, this would only serve to make his pupils dearer and nearer to him, as if they had become part of himself. It happened now, as it had never done before, that he would take them by the chin, or pat their cheek. He was all smiles and mildness in his endeavor to wash the bygone, dark cloud off the sky of Sainte-Barbe.

Mrs. Pennhallow for a day or two after the inquest had been

in low spirits; the girls had even seen her weep. They had also heard her husband laugh gently at her, "My dear," he said, "must you, now that all has come off well, shed tears because I have had a bit of a jest with an old hag of Marseilles, who was a hundred years old, and who is dead now?" They did not understand what he meant, but had watched the effect of his words on his wife. Her sallow face would lighten up now, like his own, with a kind of benevolence and triumph when her eyes fell upon her foster-daughters.

Once or twice Mr. Pennhallow talked of the time when their agreement should have expired. He had realized, he said, that life at Sainte-Barbe in the long run might become too quiet and monotonous for young people like his dear Lucan and Zosine. He would, at the end of the year, find situations for them in England, with clergymen of high rank, for he had known many of these in his young days, and his recommendation would carry weight with them. But he would never, as long as he lived, lose touch with his pupils. They would write to each other, they would meet, and how sweet would it not then be to talk of old times, even of old trouble.

Zosine was not at all inclined to forgive. She was filled with just anger against the judge of Lunel. To her he represented the Law itself, cold as ice, and without mercy toward those human beings whose existence, like her father's, lay in a sphere of beauty and imagination, or, like her teacher's, in the world of high thought. She was relentless even to gentle young Monsieur Tinchebrai. She forgot that she had ever felt sorry for him, and now spared neither the young gentleman nor the Bishop of Nîmes himself.

Lucan was silent, but uneasy at heart. She was as happy as her friend to have helped to save an innocent, noble man, and readier than her to forgive. But she felt that behind the short nightmare of the afternoon there lay a lasting, dark reality. Her old teacher had been unjustly accused, and had repelled the accusation. But what was the crime of which he had been accused? And was the real criminal still about in the world? At times her old, vague misgiving about Sainte-Barbe would come back to her. She would tell herself that it had been but a presage of the shock and the anguish, and yet it would not be put off.

She turned to what was infinitely more important to her, to the man she loved, and to her love itself. "Woman," she thought, "as long as she is free to dwell in the thought of her love, even in the thought of an unhappy and hopeless love, has a home there. If the time ever comes when it is demanded of woman, as of man, that she must forget her love to take part in the activity of the outer world, be it even in the service of justice, then she will have been driven out into the open, bleak field, without shelter, exposed to the wind and the weather. Worse than that, she will be running there like a mad creature, with disheveled hair, mocking herself and her own nature."

All the same she had the welfare of those who lived round her at heart. She took pleasure in showing Mr. Pennhallow her esteem and gratitude. When she and Zosine sat together at their studies they talked of him, of his trials and of his spiritual strength.

"But even if he has come through it all," Zosine said, "it has had an effect on him. He is changed. The meanness and malice of the world have left their mark on him. Do you remember how, when we first met, I told you that I could see on his face that he belonged to a religious sect which lived in a constant state of expectation? Patient, inspired expectation was stamped on his features, and in his manner. Now it is as if he had come to the end of his road. It is in his voice and in his glance. It is as if they both finished what they had to do. It wrings my heart to see it. And it is all due to that self-righteous, hard man of law."

Lucan smiled at her friend. "But tell me," she said gently, to turn Zosine's mind from the subject that was preying on it, "what you yourself were thinking of when you told the judge from Lunel that you had deceived your teacher? You looked so grave that you made me wonder at your words."

Zosine left her chair to come and sit beside her friend in the narrow horse-hair-covered sofa. "I have wondered, myself," she said, and twisted Lucan's long silken ringlets round her fingers, "that you have not asked me a long time ago.

"Do you still," she went on, "remember the young man who helped me when the white horse that I called Mazeppa threw me off?"

"Yes," answered Lucan in surprise.

"I have met him again," said Zosine, "during all that time when you had become so silent and absorbed in your own thoughts. He was not a groom from Joliet, as we took him to be. He is the master of Joliet. He is Baron Thésée de Valfonds."

Lucan dropped her work and turned to gaze into Zosine's face. "You have met him!" she cried. "You have talked with him! What have you talked about?"

"God, Lucan," exclaimed Zosine, "how I have regretted that I left my riding-habit in England. For we have talked mostly of horses. But sometimes we have talked of other things as well."

Lucan did not at the moment know why her friend's confession almost made her laugh. Was it this young man, and this romance, that Zosine had had in mind when she had told her fairy tale in the woods? She seized Zosine's hands and pressed them down in her lap.

"Have you seen him many times?" she asked breathlessly.

"We did not arrange to meet," Zosine answered and hung her head in a playfully penitent manner. "But I think that he knew what time I came to feed the horses. He is a very extraordinary person, Lucan," she continued. "You remember what Baptistine told us—that he had never been outside his province? He is dressed in a blouse, like a woodcutter. But I have seen many young gentlemen in London, and in Paris, when I traveled with Papa, who had pretty high ideas of themselves and their nice ways. And I have never met anyone who carried himself, or who talked as beautifully, as he does. I am sure that no gentleman of the Court of France is more free-born or noble. I have never till now realized that the blood itself, in the veins of a person, means so much. When I have sat with him at the fence, talking of horses, I have felt that his ancestors, for many centuries, have been obeyed by everybody, and that they have talked to, and danced with, queens and princesses. Is that not extraordinary?"

"Has he proposed to you?" Lucan asked.

"No, why should he propose to me?" Zosine answered. "We were just playing together, he and I. I have had to be serious for such a long time; it was nice to play with him. I did not even tell him my name. I told him that I was called Hippolyta, for she was the Queen of the Amazons. And it fitted in well, when he permitted himself to be named Theseus. But he thought the name too long for my little person. He called me Mademoiselle Lita."

"But he may not have been playing," Lucan said smiling, "and if he wants to marry you he will have to propose to you some time."

Zosine was silent for a moment. "We are not going to be married," she said.

Lucan let go her hands. "What are you saying?" she exclaimed. "I admire and esteem you so highly. You do not mean to tell me that you are in love with a man, but that you will not marry him."

"Nay, but you must understand me," said Zosine, as, after her habit, she laid her folded hands on Lucan's shoulder and her cheek upon them. "There are two reasons why we could never marry, even if he did indeed propose to me.

"The first of them," she said slowly, "is, that he is too good for me. Do you remember, when we read about the crusaders, how we pictured them riding away to the Holy Land from Joliet? And how we imagined that the Maid of Orléans herself had a knight from Joliet as her companion in arms? It was true. The barons of Joliet have been such knights and great lords for many hundred years. A lord of Joliet does not marry a foreign girl who is staying at Sainte-Barbe, and who has got no home of her own in the whole world."

Lucan thought of Zosine's many admirers in England, and of how she had shone at the ball at Tortuga, and her heart became heavy for her friend's sake. "And what," she asked, as she put her arm round Zosine's waist, "is the second reason?"

"The second reason," said Zosine and sat up straight in the old sofa, "is that I am really too good for him. I have traveled and have seen the world. I have promised myself to visit every country on the earth. Must I then, till the end of my life, sit in the same old chateau of France, watching my husband plowing the soil, and myself herd the geese? And must I buy all my bonnets at Lunel?"

Lucan did not know whether Zosine was speaking earnestly or in jest, nor whether she herself was to laugh or cry. She once more drew her friend's head down on her shoulder. "Oh, Zosine," she whispered, "how different we are, you and I! You are right when you say that you have been spoiled all your life. But you are no less dear and sweet for all that. I myself could sit in a low, lonely hut and feel that I was the richest and happiest girl in the world, if I had the man I loved with me there." She was so violently moved by her own words that she had to stop for a moment. "But you," she continued, "you demand so much of life. And you will get it too."

"How strange it is," Lucan reflected, while they sat thus silently and lovingly together, "that Zosine and I should each have a romance, and keep it secret from each other. A romance that will always remain a secret, kept in our own hearts! But to Zosine," she added sadly in her thoughts, "it will remain a secret because she chooses it to be so. I myself have no choice. And that is as it ought to be! She has been born to be loved by everybody. I am only a girl like all other girls. In any case," she finished her course of thought, "I thank God that nothing now stands between my friend and me.

"And yet," she again thought, after a while, "I shall never never quite understand that the girl whom Noël loves does not love him in return."

A few moments later the girls heard Mr. Pennhallow and his wife come back from their walk, and talk together in the dining-room.

"Do you not hear," Zosine asked very quietly, "in their very voices that they are changed? They have come to the end of something. They are balancing up their books of account."

"And do you not remember," Lucan asked thoughtfully after a moment, "that, on the morning after your ball, you declared that danger had a kind of fascination in itself, a power to exert all one's faculties? And that it was when danger was over that one's strength gave way, yes, that one sits down to die?"

Zosine was silent for a minute or two. Then she stood up. "Yes, I remember it," she said. "But then I had known for a long time that there was danger. Then I had been deceiving all the world for a long time. Then it was a game." She went to the window and came back again. "And I played the game," she exclaimed, "to save Papa, and out of love for him. You knew that, Lucan; tell me that you knew it."

"You know that I knew it," said Lucan.

"Has the Baron de Valfonds," she asked, as again she took up her work, "ever met Mr. Pennhallow? Or is Sainte-Barbe still estranged from Joliet?"

"The Baron de Valfonds? Thésée?" Zosine exclaimed. "No, I do not think that the two have ever met. It is singular, when you remember that the master has lived here for seven years! What would they think of each other?"

16. converse in the night

LUCAN was in bed and already halfway between dream and reality, in her old school, and arranging the collection of butterflies in her class-room. She was abruptly torn out of her dream by the noise of a falling chair close by and, the moment after, by Mrs. Pennhallow asking just outside the door, "What was that noise?"

From inside their room Zosine answered, "I wanted to get a glass of water. I upset the chair in the dark."

Still half asleep, Lucan thought, "What is Mrs. Pennhallow doing in the corridor in the middle of the night?"

After a while the dream returned, but now it was changed. Now Noël was catching butterflies, and she herself was a butterfly. She was happy to flutter close round him, without appearing unwomanly or coquettish, but she was caught, and his net was over her head. The choking sensation once more woke her up, and she realized, in a moment, that Zosine's hand was fumbling over her face, and closing upon her mouth.

"Be still," Zosine's voice whispered into her ear. "Make room for me in your bed." Amazed and alarmed Lucan withdrew to the wall, and Zosine slipped underneath the cover without a sound. She put her arm under Lucan's head, and pulled it toward her, drew her breath deeply, and lay for a minute without a word.

"You must not move," she whispered. "I have something to say to you." Lucan felt that Zosine was trembling from head to foot. It made her tremble for a moment, but she dared not move or ask any questions.

"It is all true!" said Zosine.

Lucan would have asked her what it was that was true, but could not utter a word, "Yes, it is true," Zosine whispered again, and her voice was so revolted and terrified that the whisper became a groan. "All that the old man was accused of by the judge, he has done!" She again gasped for breath a couple of times, and pressed Lucan's head closer to her mouth. "Be still," she said.

"I understand it all now," she said. "I shall tell you all.

"The master has had the young girls here that they talked of. He has also sold them. I do not know what it means, I did not know that one could sell white people. But it must be possible to do, and he has done it. The girl in the boat, of whom they spoke, came from here. It is not true that there have only been three girls here. There have been many, many, and he has sold them all. What happened to her has happened to them. He had given her something strong to drink that day, and the men who were with her were those to whom he had sold her. Or else they were his helpers. He is worse than the worst."

Lucan freed her mouth of Zosine's hand. She had been awakened so suddenly, and what she now heard was so dreadful, that she could not possibly believe it straightaway. She tried to calm Zosine.

"Nay, Zosine, be quiet," she whispered. "You have been dreaming. Stay here in my bed tonight." But in the whispering itself, in the dark, there was something horrid which made her own voice unsteady.

"It is true," Zosine repeated. "It is all true. But do not let them hear us talking together. We must wait for an hour more, until they believe we are asleep."

"They cannot hear us in here," said Lucan.

But Zosine really let an hour pass, and this interval of time was strange to Lucan. Then she spoke again; she was calmer now and her voice was firmer and harder.

"That was what they wanted us for, you and me," she said. "They had been informed that some of the things they had done have been brought to light. They were suspected. Therefore they got hold of us in England. They gave ample time to the task. They were kind to us. They taught us many good and great things, and took trouble about us. It was all in their plan. Yes, every single word and deed was planned beforehand. We were to have faith in them, and to look up to them. We were to be at hand when the moment of their accusation came, to give evidence for them, to help and save them. And it all happened as they calculated. We have indeed saved them."

Lucan tried to sit up in bed to compose and collect herself. But Zosine held her back.

"No, Zosine," she moaned softly, "no, Zosine." She would not believe that her friend had gone mad, and in her madness gave herself up to dreadful fantasies. But neither could she stand to gaze down into the abyss which Zosine's words, if she were to believe them, opened up before her. And at the same moment, from far away, her own vague distrust of Sainte-Barbe returned.

"Must they not have terrible, cold hearts," Zosine again whispered, "to figure out everything like that? And to go on, day by day, carrying out their scheme."

Once more a long shiver ran through her, and her teeth chattered. "Oh, they took their time, Lucan, they took their time. It was not the return of Christ they were waiting for, it was their own hateful triumph. They knew what was to come. No human being could have answered every particular charge as they did, without having thought it all out beforehand. Somebody has warned them, and told them at what day and at what hour the blow was to fall. And they sat there, and laughed in their cold hearts, as they listened to everything coming just as they had expected and arranged it."

"It was better," she whispered after a pause. "O God, it was far better if we ourselves were in danger from them."

"Are we not that then?" Lucan asked.

"No," Zosine cried out. "No girl in the world is safe from them. But we two are. Is it not a degrading, a sickening knowledge that we two are safe from them? We are their two little canary birds in a neat little cage. They give us birdseed, water and clean sand with great care, and never for a day neglect their task. Who shall dare, when they see the little birds hopping from perch to perch and singing out their happiness and gratitude, to call their master cruel and inhuman? We are to tell people of their kindness. In time to come we are to go back to England and sing their praises there and to remember them in our prayers all our life. What hearts they must have, to teach us what is right and good! And the most horrible thing of all, Lucan, is that they do really feel tenderness for us. They feel gratitude now, because we have saved their life, and because we have given them all that pleasure of their gruesome joke."

"God. Zosine," said Lucan, "if you are right, if all this is possible, what are we to do then?"

Zosine did not hear her, but continued in her own course of thought. "I understand everything now," she said. "Yes, everything! But I shall never understand that human beings can be like that. How can they murder one girl and take tender care of the other? Yes, it is true that it sometimes came difficult to his wife, for she is not so strong as he. When she sat and stared at you, and at your golden hair—as golden as that of the girl in the boat—it was difficult for her not to clutch at you there and then. She was figuring out your price in her head.

"But he!" she whispered, and her voice was almost choked by horror and loathing. "But he! He could keep to his resolution without wavering a single minute. He was so sure of himself that he would not even send for us, but was waiting for the moment when the little, simple inspector himself struck on the idea of examining us. And, Lucan, I have looked up to him; he has represented to me so much of the greatness and wisdom of the world. I have even loved him. And his whole being is mendacity. He lives on lies, and thrives on them. It is a lie that his uncle has stood up against the Negro trade. He is more likely to have bought and sold the poor miserable black men himself. There are more lies here, many more, that I do not know yet."

"But Baptistine?" Lucan asked faintly.

"Baptistine," said Zosine, "was she not the perfect tool for them in their evil work? She is as hard as stone. She hates all people, she would be pleased to see young girls sold."

"But Clon?" Lucan asked again, almost in a wail.

Zosine was silent for a moment. "Who knows what they have done to Clon, poor, unhappy boy?" she said. "He has been to prison, they say, but they will not tell us for what crime he was sent to prison. Perhaps they themselves have lured him into that crime; perhaps it is something far worse than we suspected. Since then they have frightened Clon with the thought of prison. That has been their way, to scare and frighten everybody."

"But if what you tell me is true," Lucan again said in a trembling voice, "what are we to do then, Zosine?"

This time Zosine heard her, and was torn out of her own thoughts. "What are we to do?" she repeated slowly, and a second after broke out with great energy. "We must get away from Sainte-Barbe. I shall die if I stay here. The sight of these people suffocates me. Should we let them touch us? We must get away at once."

"But will they let us go?" Lucan asked. Zosine thought her question over.

"No," she said, "they will not let us go. How could they do that? They will keep us till the end of the year, and be kinder to us than before. They will spoil us, they will take care, when the year is out, to find good situations for us, so that we shall ever speak well of them. The thought of that only is too dreadful. They even do not want to lose sight of us; we are so dear to them. No, we must fly from Sainte-Barbe."

"Fly," Lucan exclaimed. It was as if her life was to be a flight. She was chased from one place to another.

"I have still got my gold watch and the chain to it," Zosine said after a time. "It has been my Mama's. The name and the family crest of her own mother are engraved on it. Papa has told me never to part with it. But Papa himself would not have me speaking and smiling to such people as they with whom we are now staying. We can sell it in Peyriac, and we shall probably get enough for it to be able to travel back to England."

The word "England," and the thought of England, moved Lucan deeper even than Zosine's horrible information. Was she to return once more to Noël's nearness, to tread the same ground as he, maybe to see him again? She tried to realize what it would mean. In a way it would make no difference. He did not love her. When he drove past her with his young wife, he would hardly recognize her. Or if he recognized her, it would be as Zosine's sister. And of all this Zosine knew nothing, and she could not tell her of it. She was silent for a long time.

"And if," she said at last, "what you believe is not true, and we are doing these people a great wrong, what then? It would be strange, Zosine, that two girls should understand these things better than a judge. And what is to become of us in England?"

"Oh, but it is true, every word," Zosine cried. "You cannot believe it because you are so good and because you have never deceived anyone. You are almost an angel, Lucan. But I, I am no angel. I have myself deceived people. It was when, last night, we talked of Papa's flight, and of the way in which I was then misleading everybody, that I first understood how this old man and his wife could have made up their minds to deceive, and have persisted in it. But I did it out of love. I lied to save a human being, my Papa. You will understand it, Lucan? You will have faith in me still?"

"Yes, I will have faith in you, Zosine," said Lucan, touched by her friend's appeal. "I will have faith in you. I will believe that you are right here too. Let us fly from Sainte-Barbe."

They remained perfectly still for some time, their heads close together on the pillow. "But how are we to get away?" asked Lucan.

"We must get away, whatever it will cost us," said Zosine. "There is a diligence leaving Peyriac late in the evening. Now that Mr. Pennhallow and his wife are so pleased with us, they will surely allow us to go for an evening walk."

"And what is to become of us in England?" she asked.

"I will look up Olympia. I have thought much of Olympia tonight. Her own people, her brothers and sisters, were sold by us, and we have wronged them greatly. I will beg Olympia's forgiveness.

"We must get away, Lucan," she exclaimed once more, "tomorrow or the day after, or I shall die. We must play a part tomorrow, and conceal our feelings, so that they will not realize that we know of their wickedness. God, we shall have to say good morning to them once or twice more."

Lucan's thoughts had turned from her own lot to that of her friend. "But you yourself, Zosine," she said very softly, "can you leave France so easily? Can you leave Joliet?"

Zosine lay quite still in her arms. "Yes," she whispered back. "How could I see him again, while I am in these wicked people's house, eating their bread, and with the brand of their evil eyes on my face? He, who is so honest, and who knows only what is fine and noble in the world! Here fate must decide for me. If we are to meet again, we will meet. But I must get away from here. I feel as if the lies of this house were sticking to my whole body, like mire." She was silent again for a minute. It was," she said, "when you asked me if Thésée had ever met Mr. Pennhallow that I saw the old man with Thésée's eyes, and understood all!"

She laid her arm firmly round Lucan's neck. "Oh, thank God that you are here, Lucan," she said. "I myself might be lost in this vile world. But you are my sister now, as Papa said. He always knew best. And sisters can never desert each other."

17. rosa

A HOUSE or a landscape looks different today from what it did yesterday, when, in the course of the night, you have resolved to leave it.

Lucan came home from Peyriac after having sold Zosine's watch to the old second-hand dealer in the village and stood still on the road to gaze at the long, pink building, as if she saw it for the first time. The sale of the one article of value that the girls owned between them had been confided to her, because Zosine never in her life had tried to sell anything, while she herself, from time to time, after her mother's death and when conditions became particularly difficult for her father, had disposed of some object that might be done without, to acquire another more urgently needed. She had received two hundred francs for the watch and chain, sufficient, she thought, to take her and Zosine to England. The money at this moment was in the reticule on her arm.

The preparations and the flight occupied Lucan even more than the dreadful things which her friend had confided to her. For when Zosine was not present, it was almost impossible for her to believe in them. It went against her whole nature to believe in so much wickedness.

Zosine, when they rose in the morning, had declared that she had a toothache, and had wrapped a woolen shawl round her head. Lucan, wondering at her friend's invention, had understood that she wanted to avoid speaking to her housemates and to hide her pale face from them. She felt more alarm and dismay on Zosine's behalf than on her own. It was distressing to see the giddy girl so deadly still.

Now, as soon as they were alone, Zosine questioned Lucan on the result of her walk, and in great haste began the preparations for their flight.

She was possessed, as with a fever, with the idea of getting away from Sainte-Barbe, and, far more than with fright, with an abhorrence that almost seemed to choke her. When Lucan begged her to show prudence, she turned upon her with such passion as if she suspected her of defending the people from whom they were going to fly.

Although the girls had only brought modest luggage with them from England, their traveling-box was still too big to be taken out of the house unnoticed. But Lucan, besides, had a little old traveling-bag, the same which she had tied round her waist when she climbed down the balcony of Mr. Armworthy's house. In that they could pack the most necessary or valuable things they owned. At night Zosine would secretly bring it out and hide it in the wood, so that next evening they could find it there, and take it with them to the diligence.

They had had their lesson as usual. But in the afternoon they tried to arrange it so that one of them should continually remain in Mr. Pennhallow's company, while the other prepared their flight. This last task fell to Lucan. Zosine at first had declared that she would take nothing with her from Sainte-Barbe, just as she had once refused to take anything away from Tortuga, and when at last she was persuaded to take a few things, she asked Lucan to choose and pack them for her. For a second time Lucan, disturbed and heavy at heart and faced with an uncertain future, packed her nightgown and shoes in the bag, and now added Zosine's to them.

Through the door she heard Mr. Pennhallow read aloud to his wife and Zosine, and a little later the clock in the dining-room struck three. One of the drawers of her old chest had got stuck, and as she lifted it out, a piece of paper fell down behind it. It was a letter, written on a peculiarly colored yellow paper, and crumpled up, as if the receiver, in surprise or anger, had squeezed it and thrown it away. Neither Lucan nor Zosine had received any letters at Sainte-Barbe. It must have been forgotten in the drawer before they arrived here.

Lucan smoothed out the paper to see if she was to give it to Mr. Pennhallow or to Baptistine. She meant to read the heading only, but farther down in the letter a word, the name "Rosa," caught her eye. She read the letter through. It ran as follows:

Most honored and venerable Sir, my ever dear master, I am writing this letter with trembling pen and heart. I beseech you, when you read it, not to crush me under your displeasure, but to put yourself in the place of the most humble of your servants.

Do not suppose, my master, that I have forgotten the gratitude I owe you ever since you lifted me out of a miserable position, where my brilliant education was no good to me, to my present circumstances. Do not suppose, either, that I have become unworthy of, or that I have betrayed, those great ideas into which you have initiated me. Remember, I implore you, the instances in which I have carried out these ideas to your satisfaction. Recall, at this moment, the cases in which you yourself have deigned to praise my zeal and perseverance in your service.

Further, allow me, my master, to observe that the practical execution of a matter may present other aspects than the pure idea and principle of it.

You, my benefactor, in your devotion to the great ideas and principles in our concern, have attached an essential importance to virtue, innocence and purity. But your humble and obedient servant, in the practical, everyday administration of the same concern, has come to learn that virtue, innocence and purity may become disadvantages instead of assets, may occasion difficulties, and may even bring about heavy losses.

These things I write down in the hope of moving your heart to forbearance, before passing on to the statement of the following sorry affair.

The girl, whom you last sent us here (Rosa, Scottish, aged 18) has caused us such heavy losses. From the enclosed you will be informed of the exact extent of the same. This girl was unfit for use. I beseech you to believe that I had recourse to all measures, that I have not spared myself, but have had patience with her, and have held out for a longer time than any other person could have stood. But this girl was like the insane, who do not really feel what is done to them. If the other girls in the house spoke to her, she struck them. To spite you, my master, and myself in our business, this girl took a candle that I had given her and burnt her face with it. After thorough consideration I came to the conclusion that there was here nothing more to be done. My struggle was hard, for I was aware that you might think me forgetful of your great ideas, and of your will in our concern. All the same I once more implore you to believe that it was in the firm conviction of doing what was best for you as well as for me that last Tuesday evening I laid a rope round the neck of this girl, and put an end to her. On Wednesday, at noon—for at night there is no peace for such things in the house—I had her buried in the cellar.

I have only one more thing to say. I implore you to remember that we are lonely, you and I. The others who work with us do so for the sake of earthly gain. Only I have understood something, a little, of the immense ideas which move you on. If you destroy me, you will be alone.

I am, Master, your faithful and humble dog, which licks your hands, and follows in your footsteps,

Pedro Smith

Lucan read the letter through two or three times. Its contents at first were altogether incomprehensible to her. As they began to collect themselves and become clear to her mind, she felt that her scalp and her hands became cold as ice, and that her knees trembled beneath her, so that she had to sit down. For a long time it was to her as if she were sinking, ever deeper, into a darkness, the waves of which washed over her head.

When slowly she came to, she was at first seized with fear that she might have screamed out loud. But from the sound of the continued, quiet reading aloud in the next room, she gathered that she must have remained silent in the midst of her terror. She tried to tear the letter into small bits, as if to prevent anybody else from sharing her abhorrence, but her hands were strengthless. A choked, feeble sob broke from her lips. It seemed to her that she could not possibly remain in the same world as this letter. It annihilated her, like a mill-wheel, that would grind her down and crush her. After a while she tried to read it once more, but the lines became blurred before her eyes.

While she sat like this, the door behind her was opened, and Zosine came in. Lucan heard her friend say, "They have gone out. Let us make haste while they are away." But she did not understand what the words meant. "Why do you keep so still, Lucan?" Zosine's clear voice again asked, and a moment after, "What is it you are reading?" Lucan made a faint attempt to put the letter away, but Zosine had already snatched it out of her hands, and read it. Slowly, gathering all her strength, Lucan lifted her eyes up to her face.

18. the skein of green silk

ZOSINE turned toward her friend, her face white as chalk, her mouth open. Her hands sank down, and for more than a minute the two girls stared at each other. While they stood like that a shadow glided past the window. It was Mr. Pennhallow out on his afternoon walk.

Zosine cried out, "You see!" And again, "You see!" To Lucan, there was salvation in Zosine's presence, after the hours which seemed to have passed since she read the letter she had found. She rose from the chair and clung to her friend. The two girls, supporting each other, crept to the window to read the letter through once more.

Just as they had finished the reading, a knock on the window-pane close by made them start. Mrs. Pennhallow was standing outside, in hat and shawl, ready for her walk, and through the pane she gave them an order about the cleaning of the lamps, which they were to pass on to Baptistine. As the little old woman stood there, with the light behind her, and her big bonnet on, the girls from inside the room could not quite distinguish her face. In the midst of her speech, she suddenly stopped. Then she turned and walked on, and they heard her open and shut the door in the garden wall.

At the same moment, Zosine fell down on her knees, her face and hands on the yellow paper. She kept lying thus immovable for such a long time that in her horror Lucan for an instant imagined that her friend was dead, and she herself left alone. She put her arms around Zosine's shoulders, and tried to raise her up. "Zosine," she moaned, "Zosine."

Zosine slowly rose to her feet, giddily and deadly pale. "Did she see our faces?" she whispered. Lucan did not understand her, and Zosine repeated, "Did she see our faces?"

"I do not know," said Lucan.

"No, but we must find out," said Zosine, "for it is life and death to both of us. My shawl will have hidden my own face somewhat. And you did not turn all round toward her." She took up the letter, and pressed it toward her. "We will soon know," she said, "for she will come back again soon.

"In any case," she went on after a moment, "she has seen the color of the paper, and will have recognized it. I dare not tell her that we have not seen the letter. I dare not tear it up either. What am I to do with it?"

After a time, she said, "Give me that skein of green embroidering silk there on the window-sill." Lucan handed it to her, and Zosine placed the letter on the table, smoothed it out carefully, and then folded it up again and again, until it was but a narrow slip. Still with the greatest care and precision, she wound the green embroidering silk round it, until all the writing on the paper was covered, and put the reel away on the table. Then, in the same slow, somnambulant and deadly sure fashion, she loosened the shawl off her head, and sat down on a chair by the window. She spoke not a word, neither did Lucan speak or question her friend, until they again heard the door in the garden wall open and close upon the two old people of Sainte-Barbe. This time they walked up to the house side by side, but they did not seem to talk together.

"Take that book on the table," said Zosine in a quiet and clear voice, "and read to me from it." Without realizing what she wanted, Lucan took the book and opened it. It was a volume of Wordsworth's poems. In a faint, trembling voice Lucan read aloud from the page where she had opened it:

"The dew was falling fast, the stars began to blink;
I heard a voice; it said, 'Drink, pretty creature, drink.'
And, looking o'er the hedge, before me I espied
A snow-white mountain-lamb with a maiden at its side."

They heard somebody moving in the dining-room, and presently Mrs. Pennhallow softly opened the door and entered the room.

She remained standing there, her eyes on the two girls, and Lucan, who realized that Zosine meant her to continue her reading, read on:

"Nor sheep nor kine were near; the lamb was all alone,
And by a slender cord was tethered to a stone . . ."

The old woman came up to the table, and in her immediate nearness, it became impossible for Lucan to go on. She laid the book down.

"It has begun to rain," said Mrs. Pennhallow. "We had to give up our walk." The girls did not answer. "What is it you are reading?" Mrs. Pennhallow again asked, and it seemed to Lucan that her voice was vibrating slightly. Lucan handed her the book. "It is a pretty poem," said Mrs. Pennhallow. She let her eyes run round the room. "You have been putting your drawers in order, lasses," she said. "That is very nice and neat."

The girls' traveling-bag had been pushed back underneath Zosine's bed, but one or two drawers in the chest were still half opened. Lucan tried to answer, but her voice failed her.

"No," said Zosine quietly from the window, "we have been looking for a piece of paper to wind my skein of green embroidering silk onto."

"And did you find any?" Mrs. Pennhallow asked.

"Yes, we found an old letter," said Zosine. "It was quite useful."

"What was the letter about?" Mrs. Pennhallow asked, and once more Lucan seemed to hear a slight quiver in her hoarse voice. "It was a business letter," Zosine answered. "Somebody was regretting some loss. Perhaps we ought not to have taken it."

"Where is it?" asked Mrs. Pennhallow.

Zosine looked round for a moment, her eyes fell upon the letter, round which her embroidering silk was wound, and without a word she handed it to the old woman. Mrs. Pennhallow took it, and looked from one of the girls to the other.

"I have for some time been looking for an old letter," she said, "and I could not find it. I will unwind the silk from the one you have found, and give you another reel instead of it." With the letter in her hand she left the room.

A few minutes after, Zosine drew her chair close to Lucan's and put her arm round her neck. While she spoke, she kept looking down into Wordsworth's volume of poems, which was still open on the table.

"Now we cannot talk together any more," she said very low.

"Not talk together?" Lucan whispered back, terrified.

"No," said Zosine. "It is not enough that they are not in the room. They can hear us through the walls. They will be here even if we do not see them. We cannot talk together at all any more."

Lucan sat dumb. "But it is only for twenty-four hours," she at last whispered in despair. "Only till tomorrow night. After all, it is only twenty-four hours."

"Yes, twenty-four hours," said Zosine.

The terror and the wild, blind thought of flight, of getting away from this house, which had filled Zosine and which her friend had not understood before, now took hold of Lucan herself. Time after time she felt that she grew cold as ice, and that her teeth chattered. She would not let Zosine see her weakness. She would have stood up to finish the preparations for their flight, but she had no control of her limbs. She had thought out carefully what things they were to take with them; now she could no longer remember them. Nor was there now any need for it, she reflected, for it would no longer be possible for them to bring out their traveling-bag and hide it in the wood. They must fly as they were. And what did it matter, if only they could get away from the house of murder, which closed round them on all sides? If they could only reach the diligence in Peyriac, she thought, they would be saved. Or could Mr. Pennhallow and his wife pursue them, even there, and insist on having them back?

O God, Lucan thought, if Noël had loved her, as she loved him, or if he had only felt toward her as a friend, they might have taken refuge with him. He was so fearless and strong. Without really making clear to herself how it should be worked, she felt sure that he would have saved her and Zosine. She gave freer course to her thoughts now that she could no longer speak.

The two girls had to sit down at table for supper, and to pass the evening in the company of their foster parents. Lucan knew that Zosine expected her to be as calm as herself, and collected all her strength not to disappoint her. It was hardly possible for her to eat or drink. Many times in the course of the evening she felt that she was changing color, and while after supper the housemates sat by the fireplace, she once or twice got up, unable to remain in her chair. But Zosine's eyes, which rested on her, forced her back again every time.

In the midst of her own terrible agitation, she felt that Mr. Pennhallow and his wife, too, were chary of words. They looked from her to Zosine, and at each other. Baptistine herself, who brought in the dishes, seemed to be aware that something was amiss, and was darker and more reserved than usual. It was raining, as on the night when Noël had been at Sainte-Barbe and had told his story. Then Lucan had felt his presence as a safeguard against all evil. Now that happy night seemed infinitely far away; an abyss lay between it and the present moment.

Lucan heard Zosine talk as she used to, and wondered how she found strength to do so. Zosine told Mr. Pennhallow that, to please him, she had learned a long Latin poem by heart. Standing erect before the fireplace, she recited it from beginning to end in her clear voice and without a fault. Mr. Pennhallow was cheered by the declamation, and himself delivered a long classic poem. Later on, he made his wife follow his example. In the course of the evening the atmosphere in the long dining-room of Sainte-Barbe grew peaceful and genial as usual, and even more lively. Lucan mechanically followed the talk of the others. From time to time she lifted her eyes toward the old clock, and thought, "Now there is so much less than twenty-four hours left."

Even when the company parted for the night, and the young girls were alone in their bedroom, Zosine went on chatting for a time, as always while they went to bed. There was a key in the door, and it was impossible for Lucan not to turn it, but Zosine without a word turned it back again. They undressed as usual, and dared not take shelter with each other in the same bed, for anybody listening outside must hear both beds creak under their weight. The moment came when they must blow out their candle, and then Zosine too grew silent and very pale. The slight flame seemed to be their last protection. When it was put out, the girls, sitting up in their beds, each squeezed against a corner of the room, were seized with the consciousness of the darkness round the house, and the long distance to any other human dwelling place, and with a new, awful idea: would they survive this night? If those who were listening in the other room had indeed realized that their secret was known, would they not make use of the night to lay a rope round their necks, too, and put an end to them?

19. zosine's resolution

THE hours went by with infinite slowness. Once or twice in the course of the night, the girls seemed to hear somebody moving in the corridor outside their door. Then the house once more became dead silent. Lucan was cold, but dared not lie down under the cover. She knew that she had been weeping; her face had been bathed in tears and had dried again. She did not hear a sound from Zosine's bed. When the first pale light of dawn drew the outline of the window, the girl's strength suddenly gave way. She tried to keep her eyes open toward the light, to see it wax clearer, but they fell too. Still half sitting up, and leaning against the wall, she fell asleep as if she had fallen into a faint. For some time sleep itself was filled with horrors; it seemed to her that she was drowning or was being buried alive. But after a time it closed round her like a deep and merciful darkness.

When she woke up, it was morning. A faint sunshine colored the wall. Zosine slept, with her face pressed into her pillow.

Slowly the happenings of yesterday came back to Lucan with awful significance. And upon them followed, like the first faint ray of light, the certainty that this dawn was her last at Sainte-Barbe. No longer did a night lay between her and liberation.

As she let her eyes run round the room, she saw that her own traveling-bag beneath the bed was gone. Was it possible, she thought, that Zosine, while she herself had been asleep, in the rain, which would have drowned all sound, would have dared to carry it out, and to have taken the first step toward their flight and their freedom? Lucan's profound devotion and admiration for Zosine made her heart swell, and gave her new strength.

She would not despair, as long as she had her friend with her. She would give her destiny into Zosine's hands.

Lucan had a small book which had belonged to her father, and in which there was a verse or a maxim for each day of the year. Although there was so little room in the traveling-bag, she had put it down there yesterday, she had never till now gone anywhere without it. As she sat up in bed, her elbow hit something hard, and she saw that the small book had been stuck underneath her pillow. She almost believed that she was dreaming, and took it up. A piece of paper had been put into it. As she unfolded it, she saw that a few uneven lines were written down on it in pencil.

"*I am writing this in the dark,*" they ran. "*I will help you to get away but I myself cannot leave Sainte-Barbe. Tear this up.*" It was signed "*Zosine.*"

Lucan remained perfectly immovable, until her friend stirred and woke up. When Zosine was quite awake, she sat up in bed, and looked back at Lucan, and at the book in her hand. She grew very pale, and slowly and solemnly nodded her head twice to her. Then by a sign she gave Lucan to understand that she must destroy the letter, and silently followed her movements, while she tore it up in little bits. For a long time the two girls gazed at each other, Lucan with bewilderment and despair in her clear blue eyes, Zosine with a strange calm and determination in her pale face.

It was still so early that they dared not exchange a word. But as they got up at the usual time, and as the clank of the water jug or the clatter of a chair being moved, might serve to cover their low whispers, Lucan seized Zosine's wrist and pressed it to her bosom. "Zosine," she whispered, "explain yourself to me. You are not mad? I do not understand you."

"I have taken my own things out of the bag," said Zosine. "I will bring it out for you, if you want me to. But I will not go away myself."

"Why will you not go away?" Lucan cried.

Zosine closed her eyes as if in sharp, bodily pain. "I cannot go," she whispered back.

"Who holds you back here?" Lucan asked despairingly. At the moment she feared that their terrible experiences might have deranged her friend's mind. Zosine did not open her eyes; her young face was as white and still as if it had been cut in marble. She tried to speak, but the attempt seemed to hurt and pain her, and it was more by the faint movement of her lips than by any sound that Lucan caught her answer.

"Rosa." Zosine whispered. Then she softly pushed Lucan away.

They dressed in complete silence. When they had finished, Zosine went to the bookshelf, took out a book, and handed it to Lucan.

"Hear me repeat this," she said in a loud, clear voice. "I am not sure that I know it quite by heart." She stood up erect before Lucan and a little lower than before, but in the same clear and calm voice recited:

"O all you host of heaven! O earth! What else?
And shall I couple hell? O fie! Hold, hold, my heart!
And you, my sinews, grow not instant old,
But bear me stiffly up! Remember thee!
Ay, thou poor ghost, while memory holds a seat
In this distracted globe. Remember thee!
Yea, from the table of my memory
I'll wipe away all trivial fond records,
All saws of books, all forms, all pressures past,
That youth and observation copied there;
And thy commandment all alone shall live
Within the book and volume of my brain,
Unmix'd with baser matter: yes, by heaven!
O most pernicious woman!
O villain, villain, smiling, damned villain!
My tables—meet it is I set it down,

That one may smile, and smile, and be a villain . . .
Now to my word;
It is, 'Adieu, adieu! remember me.' . . ."

She looked up at Lucan with a glance at the same time humble and severe. "Is it right?" she asked. Lucan let the book sink.

After a long silence Zosine said very slowly in a voice so low as to be almost inaudible, "Once they have betrayed themselves, and that proof we had to give up to them. But they will betray themselves again. Sooner or later they will give a new, decisive proof of their wickedness into my hand. That I shall keep. And I cannot desert her till this has happened. She was a girl like you or me, eighteen years, like us. She took a candle which she had given her, and burned her face with it. And she was like you, Lucan. She had a lovely face like yours. Now she is waiting for you and me to see justice done to her. She expects us to avenge her."

"Of whom are you speaking?" Lucan asked.

"Of Rosa," said Zosine.

The girls found no opportunity to talk together during their lessons. Later on, while they were sewing in the dining-room, they noticed that their adoptive parents would never today leave the room both at the same time, but that one or the other of them would always remain with them.

In her work-box Zosine found a bag of little colored glass beads, and, as if to pass time, she set about to string them. It happened that the girls, for a few moments, were alone in their corner of the room. Zosine stretched out her hand to her friend. "Look, Lucan," she said. She had put a small ring with three beads on her finger.

"Do you remember," she said, "that Papa told you how his sisters had rings made of stones, the initials of which formed the word 'one'?"

"Yes," Lucan answered, without grasping her friend's meaning. "I have made myself a ring like theirs now," Zosine said. "My beads are not worth as much as their precious stones, but they mean the same thing. Will you, too, have such a ring?"

"I?" Lucan asked.

"Yes," said Zosine. "Then it will mean 'one' to us as well. Then the three of us will again hold together."

"The three of us?" Lucan asked.

"Yes," said Zosine again.

"You and I," said Lucan, "and who else?"

"Rosa," whispered Zosine.

Lucan grew very pale. "Then God help us," she said. "I will not desert you. But God help us now."

PART THREE

the buried treasure

*

1. masks

FOR two days but few words were spoken at Sainte-Barbe.

The girls did not talk together; they felt that they were being watched. If they were left alone in the room, Zosine's gaze always crdered Lucan to go on speaking, as if other people had been present. They would discuss everyday matters for a while, and then sew on in silence. More than once it then happened that they heard Mrs. Pennhallow, who had recently said good-bye to go to Peyriac, stirring in the next room.

Nor did the two old people speak much. They would sit in the dining-room, each absorbed in a book, and in complete silence, for many hours. They went for their walks, but as far as Lucan and Zosine could follow them with their eyes, they seemed to keep step without talking. They came home and entered the house, but no word between them told of their arrival. They had suspended the lessons for a week; they were, they said, waiting for new school books to arrive from England.

The meals were very quiet. Sometimes Mr. Pennhallow would break the monotony with a mild little joke; sometimes Zosine would answer him. But soon after they all fell back into their own thoughts.

Lucan clung to Zosine. Away from her friend she felt like a person who has lost his way in a dark wood.

She thought, "When we were in London, and looking for a situation, Zosine kept close to me, and was uneasy when she did not see me. She left all decisions to me and placed her destiny in my hand. Now it is I who hold onto her. For then it was a question of earning our bread, and of that I had some experience, but she had none. But of the task which she has now undertaken, I know nothing, and I do not understand her any longer. Revenge! What is revenge? It does no one any good; it is a cold, barren thing. I did not want to revenge myself on Mr. Armworthy, however angry I was with him. I am afraid I know no better than to fly from evil whenever I meet it."

"But from here I will not fly," she further thought. "It is true that I am no heroine. I am scared here. I hardly dare to turn my head for fear of what I may see, I hardly dare to sleep. But I will not fail Zosine. I would have given her the man I love. I may well die with her then, if that is what she wants."

Still, after a couple of days, conditions were changed. Mr. Pennhallow and his wife no longer kept their eyes on their adopted daughters. They even encouraged them to leave the house, and to go for long walks wherever they liked. For the fresh air, they said, would do them good, and the beauties of nature would make them forget the happenings that had frightened them. "You ought," the old people said to them, "today, in the fine weather, to walk as far as Neuvéglise, where the diligence to Paris makes a halt, and from where there is a beautiful view." When the two girls returned, their foster-parents would exclaim in surprise, "Are you already back?"

On the roads across the fields and through the woods, the girls talked again.

"Have you ever," Zosine asked, "been at a bal masque?"

"No," answered Lucan wonderingly.

"It is great fun!" said Zosine. "You dance in a mask, with a masked young gentleman, and you believe that you know who he is. He, too, believes that he knows who you are. But none of you can be certain of the matter."

It was a clear day, but the wind blew, chasing the clouds across the sky and swirling the girls' clothes round their slim, straight figures. "Why do you talk of bals masques?" asked Lucan.

"Because we ourselves are holding a bal masque at Sainte-Barbe, these days," Zosine answered.

"Do you not see," she added after a moment, "why the old people make us walk as far as Neuvéglise, where the diligence to Paris makes a halt? It is to give us an opportunity to go away. They will go on giving us such opportunity for a few days or for a week more.

"Yes, it is a merry masquerade," she went on. "We have got our masks on, and the old people have got theirs! We do not know if they have recognized us, and they cannot tell either whether we have recognized their murderers' faces behind their masks. But now, out here, under the clear sky of God, I will tell you of what things they are still in doubt, and what things they know for certain. And I will tell you, too, what they are today brooding over and wondering about, as they sit in their chairs at Sainte-Barbe.

"They do not know for certain whether we have recognized them, whether we know that they are murderers. And even if, to be on the safe side, they reckon with it, they cannot be sure that we know that they know that we know that they are murderers! But of one thing they are sure: that the only proof we had against them they have got back from us. And they know for certain, too, that as long as we have got no other proof against them, they have nothing to fear from us.

"And they wonder, and rack their brains to find out, why we stay on at Sainte-Barbe.

"So," Zosine finished, after they had walked on a bit, "the outcome of all this is that the four of us agree very well about things. If we want to run away, they will be pleased to help us to do so. We will then go back to England and tell everybody there that we have been scared out of our life at Sainte-Barbe. And they, on their side, can make a judge and his inspector swear that there was nothing whatever to be scared about. Our conduct will then go to confirm what the two good old people have already sadly learned in life: that light-headed girls will run away from their benefactors, no matter how kindly they have been treated! We would do them much good by running away from Sainte-Barbe.

"But if instead of running away, we should choose to remain with them," Zosine went on, "what then? Why, then they will be only too happy to keep us! For it may mean one of two things to them. It may mean that we have been so young and simple that we have never seen anything but what they meant us to see. They will then keep us till the end of our year, as they meant to do. We shall still be their little canary birds, tamer and gentler even than before, and they will look after us with even greater care."

"And what is the other thing that it may mean to them?" Lucan asked in a low voice.

"The other thing," cried Zosine, looking up briskly, "which they may conclude from our holding on to Sainte-Barbe, is that the tables have been turned, and that now we are chasing them. The canary birds are out of their cage, and on their track. And they will never leave the blood-trail till they have hunted them down, till they are dead!" Zosine was crying these last words out half laughing, half in horror. "They do not yet believe in this possibility; they are thinking it over at this moment in their chairs. But they are clever. They will find out today, or tomorrow, or the day after. And then," she said, and stood still, "then, Lucan, they will never let us get away from Sainte-Barbe alive."

They had walked so fast against the wind that they were both out of breath. Now they sat down on a slope by the road, under a chestnut tree, where there was shelter and where the afternoon sun shone on the dry grass.

"Zosine," said Lucan after a long silence, "are you aware of what you are doing? For a few days more, you say, they will still allow us to fly from Sainte-Barbe. But you refuse to fly. Sooner or later, you say, they will furnish another, final proof of their wickedness. But this proof may be final to you and me as well. For it may mean the death of us both. Consider that the people with whom you are dealing are infinitely more clever and cunning than we. Do not forget that they have got blood on their hands."

"Nay, that is what I do not forget," said Zosine.

"I am always thinking of Rosa now," she said after a while. "Wherever I am, I feel that she relies on me. She was friendless, in the hands of monsters, but she would not give in to them. When the other girls talked to her, she struck them. I have dreamed of her, and on waking up in the morning I have seen a red ring round my wrist. It was the mark of Rosa's fingers, where she had held on to me."

Zosine folded her hands in her lap, and looked at Lucan very gravely. "Take the diligence here at Neuvéglise," she said slowly, "and take the two hundred francs which we got for the watch. Then I will return alone to Sainte-Barbe."

"Do you think so badly of me?" asked Lucan, and her eyes filled with tears.

"I will tell you a story," said Zosine, "which my old French dancing master once told me. Near his home, in the mountains, there was a cleft named 'The Knight's Leap.' A young knight was here pursued and taken prisoner by his enemies. 'If only,' he cried, 'I had had one minute more! Then my good steed would have jumped the cleft, across which you could never have followed us.' The leader of his enemies laughed, and answered him, 'If you can indeed jump this cleft, you shall be a free man, and your whole province shall be spared. For no steed in the world can jump it.' The young knight again mounted his horse, made it back up, and then set it into a gallop. And the good horse realized what was at stake, and in a mighty leap crossed the cleft! Since then it is called 'The Knight's Leap.'

"And old Monsieur Dumont explained to me," said Zosine, "that in this world there are two kinds of courage. He called them the aristocratic and the bourgeois courage. The bourgeois courage belongs to the man who, without trembling, will give his life to a cause dear or sacred to him. But the aristocrat loves danger for its own sake. There would, he said, be many good burghers who, to save their town, would unhesitatingly have thrown themselves into the cleft. But the leap they would not have taken.

"I have myself read a story," she continued, "of two men who had been sentenced to death by the Sultan of Turkey. The one was a pirate, the other a peasant who in hard times had stolen seed-corn for his field. The Sultan was a great chess player. He now gave the prisoners a last chance. They might play a game of chess under the gallows. The winner would be set free, but the loser would be hanged. The pirate at once was ready to sit down to the board, but the peasant declined. 'Nay,' he said, 'I would rather be hanged in peace.'

"But in order to love danger," said Zosine, "one must, I think, have something hard and dangerous within one's own nature. Therefore you have not that kind of courage, although you are so much braver than I. I myself all my life have been a spoiled, hard girl. Only in the company of an angel like you, Lucan, I have lately tried to become a bit of an angel myself. I have worried my Papa, tormented good old Olympia, and tortured my admirers. It falls to me to fight the evil old man of Sainte-Barbe."

On the same evening, when after supper the small party at Sainte-Barbe was gathered round the fire, Mr. Pennhallow kindly asked the girls whether they could play chess. They both knew the game. Lucan's father had taught it to her, and Zosine's Papa, when the two were alone at Tortuga, had played it with his daughter.

The master the first night played against Lucan. She was a sensible, thoughtful player, and the game dragged out a long time. Still, Mr. Pennhallow won all three games from her. The next evening he played against Zosine. Also this time the old man checkmated his opponent three times. He had watched the game closely. When they had finished, he folded his big hands on the board and looked at her across it with a little tender smile.

2. father vadier

ON the very last of the walks, which Lucan and Zosine took together at the invitation of the old people at Sainte-Barbe, they came past a pretty and stately old farmstead named Le Haubourdin. It was the nearest house to Sainte-Barbe, and there was a distance of a mile between the two places. The girls stood still in front of the farmyard, and looked into it. A small girl was just driving a flock of goats across it. As once more they walked on down the road, a barefooted boy came running after them. Father Vadier, he said, was on a visit to Le Haubourdin, and begged to speak to them. They looked at each other, and, wondering, followed the boy back to the house.

Father Vadier himself came out of the house to greet them, and asked their forgiveness for having interrupted their walk. For a long time he had wanted to meet the young ladies of Sainte-Barbe. He had caught sight of them from the window, but had not, he explained with a smile, held himself capable of catching up with them, and so had taken the liberty of sending the boy. Now he asked the girls to step inside the house.

Father Vadier was still a young man, with a broad, sun-burnt face, red cheeks and clear, quiet brown eyes. He had a grave, courteous manner, and a very fine youthful voice. He was himself a farmer's son of the neighborhood, and the mistress of Le Haubourdin, whom he had come to visit, was his mother's sister.

Within the house the girls were respectfully and cordially welcomed. The old farmer and his wife spoke the dialect of the province, and they were somewhat embarrassed to receive two foreign young ladies. But the family gathering in here had obviously, till this moment, been so hearty and gay that it was not easily affected by any interruption; the wrinkled old faces still wore the bright and happy expression of a moment ago. All the same, there was a certain reserve and prudence in the manner of the French hosts toward their guests, and Zosine thought, "It is because we come from Sainte-Barbe." Some children in the room stared at the pretty visitors with surprise and wonder.

It was a curious thing to Lucan and Zosine to find themselves once more in a circle of people, related to one another and belonging together. The people of the farm, while they showed due respect to Father Vadier, jested with him, and he with them.

Lucan was strongly impressed by the happy, homely atmosphere of the house. "Please God," she thought, "that Zosine might come to have confidence in these kind, honest people, and turn to them for help."

The room was plainly furnished, but as the English girls gazed round it, their eyes met more than one old solid and pretty French heirloom. The white-haired peasant invited them to take a glass of wine from his own vineyard, and for a little while they talked together of the wine, the weather and the neighborhood. But after a time their hosts got up, excused themselves and, taking the children with them, left the room. The girls were alone with Father Vadier. The priest's face and voice changed and became graver. He too, to begin with, seemed a little shy of the English girls, but his natural candor, and his zeal in the task he had taken upon himself, overcame his shyness.

The demoiselles, he said, must forgive him asking them a few questions, for he was talking on behalf of a dear and honored *penitente*. As they would know, he continued, he was acquainted with most people of the neighborhood. Some time ago he had happened to be chatting with the old second-hand dealer in Peyriac, and the old man had shown him a very fine watch, which he had newly purchased. The watch had a name and a crest engraved on it, which were both well known to both the priest himself and to Madame de Valfonds. In great agitation she had sent for the old man, and had questioned him on the matter. He explained that he had bought the watch from one of the young English misses at Sainte-Barbe. But through such information as Father Vadier had acquired, he was aware that the name on the watch was not that of the sisters. Now he asked them if they would kindly tell him what they knew of the watch, and how it had come into their possession.

While Father Vadier spoke, his clear gaze rested upon one or the other of the girls' faces. It was very gentle, but earnest and serious; it scrutinized them. Both Lucan and Zosine thought, "There have been rumors about Sainte-Barbe. People have come to know of the police's visit there. Now Father Vadier is considering whether he will believe us to be victims or accomplices." Zosine in her mind wonderingly added: "It would be a pretty thing if I were to be charged with complicity in my own murder, and in the theft of my own watch!" But they kept quite still, and Father Vadier had not expected to find them so silent.

"Have you not sold the watch to old Pinbrache of Peyriac?" he gently inquired.

"Yes," Zosine answered. "It is my watch."

"And you are familiar with the inscription on it?" Father Vadier again asked.

"Yes," said Zosine. "The name is 'Zosine d'Acier de l'Orville.' And the device is: '*Durior Ferro. Purior Auro.*' It means: 'Sharper than steel. Purer than gold.'"

"But it is not your own name or device?" asked Father Vadier.

"It may be my own device," Zosine answered gravely. "But it is not my name."

"There is something, then, that I should much like to know, Mademoiselle," said Father Vadier. "You sold the watch very cheap to old Pinbrache, and he gathered that it was important to you to get the money at once, in great haste. Was the reason for this that you were in need of money and could not admit it? If so, I beg you to have trust in me. I might help you, if you would so far honor me. Or were you keen to get rid of the watch as quickly as possible?" His question came quicker than before, and he looked hard at the girl to whom he spoke.

Zosine thought his question over. "I cannot answer you," she said.

Father Vadier gave Lucan a short glance, and she faintly shook her head in reply. He once more turned toward Zosine, but for a few minutes he did not speak.

"Mademoiselle," he said at last, "I beg you to listen to me. I do not speak without having given the matter my full consideration. There is one more reason for my inquisitiveness. This interview may be of great concern to people whom I hold dear and esteem highly. It may be of great concern to you yourself. I speak so freely in your sister's presence because I assume her to be acquainted with the things of which we speak, and also because it may prove useful for you to consult her in the matter. I believe that you have both, under circumstances of which I have no knowledge, become entangled in difficulties too heavy for young maidens like yourself. You may rest assured that what you may here deign to confide to me, I will never, without your own permission, mention to any human being. But first of all, I myself want to tell you something.

"You may have been told," he continued, "of a particular tradition in the Valfonds family, according to which no one of that name will ever leave the province of their feudal estate. Baron Thésée's father observed this tradition. He himself has already at his first communion vowed to observe it. On the same occasion he promised that he would not, without his grandmother's permission, marry any lady unwilling to undertake the same obligation, and to remain in our province all her life. I am," Father Vadier went on after a short pause, "acquainted with the origin of the tradition. Baron Thésée knows nothing of it. But he is a noble young man. He would never break a promise.

"Baron Thésée," he said, "a few months ago fell in love with a young girl. He wishes to apply for her hand. But as I have already told you, he is a noble, high-minded youth. He would not expose the lady whom he loved to the risk of being met with distrust in his family, or at Joliet. Still less would he enter into any intrigue with an innocent young girl. He has taken his grandmother into his confidence, as well as myself, who have known him since he was a child, and who have for a long time been Father Confessor to him and to the lady of Joliet. He has given us both to understand that he will never marry, if he cannot have this young girl for his wife. With deep regret I have, for the first time, watched a conflict between people who, till now, have given the whole province an example of firm and sacred solidarity.

"The Baroness de Valfonds is a lady of rare spiritual strength. She may not be without prejudice of rank, but she has the happiness of her grandson most at heart. She would be ready to receive any good, innocent girl, who loved him, into her home and family. But a young lady who was in some way connected with the name and the crest engraved in the watch would be welcomed at Joliet with particular warmth and tenderness." As before, Father Vadier made a pause, and as before, Zosine remained silent. Lucan saw that she had grown very pale. In the heavy, wooden chair she looked slight and childlike.

"There is," said Father Vadier, "something in your situation which I do not understand. But I have some experience of the world, and some knowledge of human nature. I believe of you, my child, that you are an innocent, noble girl. Will you let me take you to Joliet, to Madame de Valfonds? Will you open your heart to her or to me? Are you not in need of such friends as you would, then, find in both of us?"

Zosine looked at Father Vadier as gravely as he at her.

"Father Vadier," she said, "my Mama was a Roman Catholic. She made Papa promise that I should be brought up in her creed. But when she died, his family in England objected to her wish, and as the matter did not mean much to him, he gave in to them. I am a Protestant. But for the sake of my Mama, —and," she added, "of my old nurse, who has often talked about the Saints—I regard the Church and her priests with reverence. I would never try to deceive you.

"I cannot come with you to Joliet. I have got an obligation toward a person at Sainte-Barbe whom I can never fail. That person is expecting something from me, of which I cannot tell Baron Thésée or his grandmother. I understand that he cannot break his word. And he, too, will understand that I cannot break mine. Will you," she finished, with trembling lips, "be good enough to tell him this from me? And will you say good-bye to him from Lita?"

Father Vadier for a minute did not take his eyes off her face. "A person at Sainte-Barbe?" he repeated.

"Yes," said Zosine.

Father Vadier took her hand. "My child," he said very gently and solemnly. "Are you happy at Sainte-Barbe? Is it a good place for you and your sister to be in?"

Zosine had risen, but she stood with her head bent and still looked like a pale child.

"I do not know as many people of the neighborhood as you do," she said. "But I have talked with Baptistine, Baptistine Labarre, of Sainte-Barbe. I am aware that Joliet and Sainte-Barbe can have nothing to do with each other. And that it has been so for a very long time. And I, I belong to Sainte-Barbe."

Father Vadier in silence saw them out of the house. As he gave Zosine his hand in good-bye, he said, "Send for me, if ever I can be of use to you."

While the two young girls walked away toward Sainte-Barbe, he kept standing outside the house, and followed them with his eyes.

3. mr. pennhallow goes on a journey

AS has already been told, Mr. Pennhallow made pretty little pictures of landscapes and flowers. Lucan, who as a child had been taught to sketch, often wished that she could draw anything as neat and graceful. But he also, at times, when he was sunk in his own thoughts, let his pencil run over the paper, and produced strange pictures. Once or twice Lucan and Zosine had found such drawings on the school table. They had wondered, smiled a little, and at the same time felt a particular slight shudder at the sight of them. They might, they thought, have been drawn by a person in a dream or a nightmare. There were human figures in them, but they were supplied with new fantastic features and limbs unknown to the girls. Zosine once said that they were like some old, dark idols which the Negroes on Santo Domingo had carved in black wood, and which Olympia had brought with her.

One evening, the next after that on which he had been playing chess with Zosine, the old man amused himself in this way by making lines on a sheet of paper. From time to time he looked up casually at the one or the other of his pupils, so that Lucan, with a certain uneasiness of heart, imagined that he might be drawing a portrait of her. This evening Mr. Pennhallow and his wife were unusually pensive and absent-minded. He was a long time over his drawing. In the end he gazed at it and pushed it across the table to his wife. She gave it a glance, and then a longer glance, and was seized with a fit of chuckling so vehement that she had to hold her handkerchief to her mouth. The drawing remained lying on the table. Many times in the course of the evening the old woman fixed her eyes on it, and each time seemed more pleased with it. Her arms and legs moved jerkily, and once, when she had studied it for a long time, she rose and went out of the room.

Early the next morning the girls heard from their own room that their foster parents were up and busy in the dining-room, where they had sat last night. They pulled out drawers, turned over papers, and the while talked low and violently between them, and as Lucan and Zosine listened, they heard them poke up the charred wood in the fireplace. They also called Baptistine in, and seemed to ask of her a series of hasty questions. When the two girls came into the dining-room, they both noticed that the old people stared at them stiffly and piercingly. They understood that something, they did not know what, was occupying their minds.

In the course of the morning, Mr. Pennhallow and his wife went into their room and remained there for a long time. A little later, the old man wrote a letter, and sent Clon off with it, but called him back before he had gone out of the garden gate. About dusk he went out of the house himself, and was away for a long time. In his absence his wife was silent and restless. And in the evening, after their pupils had gone to bed, they stayed up late, moving and whispering in the dining-room.

About noon the following day, Mr. Pennhallow called in the girls and informed them that he and his wife would have to leave Sainte-Barbe for two or three days. They had received a sad message, which made it necessary for them to go to Marseilles at once. An old fellow-student of Mr. Pennhallow's, who for many years had been a missionary in China, was on his way home to England in a state of mortal illness, and fervently wished to see his friends for a last time. They would leave Sainte-Barbe on the same evening, to take the late diligence at Lunel, and had ordered a peasant of the neighborhood to drive them to the town. Mrs. Pennhallow went to her room to pack their things. She was pale, and her hands trembled; the sorry news, Mr. Pennhallow said, had moved her deeply. He himself kept on sitting with the girls for a while, and talked to them, mildly dwelling on the idea of death, which will so often be near when you are least thinking of it.

Shortly after, the old woman returned to the dining-room, and gave her daughters new instructions. In her grief, she said, she had forgotten that she had today intended to walk out to a village named Vaour which lay about five miles from Sainte-Barbe in the opposite direction to Lunel. Here lived an old Englishwoman who had once been a governess at Joliet itself, and who was now ill. Mrs. Pennhallow had meant to bring her some good soup and a bottle of mixture. Now that she had been called away from Sainte-Barbe so unexpectedly, the girls would have to take over this duty. Baptistine would go with them to carry the basket, but they themselves would act as true Christians in visiting their sick countrywoman. The young girls had no idea of what their foster parents' sudden journey meant; they had never heard of any English lady in Vaour, or seen Mrs. Pennhallow pay a visit of charity in the neighborhood. They were seized with surprise and alarm, but dared not look at each other. They would rather have been without Baptistine's company, but Mrs. Pennhallow insisted that without her they would not be able to find the road to the village. They would have to start on their walk to Vaour at once.

As the girls would not be back at Sainte-Barbe before dark, and Mr. Pennhallow and his wife would by that time already have left the house in their peasant's carriage on their way to Marseilles, the old and the young people must take leave now. The old couple were a remarkably long time saying good-bye, although they were to be away for a few days only. It was as if they took a quite particular pleasure in the parting scene. Mrs. Pennhallow sat down with folded hands, and listened with a singular expression of content or suspense, while her husband minutely instructed his pupils as to their behavior in his absence. Were they, the old man asked, afraid to be alone in the house? If so, of what were they afraid? Would they, he added with a smile, miss him and long for his return? He added a number of detailed directions, and seemed to hesitate to devise still more. He and Mrs. Pennhallow went to the gate to see their pupils off. When the two girls and Baptistine were already outside the wall, the old woman called Lucan back and gave her a long, deep and scrutinizing glance, the same glance which, in the morning mist outside the inn, she had once given the pretty girl. As the girls walked down the road, the two old people kept looking after them from the gate in the wall.

Out in the fields the air and the landscape itself were already marked by the coming autumn. The colors were faded, the road covered with dry leaves from the trees. It was cold, and the gray clouds seemed to hang low above the earth. The two girls walked on in silence, puzzled in their minds. They asked themselves if there was really a place named Vaour and an old sick English lady there. They wished that they could have talked together in English, but Baptistine walked beside them, so solid and watchful in her heavy shoes that they had not the spirit to do so. Little by little the road and the view took hold of their thoughts; they had never till now been so far out on this side of Sainte-Barbe.

Vaour, when at last they got there, turned out to be a small, gray village at the end of a road with stone walls on both sides. Here, in a small, neat room above a baker's shop, they really found a very old English miss, like a relic of a distant, forgotten past.

Miss Pinkney was not ill, but dry and spare as a mummy, and in her second childhood. She did not recollect Mrs. Pennhallow's name, but shook her head when it was repeated to her, and it was not possible for the girls to explain to her who they were themselves. Later on she called them by names which they did not know, and evidently took them for a couple of ancient pupils in England. She had a few English books in her room, between the flower pots and the bird cage, but she had almost forgotten to speak English; the words only slowly and brokenly came back to her. Lucan looked round in the small room, and reflected that she herself might some day come to sit in this same way, like a small bit of human wreckage, washed into a quiet corner of existence by many winds and currents, and forgotten there.

But as they named Joliet, a delicate blush mounted into the

wrinkled cheeks, and Miss Pinkney began to talk with much life and for a long time. She obviously believed herself that she was recounting a great many things of interest about the castle and the family there, but only a small part of her long speech was intelligible to her audience. Very old events were taken out and held up, as from a drawer. The old governess was scandalized at the thought of General Buonaparte, who had had himself crowned as emperor, and was looking forward to the time when the legitimate Royal House of France should return, and once more set the country in order. She talked of Baron Thésée, so that Lucan threw a quick glance at Zosine. But they soon realized that it was the present lord's grandfather, the old Baron who had been murdered, whom she saw before her. Of him she spoke with passionate affection, as of an infatuation of her youth. But when they named his wife, whom they themselves had seen at Peyriac, she became dumb.

In the course of the afternoon a strange little incident took place. Zosine mentioned her companion as Madame Labarre of Sainte-Barbe. At the sound of this name the old maid grew deadly pale, as if she was going to faint, and when she had come to, she endeavored to show Baptistine out of her room. Zosine, though, succeeded in turning her mind to pleasanter things. There stood a little old spinet by the window. Zosine asked Lucan to play to them. Lucan sat down by the spinet, and in her sweet, clear voice sang a couple of old English songs. Now Miss Pinkney forgot her anger and melted. In the end she herself, in an almost inaudible, but pure little voice, joined in the ballad of "Annie Laurie."

When, on Baptistine's request, the girls rose to say good-bye, the old miss stared at Zosine, and radiantly exclaimed, "Oh, Madame, is it really you! How happy I am to see you!" At last, she saw her young visitors down the stairs, and from the baker's shop bought them a big cake to take home with them. Here once more she called them "Fanny" and "Elizabeth."

It had begun to blow and rain, and the wind and the rain increased as the small party walked home. But it was such a long time since the girls had sung a song; it had stirred forgotten chords in their hearts, and for a time on the road they went on singing the songs of their home country. The while it occurred to Lucan how lonely and hard Baptistine's position in the world must be, she tried to make her talk, and tell them of her youth. But Baptistine gave but short, sour answers. Her feet were sore from her long walk, and she was not in the mood to speak.

It was almost dark when they once more came within sight of Sainte-Barbe. Against the dark sky the old farmhouse drew its darker outlines. Lucan, who had once painted a small picture of the farm from this side, stood still for a moment, and exclaimed, "How different things do look in the evening, from what they do in the daytime! I should say that something was altered here. Yes, it really looks as if the stack of firewood by the gable is now in another place, and nearer to the house than it used to be!"

Here Baptistine hurried them on. She was content to be home again, and for the first time spoke of her own accord, although more to herself than to the girls. "Is there now. I ask you," she grumbled, "any sense in making a fuss, and chasing people out in the rain, for the sake of a bit of paper? I may have burnt it or I may not have burnt it. Nobody would care to make a keepsake of any of those pictures." The girls did not understand what she was talking about, and only later in the night recalled her words.

4. Where is my bonnet?

THE three wayfarers were wet and tired. Baptistine herself probably felt that something was needed to reanimate them, for she brought a bottle of her home-made cordial and made each of the young girls drink a big glass. The wine was strong. It sent a pleasant warmth through their veins, and went a little to their heads. Baptistine wanted them to have a second glass, but they themselves decided to wait until supper.

Lucan did not easily swing over from one mood to another; Zosine's violently changing emotions always surprised her. She did not, tonight, understand the mighty feeling of release and liberation which filled the girl at the idea that she and her friend were alone in the house. Before she had taken off her wet clothes, and while Baptistine was laying the supper table, Zosine went to and fro from the girls' own room to the dining-room and kitchen, gazed round in each room and drew her breath deeply. Her face was shining.

"Alas, Zosine," said Lucan, "we do not know yet how matters really stand with us. We cannot tell what the old people's departure means, or what they will be hiding behind it. It is only a short respite in which you now delight."

"Yes, it is so," said Zosine, "but this short respite was necessary to me. I can draw my breath freely in it. It is as if there were a large, black, deep sea round us on all sides, but in the middle of it we have, all the same, saved ourselves ashore on a small island. The extent of our island is terribly narrow. In the one direction it is only this room, in the other a few hours. But it is an indescribable happiness to have got ashore on it. We can sit beneath the trees; we can run in the grass. I have struggled so hard against the current and the waves! If we had not found this refuge, I think I should have died.

"Tonight, and until tomorrow morning," she continued, stood still for a moment and then again walked on, "I will forget the two old people of Sainte-Barbe. I have thought too much of them altogether. And you cannot imagine how their eyes and their evil breath have come near to poison me. The old man himself has told us, how the python, to swallow its prey, must first pour it over with its slime. Just in that way I have felt that their whole being did stick to me, yes, that I was myself going to become part of them! Tonight I will wipe them out of my mind. I will be myself again, Zosine Tabbernor!"

Lucan sat still and gazed at her friend. Was she not herself, she thought, more thoroughly poisoned than Zosine, who all the time had been in activity, and ready to fight? At times it seemed to her that she understood more of the nature of the wickedness, which surrounded and threatened them, than Zosine, and she could then feel with a kind of horror, as if this understanding did in itself draw her farther away from the other girl and nearer to the old people.

"Who is Zosine Tabbernor?" Zosine exclaimed. "A silly worthless girl, a little spoiled baggage! Yes, but all the same a truthful person. I have thought a lot of my Papa ever since we found the letter of Pedro Smith. Many people, even his own relations, blamed Papa and held him to be a frivolous man and a sybarite. But nobody has ever said about him that he has betrayed a friend nor been cruel to anyone weaker than himself and in his power. I will be Zosine tonight, Papa's spoiled daughter, in order to get strength to master the cruel old man when he comes back."

Lucan rose from the sofa and went to the window. "What terrible weather," she exclaimed. "Hear how the wind blows and how the rain beats against the windowpanes. And we shall have to change our clothes, Zosine."

Zosine looked round the room. "Now we will first put a log on the fire," she said, "and light all the candles. Look, Baptistine has set Miss Pinkney's cake on the table, and left her cherry brandy there too. We will have a cozy evening at Sainte-Barbe tonight! For some hours it is, once more, to be the old Sainte-Barbe from before 1793, a place where good, honest people feel comfortable and at home, where one can sit before the fire and talk of beautiful, happy things."

While she talked she had begun to take off her wet clothes, she also helped Lucan to get rid of her soaked cloak and smoothed her friend's long golden ringlets, which the rain had darkened.

"We will be fine tonight," she cried. "Away with those frocks, in which the old people have seen us every day. We will put on our nice frocks, in which we traveled from England. Then it will be as if we had just this morning arrived at Sainte-Barbe, and as if nothing had ever happened to us here. We will be ourselves once more, as if we had never met the old parson and his wicked old wife!"

The two half-naked girls, in the light of the candle, looked at each other. They were so young that the idea of a pretty frock put their minds into strong motion. They felt at this moment, both and in the same way, that during these months they had wronged their youth and their womanhood. The glance wherewith Mr. Pennhallow and his wife had eyed their beauty in the end had made them afraid of it themselves. Now each of them saw it again, reflected in the eyes of the other.

In all matters with which they had occupied themselves during their stay on Sainte-Barbe, their old teacher had been so much their superior that he had annihilated them beneath his learning and insight. They should not, they now thought, have let themselves be persuaded to lose themselves in history and philosophy, or to forget that they still had big eyes and small feet.

Zosine's pretty hair, which had been cut off, had by now grown out a bit again. She wanted to put it up according to a fashion which she had seen in a reproduction of an old painting in her Papa's house. While she was arranging it she went, half dressed, from the bedroom to the dining-room, where there was a looking-glass between the windows. From the dining-room she cried to

Lucan that she must take out their frocks and their fine shawls. They would even put on their bonnets tonight! One of them was trimmed with white ostrich feathers; the other was made of brown checkered silk with a delicate white frill below the edge, which, in a highly becoming fashion, framed the wearer's face. Lucan was free to choose which of them she would.

"I remember well," said Zosine, while she rolled her curls round her slim fingers, "when I bought each of them. The one with the feathers was terribly expensive. The other one Aunt Arabella chose for me when we were to drive to the races of Newmarket. Lady Flora Hastings had a bonnet just like it. Olympia thought, that she was the Queen herself and was very proud on my behalf. Alas, my dear good Olympia! And now my hair is done, do fetch me my bonnet!"

"I cannot fetch it," said Lucan. "I cannot find it anywhere!"

Zosine, who rarely kept her things in order, hastened to excuse herself. "I have not touched it, or even looked at it, since we came here," she exclaimed. "It must be where you yourself put it, together with our shawls, shoes and gloves." Lucan came out from the bedroom, still very lightly dressed in her chemise and her fustian petticoat, like a picture of an angel, and quite bewildered. "But neither our shawls nor our frocks nor gloves are here," she stated.

"Oh, nonsense," cried Zosine incredulously. "They must surely be there, if you search well."

"Come and see for yourself," said Lucan.

The two girls had only a few drawers in which to keep their clothes, and soon had looked through them all. But however much they looked, opened and shut the drawers and gazed at each other, they found neither their hats nor their frocks. Every single piece, which they had had on, when they traveled from England to Sainte-Barbe, and which had been laid aside so carefully by Lucan, was now gone. Only their little pretty shoes were left, and looked quite forlorn.

They stood perfectly still, struck with the deepest wonder and surprise. They could not possibly explain matters to themselves. The solutions which at first, as in a glimpse, showed themselves to them, seemed so fantastic that they came near to burst out laughing. Had Mrs. Pennhallow been borrowing their bonnets to impress the old missionary in Marseilles?

But after a few minutes they became grave. Here at Sainte-Barbe inexplicable things might be expected to have a terrible explanation. Almost at the same time the same idea came to each of them, and as their eyes met they understood each other, as if they had expressed it in words. Zosine, who had grown very pale, nodded her head.

"They are exactly of the same height," Lucan exclaimed, "and just as tall as we are."

"And that," Zosine added a moment after, "was why they chose to go away by the night coach from Lunel. In that coach it is dark; no passenger can see the face of another. If they have pulled down their veils nobody will have had the least suspicion about them. Nobody will possibly have doubted that it was you and me who were going away by the coach."

"And that," said Lucan after another pause, "was why they sent us away to Vaour with Baptistine."

Zosine stood silent for a long time, so absorbed in her own thoughts, so strained and brooding that she no longer saw Lucan, nor heard what she said. "But our shoes they could not get on," she said at last.

5. a visit in the evening

A HEAVY burden of fear, trouble and despair, which for a long time, day and night, rests on the mind of the human being is not lifted away in a moment. For some minutes Lucan felt stunned and giddy, thrown from side to side, as when she traveled over the water from England to France. But the warm room with the clear flames in the fireplace and the lighted candles, with the white tablecloth and the cake and wine bottle at the table, and Zosine's own happy released mood a short time ago, everything seemed to prevail upon her to take confidence and hope. She looked at Zosine, blushing, with gentle radiant eyes.

"They have fled!" she cried. "They have gone, Zosine!"

"What are you saying?" Zosine asked.

"Oh, yes, they have gone from here forever," Lucan repeated. "They have fled from Sainte-Barbe in our clothes! They had caught fright of us," she continued, and the reflection of a smile went over her face, "and they have at last realized that we knew everything!"

"Do you think so?" Zosine again asked.

"It must be so," said Lucan once more. "If not, why should they hide their departure so carefully, and go off in the middle of the night? We never did believe their tale of the old sick missionary. But we did not guess that the thing they hid behind it—that this was a flight!"

Once more the girls were silent, while fumblingly they tried to find a foothold in these new, overwhelming circumstances.

As to Lucan, it was not only the horror and the dismalness which seemed to have happily departed from her. It was even more than this: that fatal task which Zosine's resolution had laid upon them both and which she herself had feared and doubted. The retribution which Zosine had insisted upon fulfilling, and which she could not give up, was now indeed fulfilled. They were free.

Almost at the same moment Lucan exclaimed, "We are saved!"

And Zosine, "They have got away from us!"

Lucan put her arms round her friend's neck and felt her cool, smooth, naked shoulders against her own cool, smooth, naked arms. "Oh, God, Zosine," she cried. "Let them go away! They are homeless now, terrified. They are hiding their faces. Are they not punished now, then?"

Zosine remained silent, looking round with dark and deep eyes.

"They will never more be able to commit any crimes," Lucan said. "Surely you yourself must see that this flight of theirs is just that new and decisive proof of their guilt for which you have been waiting. Now we can go to the judge in Lunel and tell him everything. He can no longer doubt what we tell him, when he hears, that the old man and his wife have gone away in our clothes. The postilion and the travelers themselves will tell him that they have done so."

"The postilion and the travelers," Zosine said very slowly, "are now certain that it is you and I who have fled!"

Until this moment Lucan, in this gruesome matter into which they had been drawn, had followed Zosine, and had continually been in fear of her friend's hasty and impetuous disposition. Zosine at first had made her believe in the horror and the danger at Sainte-Barbe, and later on, even although she had never quite understood her, she had held her back there. During all the time Lucan had been irresolute and uncertain of herself. Now it seemed to her that she did once more sight the straight trodden road before her, and that she must also be able to show it to Zosine. She talked gently and impressively to her friend, just as she had done on the first day after the catastrophe at Tortuga, or just as, long ago, she had talked to the blind child of Fairhill.

"Surely," she said, "surely the police will search for them in Marseilles. And do you not see that the judge of Lunel will know better how to pursue and overtake them than two girls would ever be able to?"

"Why have they suddenly taken such fear of us?" Zosine asked in the same way as before.

Lucan thought her question over for a moment.

"They think," she said, "that we have found some proof against them. Do you not remember that yesterday morning they were here in the dining-room and that they seemed to be looking for something? And Baptistine," she continued slowly and thoughtfully, "today on the way home from Vaour mentioned a paper which had been lost and which had caused them great anxiety. I believe," she concluded after a while, "that she was thinking of that drawing, to which the old man gave so much time and which he showed to his wife. They both laughed at it. They were absent-minded the night before yesterday; they may have forgotten it and they must have thought that we had found it and kept it. Yes, that is why they have suddenly become so afraid of us! Do you not think so too?"

At Lucan's question Zosine's face took on such an expression of abhorrence that she herself was struck aghast at it. She realized that Zosine was at this moment trying to picture to herself that piece of paper which, had it been viewed by others, would have been sure to betray the criminals. In haste, she tried to drag her friend's thoughts away from it, and on to other courses.

"They told us that they would be absent for two or three days," she said. "That would have given them ample time to get away. They could not possibly know that you should want to put on your bonnet tonight. They have gone now, and we are safe!"

"I had not imagined," Zosine said, as slowly as before, "that things were to happen in this way. I did not imagine that this was what Rosa was expecting from us!"

"Zosine!" Lucan cried. "For God's sake, call back your thoughts. They are running on the track of the old wicked people, as if you could not possibly let them go. Remember that you have now triumphed over them, Zosine. What more evil can they possibly do in the world, when they must forever hide themselves, and can never again tell their names? Now you must forget them. You must put them out of your mind. If not, they will have succeeded in drawing you with them into that horrid darkness and loathsomeness which belongs to them. Nay, I have a right to adjure you like this," Lucan continued in great agitation, "for I should never have failed you, if things had happened in a different way. I would have been as staunch and loyal to you as you yourself would have been to Rosa!"

She had pushed Zosine a little away from her in order to see her face. At these last words she again pressed her closer to herself. In a while she felt that her friend was drawing her breath deeply and freely.

"Yes," she said, throwing back her curls, which had fallen forward over her face, "I will believe that it is as you tell me, you brave, loyal girl. I will do anything you ask me."

While they were standing like this, closely twined together, with happy, clear faces, the bell of the door in the garden wall rang. It was a faint and broken tinkle, and through the rain and the wind the sound was only just audible. Still, neither of them could doubt that they had heard it. They stiffened in each other's arms, while they waited to hear the ring repeated. Who was pulling the bell-rope here, so late at night?

The ringing was not repeated, but a little later they heard Baptistine talk to somebody. They had thought that Baptistine had gone to bed a long time ago. A short time after, the peasant woman herself came into the room to tell them that a gentleman at the door begged to talk with the English mesdemoiselles.

"A gentleman!" the girls exclaimed, many conjectures running through their heads.

"But we cannot receive anybody, Baptistine!" they cried. "Mr. Pennhallow has told us not to let anyone in." Baptistine did not move.

"Tell him," Lucan said, "that Mr. Pennhallow is away from home."

"He tells me that he knows that already," said Baptistine.

"Do you know him, then?" Lucan asked.

"Yes," Baptistine answered. "It is M. Emmanuel Tinchebrai."

Now the girls became aware of their defective dress. In haste, without quite letting go of each other, they retired from the dining-room into their own bedroom. "He must wait," they said, "till we have dressed."

They had to redon the frocks which they had just laid away on the bed and the chair. They did not notice that these were still wet with the rain. They both asked themselves, "What on earth does M. Tinchebrai want at Sainte-Barbe, while the master is away?"

They did not see Baptistine again.

6. an unexpected ally

MONSIEUR EMMANUEL TINCHEBRAI stood before the fireplace, still with his wet cloak on his arm, and his hat in his hand, as if waiting for permission to put them away.

The girls looked at him in the highest amazement. Before the horror broke out at Sainte-Barbe, they had jested about the elegant young man and about his languishing admiration for Lucan. Since then, they had met him in this same room, as the representative of the law, a silent, correct young inspector in the old judge's wake. And now he stood before them in the middle of the night, in the storm, and with something highly unusual and important on his mind. Lucan, who remembered the attention he had paid her, kept back during the conversation. It was Zosine who did the talking.

The importance of the young man's errand was obvious not only from the circumstances of his visit, but still more from his own countenance. He had no more the pink-and-white complexion, but was so deadly pale that his fine chestnut hair and whiskers looked quite dark against his white face. He bowed deeply to the two girls as they entered the room, but he hardly looked at them, and it seemed difficult to him to break the silence. Later in the course of the conversation, he wiped his forehead, and dried his hands on his silk handkerchief, and he stuttered as he spoke.

Zosine thought, "This nice, complacent young gentleman has been driven to Sainte-Barbe against his own will by something stronger than he. Is it love? Does he come here, when the master of the house is away, to declare himself to Lucan?" She remembered how Baptistine had told them that Monsieur Emmanuel had formerly been a frequent visitor to Sainte-Barbe, but had suddenly ceased to come there. It was very unlikely that recent events should have improved the relations between him and Mr. Pennhallow. Perhaps it would be necessary for him to appear at Sainte-Barbe in secret. "But if that be so," she thought again, "he is, in spite of his audacity in arriving here at night, an uncommonly bashful lover. He stands at attention there very neatly, but it can be seen on the outside of him that he is writhing inwardly."

"It must surprise you," Monsieur Emmanuel said at last, in a harsh, strangled voice, "to see me here at this hour, and in the absence of your foster parents. But it has become necessary, inevitable, for me to see you. I have not even come by my own free will. I have been forced to it by—" He interrupted himself and was silent for a moment, "by the constant thought of you."

Zosine looked at him. "Put down your wet things, Monsieur Tinchebrai," she said, "and come nearer to the fire." The three young people sat down face to face. The supper table stood untouched with the candles and the wine on it. It almost looked as if a late guest had been expected at Sainte-Barbe.

"But how did you know," Zosine asked in a sudden vague impulse, "that our foster parents have gone away?"

Monsieur Emmanuel's eyes met hers for a second, glassy and expressionless. "How did I know?" he repeated and made a short pause. "I happened to be informed. Never mind how, now.

"I have been forced to come," he repeated, "by one permanent, obsessing idea. It has pursued me since I was last in this house. It has not permitted me to sleep. You may wonder that a subordinate dares to act without the knowledge of his superiors, yes, so to say, against their decision. I hold Monsieur Belabres in the highest esteem. But nobody, nay, nobody," he continued in a trembling voice, "can stand against the power which has brought me here. Even were I to incur the displeasure of my superiors, even were I to lose my office through this move, I can no longer keep back. My position is terrible!" Here for the first time he looked straight at Zosine, and the young girl seemed to read despair in his eyes. He had not looked at Lucan once since he entered the room; he continued to avoid doing so all through the conversation.

"No," Zosine thought, surprised, "it is not love alone; it is also the thought of his career which puts him in this terrible agitation of mind. Monsieur Emmanuel is an ambitious young man. At this moment a violent struggle between his ambitions and his feelings goes on within him." But this was the last time during their nightly conversation that the girl did thus occupy herself with her guest's state of mind. When, after a short pause, he spoke again, her thoughts made a tremendous leap.

"The inquest," said the young man, "which satisfied Monsieur Belabres, did not set my own mind at rest. I went away from here alarmed and troubled. I do not know myself what first awoke my doubt that all was good and well in this matter, but the doubt would not leave me. These last weeks have been unbearable to me. And when now I come to you here, I know well enough to what I expose myself. You will perhaps believe that I am off my head, you will perhaps laugh at me, or you will show me the door. I have come," he hesitated a moment, "for the sake of truth. There are other dangers than the one that threatens me. It is possible that you find yourself in a far more terrible danger, and that it may be in my power to avert it." He looked down and in his excessive turbulence of mind seemed to grow quite small in his chair.

"I now beseech you," he continued, "to answer me one question only. If it appears to you insane, I will go away at once." He made a long pause, and the two girls regarded him in breathless suspense.

"Has not," he suddenly asked in a low and hoarse voice, "since the afternoon when I was here, anything happened that has changed the conviction which you expressed in your evidence? Are you at this hour as certain of these old people's innocence as you were then? I implore you to answer me. Whatever you may think about me, be convinced that the answer to this question tonight means everything in the world to me."

Here Monsieur Emmanuel became silent, as if he had now, in

a way, expressed what he meant to say. But the girls, too, were silent for such a long time that he at last looked up, as if he was doubtful whether they would ever answer him.

It was, in reality, for a few minutes impossible for them to answer. They had lived in isolation and horror, and could not immediately conceive that there might be anything but falsehood and cruelty to be expected from the world that surrounded them. They hardly knew what to do with the help that was offered them.

Lucan trembled from head to foot. It seemed to her that she must throw herself on her knees before this young man, in gratitude and relief. And, almost at the same moment, a strange thing happened to her. As Monsieur Emmanuel sat there, so close to her, with the shine of the fire on his black clothes, he somehow resembled Mr. Armworthy, as he had been sitting by the fireplace at Fairhill. A man made her an offer, but it was not what it sounded. The sudden recollection petrified her; at the moment she was incapable of expressing her thankfulness.

Zosine sat up straight, her eyes shining. For a long time, which to her seemed an eternity, she had collected all her being upon one single purpose. The flight of her enemies tonight had almost struck her with awe, as if she now no longer knew what to do in the world. Lucan herself did not understand her. Her gentle, imploring entreaties a little while ago had reminded Zosine of old, happier days, had alarmed her and made her afraid of her own hardness of heart. And yet, she had not been able altogether to believe her friend. But now, here, in the dining-room of Sainte-Barbe, a human being, a stranger, spoke to her as a friend and an ally, and offered her his help.

It seized and touched her, deeply and strangely, that this ally should be Lucan's rejected lover, whom she herself had so many times mocked. He might be vain, insignificant and weak. But he had guessed her distress, and had come a long way in the night, through the storm, himself—for some reason that she did not know—deadly scared of the task before him. He offered her his service, as a brother. He begged her to receive it.

She rose from her chair and almost staggered as she stood up.

Her own voice trembled, but it was clear and sonorous. "Yes," she cried out, "yes, you are right! It is all just as you think."

She slowly got command of her voice. Her confession broke from her heart in a flow of passion.

"Yes, it is true every word!" she cried. "The two old people here at Sainte-Barbe are murderers. They are worse than murderers, worse than anybody can imagine. They have already killed a girl. An awful man, their friend, strangled her with a rope. And she was eighteen years old, like Lucan and me! Thank God," she cried again, "that I can speak freely once more. Thank God that you have come here tonight, and that you will help me. Thank God that we may now revenge Rosa, and that the evil people may die for what they have done!"

Monsieur Emmanuel drew his breath very deeply.

7. aunt arabella's letter once more

"YES, Mademoiselle," said Monsieur Emmanuel, in a voice, almost choked by horror and dismay, "you can speak freely now; you can tell me all. I am your friend. You must recount to me how, and when, you first came to suspect the old man and his wife."

"How? When?" said Zosine, and tried to search her memory. "Oh, it is a long time ago, an eternity! No one can know or understand what we have been suffering here, alone in the whole world, among people who wanted to murder us too!"

"Aye, I know, I understand," the young man answered in the same hoarse, stifled voice. "But you must take heart, Mademoiselle. It is all over tonight. And you must tell me more. What you have been feeling and thinking here is not enough. It is not enough to condemn any human being to death." He broke off, and dried his face with his silk handkerchief. "Have you not," he asked in an almost inaudible voice, "have you not a letter, some writing that you can produce, to support you in your terrible, forlorn situation?"

Zosine regarded him intensely. He was still crouching in the chair, even paler than before, and apparently even more shaken and terrified than the girls themselves. And yet his eyes, when they met hers, were changed. They were no longer the eyes of the sentimental youth, but those of the policeman. They were the eyes of the hound which had found the scent, and which now will not let go until the quarry has been run down and finished. There was no mercy in those big eyes. From them, Zosine thought, the criminals must expect no grace.

The zeal of the young man for her own cause seized her deeply and violently. She did not herself realize that she was weeping until she tried to answer him and found that she was unable to speak. Then she gave free vent to her tears. She cried without restraint, and her wild passionate sobbing shook her like a storm.

Lucan was amazed and terrified to see Zosine weep. She herself had often cried here at Sainte-Barbe, but only once before tonight, in England, had she seen her friend in tears. She understood that Zosine's sobbing did not need, and probably would not accept, any consolation. She was, moreover, herself in a state of agitation for which she could find no real explanation; if she had wanted to, she could not have formulated any soothing phrase. All that she could do was to stand up and remain standing by Zosine's side.

Monsieur Emmanuel sat perfectly immovable. After a while, quietly as before, and almost mechanically, he repeated his question. "I asked you," he whispered, "whether you had any paper to which to appeal?"

Zosine at last conquered her emotion. With her handkerchief pressed to her trembling lips, she twice solemnly and affirmingly nodded her head to the young man. A silence followed which lasted so long that Lucan turned toward her friend. The young girl stood as straight as if she had been turned into stone. She looked straight at Monsieur Emmanuel, and asked, "What sound is that?"

Through the rain and the wind they did indeed, from outside the house, hear a low, recurrent sound, a regular, dull stroke.

"Someone is digging in the garden," Zosine said.

Monsieur Emmanuel rose from his chair. He took a few faltering steps toward the window, stopped and turned, took another step, and stood still. "No," he said, "nobody is digging. It is someone cutting firewood. I know," he added, in a higher and clearer voice than at any other moment of their conversation, "that Mr. Pennhallow has before now complained of people of the neighborhood stealing firewood in the garden of Sainte-Barbe. They will have known that he was away tonight; they will have taken it for granted that everybody has gone to rest. And the wind and rain are loud here. It is a good night for stealing firewood." His voice changed into a peculiar low hiss. "I might go out to investigate if you wanted it. But it is of no importance, compared to what we are here talking about. And who can tell how much time we have left? Let them steal the firewood tonight, Mademoiselle, and let us finish our business." He turned and faced Zosine. "I understand," he said, "that you have really got a letter, a document to show against the people whom we accuse. It is, indeed, a piece of good fortune! It will decide everything for all of us!"

Zosine stood as still as before, staring with wide-opened eyes at the young man. She had lowered the hand which held the handkerchief, but seemed to breathe with difficulty. She gasped or moaned a few times with half-opened lips before she spoke. Then she said slowly, "Yes. A letter. A document. I have got it in there, in our own room. Now I shall go and fetch it. Then you can see for yourself." It was as if she was recoiling before him. She did not take her eyes off his face, as, backwards, she walked the short distance to the door, and left the room.

Lucan followed the sound of Zosine's steps. She was going farther than their room, out in the corridor and the kitchen. "Where is she going?" Lucan thought. "What is she looking for? We have no letter!"

She was alone in the dining-room with the young man. She put her hand on the chair where Zosine had been sitting, to steady herself. In the deep silence she again heard the low, short, measured blows from the garden. Once only she lifted her eyes and looked at her guest, and his own glance met hers.

She heard Zosine come back, and giddily turned toward her. Zosine brought no letter with her, but in her right hand she held the heavy kitchen axe with which Baptistine was wont to cut sticks for the fire. Without a word Lucan took a step toward her. Monsieur Emmanuel at the same moment, and likewise without a word, took a step back.

"I cannot find the letter I was looking for," said Zosine. Her own glance automatically followed the direction of that of the young man and of Lucan, toward the axe in her hand, and she seemed surprised at their consternation. "It is the kitchen axe," she said, as if explaining or apologizing. "I wanted to find out if the thieves in the garden had taken that as well. But they had not taken it." She stood for a while, brooding.

"I cannot find the letter I was looking for," she repeated. "But I know it by heart. Let us sit down, as we were sitting before. Then I shall repeat it to you from beginning to end."

She sat down before the fire, erect, and still with the axe in her hand. Her eyes shone with a strange and strong brilliance, like steel. The two others also sat down in their former places.

"Listen to me now," Zosine said, "so that you will remember it. Lucan knows the letter; she too has seen it. You ask me if we have had no letter to maintain us in our forlorn situation. Yes, we have had that, even if I cannot find it now.

"I have an old aunt in England," she said, "Miss Arabella Dibdin. She is my godmother. Aunt Arabella loves me. She will do everything in the world for me. But some time before I was looking for this situation in London, we two had quarreled for the first time in our life. She had scolded me because I was spoiled and frivolous. She would have been pleased to receive me into her house, yes, it would probably, as Lucan did then tell me, have been the happiest thing which could have befallen her, had she been able to open it to me. But I was unreasonable and headstrong. I would not listen to her. I told her that I would earn my own bread and be independent of everybody in the world. Then Aunt Arabella wrote to me, before I went away from England, and I have still got her letter. It is somewhere among my things. I have only hidden it too well."

Zosine had not looked at the others while she spoke, and she did not do so now either, when she had finished. But Lucan and Monsieur Emmanuel both stared at her face.

"Aunt Arabella wrote," she said in a high, clear and steady voice, " 'It is good and useful to get to know life. You will now have to carry heavy burdens. It is inevitable to most human beings. But preserve that dignity which consists in obeying one's destiny.' But she also wrote, 'Every one of my possessions will every day recall your picture to me.' And Aunt Arabella means what she says, Monsieur Tinchebrai, she always keeps her word!

"Then she wrote further," Zosine went on slowly. " 'For your father's sake, I will always stick to you more than to any other human being in the world, and never fail you. Even if now you are going away in spite, you cannot tear asunder the tie between us. I shall follow you, with my eyes and my heart, and always keep informed of all your doings. That you are going to a strange country will make no difference to me. People like me have got connections everywhere.'

"I was proud at the time, Monsieur Tinchebrai. I did not answer her. But I know that she will have done as she said, even if I cannot tell you exactly by what means she has managed to do so. I have had proofs of it. I am still proud. I have never done anything which I could not tell Aunt Arabella. If she could see me at this moment, she would understand me, and not be ashamed of me! She wrote, 'I did not know till now that there were such possibilities for suffering in life.' I did not know it either at that time. I did not know how much Aunt Arabella had gone through with spoiled and frivolous people. When we meet again, I shall tell her!"

In the long silence that followed upon Zosine's words, Lucan remembered, as clearly as if she had seen it before her, her friend's little morning-room at Tortuga, where she had found her standing by the window with Aunt Arabella's letter in her hand. She also recalled their talk then. At first Zosine had declared that she would never, not even to save her life, mention this letter. A little later she had laughed at Lucan's grave and frightened face, had fallen on her neck, and said to her, "In return for all your goodness toward me, I promise you that, in order to save my life, I shall mention Aunt Arabella and her letter. But only then!"

Monsieur Emmanuel sat without a word. A couple of times he tried to speak, and again gave it up. After a long time he spoke at last, "But then, Mademoiselle," he said, "in spite of all, you have had friends who were aware of your place of residence and who were keeping their eyes on you?"

"Yes, that is so," said Zosine.

8. the rope and the axe

MONSIEUR EMMANUEL had sat for a while looking stiffly at Zosine. Then he rose and automatically reached for his hat. He stopped in the middle of the gesture, stared toward the window, and kept perfectly still. But he must compel himself to keep still; the ground burned beneath his feet.

"You have friends," he repeated slowly, "you are being watched over. You will be helped! Then I am not needed here tonight."

"Oh, yes, you are needed here all the same tonight, Monsieur Tinchebrai," said Zosine. "You too have got friends and influence. You came here for the sake of truth and justice. Now you will act in the service of these ideals. Now you will speak to the judge of Lunel."

"Yes," said Monsieur Emmanuel, slowly as before. "Yes, I must speak to somebody. This singular, happy turn of things . . . For the moment I cannot quite see to what it may lead . . ." He broke off, and once more, in the same strange suspense, almost as if hypnotized, gazed toward the window. The wind and the rain were still loud outside, but the low, dull sound, which, like the beating of a drum, accompanied their rush before, had ceased.

"Now they stopped out there," said Zosine.

Lucan, who was half unconscious with uncertainty and fear, could no longer keep herself back. She lifted a candlestick from the table and went to the window to draw the curtain back and look out. At the same moment the young man seized her arm and stopped her. "No!" he cried. "No! Do not take that candle to the window! Stay here!" His touch was so repulsive to her that she almost let the candlestick drop, and she felt, with a curious emotion, that he too shuddered to touch her. He let go her arm as if it had burned him. Immediately after he staggered, so that for a second she thought that he was going to fall.

"I am not well," he said. Although it went so much against the girl to come nearer to him, she put down the candlestick to hand him a glass of water from the table, but he shrank away from her and leaned against the wall.

"In the name of God," he suddenly cried out in a trembling, harsh voice, "why have you not gone back to England? Why are you still at Sainte-Barbe?" Lucan stood dumb, terrified by his sudden passion.

But Zosine answered him, "We may be going away, Monsieur Emmanuel. We may not remain long at Sainte-Barbe."

"Yes, go away!" cried Monsieur Emmanuel, and in the light of the candle, which had changed place, Lucan saw the sweat run down his face. "Perhaps I can still help you to get away from here.

"Would it not," he asked hoarsely, after a short silence, "be better for you never to mention what we have talked about to-night? You have friends, you can live long and happily in England! Will you not give up taking any part in this matter, when once you are in safety there?"

"In safety?" Zosine repeated slowly.

"Yes," he went on, quickly and stuttering, "listen to me. It must always go against your feelings to be mixed up in a matter like this. As it goes against me to accuse my superiors of neglect. If, there, tonight, the three of us agree never to speak of it, then it might be possible—then there might still be a hope—" He almost bent double, as in piercing physical pain. Suddenly he turned straight to Zosine.

"If I advise you to do so," he whispered, "will you give me your word never to talk of the things which you have told me tonight?"

Zosine did not answer.

After another long silence he said, still almost in a whisper,

"I must go." All the same he did not go at once. He looked round the room. Once he looked at Lucan too, and she never forgot the despair and madness in his eyes. But soon after he took his hat and his cloak. "I am not well," he repeated. "I must have time to think these matters over. Good-bye. I thank you because you have received me here, and for your confidence. I bid you good-bye."

"I will light you out, Monsieur Tinchebrai," said Zosine. The young man made a gesture to prevent it, but she had already taken the candlestick in her left hand, and went with it to the entrance-door, which turned to the side of the garden opposite to the one from which they had heard the spade strokes. The rain beat violently in against her as she opened the door, but in spite of it she did not leave the doorway until she had seen her guest, almost running, the wind whirling his cloak round him, hasten down the path to the gate in the wall, and disappear through it without giving himself time to close it after him. Then she shut the door.

She put the candlestick down on the chest in the corridor and sank back against the wall. She looked Lucan, who had followed her, straight in the face.

"Now it has come as you foretold," she said. "You have been right all the time. Now we have got that new proof of the old people's wickedness which I longed for. And that proof will be the murder of you and me."

Lucan would speak, but her voice failed her. "Yes, you were right," said Zosine, "you told me to remember that the people with whom I was dealing were infinitely more clever and experienced than I! You told me to remember that they had blood on their hands. Now there will soon be no more need for me to remember it."

"Oh, Zosine!" cried Lucan. "Oh, Zosine!"

"Did you notice where it was they were digging?" Zosine asked in a quaint dead and distracted voice. "It was in the place where the big stack of firewood used to stand. You were right, too, when you said last evening that it had changed place. They had moved it away to dig our grave where it stood. Tomorrow they will move it back again. And it is I who have made you stay on at Sainte-Barbe!" She stood up straight against the wall, almost as if she had been nailed to it.

"I thought," she whispered as before, "that when I held onto Rosa, I might lift her out of the darkness. But it is you and I who will be following her down there. Now we are lost, Lucan."

"Oh, do not speak like that, Zosine," said Lucan. "We are still alive."

"Nay, you are wrong," said Zosine slowly, in deadly, cutting and merciless irony. "We are no longer alive. We have already gone; we do not exist any longer. It was not in order to get away that the two old people put on our clothes. It was in order to take us away from here. Lucan and Zosine are no longer at Sainte-Barbe; they have gone with the evening diligence from Lunel, the postilion and the other travelers will testify to it. And who will give them the lie? An old Englishwoman, whom nobody knows, who is in her second childhood, and who will not remember our names or our faces? No, we are already a long way from here, out in the dark, in the wind and the rain. I cannot tell in what place the old people have again put on their own clothes and have left you and me. Perhaps it will be in Marseilles, in a big town, where the track of Lucan and Zosine will soon be lost. But in any case we are no longer in this house or in this room. The girls who, at this moment, are talking together here are ghosts, phantoms whose bodies have long left the world of the living. Here at Sainte-Barbe there is only one place which is waiting for us, which will receive and recognize us. It is the grave which they have dug beneath the woodstack.

"Oh, I wish to God," she cried out wildly, "that it was already tomorrow! Then it will be all over. Then we will be lying still; then there will be nobody touching us. They are going to touch me before then; they are going to look at me. That is worse than death itself. Come," she said after a while, "let us move the chest here up in front of the door. After all we will not let them walk straight into the house."

Lucan would not oppose her, and together the girls dragged the heavy chest across the floor to the door. Zosine went into the kitchen to make sure that the door was locked, and here too they barricaded the entrance with a heavy piece of furniture. They became breathless with the work; there was a kind of relief in it. Zosine had laid the axe away, but as soon as they had finished, she again took hold of it. She asked Lucan to hold up the candlestick and let the light fall about everywhere, so that they could see that the shutters were all properly closed. They then discovered that across the kitchen chair, loosely coiled up, there hung a new, strong rope.

They stared at it. Lucan took a step back. A low moan broke from her lips. At last Zosine walked up to the chair. With a shiver, as if it had been a long, dead snake, she lifted up the rope and let it run through her hands. It seemed as if she could not again let go of it. "Oh, come back, Zosine," Lucan said. Zosine followed her slowly, but she took the rope with her. It trailed after her along the kitchen floor.

A long time after, when they again stood in front of the fire in the dining-room, they recovered their speech. "Do you believe," Lucan whispered, "that he knew everything before he came here tonight?" She could not bring herself to pronounce Monsieur Emmanuel's name.

"Yes, he knew everything," said Zosine. "They had sent him here to find out how much we knew. For there will always be a risk in murdering, however carefully one plans the murder. If they could have avoided murdering us, they would have preferred to let us live on. The candle in the window was the sign for them to come in."

"Still, I do not understand," said Lucan, haunted by the thought of the man, who had come to see them, "how he has ever become their friend. How could he agree to have anything to do with such evil people?"

"Oh, how could he resist them, when they wanted to make use of him some time, long ago?" said Zosine. "He may have wanted to become rich, to gain power over the people at Lunel, who disdained him, and to be able to show them his own disdain of them. But when once he had become acquainted with him, the old man has got him in his power. It was not the retribution of law and justice which tonight put him in such deadly fear. It was the master—it was the old man!" At her own word "fear," and at the thought of the fear with which their enemy had inspired his accomplice, she began to tremble; her whole figure contracted in horror and repulsion.

"But still, he has got away," said Lucan after a time. "Still, what you told him has confused him and made him less sure of his position. They now believe that we have got friends in England who are keeping their eyes on us. Perhaps they will not dare to harm us now."

"Oh, yes, they will dare to," said Zosine. "We have succeeded in confusing them for a moment. But they are clever. They will soon look through the poor little trick we have tried to play them. Aunt Arabella's letter will not save us. There is nothing in the whole world which will save us now."

"Why did you take the axe?" Lucan whispered, trembling all over. "Did you mean to defend our lives with it?"

Zosine once more looked in surprise, first at her friend and then at the axe in her own hand. "To defend us?" she exclaimed. "No, I did not think of that. It would not have helped us much! Who knows how many they are? They will have Clon with them; they will perhaps have Baptistine with them, who wanted us to drink her wine. There may be others as well outside."

"No, I did not think of that," she said after a silence. "I took it to hold steel in my hand. Steel, Lucan, is honest; it is straight and noble. You may well need to feel steel in your hand when you are talking to a man like him whom we had with us tonight. 'Durior ferro,' " she continued very slowly. "I would that it could be laid down in the grave with me. It was good to hold it. But it can help us no longer. There is nothing that can help us any more. We are lost now, Lucan."

9. olympia once more

DEADLY exhausted as the two girls were, they still stood before the dying fire for a long time, as if they had forgotten that they could sit down. They no longer talked together; they listened. Only once Lucan broke the silence, and in a sudden faint emotion exclaimed, "We might, even now, try to get away. If we could only get as far as Father Vadier's house."

Zosine answered her in a low exclamation like her own, "But they are here, inside the wall, in the garden. I will not meet them in the dark."

At last long shooting pangs and tremblings in her knees compelled Lucan to sink down into the chair where Monsieur Emmanuel had sat. Zosine then sat down too, but not next to her. With a vague alarm and pain Lucan felt that Zosine shrank away from her, in the same manner as the young man had done. She did not know that her own pure, simple nature would cause those, who were filled with the ideas of death, horror and madness, to hold back from her in a kind of awe. Zosine looked away, and once more looked back at her friend. Her dark eyes seemed very big in her pale face.

At last she asked, "What will it be like to die, do you think? What will it be like to be dead?"

Lucan at first was dismayed by her question; then her eyes filled with tears. She collected all her strength to comfort her friend. "I am quite sure that we will be happy and at peace," she said, and after a moment added, "Maybe one escapes much grief and disappointment in life, if one dies so young as we are now." She would have said more, but her voice failed her. If Zosine or she had been lying on a deathbed, she might have found gentle consoling words, but in face of the brutal, cruel death awaiting them she was mute.

"This is the third night that you and I keep watch together at Sainte-Barbe," said Zosine. "On the first night I came over into your bed to tell you that the judge's accusation was true. Do you remember? On the second night we meant to fly from here. Do you remember?"

Lucan nodded, she sat immovable, and only pressed or squeezed her fingers lightly in the folds of her frock.

"Now we have only got a short time left," said Zosine, "only long enough for me to beg you to forgive me all the harm I have done you. Can you do it, Lucan? You came to Tortuga and said to me, 'My father has died. I no longer have a home in the world, and if you will not receive me, I do not know where to turn.' It was on our birthday. And now I have brought you here, into this room!"

"Do not speak like that," said Lucan. "You are with me here. I was alone, I had no friend, when I came to Tortuga. But you have been a friend to me since that day."

"Tell me, all the same, that you have forgiven me," said Zosine.

"Yes, if you wish me to do so," said Lucan.

"Oh, if you had only gone with the diligence from Neuvéglise," said Zosine, after a while. "I myself could not leave Sainte-Barbe. But you might have been happy in England."

"I?" said Lucan.

"Yes," said Zosine, "there is something in England that you are thinking about and longing for. I have known it all the time. But for a long time I have not been able to think of any other girl than Rosa. Therefore I have not asked you. You might tell it to me now, while we are sitting here. There is no reason why we should have secrets from each other any longer. I am so selfish and restless, Lucan. It would do me good to hear of the things which you have had in your mind. For I know that it will be something good and beautiful."

Lucan did not speak at once. Her love of Noël, and the pain

which belonged to it, lay hidden in the depth of her nature. At no other time could she have lifted it up into the light. But in the face of death she might share her secret with Zosine. Very softly, as when, at Fairhill, she had told the blind child a fairy tale, she began to recount all that had happened between her and the man she loved. She remembered each word Noël had spoken in the moonlit garden, and as she repeated them, it seemed to her that her voice sounded like his own. She trembled; the moment held both agony and ecstasy. The distress and bitterness of life, and death itself, vanished in the presence of love; a faint ray of light began to shine through the darkness round her.

Zosine listened without a word or a movement, her hands folded in her lap. Her face, which had recently stiffened in pain and disgust, grew peaceful and tender. Even after Lucan had finished her tale, she for some time remained immovable.

"But, Lucan," she said at last, "how could you have been so simple and blind? Noël loves you! He has never thought of me. He has seen a hundred girls like me, and knows to a nicety how little we are worth. But a girl like you he has never met before. What does a man know about the color of our shawls, do you think, and what does he care if the white shawl is yours or mine? If the moon was up, as you say, it would have shone down on your hair, just as I have often myself seen it on moonlight evenings here at Sainte-Barbe. And your hair he could never mistake! It is true that on the way to Lunel, he talked to me—for he is used to talking to girls like me—but it was at you that he looked. And once, when he and I were alone there, he asked me about you, and I knew very well what it meant. You may take my word for it. I know something of young men in love. He loves you, and will never forget you."

Lucan had got into a violent agitation of mind, as she had now for the first time given words to her feelings. It seemed to her that she was in this hour balancing the accounts of her whole life. And now, on Zosine's words, they turned out different to what she had known or imagined. She had believed that the sum of them would be death. Was she to find that it was life itself, a truer and richer life than what people in general understand by the word? In the midst of her terror and exhaustion she reflected that it would be easy for her to die, if she could but believe for an hour that Noël loved her. She rose from her chair. As if somebody had called her, she felt that she must go somewhere, away from here.

Zosine had risen with her. "Listen," she whispered.

Heavy, measured footsteps came up the path from the garden gate to the house so slowly that both the young girls, before the steps reached the door, had time to think: "The visitor who comes has been inside the wall. For we have not heard the gate opening." The moment after a mighty fist struck the door of the house. Now the time had come. They were to wait no longer!

Zosine seized the edge of the table in front of her, and again let it go. "No," she said, "I cannot stand here, waiting for them. I will go out and meet them."

Lucan followed her a step or two, and then stood still. She could hardly feel the ground under her feet. Her eyes sank, and she whispered a prayer which she had been taught as a child and had never since remembered.

A deep, booming voice, which the girl thought she had heard long ago, in a dream, impatiently and angrily cried out a few words on the other side of the door. She heard Zosine answer in a hasty and wild cry, and then once more the voice from outside. Then the voices mingled. Zosine spoke, and in the next moment the room resounded with the long, terrible, trembling shriek which she gave.

"Lucan, come here," she wailed. "Help me! Come and help me to move the chest!" Lucan leaned to the wall. She would have come to her friend's aid but even now, when it seemed to her that she was already dead, she was petrified by the thought of violence and of brutal, savage handling. She heard Zosine shove or drag the heavy chest over the floor, and herself stumble over it; she heard the entrance door flung open, and the noise of the wind and the rain increase for a moment. The light of a lantern, in the hand of the visitor, reached her through the doorway. In an intense effort she made a few steps forward.

Through the open door, in the half-light of the corridor, she saw a colossal, shapeless, almost inhuman form half crawl, half toss itself forward across the chest with which the entrance-door was barred, and Zosine throw herself upon it. In the next moment the two figures were merged into one, and Zosine cried, "Olympia! My Olympia! It is you, Olympia!"

"Yes, indeed it is your Olympia," the old Negress answered in her mighty, sonorous voice, half smothered in Zosine's embrace. "Sure, it is me, my lamb, my evening star. Let me go! You throttle me, you tear off my head. Is there any sense in that?" The sound of many ardent smacks interrupted her speech. "Let me stand on my legs. What is the matter here? Do people always bar the doors like this here in the country of my missus?"

"Yes," Zosine cried back, "bar the door, and push the chest back on it! There are enemies outside! We are in great danger, Olympia. Let me look at you! Hold me fast! Olympia, how have you come?"

The huge dark, female figure had found a foothold on the floor, although her frock and cloak were still caught in the iron work of the chest and left to view two legs heavy as door-posts. Soaked by the rain, splashed with mud, and with her bonnet pulled askew over her face, Olympia freed herself of the chest, slowly stepped over the threshold, and looked round.

"Well, you have got a fire here in any case," she said. "You are as white as two shifts! At times, after all, it is best to be black! I knew well enough, in the coach and on the road, I knew well enough that you were in danger. Tell me now who it is who wants to harm you. Oh, I was dying, I was dead with longing for you, my chicken, my angel, you the neat, sweet little finger of Master Theodore! Oh, I could eat you up! Sweetheart, let me feel my little puppet in my arms again! If Olympia cannot save her, she can die with her!"

"How have you come?" Zosine cried again.

"Aye indeed," answered Olympia, "it would be an easy matter to keep me away from you! When the cart, which I hired in the village, could not drive me any farther, because a tree had fallen across the road, I picked off one of its lamps, and I crawled over the thick trunk of the tree, and walked on in the dark."

"Was there," Zosine asked breathlessly, "nobody on the road? Did you meet nobody by the house?"

"Yes, indeed, I met a young gentleman on the road," answered Olympia. "Why was he running as fast as he could? Was the devil at his heels? I asked him my way, and held up my lamp, but when he saw my black face in the light of it, he shrieked, as if I had stuck a knife into him, and ran on. People," she said, "are madder in England than on Santo Domingo. But they are still madder in this country than in England. What are you afraid of tonight?"

The girls now remembered that Monsieur Emmanuel, in his hasty flight from the house, had left the gate in the garden wall open behind him, and realized that this was why they had not heard the garden gate being opened or shut.

10. news from england

"BUT if nobody stopped you," said Zosine very slowly, staring at Olympia, "and if you have seen nobody near the house, then they may really have gone away. The light in the window was the sign that they had agreed upon between them. When the candlestick was put down there, it meant that Monsieur Tinchebrai had got his information, and then those who waited for him in the dark were to come in and kill us! But no candle has been put in the window! And Monsieur Tinchebrai ran away, without letting them know what he had found out. Now they are uncertain; they are perhaps consulting among themselves, and waiting. Oh, they will come back, do not doubt it. But perhaps they will give us an hour or two still."

"Who are the wicked people who want to hurt you?" Olympia asked, rolling her dark eyes and showing her teeth. "Who is coming? Against whom have you barred your doors? They shall not get near you as long as I have got nails on my fingers or teeth in my mouth. Let me hear who they are."

"Yes, I will tell you," said Zosine, and drew her breath deeply. "But I will not tell you at once. If we have an hour left, Olympia, then in this hour let me hear the name of England, and of the people who live there. Let me remember that there are men and women who speak the truth, and who love me. Who has sent you, Olympia?"

"Oh, it was a pity. It was enough to break your heart," said Olympia. "It was all wretchedness and misery in England. Miss Arabella grieves and grudges. She is worrying day and night. If you saw her, you would weep over her. She will say nothing about it, but she dies from it.

"At first," she continued, "one could still stand it, although it was hard enough to be in her house. For she would not give a farthing out. She thought that when she had died from grief and starvation, you would perhaps forgive her, and accept her money. My God, she has never had much flesh on her, the poor girl, and now it is as if a stick was walking inside her frocks and shawls. Her servants starved, and gave notice one by one. Her old butler and myself were the only people who remained with her. For there must be someone to look after her. She had holes in her shoes, and no fingers in her gloves. And still, long ago, when she was young, she was the most elegant lady that we saw in Master Theodore's house. But it became worse still, when she heard from Master Theodore in Santo Domingo—"

"Has she heard from Papa?" cried Zosine.

"Yes, from Papa, from Papa himself," said Olympia, "and she heard that it was well with him. For now the tobacco has been harvested. He is rich again, and can pay everybody what he owes them. From that moment Miss Arabella would no more get up in the daytime. 'I am ashamed to meet the light of the day,' she said, 'for when he comes back to England, and asks me about his daughter, what am I to answer him? I have forgotten that I am an old woman. I have thought, spoken and written like a schoolgirl! What is my destiny to me? You have no destiny when you are fifty years old!' We had to work and eat at night, and in the daytime all the shutters of the windows were closed.

"Then," said Olympia, "I went to Master Ambrose—"

"To Ambrose! Where is Ambrose?" cried Zosine.

"Master Ambrose is married now," said Olympia. "He has become a genteel gentleman, so sad and melancholy that all people must respect him. Does he play any pranks now, or keep race horses, or send flowers to young ladies? Oh, my God, no. He is just like a blessed little baby that thinks of nothing but his food. 'What are we going to have for dinner?' he asks, when he gets up in the morning. In Master Ambrose's house I had a decent meal, a nice, fine meal for the first time in many months, for his lady was away, and he had a chair set for me by his own table. He looked through all his drawers, and there found the name of the lady who was called Mrs. Quincy, and in whose house you had last set your dainty little feet. I went to Mrs. Quincy. At first I offered her a hundred guineas, if she would tell me where you were, and later I threatened to cut her throat."

"But she did not know where we were," said Zosine.

"No, she did not know where you were," said Olympia.

"How did you find us then?" Zosine asked again.

The old woman's black face suddenly became empty and expressionless. It was as if a door had been shut. "Who of you," she said, "knows our ways? Black people have got their own souls and their own noses. Of that we will not speak. And this time," she added, more to herself than to Zosine, "somebody from the old time came and helped me. They came from far away to show me the road. The Negro to whom I was married came, yes, my own baby laughed and jumped a little ahead of me where I walked. But why they came I do not know. And at last, tonight, I smelled your danger and your fear. And do you think that any human being could then have kept me back or made me turn? But all this is nothing for nice young ladies to ask about, or listen to."

To Lucan's ears Olympia's account sounded fantastic and almost insane. But Zosine was used to the black woman's ways, and knew that to her, people and events did not look the same as to others.

"But you ought to have turned back, Olympia," said Zosine. "You have searched so untiringly, and you have traveled so far, only to die with us in the end. Oh my poor Papa! What good does it do him to have grown rich again, and to have got back his good name, over which we have grieved so sadly, if in the meantime I shall be dead? The house to which, with so much trouble, you have found your way, Olympia, is named Sainte-Barbe. It is a murder-house! The people who live in it went away yesterday, only to return tonight to kill us. While you were driving with the diligence, or crawling over the fallen tree, they were digging our graves outside in the garden."

"Now you must tell me," said Olympia, "what they are named, and how everything has come about."

"Yes, I will tell you," said Zosine. "Lucan knows it too. Lucan has been my friend here, Olympia. While we were living at Tortuga, you were not nice to her, but now you ought to go down on your knees and kiss her hands. And there is," she went on with trembling lips, "another girl, of whom I shall tell you. But you have come a long way, and you are so old and fat, you must be tired. I will give you some wine. We have also got a cake. Then you may eat and drink, while I tell you my story, so that you shall not go to sleep."

The old woman really drank the cherry brandy, and ate up half of the cake, while she waited for Zosine's tale.

"Olympia," said Zosine, "I do not like to tell you these things at all. They are dreadful to hear. Do you remember, when I was a little girl, that I read aloud to you from my fairy-tale books, because you could not read? There were ghouls in them, werewolves, trolls. Sometimes you screamed aloud and almost fell down from your chair. But those were only fairy tales. These things are true! You do not know how one feels when one realizes that they exist in the world."

The Negress listened perfectly motionless. With a huge hand on each thigh and half-shut eyes, she watched or lurked for each of Zosine's words.

"This old man here and his wife," said Zosine, "lured young girls to their house, like big spiders in their web. They did dreadful things to them, which I do not understand. They sold them across the seas to other people, horrid like themselves, who killed them. There was a girl named Rosa, just as old as Lucan and me, to whom they did this. She was brought to the house of a ghastly man, where she had no friends and no merciful people to help her. And there the man strangled her with a rope and buried her in his cellar. He wrote it all to the old man of Sainte-Barbe, and I have read the letter myself!"

Olympia thought this tale over for a moment. "What!" she cried out in a deep, vibrating voice, like the growl of a big angry animal. "Did the old man sell white girls in a market for money? Just as we were sold?"

"Yes, just like that, Olympia," Zosine answered.

"Oh, may the Almighty God strike him then, split him, grind his bones to flour!" roared Olympia. "I will hold my ears, I will swoon, nobody can stand listening to you, when you tell them such things! What? Did he send white girls across the sea, away from their Papa, into the hands of foreign traders? No, go on all the same," she cried, "let me hear everything! I shall not die from it yet, not till I have spat into the old man's face!"

Zosine went on to tell her of Monsieur Emmanuel's visit, of her own device about Aunt Arabella's letter, and of his wild flight from the house, up to the moment when from this room the two forlorn girls had heard Olympia's own steps on the garden path. She told her tale in a confused, abrupt way, but her old black nurse followed it, word by word, and seemed to understand it all.

"Oh, you are clever," she said, and nodded her head. "You are as clever as Master Theodore himself, when he talked to the people who meant to harm him. You can purr as a cat, even with a big fury in your heart. You have scared your enemies, the wicked people, so that perhaps now they dare not come back. When it grows light enough to see the road before us, we will go away from here, and you are never to see this bad house again."

Lucan took courage at Olympia's words, she exclaimed, "Yes, Zosine, when it grows light, we may get away. We may go to Father Vadier's house. He will help us."

"But is the old man then to get away from us?" Zosine asked slowly.

The black woman had risen. Her stout arms were hanging down; she opened and shut her hands and panted heavily.

"No, he is not to get away from us," she said. "Now old Olympia begins to understand. Many, many nights since Master Theodore went away from me, I have lain awake and grieved that I was not dead. But now I see that it is good for something. I have lived for seventy years, and some of them have been long to get through, but they were not too many. With a rope, you say?" she went on. "They strangled the girl with a rope? And now they have got another ready for you? Let me have a look at it. It is a good, new, strong rope. It will be a joy to lay it round the neck of the old man." She shifted her weight from the one foot to the other, and rolled her eyes, so that the whites in them gleamed.

"I thought so," she cried. "I thought there would be a hook in the ceiling! It has been waiting for him a long time. And tonight I will hang him from it."

"Olympia, what are you saying?" cried Zosine. "You are old. I can knock you over with one hand. You puffed and panted every day over the stairs of Tortuga. How can you imagine that you can stand your ground, even against one single old man? And would you touch him?" she added with a shudder. "You would not touch him, Olympia!"

"Now you be silent, my little doll," said the old woman. "Of these things I know more than you do. The stairs of Tortuga? I am going to take a higher step tonight!"

She dragged the stool, on which Lucan had sat when she had read aloud to her teacher, from near the fireplace out into the middle of the floor. Staggering on her feet she heaved her heavy body on to it, and fastened the rope that Zosine had brought in from the kitchen to one of the two hooks in the ceiling of the room. She made a running noose on it, and bit into it. Lucan could not get her eyes away from her, so strange and ghostlike did the black woman look on the stool. When she stepped down from it, she swayed and shut her eyes. Zosine ran up to her, put her arms round her, and sat her down in a chair. After a minute, Olympia once more opened her eyes and stared at the rope that hung straight down from the hook.

"It is the big snake!" she said in a dull voice.

"Are you ill, Olympia?" Zosine asked.

"No, my little one," Olympia answered. "Now I am well. Now let him come home."

11. mr. pennhallow comes home

SAINTE-BARBE'S cock crew. The morning came. Lucan and Zosine had been sitting on the sofa, each to her side of Olympia, and Zosine with her head on her shoulder. The old Negro woman's body radiated a kind of warmth and hope. Close to her the girls had even, in the course of the night, fallen from time to time in a short doze. Olympia had pushed off her wet shoes and sat with her feet on the fender to dry them. Now the fire had died out, and the candles on the table had burned down. In the gray light of dawn one could already dimly distinguish the outline of the windows on the wall, and of the two big cupboards in the room. The wind had decreased, and the noise of the rain was no longer heard in the room.

Somewhere in the house a door was opened. Without moving, Lucan and Zosine looked at each other. A series of other faint sounds followed, and at the same moment one idea ran through the minds of both girls. They remembered the cellar under the house and the narrow stair leading from it to the corner of the corridor. It had not been in their thoughts during the night.

The cellar of Sainte-Barbe was no longer in use. There was an outside door to it, in the gable of the house, opposite the gable where the wood-stack stood, but it had been locked and barred for almost a hundred years. Only once, shortly after their arrival, the girls had been down in the long, dark vaults. This deep cellar was older than the rest of the building and had been the most important part of it at the time when Sainte-Barbe still had its own vineyards. The young English girls had looked at the heavy casks and had wondered at the thickness of the walls, and at the fact that no sound from above found its way down here.

Either, they thought, the visitor who now moved so softly in the house, came from outside it, and would perhaps have chosen his way because he did not want to walk past the wood-stack. Or else, they thought again, he had been in the house for many hours, from before the moment when they had lighted Monsieur Emmanuel out, and had begun to strain their ears for any new sound in the dark. No noise of comings and goings above would have reached him down there. Or he might perhaps just once, like a distant vibration in the night round him, have caught Zosine's long, wild shriek when, through the entrance-door, she recognized Olympia's voice.

Quiet, deadened steps came along the flags of the corridor. At the sound of these steps Olympia sat up straight. She listened again, and Zosine felt how her mighty body stiffened beside her. A moment after, she rose. Without the slightest noise, and with a singular lightness, like that of a big black cat, she glided along the wall to the corner between the door and the cupboard, where her figure became almost indistinguishable from the dark wall.

He who came was in no hurry. At first he walked toward the door of the dining-room. But he stopped outside it, as if hesitating, and took a few steps down the corridor to the door that led to the bedroom of the two girls. Lucan and Zosine listened to his movements with every nerve and fiber strained, so that it seemed to them that they were following them with their eyes. He stood still for a long time outside their door, as if to make certain that no sound came from inside it. Then he slowly turned the door-handle. On the threshold he once more hesitated, craned his neck before he crossed it, and gazed round the little room. The two untouched beds caught his eye, and he nodded his head. Still without a sound, he went to the window and drew the curtain. The daylight gave him the confirmation he wanted: no one had slept in this room tonight. His instructions had been carried out, what was to be done had been accomplished. He was right to have come home. He nodded once more and cleared his throat. The girls had already recognized Mr. Pennhallow's footsteps. In this short noise, a little approving chuckle, they now recognized his low, hoarse voice. A moment after, the door of the dining-room was quietly opened, and the old man poked in his head, and threw a watchful, piercing glance around him.

When they had heard the door from the corridor to their bedroom being opened, both the young girls had sunk from the sofa onto the floor. Lucan lay with her face on the sofa-seat; Zosine squatted in front of it with her arm upon it. They were hidden from the comer by the tall back of the sofa, but between it and the wall Zosine could follow him with her eyes.

The old man looked exactly as he had on the day when he gently turned the handle of Mrs. Quincy's door and entered the office in London. He had the same long, black coat on, the heavy shoes, and the old, tall hat. He came in as meekly and unpretentiously as then, and his little bland smile just as then gave the impression that he might smile deeper than other people, but was subduing his mirth, out of some particular leniency toward the people at whom he smiled. On that day Zosine had put her handkerchief to her mouth to hide her laughter; now she bit her lips to stifle a shriek.

Mr. Pennhallow slowly let his eyes run round the dining-room. He came from a room where he had let the light in, and it took him some time to distinguish the objects in here. For a minute he gazed at the supper table with the burned-down candles, and at the chairs pushed back from it. Just as in the bedroom, he went to the window, and pulled aside the curtain, and the dim morning light fell upon his face. It was gray as usual, and even more devoid of color. Whether he had spent the night in a diligence, or in the cellar of Sainte-Barbe, he had not slept much. The old man was tired. But as he looked round the room, a little delicate blush of content mounted into his leaden cheeks. He ran the tip of the tongue over his lips.

At this moment, when his old, happy face was lighted up by the dawn, Olympia from her corner by the cupboard gave a long, terrific roar, as if the big wild animal, which a short time ago had growled in front of the fire, now made its mighty, deadly leap. "Papa le Roi!" she cried.

Mr. Pennhallow, in his surprise, took a short step back, and the faint color sank from his face. But immediately after he was quiet as before, and his pale eyes met the eyes of the woman.

"It is Papa le Roi!" Olympia once more roared from the middle of the floor, swinging her arms, and throwing her body forward and back. "It is the gray man from the woods who has come back!"

Zosine had stood up automatically and without knowing what she did. Behind Olympia's colossal wild figure Mr. Pennhallow caught sight of her pale face, and for a second his eyes glinted. Zosine never forgot this glint; for many years she dared not recall it, and later she thought, "It was the eyes of a snake which realizes that it has missed its stroke." Then he once more turned away from her. As calmly as if nothing unusual had happened, he went to the second window of the room, and here too drew back the curtain. He slowly measured the Negro woman with his eyes, but for another minute remained silent.

"Who," he at last asked the girl very gently, "have you let in here tonight? Has this unhappy, mad black woman sought shelter at Sainte-Barbe in the storm? If so, it was right and charitable to open the door to her."

Zosine did not answer. She felt with a horrible giddiness, that the old man, if the two had been alone in the house, once more could have forced her back into the world of lies and deceit, in which they had been living together for months. But Olympia stood on the floor between them like a solid and unshakable reality, and her shriek still re-echoed from the walls. Olympia belonged to Tortuga and to Zosine's old life. She would at this moment have died for her master's daughter, and she had bellowed her accusation into the face of the old man. The Negress spoke and behaved like a mad woman, and still it was her presence which drove back the falsehood at Sainte-Barbe, as now the morning light was slowly driving back the darkness into the corners of the room.

"Why," asked Mr. Pennhallow, "are you up so early? What has been going on in this house tonight?"

Zosine did not answer this time either, but she looked straight at him. For the first time her young face expressed the hatred, the loathing and the contempt with which he inspired her. There was a franker and deeper threat in the girl's glance than in the black woman's furious accusation. The old man's own long gray face was changed beneath it, the smile on it widened, and became almost sickly in its mildness, a grin. He seemed to writhe back a little toward the window-sill.

"Aye, my dear young friends," he said, "now we will talk together of what has happened here tonight. And of what is going to happen here today."

Olympia suddenly stopped her wild war dance and stood immovable, like a majestic, dark statue. Then she took a step toward the man before her, and stared at him.

"Where do you come from?" she cried in a deep, ringing voice. "You gray man who ate my child! You were as old as you are now, fifty years ago. Could you no longer lie still in your grave?"

12. the rope once more

MR. PENNHALLOW did not look at Olympia, but again let his glance run round the room. It passed Lucan's crouching figure by the sofa, and, in the middle of the ceiling, was caught by the rope in the hook. He broke into a long, noiseless laughter.

"What have you been doing here?" he asked. "What comedy is it that you have meant to play? Come, tell me all about it."

Olympia fumbled in the folds of her clothes, and pulled out a heavy object. It was a big old pistol. It was with this same pistol that, at Tortuga, she had meant to defend her master's life. In the silence of the room there was a short, sharp click as she cocked it.

"No!" she said. "No! It is you who are now to tell of all the evil that you have done. I shall not shoot before you have finished. Did you eat my child? Was its flesh sweet to your mouth? Were you going to sell Master Theodore's child, you devil and swine from the slavers, as you sold the pretty black girls? Yes, think the matter well over. For I am not going to let you off. This time you would have to gnaw the flesh off your own fingers before I let you off!"

The master again laughed gently, as in his own thoughts.

"There!" cried Olympia, and pointed with the pistol at the stool beneath the noose. "You shall stand up there, and tell me everything!"

"There?" said the old man. "On my own stool? The stool on which my little pupils sat when they read pious stories to me?

Aye, it is a worthy pulpit for the sermon that I am going to preach to you."

He stood up on the stool, all the while smiling gently, as if he was humoring a party of dear children by joining in their play.

"Lay the rope round your neck!" cried the Negress.

"Round my neck?" said Mr. Pennhallow. "Aye, I will put it round my neck. I have a mind to know for myself how it feels there. It is a graceful clergyman's collar. Is it now as you want it? Then we will have a talk together. And I think that we are all going to enjoy it."

He really placed the rope round his neck. His face was ashen, and his big, dark hands, that hung straight down, trembled. But his mild, quiet dignity did not leave him, even as he stood so, with the wild woman's pistol pointed at him.

"You simpletons," he said very slowly, "you fools. I will enlighten you, and show you the black hole, at the edge of which you stand. In your ignorance you imagine that you can harm me. But no human being can do me any harm. When you pull the trigger of your pistol, you old black hag, you will hear a click, and nothing more. It is not me, it is you and your lasses who are in danger here. Yes, you are in a more dreadful danger this morning than you have ever been! My heart bleeds for you.

"Why should I not," he went on, "answer you as politely as I answered the old judge of Lunel, who came here with all the greatness of the law, and went away with an apology? I have never refused to answer the questions of honest people. But I have got more things to tell you than you have to question me about.

"You have been afraid to die tonight, and you rejoice now, because you have managed to escape death. But there is something that you will not escape. It is the living death of insanity. You, my old mother, may hold yourself to be safe from it, because you are already insane. But still it will be a sad thing for you to see the girl, whom you came to help, more mad than yourself, a maniac, who shrieks when she sees you, and bites you when you try to cuddle her. And from that you will not be saved.

"I myself," he continued, and although his teeth were chattering slightly a delicate, clear light spread over his face, "am safe and happy wherever I go. No human being can take away my heart's content from me. The bargain which I have made is too firmly consolidated for that.

"But you, my children, have got many things to fear. You were afraid to die, you, who are virtuous and chaste, and who believe in Paradise. I tell you that life to you will be worse than death.

"It is not I who am going to harm you, my children," he said. "You will take care of that yourself. Believe me, I know pious people and their consciences. My father and my grandfather, and my great-grandfather with them, were good, pious people, and prophets to their congregations, in my cold home country. Their consciences left them no peace, and permitted them nothing in all the world. It had got stronger and more delicate instruments to torture them with than those that I have handled in the vaults of the old prisons, and in the hands of their conscience they were as naked, pinioned and gagged as the people who were brought down there.

"Alas," he continued slowly, "they had to forsake everything; they had to starve their bodies and souls to death at the bidding of their conscience. What infiinite penance they must do for the pale pleasure of a moment. How did a small, unchaste thought pinch, flay and scorch them all through their long nights. Their conscience drew deep furrows in their faces, like the scars after the hot irons. It put out their eyes and made them tremble in the dark. And their bitter, undying envy of those who were not slaves of their consciences stuck in them, like the poles on which the victims of old days were impaled, and made their souls grow gangrenous round it. Verily, I know the torments of pious people better than anyone else in the world.

"And do you now, my foolish little children," he asked again softly, "believe that you can kill a human being, and live on after it? I myself, I tell you, am well enough here on my stool. The rope is an old friend of mine, and has been useful to me before now. I flatter myself that I look well and in harmony here. But how will I look, later on, to you, in your dreams at night? You will be sick when you clasp a necklace round your own necks. How many times a year will you faint at the sight of blood?"

Lucan had risen. Unable to listen any longer to her old teacher, she stood for a moment, deadly pale, before him, and then staggered toward the door of her room. But he stopped her with a gesture.

"Come here, my little guileless daughter," he said. "I have got a letter in my pocket which I have kept for you. Take it and read it." He took a letter from his pocket, and handed it to her, but as she did not move he let it drop to the floor. "Your lover in England will come over here to fetch you," he went on, and smiled at her. "He is free once more, and nothing will prevent you and him from marrying and being happy. Is your wedding-ring, then, to stick to your finger with blood? Your child will be born with another red ring round its throat, and he will ask you where it had got it from. When you teach it to read, it will be the letters of our old school books at Sainte-Barbe, which will turn up, and form themselves into hideous words. I will be standing behind you, on this stool, with the rope round my neck, when you gaze into the looking-glasses of your pretty rooms, until, squealing, you break them all with your fists, and your husband will have to shut you up, with shutters to the windows, and a strong woman to put the strait-jacket on you. It is then that, like my other girls, you will be taught to yearn for the river, for the deep well, for the rope itself."

He stood for a while in silence, and again his face shone.

"I have told you," he exclaimed, "that I am safe wherever I am. Everything is permitted me. My happiness cannot be affected by outward things.

"The happenings that have shocked you," he continued, "and which have upset your peace of mind, my little children, were nothing but small attentions toward the power which I serve, and which has thus made me safe. They were jokes by which, from time to time, I expressed my gratitude. My old uncle, whom you remember, black woman, and for whom you mistook me, likewise from time to time showed his zeal in the same service. When he tasted the flesh of your child, good mother, it was to amuse his master. When I sent my girls to my own places it was in the humble hope of making him smile. Alas, the hope sometimes deceived me, as it did with your friend Rosa, and I was a little ashamed of myself, a little bashful before him. But I have been in luck too. I have succeeded in amusing him. I have seen another of my girls, when she had come to the end of the road onto which I had set her. The pink, sweet-scented rose from the English garden had become black and charred, and its smell gave offense. There evil had taken root, and had spread nicely. I have often since then thought of her with pleasure. I will think of her now."

"Stop him, Olympia!" cried Zosine, her lips white.

"But these things were only trifles," said he. "I have given him a richer gift, when I gave him my own soul. We know it well, he and I. See, then, how true he is to his faithful servants, see how all things join to be good in his sight. For it was to you, Lucan and Zosine, that I was a father. When you had no home, and no friends, I gave you shelter under my roof, I became your friend. I taught you wisdom, and opened your eyes to the greatness of the world. You two I would never have harmed. I was in earnest when I told you that I would send you into the houses of good, pious people, of bishops in England. I was in earnest when I said that we should meet again, and talk of great and sweet things. You yourself, on your own, have found the path to lies and deceit, and to murder.

"Maybe," he added with a little smile, "maybe you imagine that I shall have to pay for my happiness on earth in another life. You are much mistaken, my children. My pleasure is to last forever and ever. How can it be otherwise, when I shall come to a place where all is in accordance with myself, and filled with the same spirit as that which lives in my own heart? I shall meet my girls there again! They will howl at me once more, and I shall laugh at them again."

"Oh, stop him, Olympia!" cried Zosine.

Olympia lifted her huge arm, and took aim.

In the other room Lucan had sunk on her knees. Now she jumped up, and came running into the dining-room.

"Zosine!" she cried. "Olympia! You must not kill him! Do you not see that he is right? We cannot live if we kill him. None of us can live!"

Beside herself she seized the old woman's arms, and clung to her. In a violent movement Olympia shook her off. There was a short, sharp noise as the pistol missed fire.

"Aye," smiled the man on the stool, "the powder will have become damp in the rain tonight. Take your time, my black sister, try the other barrel, and after that, load your pistol once more. It will click on you again, and again!

"But first," he went on, "listen to me, woman of Santo Domingo, for I am longing to have a talk with you. Do you know yourself so little that you believe that this is what you want? Have you forgotten the old black nights of long ago, of your youth? Come, I will call them back to you.

"We might talk together," he said, "of the goat without horns. But I will tell you of a finer gift, which you may bring to him whom you have served before now, who will not have forgotten you. Give him, tonight, the lamb without a speck, the little white lamb which you have yourself fed and fondled and which trusts you, and seeks her refuge in your bosom! Why, do you think, were you allowed to find your way to this house, and to be with me and her at this hour? On that dark road, who was your leader? In your own heart you guessed, then, and you know now, that he is ready to grant you a sweeter ecstasy and a deeper pleasure than you have ever experienced. He is waiting for you. Is he to wait in vain?"

Olympia had cocked the second hammer of her pistol, but slowly her hand sank down. Once more she raised it, and once more it sank. For the third time she brought it up, and for the third time, as if forced down by a heavy weight, it sank to her side. She covered her face with her left arm, as, for the last time, she raised her arm and, blindly, took aim at the man in front of her.

"Oh, Olympia! Oh, Zosine!" cried Lucan. "Have pity on him! Do you not see that he is off his mind? He is not as evil as he thinks himself! And even if it was so, there is forgiveness for all human beings! There is an infinite grace in the world. There is grace for him too. Have pity on him! Have mercy!"

Her beseeching voice was choked by her emotion at the same second as a terrible shriek from the old man's lips re-echoed from the four walls of the room.

"What!" he cried. "What! A young girl begs forgiveness for me! A maiden cries grace for me! It is Rosa who prays for me! It must not be. It is the one thing which must never be. Stop her! Silence her! Knock her down and make her stop! Chase her out from here! Away! Away!"

"Yes. Grace!" Lucan cried and fell on her knees.

Their master lifted his hand as in rending, unbearable pain, and shook his broad forefinger in the air in front of her. His face was distorted. He opened his mouth wide and made an effort to shriek again, but his lips were stiff; froth ran down them. He held both hands to his throat and to the rope there, and in one great movement, as if he fled from an advancing, devouring fire, he stepped over the edge of the stool.

A dreadful sound, a raw and raucous rattle broke from his throat. For a moment his feet struggled in the air, and his body spun in the empty space. Then the swinging of the rope decreased and stopped; it hung straight down from the ceiling as before, with a heavy, dead weight at the end of it.

Zosine, like Lucan, had sunk on her knees beside the old black woman. She hid her face in her clothes. But Lucan, still trembling, with wide-opened, clear eyes, stared at the face in the air in front of her.

"Yes. Grace!" she whispered, without knowing that she spoke. "Forgiveness! Mercy!"

13. ~ two letters

WHEN Lucan, as it seemed to her after an eternity of darkness, rose from the floor, her soul held but one single thought: "Away!" Away from Sainte-Barbe, the place that was forever cursed. She took Olympia's hand to draw her and Zosine with her on her flight from the room and the house.

The old black woman did not move. When the doomed man before her had uttered his last cry, she herself had opened her mouth wide, in a long, dumb shriek toward him. But as he stepped over the edge of the stool, and his body, in the sudden, convulsive swinging of the rope, passed close to her, her mouth fell, her arm with the pistol once more sank down, and she stood as if she had been turned to stone. After a minute she whispered a few words in a strange, guttural language, and solemnly crossed herself three times. Lucan turned to Zosine.

Zosine lay in a heap on the floor, so deadly still that a shiver of terror ran through her friend. Lucan tried to raise her to her feet, but she hung lifeless in her arms, and her eyes were big and dark, as if her body were imitating the body in the rope. Her eyes reflected the last sight that had met them, so that they would now be blind to all others. Lucan cried out her name, and supported her drooping head, but Zosine did not seem to hear or to feel.

At last the old woman slowly turned round toward the girls, and stared at them. The rigidity of her limbs dissolved. She pushed Lucan aside, and with an extraordinary display of strength lifted Zosine in her arms. Her face changed and shivered. Two big tears rolled down her heavy cheeks as she held the girl to her bosom and broke into a low, soft and wild babble, as if she were cuddling a small child.

"Oh, my baby," she cried. "Rest your head on these dry breasts, as you did when they were full! Stay with the black woman, and suck away her great sins as you did before! Smile at her again, my little child, and call her again your lump of black sugar! Oh, my baby!"

She carried the girl almost to the door, and Lucan followed her. None of them thought of putting on a bonnet or a shawl. They fled as they were, in their rain-splashed and crumpled clothes.

They did not consult, either, about where they were to go. But Lucan had twice named Father Vadier. Her thoughts hastened to his house.

Before she left the room she threw a last bewildered and sad glance round her, and on the floor caught sight of the letter which Mr. Pennhallow had held toward her, and which she could not take from his hand. She had hardly heard what he had said about it, but she dimly felt that a letter from England ought not to be left in this room. At the last moment she picked it up from the floor.

With Olympia's help she again dragged the heavy chest away from the entrance door. While they worked with it, Zosine stood leaning against the wall, deadly pale and dumb.

As long as she lived Lucan did not forget the fresh air of this morning, as it met her when she opened the door. It was quite light now. Above the fields a thin mist floated; the landscape was calm and serene. The trees were dripping with rain, and there were puddles of water in the garden path.

In order to support Zosine, Lucan had to free herself of the letter that she still kept in her hand. She gazed at it, uncertain of what to do with it. "But there are two letters here!" she exclaimed.

The one letter was from England, and bore her name. It had been opened. The other had no stamp and was not closed. Lucan would let it drop, but Olympia stopped her. "No," she said, "there may be something that one ought to know written on a paper. Read it, you who can read!"

The girl looked at the letter. She recognized Mr. Pennhallow's handwriting, which she knew so well from their lessons, and trembled to read the words which he had written down. The letter only contained a few lines; they ran:

"*Come to Sainte-Barbe at once. I have got a piece of information for you, about which we will have to come to a decision.*"

It was not dated, but it was addressed to Monsieur Emmanuel Tinchebrai, at Peyriac.

Lucan thought the matter over. "This is the letter," she exclaimed, "which Mr. Pennhallow wrote yesterday, or the day before—I can no longer keep account of the days. He gave it to me, to tell Clon to bring it out. But almost at once he called it back again. He went himself, instead, with the message it contained."

Out here, in the clear morning air, she could not realize that the information, of which the letter spoke, was the information about Zosine's and her own knowledge of the crimes at Sainte-Barbe, and the decision which was to be taken was their sentence of death. She was about to tear up the letter when Zosine took her hand. "No, wait!" she said, and for a minute stood silent, looking at the paper.

"Somebody," she said at last, very slowly, "is to come, some time, and find Sainte-Barbe as it is now. Let it be him then. He will believe that the letter has been written this morning. Monsieur Tinchebrai is in the service of the police. Let it be the police itself, which first opens the door here."

"But how are we to send the letter to him?" Lucan asked. It took Zosine a long time to answer, as if her brain was working with infinite difficulty. "We must give it to somebody whom we meet on the road," she said.

Just as she had finished speaking, she and Lucan caught sight of a human figure by the garden wall. It was no wonder that they had not noticed him before, for he stood perfectly still, his blouse, shoes and hands were so pasted with clay and mud, and his face itself so moldy, that his form seemed to be one with the wall. It was Clon.

The boy leaned half against the garden wall and half upon his heavy spade. He was soaked by the rain, and looked as if he could hardly keep upright. He stared with wide-opened eyes at the three women, but seemed too ill and exhausted to take in what he saw. Even Olympia's unexpected and strange figure only made his mouth widen in a kind of dead grin, as if he did not believe his eyes.

Zosine looked at him. "Clon," she called gently, "come here, Clon!"

Clon hesitated, and looked as if he wanted to run away. All the same after a moment he put down his spade and, half sideways, came a few steps nearer.

"Speak to him, Lucan," said Zosine. "He understands you better than me. Tell him," she continued, very slowly, as before, "that he is to go down to Monsieur Tinchebrai in Peyriac, with this letter from Mr. Pennhallow. He is to deliver it at his house, and to go away again at once, without speaking to anybody."

Although she did not understand what Zosine wanted, Lucan repeated her order to the boy, and put the letter into his clammy hand. It shook as he took the paper from her. "He is ill," Lucan thought. "He has been standing out here all night. He has fever!" Clon read her compassion in her eyes and shrank away from her in such obvious fear of being spoken to again or of being touched that Lucan grew silent and left him alone.

She looked down at her own letter. She did not know the handwriting, and wondered who would write to her at Sainte-Barbe, from England. Slowly and dimly Mr. Pennhallow's words came back to her, and she threw a glance at Zosine, as if to get them confirmed by her, before she put the letter into the pocket of her skirt. While they walked down the road and through the forest she twice put down her hand to feel if it was still there. But it was not until two days later that she took it up and read it. She then found it to be anything but a neat and well-proportioned letter. It was short in itself, but had a very long postscriptum. This is what she read:

Miss Lucan Bellenden.

Am I worth that you should read a letter which I have written? I have asked myself this question many times. But it is for you to decide upon it, as it is for you to decide upon everything in my life. I am a young man of little merit or virtue, a rough sailor, perhaps a sinner in the eyes of God. But just as, on the sea, any merchant boat or whaler steers her course by the stars, I must, wherever I am, steer my course by your will.

I write this letter to impart two things to you.

I first beg your permission to tell you that I am free. The word which bound me when I met you in France has been given back to me. If it had not been so I should, I trust, in the thought and memory of you, have kept it. But the lady who was to have been my wife has found, God bless her for it, the richest old man in England, who better than I can give her what she wants in the world. This is the first of the two things which I wanted to tell you.

I next beg your permission to come to France to see you one single time more. You will ask: Why should I let him see me? And I can give no reasonable answer to your question. But at times, lately, a strange thing has happened to me. Against all reason—for I know in what good and safe care you are—I have felt that you might need protection. And you will not, I think, be so hard as to order me to bear this presentiment in silence and with patience. But out of compassion, from your mild and kind heart, you may send me just one word in reply to my prayer.

I have the honor to be, until death,

Your obedient servant

Noël Hartranft.

P.S. Miss Bellenden. You have never heard me say one sensible word to you, with the exception of the very last sentence in the garden. If it were possible that you would allow me to repeat this sentence every day of my life, not in words, but in all my doings, you might perhaps in the end come to think better of me.

P.P.S. Miss Lucan. The very last thing I would have happen is that you should find me preposterous or conceited. Do not be-

lieve that, because you are kind enough to read this letter, I shall take your kindness to be more than you mean it to be. I swear to you that, as I write, I am the humblest person on earth. But I realize myself that, in spite of this, my letter will betray to you that sky-high hope, that indescribable joy which fills me at the idea that I might help, serve or gladden you in any possible way.

P.P.S. I have re-written this letter many times, but have not succeeded in improving it. So I finish it now, in order that it shall not further anger you.

Your servant

Noël Hartranft.

When Lucan, Zosine and the old Negress had gone a bit into the wood they sat down on a slope, to let Zosine rest.

Zosine looked round her and said, "Clon and I are much alike, after all." Her voice was so toneless and distant, and her words in themselves so strange, that Lucan found nothing to answer. A little later Zosine added, "And no wonder!" This time her words clearly expressed her thought, "For we are both murderers!" and Lucan's heart for a moment seemed almost to stop with fear and pity for her friend's sake.

14. joliet

FATHER VADIER'S house, which Lucan and Zosine had often passed on their walks, stood a little to itself at the end of the village. It was surrounded by a garden and a low wall of gray stones. A big mulberry tree shaded the gate. The house itself was gray, low and humble, and the roof sloped down on one side. As the young girls and the Negress were approaching it by the road, a fine carriage and pair were waiting outside the door. Father Vadier himself was standing beside it, talking to the coachman on the box.

Father Vadier looked toward the three women, and shaded his eyes with his hand, the better to see them. He interrupted his talk with the coachman and went a few steps to meet them. He greeted them kindly and took Zosine's hand. "Come and sit down, Mademoiselle," he said, and led her to a stone seat by the wall. "I am happy to see you at my house."

Lucan was struck by the idea of how strange and dismal all three of them must be looking in the daylight. Zosine sat down mechanically as a doll and pale as a corpse. Olympia sank down beside her; her clothes were tumbled and soiled by the mud of last night. "And I myself," the girl thought, "am surely looking as bad as they." She kept standing erect, face to face with Father Vadier. She reflected that now she would have to tell him all that had happened at Sainte-Barbe. She remembered that pale, hard-faced clergyman in England who had conducted her own father's funeral and had questioned her so sternly on the orthodoxy of the man of science, and had seemed to doubt his hope of salvation. Trembling, she collected all her strength to meet Father Vadier's questions and to defend her friend.

But Father Vadier did not ask her any questions; he only raised his voice a little and called toward the house. "Brigitte," he said, as a peasant woman in a white cap, and with a round rubicund face, appeared in the doorway. "Please bring us some cups of good strong coffee. The young ladies, who have come to see us, are tired and in need of a warm drink."

Lucan thought, "Does he not want us in his house?"

Father Vadier went back to the coachman to give him a short order, and then kept standing before the seat, while Brigitte brought and poured out the coffee. To the young girls it appeared almost impossible, on this morning, to do anything as trivial as drinking coffee, and Zosine could not lift her hand to receive the cup. But Father Vadier made Brigitte hold the cup to her lips, and with a little smile urged her to swallow the hot, strengthening drink.

"And now," he said gently, "you must come with me to Joliet."

A sudden long shiver ran through Zosine's body. "You and your sister," Father Vadier said to Lucan, "and this woman, who I understand is your companion or maid, will all be welcome at Joliet. Your sister is not well. You must change your clothes, and you both want better care and tending than I can render you here. It was by a happy chance that Madame de Valfonds did this very morning send her carriage to my house."

Zosine had risen from the seat. "No," she whispered, "I cannot go to Joliet. I must move on. You must let me move on." But she wavered on her feet, and could make no step.

Father Vadier took hold of her arm and supported her. "Yes, my dear young lady," he said, "you must follow me to Joliet. There you will be well looked after. The mistress of Joliet, ever since she saw you at the feast of the vintage, has felt a live sympathy for you. She will wish to talk with you, and to hear all about you."

Zosine looked at him. "Will the mistress of Joliet," she said slowly, "wish to hear all about me?"

"Yes, my child," said Father Vadier.

She kept standing immovable for a while. "Let it be as she wishes, then," she said. "Let us go there."

It was to Lucan as if she were dreaming, when, the morning after the terrible night, she drove up the long avenue to Joliet, among the groups of old trees and the terraces at which she had often gazed from a distance. Olympia, as soon as she had taken her seat in the carriage, had fallen into a sudden, heavy sleep, and was moaning and sighing in it. Zosine kept as still as if she neither heard nor saw anything around her. Once she ran her hand over the smooth cloth of the carriage seat, and then looked at her fingers as in surprise or wonder. Father Vadier kept up a light, gentle conversation with the girls while they drove on. He talked of the storm that was now over, and of the sun that was just breaking through the clouds, and he showed them an old tree in the park, in which the philosopher Montesquieu had cut his name.

"Baron Thésée," he said, "has gone away from Joliet for a few days to his relations in Nîmes. His grandmother has been uneasy in his absence. She is old and needs peace in her house and in her heart. She was anxious last night, and unable to sleep. This is the reason why, this morning, as a couple of times before, she has sent for me. But she is not aware that I am bringing two young visitors to her house."

At the foot of the stairs to the long white building Zosine again trembled violently and gave Father Vadier an imploring glance. He took her hand and reached his other hand to Lucan. Olympia remained on the terrace. In the hall Lucan saw how the footman, who opened the door to them, was suddenly turned to stone at the sight of her huge and strange figure.

The long room into which Father Vadier led the two girls was light and airy. So many beautiful things here seemed to receive them with kindness that Lucan's eyes filled with tears, as slowly and timidly she gazed round her. But the next object which met her eyes took away her breath. It was a painting of a young lady in a green garden, and with a basket of flowers on her arm, and this young lady, in face and figure, and in the happy and confident smile with which she seemed to meet the onlooker, was so like Zosine that Lucan came near to crying out her name loudly. Even the careless fashion in which her brown hair was tied up was the same in which, the evening before, Zosine had arranged her own pretty hair. How wonderful to meet Zosine here on the blue wall between two of the tall windows! And, alas, how sad the contrast between the happy graceful painted figure, in the idyllic surroundings, and her friend's exhausted and broken form.

By the window in the farthest end of the room an old lady sat in a deep armchair. A younger, thin and stiff woman, that same lady companion Lucan and Zosine had seen in the carriage at Peyriac, was arranging her cushions, and at the sight of the visitors drew back behind her chair.

"Madame," Father Vadier softly and respectfully addressed the old lady, "I am bringing you the two young English misses who have been visiting your neighborhood. They have left Sainte-Barbe. Something that has happened there—what, I do not know—has shocked and frightened them. They stand in need of that shelter from the turbulence and sadness of the world which Joliet can grant them."

Madame de Valfonds looked up at the strangers, surprised and, after the habit of very old people, with a kind of reticence.

The mistress of Joliet was a highly dignified and graceful woman. It was still evident that in her young days she must have been beautiful and spirited. But she had grown older since the day when girls had seen her at the vintage; her noble face and delicate hands were almost transparent; the dark brilliant eyes lay deep in their sockets. With the assistance of her companion she rose from the chair, advanced a step, and greeted the priest and the girls with dignity and courtesy. Her glance for a moment rested with pleasure upon Lucan's lovely face. But as it fell upon the face of Zosine the old lady stiffened.

"I have heard your name, young ladies," she said after a long time, in a clear, quivering voice. "But you will forgive me that I do no longer remember it. Be kind enough to tell me what you are called."

Her eyes did not leave Zosine's face. The girl drew her breath deeply. "My name is Zosine Tabbernor," she said.

Madame de Valfonds grew very pale, her eyelids trembled. "After whom," she asked slowly, "are you named Zosine?"

"After Mama," Zosine said, "and after her own mother."

Madame de Valfonds lifted her hands to her heart. "And what was your grandmama named more than Zosine?" she whispered.

"Grandmama was French," Zosine answered, "and her name was d'Aciers de l'Orville."

A clear, deep blush rose into the old lady's cheeks, her face shone, although at the same time her eyes were filled with tears. "Zosine!" she cried out.

The sudden strong emotion, the joy, and an overwhelming abundance of recollections for a moment paralyzed the old woman and nailed her arms to her sides. At the next moment, in a majestic and ecstatic gesture, she raised them both, stretched them out, and closed the girl in them.

Zosine sank into the old lady's embrace, but only to tear herself away from it.

"No, Madame," she said, "you must not touch me."

"Oh, do not call me Madame," Madame de Valfonds exclaimed, the tears streaming down her face. "We are of one blood. Your grandmama was my beloved, lost cousin and friend. Call me Grandmama, in her place."

"Madame," Zosine moaned, "you must not embrace me. Madame, I have killed a human being! I killed him in the cause of justice. He was evil, a murderer. But I cannot remain at Joliet. Let me go, let me get away. Grandmama!" she suddenly cried out in a terrible, shrill voice, "I will die if you touch me!"

Slowly the comprehension of something strange and fatal seemed to penetrate into the old lady's mind. Her face became grave and attentive. But as she regarded the young girl, who, wavering, turned away from her, this shadow once more gave place to a proud, deep, generous tenderness. She held out her hand toward her. "Zosine!" she exclaimed, "Zosine! 'Durior ferro—' " Zosine's dark, wide-opened eyes for a last time stared into those of the old lady.

" '—Purior auro!' " she cried out loudly and clearly, as if hardly aware that she was speaking. And she would have sunk to the floor, if Father Vadier had not quickly laid his arm round her and held up her unconscious body.

15. madame de valfonds' story

"ZOSINE D'ACIERS DE L'ORVILLE was the daughter of my father's sister. Zosine, as you know, was the name of King Tigranes' queen, whom Pompey made walk in his triumphal procession into Rome. My father's sister had acted her part in a tragedy at Court, and had had such a success in it that she named her infant daughter after her role. My cousin and I were much like each other. We played with the same dolls, and we were brought up in the same convent. I had been married for two years, and Zosine was engaged to be married, at the time when the Revolution broke out in Paris, and drove many people into exile, and Zosine's future husband was among them. He came to Joliet, where she was then staying, on his way to England, and our own priest married them in the drawing-room. Before they went away, my cousin promised me, with tears, that when the terrible times were over, she would come back to Joliet. Do you not think now, my Zosine, that it would be a reasonable and sweet thing if, here at Joliet, you should render my last years as happy as your grandmother rendered my childhood and youth?"

It was Madame de Valfonds who talked in this way to Zosine in the young girl's room at Joliet. Zosine had slept for a few hours, but had again got up and had dressed. She now sat, very pale, by the window, and listened to the old lady in the armchair opposite to her.

"I cannot remain at Joliet," she said after a long pause. "It must not be a girl from Joliet who is examined by the judge at

Lunel, and at whom the people of Peyriac point their fingers. You must let me go away from here."

"There is no finger in the province," said Madame de Valfonds, "that will be pointed at a girl from Joliet."

"No," said Zosine, "none but her own." Once more the two women were silent for a long time.

"Do you know," said Madame de Valfonds with difficulty, "that my grandson has confided to me that if he does not get the girl he loves, you yourself, for his wife, he will never marry? Do you want a name, which for many centuries has been written in the history of France, to be wiped out of it?"

"I cannot see him again," said Zosine. "At the time when we knew each other, I was innocent and happy. The horror, which kills me, had not then got into my life. It is better that he should remember me as I was then. You must give me your permission to go away from here."

"My grandson," said Madame de Valfonds in strong agitation of mind, "in his heart blames me, because you have kept away from him, and because you see each other no more. He has always loved me. He is the apple of my eye, an angel. Will you allow a child of Joliet to hate his grandmother? Oh, Zosine, I have suffered agony all this time for your sake. Now I implore a young girl from another country to remain long enough at Joliet for my grandchild to speak to her. Will you refuse my prayer?"

"I cannot remain at Joliet," said Zosine. "I would see him and talk with him if it were possible. But it cannot be. I have not been at Joliet for even twenty-four hours. But I believe that in this short space I have understood things more clearly than ever before in my life. I feel that here live good people, who are kind and helpful to one another, that here nobody hates or lies, but that all work together to the same purpose, and that it is this that has made Joliet a righteous and happy place. The furniture, even, in the rooms, and the trees which I see from my window, have told me so. I will not bring the consciousness of evil and falsehood into this house. The looking-glasses of Joliet shall not reflect a face which has been as pale and dark with hatred as mine. I have lived too long at Sainte-Barbe. Madame! Grandmama! you must let me go away."

The old lady sat for a long time without a word. Zosine looked at her, and with surprise noticed that a deep and delicate blush mounted into her face, sank back again, and left it as pale and clear as alabaster.

"Zosine," Madame de Valfonds asked, "do you not think that a woman may sin in a more dreadful way than by hating?

"I will tell you a story," she said after a while.

"Zosine," she said again, "you know, I suppose, the tradition in our family, which does not allow any de Valfonds to leave his province. I myself have not left it for fifty years. My son never till he died set his feet outside Languedoc's ground. My grandson, too, has kept the tradition faithfully. Now I will make you a promise, which never in my life I have dreamed of making anybody. If you marry my son, I will give up this tradition, and you and he may go together to see all the beauty of the world.

"But in order that you may realize what it costs me to make you such a promise, and in order to show you the trust I have in the granddaughter of my Zosine, aye, in order to make you belong to Joliet, I will now tell you how this tradition first came about. I myself, till now, have only told this tale to a single person, to Father Vadier, twelve years ago, on the day of my grandson's first communion. When I speak to you here, it seems to me that I am going back to the days of my girlhood and talking to my young cousin Zosine.

"There was a lady of our name," she began, "who was married to a gallant and generous husband, many years older than herself. They had a son. Her husband, the lord of Joliet, was a true nobleman, the squire of his land, and the father of his peasants. He knew every oak tree in his woods, every brook in his meadows, and every child in his villages, and he had the welfare of each of his tenants more at heart than his own. He was loyal to his King, he had never told a lie, and he did not believe that other people could lie to him.

"But his young wife was bored at Joliet. She dreamed of travels and of romance; to her the daily life here seemed too monotonous and simple. She was a brilliant and passionate young woman, in her idleness she began to read the new philosophers and to play with the mighty and dangerous ideas of the day. Soon she did not believe in the Divine Right of Kings, and hardly in the grace of God itself. She called King Louis weak, and his family depraved. When the Revolution raised its head in Paris, she read about it with enthusiasm, and became infatuated with its great men and its coryphaei. Her husband at first smiled at her folly, but little by little, as times grew darker, and she herself more obstinate, it alarmed him. He took care that, in case of his own death, the guardianship of his only son would be withdrawn from his wife and entrusted to his cousin, who was an ecclesiastic of high rank. The young mother loved her child; she was broken-hearted and indignant at her husband's decision. Husband and wife became estranged and the child became an apple of discord between them.

"At that time a young man came to Joliet on his flight from Paris. He was a Prince of the Royal House, but his name I cannot tell you, for I have vowed that it should never pass my lips. For three weeks the lord of Joliet hid this young man in a pavilion in the garden, and waited upon him there himself, so as not to expose any of his servants to danger. His wife at first would not join him in the task, but later on she consented to do so out of curiosity, and because the time was so full of great events that she felt she must play her part in some of them. She carried the fugitive's meals down to the pavilion and entertained him there.

"As now the young Prince had got nothing else to do, in the midst of his danger and misfortune he resolved to seduce his benefactor's wife. She was not much more than a child, and without knowledge of the great world. When he told her of his everlasting and unconquerable love, she believed him. At last she granted him admittance to her bedroom on a night when her husband was away at one of his farms.

"On that same night Baptiste Labarre, of Sainte-Barbe, betrayed the fugitive to the commissary of the Convention, who stayed there, and the soldiers of the Revolution came to Joliet to look for him. Baron de Valfonds was arrested on the road, and brought back to his own house. The commissary had the doors of the pavilion broken open, and they found it empty, but they also discovered that somebody had been living there, and they now set about to search the chateau itself.

"In the end they came to the room of the mistress of the castle. But as she was known to be an adherent of the ideas of the Revolution, they did not break into it, as into the other rooms, but their officer knocked at her door. She opened it to him, in her nightdress, and her hair loose, and she saw that the soldiers in the corridor held her husband between them. They only put a few questions to her, and took but a swift survey of the room.

"Still, they decided that they had sufficient proof against her husband to judge him, and informed him that he must go back with them to Sainte-Barbe.

"The lord of Joliet then asked them to draw back a little, while he spoke a few words with his wife, and this demand was granted him. He said to her, 'I have seen that the portrait of my mother in your bedroom is hanging askew on its hook. I understand that, at the risk of your own life, you have fetched our guest from the pavilion up to your bedroom, and have hidden him in the secret closet behind the picture. I beg you to forgive me that I have ever doubted your loyalty to me or to the good cause. We have now but little time left. In the drawer of my writing-table you will find the letter which deprives you of the guardianship of our child. Take it and tear it up before the eyes of these people.' For his own hands, Zosine, were tied with a rope. 'It will be the best thing,' he further instructed her, 'if early tomorrow you make our guest dress in your own clothes and drive away in your own calèche. Let down the hood, and let the carriage drive slowly through the avenue. For these people may come back here to look for him. Tell him that I am proud and happy to die for him.' The soldiers laughed and the commissary of the Convention applauded when the young woman did as her husband bid her, and tore the paper up. 'And now, my wife,' said Baron de Valfonds, 'I beg you to govern Joliet, and to bring up my son in the same spirit as that in which you have acted tonight. For it answers well to the name of Valfonds. Last of all I humbly beg you, as a token of your forgiveness, to bend to me, and give me a kiss of farewell. We two are not to meet again.' Immediately after, the soldiers carried him away.

"The lady of Joliet, after her husband had left her, sat for a long time in front of the picture in her room. She thought, 'I will not open the door, but leave the prisoner to die from starvation and thirst behind it.' But in the course of the night she remembered her husband's words, and took out the key of the secret closet.

"Seven times she put the key into the keyhole, and seven times she took it out and laid it back. She thought: 'How am I to meet the light of day tomorrow, and of the mornings to follow? What face will the looking-glasses of Joliet show me?' But when it began to grow light, she made up her mind to live as her husband had told her, for the sake of Joliet. 'None of my descendants,' she said to herself, 'from this time shall leave our province, to be corrupted by the outside world. We will dig down our hearts in the soil of Joliet until death.'

"At sunrise I opened the door to the closet. Yes, Zosine, I myself was this woman, and the man, whom they brought away to Sainte-Barbe, his hands tied with a rope, was my husband. At sunrise I handed my guest the silk frock, the petticoats and the fichu, which I had taken out for him, and I said to him: 'Here are clothes suitable for Your Royal Highness. For as you see, these are women's clothes. For your sake a man has been shot tonight!'

"He was in danger; he was in a hurry. All the same, when he was dressed, he said to me: 'I am not going to leave Joliet without a kiss.' For till then I had never kissed him.

" 'I have,' I said, 'upon my lips the kiss of Baron de Valfonds, whose last words were, that he was proud and happy to die for you. It would ill befit your royal honor and dignity, should that kiss be wiped out by any other kiss in the world.' "

16. all is quiet at sainte-barbe

TOWARD evening on the day after she had come to Joliet, Lucan sat in her room and sewed, making fast a flounce of her frock which she had torn off in moving the big chest at Sainte-Barbe. Zosine was in bed in the adjoining room. She had fever. From time to time she fell into a short drowse and moaned in her sleep, but when she woke up, she was silent. "It is well," said Lucan, "that she has realized that she is too weak to travel. But how is her mind to gain back its peace and strength?" Zosine wanted to be left alone. She gazed at Lucan with dark, dumb eyes.

Olympia had lain in a deep, deathlike sleep ever since she had come to Joliet. Lucan herself passed the days in a strange, dreamlike condition of mind, in which she could not quite distinguish between the past and the present. When Madame de Valfonds spoke to her, she found no answer. She did not know what the future might bring, nor how much part she herself had had in the tragedy at Sainte-Barbe. When her mind turned to England, and she bethought herself of what her friends there would think or say, when they heard that she had been examined and judged in France, it became blurred or seemed to shrink from the subject. She could no longer clearly realize, or decide about, her own destiny. She must now leave that to others.

Several times in the course of the day carriages had driven up before Joliet, and people had got out of them. Father Vadier had visited the old lady. Lucan was waiting to hear what had been discussed and decided. While she sat and sewed, Father Vadier came into her room. His face was very still as he saluted her and sat down opposite to her.

"I have something to tell you and your friend," he said, "in case Mademoiselle Zosine has so far regained her strength as to be able to hear me." Father Vadier and Madame de Valfonds now knew that Lucan and Zosine were not sisters.

"How can she possibly regain her strength?" Lucan answered sadly. "For so long she has devoted it all to one single cause, as no other girl in the world could have done. And in what horror did it not all end!"

Father Vadier for a time sat still, looking at her. "Mademoiselle Lucan," he said, "will you recount to me all that has happened to you and your friend in France?"

Lucan grew a little paler. "Yes," she said.

She folded her hands in her lap. It was a good thing, she thought, that it fell to her, first, to tell of the happenings at Sainte-Barbe. Zosine would have accused herself so violently.

In her report she went back a long way, till her first meeting with Mrs. Pennhallow outside the inn at Staines. Slowly and conscientiously she went through all that had happened to her since then. Even to talk about it was like a dream, and in this dreamlike atmosphere she could relate it all, as if it had happened to some other girl. She could even, with only a faint shiver in her voice, quote the letter which she had found in Mrs. Pennhallow's drawer, and recount what had happened on her last night at Sainte-Barbe. When she had finished her tale, she looked straight at Father Vadier and waited for his judgment.

Father Vadier remained silent for a long time. At last he said, "It will, all the same, be necessary for me to speak to your friend. I understand that she is suffering now. But there is no other way out for her than to tell the truth to someone. I believe that it is, at this moment, what she wants herself." They heard Zosine move in the next room. "Go in to her," said Father Vadier, "and let me know if I can come."

Lucan went in to Zosine. "Whom did you talk with?" asked Zosine.

"With Father Vadier," said Lucan. "He has got something to tell us."

Zosine drew her breath deeply. "It is a good thing that he has come," she said. Lucan arranged her pillows so that she could sit up, and pulled an armchair up to the bed. It was dark in here; Zosine asked her to light the lamp. As Lucan lifted the globe onto it, she noticed, with a heavy heart, how pale and feeble her friend looked.

"Yes, it is a good thing that you have come, Father Vadier," said Zosine, "for here they all believe that I can go on living among other people, as before. But that is not possible. For I have driven a human being to death. Time after time, during these last months, I have dreamed that I saw the old man with a rope round his neck. And my dreams have been powerful, Father Vadier! In the end he had to put it there. Listen to me. I will tell you all."

"You need not tell me what has happened at Sainte-Barbe," said Father Vadier. "I knew it already before I came here to-night. We will talk together of what you are to do now."

"Do not think that I repent of what I have done," said Zosine, and moved her head on her dark hair that was spread over the pillow. "For I would do it again, if once more I came to Sainte-Barbe, and all things were as they were then. The old man deserved to die. It was but just and right that he must die. But do you know, Father Vadier, that justice is a terrible thing? The person who cannot give up the idea of justice in life, and who comes face to face with a human being as evil as the master is himself doomed. He is cast out from the society of innocent, honest people. The innocent, honest people here, Father Vadier, Madame de Valfonds and Lucan, think that I can go on dressing, walking in the garden, sitting by the lamp, sewing with them. But it is impossible, Father Vadier. I might perhaps keep alive in a prison cell. But if I stay here, I shall die!"

"My child," said Father Vadier, "I came here to tell you something. Listen to me now.

"Early yesterday morning, a letter was brought to Monsieur Tinchebrai in Peyriac. It came from Sainte-Barbe. His housekeeper knew the messenger. When he had read it, Monsieur Tinchebrai told her that he had to go away on matters of importance, and he did not come back. Nobody has seen him since. But I take it that he went to Sainte-Barbe. When, later in the day, and after I had taken you up here, I myself went to Sainte-Barbe. The door was open, but there was no sign of life at the house. In the long dining-room I found what Monsieur Tinchebrai must have found there. On the two hooks in the ceiling hung your master, Mr. Pennhallow, and the woman who called herself his wife. They had both been dead for several hours. I gather that the woman had come home some time after you yourself had left the house, and that, at the sight of the dead man, she has put an end to her own life. The rope from which he had hanged himself was long enough for the two of them. She had cut it with an axe which lay on the table.

"Alas," Lucan thought. "Poor unhappy woman! She could not bear to live when he had died. But in his last hour, when he spoke to us, he did not once mention her name."

"In the house," Father Vadier continued, "there was ample evidence to prove what had driven those two to death. The judge of Lunel, who showed great consternation and dismay at the discovery, has opened their safes, and there has found proof of a long series of inconceivable misdeeds. Although Mr. Pennhallow's name was not known to the police of France, they had for a long time been on his track, and if they had got hold of him, the law of the country would inevitably have sentenced him to death, as he has now done himself. From papers and letters found in the house it was also learned that the couple at Sainte-Barbe were not husband and wife, but brother and sister.

"There will be no inquest and no verdict in the case, Mademoiselle Zosine. Madame de Valfonds and I have spoken with Monsieur Belabres. He has come to see the sad case with our eyes. By a singular coincidence he himself has just been informed by the postilion at Peyriac that, on the evening before the tragedy, you and your friend had left Peyriac on the diligence for Les Matelles, where one changes for Marseilles. Without doubt, Monsieur Belabres explained to me, it is your flight from his house which has convinced Mr. Pennhallow that you knew of his crimes. And it is this conviction which has turned the blood-stained hand of the murderer against himself. Baptistine Labarre was no longer at Sainte-Barbe."

For some time all three were silent.

"And Clon?" whispered Lucan.

"The boy from Sainte-Barbe," said Father Vadier, "was found in a shed where he had sought shelter on his return from Monsieur Tinchebrai's house. In his delirium he has told us many things of what happened there last night, and during all the time that he had been in Mr. Pennhallow's service. He seems to have in some way attached himself to you, Mademoiselle," he added, turning to Lucan, "but he does not remember your name. He calls you Mademoiselle Rosa. He declares that he would not take part in your murder, but that he was forced by people whom he calls 'the others.' When for a long time he had waited in vain for that light in the window, which was the signal upon which he and these others were to enter the house, he went round to the other side of the building, and kept standing there all through the night in the wind and the rain. It is uncertain whether he is going to live. All is quiet at Sainte-Barbe now."

All was quiet, too, in the room at Joliet, when Father Vadier had finished speaking.

He himself was the first to break the silence. "You ask me, Zosine," he said, "whether I know that justice is an awful thing. Yes, in our own unworthy hands, it is an awful thing. And revenge will crush the individual who takes upon himself to execute it. To exercise justice the law and the authorities have been empowered to judge the criminal and carry out the judgment, without hatred or vindictiveness, on behalf of the whole human community. It was but just that the evil man must die. But it was sinful arrogance in you to install yourself as his judge.

"But do you not see, Zosine," he went on, "that God in his mercy, at the last moment, saved you from becoming so? You are not guilty of the death of any human being, and no prison will open its doors to receive you. In the hand of the self-appointed judge, the pistol clicked. It was mercy, in the person of this good girl, which frustrated your rancor and defiance, and which killed the evil man. His dark spirit could not suffer the ray of light of forgiveness. And before the intercession of a young innocent girl, he shrank back, and sank into the abyss.

"Your friend has told me," he said, "that Mr. Pennhallow's last horrible cry was, 'Rosa prays for me!' Does this not show you, that Rosa, whose cause you have taken on, and whose agony you meant to revenge, was more powerful than you yourself? She asserted a higher and purer justice, at the moment in which she renounced her revenge, and showed mercy!"

He took Lucan's hand and led her up to Zosine's bed. "Zosine," he said, "you are to kiss your friend now, while I look at you."

Deeply moved and touched, Lucan bent down to Zosine. She felt her cold cheek against her own.

"You are not cast out from the society of innocent and honest people, Zosine," said Father Vadier. "You are to live among them as before. And, among them, you are to learn to accept, and to show, mercy."

When Lucan had sat by Zosine's bed for a while, and had seen her pale stiffened face soften, so that once more she looked like the child who had slept in the bed next to hers, a long time ago at school, she had a sudden impulse. "I will go in and read my letter," she thought.

In the course of time the people at Joliet learned that late at night a young man had come to the Bishop of Nîmes' house, and had demanded to see him. Shortly after, the stranger had left the house hurriedly, and as if in confusion and despair. The conversation had deeply shocked and shaken the Bishop. He lay ill for a long time after it. The stranger was not seen again.

17. do you not believe it

WHEN the first Zosine, during the days of the Revolution, had come to Joliet, she had brought her whole trousseau with her. But times were too unsafe, and every hour too precious, for the newly married couple to carry with them a whole wagon-load of boxes and chests. The young wife parted with her treasure with many tears. "How," she thought, "can one live without fine linen and lace?" Her cousin had the chests taken up to the attic, and the two young women had comforted each other by depicting how, in times to come, they were to open them together. Since then the heavy chests had collected the dust of almost a half century in the attic of Joliet.

Now Madame de Valfonds had them carried down again. For all that they contained belonged to the young Zosine. Zosine's arrival and presence at Joliet had strangely agitated the mind of its mistress. It was as if her own youth had returned and taken her house into possession. The old lady did not always clearly distinguish between past and present. Zosine had come back again! What joy! The ancient love of the friend of her childhood, the new delight at the presence of youth and beauty in the rooms of the old house, and the sweet hope of a beloved child's happiness which they carried with them, were all merged in her mind into a curious, ecstatic kind of passion. Still, a shadow was thrown over her happiness: for reasons incomprehensible to her, it was uncertain whether Zosine would remain at Joliet. When she was a young mother, Madame de Valfonds, against the custom of the day, had insisted on suckling her baby, and it had then happened that the child would not take her breast when she offered it to him. The old distress was now once more renewed, and in the same way in which she had then grieved over and coaxed her little son, the old lady now grieved over and coaxed the child of her friend, who seemed unwilling to accept the breast offered to her: life, and the happiness of life, itself.

She had the chests put into Zosine's rooms, and begged Lucan to make her look at their contents. "She no longer," she declared, with tears in her eyes, "believes that she can live and be happy." Lucan felt that in her heart the old lady added, "And what on earth will comfort and cheer up the heart of a woman, if fine linen and lace cannot do so?"

Before Zosine's armchair Lucan held up piece after piece, and while she did so, remembered how, at Tortuga, she had seen her friend empty wardrobes and drawers of things almost as fine as these, and throw them about the room. "Alas! she is changed!" she reflected. "At that time she had in the turn of a hand settled the value of all things in the world, and she had accepted or rejected them according to her own mood. But now she hesitates and looks at them listlessly. She gazes at the trousseau, at the loss of which her grandmother once wept bitterly, and asks herself, 'Is it worth having?' " Her friend's grave dark eyes rendered Lucan heavy-hearted.

"Is it all mine?" Zosine asked at last.

"Yes, it is yours," said Lucan.

"Then you take it, Lucan," said Zosine. "You are not to come to Wanlock Hall as an empty-handed bride. If your Noël sees my name on it, tell him that you have had it put there so that you and he, when you lie down to sleep between the sheets and upon the pillows, will sometimes remember me."

"Do you think," Lucan cried, laughing, "that I want twelve dozen nightgowns? I, who have never in my life possessed more than six!"

"Oh, but you do," said Zosine. "You are to live to make all people round you happy, until you are a lovely old lady, and have worn them all out. And you are to be content and happy, yourself, in every single one of them."

Lucan laid down the thing she had in her hand. "And you yourself, Zosine?" she asked. "Do you not believe that you may be happy?"

"That is what I do not know," said Zosine, but at the sight of Lucan's discouraged face she added, "I am not unhappy. I am no longer in despair. But I am not the same girl that I was, and I do not believe that I can ever live in the same way as then. If only I had had my Mama's religion, I should now go into a convent."

"Do you know," Lucan asked, "that Baron Thésée has now finished his journey, and is coming back tomorrow?"

"Yes, his grandmother told me so," said Zosine.

"Then you will see him, and talk with him?" Lucan asked softly.

Zosine did not answer at once. "If I see him again," she said, "I shall be able to answer the question that you put to me a moment ago. But can I see him again? In what place in the world can we two meet and speak together?"

"Oh, yes, Zosine," said Lucan, "you and he will meet, be sure of that."

Baron Thésée de Valfonds came home to Joliet the next day. Still in his big traveling cloak, he entered the drawing-room, where his grandmother and Lucan sat at their needlework. The old lady went to meet him and embraced him.

She began to tell her grandson all that had happened while he had been away, in the slow manner of very old people. She confused the order of events, and had to appeal to Lucan. She would not dwell on the tragedy of Sainte-Barbe, as if she had once and for all time wiped the old farmstead off her mind, and would not approach it even in thought. But she told him the story of the girls' arrival at Joliet, of Zosine's connection with the watch found at the old second-hand dealer's shop in Peyriac, and of the miraculous discovery of her kinship to the house of Joliet, and repeated little details of her tale many times. When she came to the end of it, the old lady deliberately let her report drag. She dreaded her grandson's eagerness, but still more the moment of Zosine's decision. Zosine was not well, she said. She had been in bed since she came to Joliet. She would now find out whether the girl was ready to receive a visitor. She rose and went out of the room.

Lucan was alone with the young man. She remembered his face and figure from their first meeting by the enclosure, but as he now saluted her so gently, and as, after his grandmother had left him, he talked to her as to Zosine's sister and friend, she was struck by a peculiar nobility and openness in his carriage, glance and voice. He was very young, most likely only a year or two her senior. She now understood her friend's words of long ago, that it must have taken more than a generation to produce this balanced, unassuming manner. He asked her a few questions about their stay at Sainte-Barbe, and she gathered that he had already seen Father Vadier and heard of it from him. He grew pale while she told him of the danger and distress which the girls had gone through, but she herself became easier at heart while he listened to her. "We two are going to be friends," she thought. A moment after, another thought ran through her mind. "Yes," she said to herself, "after all, one can understand that Zosine could love him, even after she had met Noël at Sainte-Barbe!"

In the midst of their talk, Madame de Valfonds returned to the drawing-room, followed by Olympia, and in the greatest alarm and distress. Zosine was not in the room, and they could not find her anywhere in the house. When the girl had heard the carriage drive up in front of the door, she had made Olympia dress her in great hurry, but while she sent away the black woman on some errand, she had gone out, and Olympia did not know where.

Both Madame de Valfonds and Thésée looked at Lucan. The girl tried to set them at rest. "Perhaps," she said, "she has gone down into the stable."

At the same moment a terrible apprehension caught hold of her. In the stable, she knew, there was a deep well, dating from the time when that building had been the main stronghold of old Joliet. She had herself listened to Mr. Pennhallow's last, mocking warning to her and Zosine, while he stood on the stool, with Olympia's noose round his neck.

Did these words now re-echo in Zosine's ears, so that she could not let the young man, whom she loved, put his ring on her finger, and dared not look into a mirror? Was the old man's low, luring voice drawing her with him? She felt that she grew pale, and that something in her face terrified the others.

But the young man had already jumped down the tall stone stair to the courtyard. Lucan tremblingly followed him with her eyes on his way across to the stable.

The stables of Joliet had always been the pride of the place. Through the windows the afternoon sun fell upon the shiningly groomed horses and the gold letters of their names above their boxes. In the box by the white horse, which she had named Mazeppa after her own father's riding horse, Zosine was standing. She held the horse by the forelock, and was feeding it with sugar from her hand.

The stable air and the smell of the horses met Thésée as well-known and friendly things, and the sight of the girl with the horse was so pretty that it made him stand still for a moment. Zosine did not look at him.

"Lita," cried Thésée, "why have you fled from me?"

Mazeppa turned his head, and neighed softly, when he heard his master's voice, but Zosine did not look up or answer. "Lita!" the young man cried again. "You have made me suffer terribly for your sake." He took a step up in the box toward the girl, but at the same moment she dived under the neck of the horse, so that she now stood at the other side of it.

"You would not answer me when we last met!" he exclaimed. "And you never came back again! Was it not enough that I must grieve and long for your sake? Now I know that you have been in danger, and in deadly fear, here on my own soil. And you did not send for me!" Again he went toward her on the other side of the horse, and again she dived under its neck, away from him.

"You told me yourself that we might be friends," he said.

"Who has the right, here at Joliet, to protect an innocent girl, and to punish her persecutors, if it is not I? If it is not I, who love you!" Both the young people were in the most violent agitation of mind, and the white horse between them pricked his ears at the unusual ring in the voice of the young man, and stopped rubbing his muzzle against Zosine's trembling hand, as she stopped to caress him.

"How are we to live after this?" Thésée cried again. "How can I ever forgive you?"

Exasperated by her silence, he put his hand on Mazeppa's back, in one sudden, long movement he swung himself across the horse to her. So as not to knock her back against the stable wall, he had to fall on his knee in the straw. Still in this humble attitude, seizing both her hands and drawing her toward him, he repeated, "How can I forgive you?"

Zosine, who knew something about horses, had lost her breath at the swift, audacious leap. She left her hands in his and looked straight down at him. The moment after she whispered, while something within her throat, a sob or laughter, half choked her voice, "Yes, I know how we are to live now, after I have talked with Mazeppa! He tells me that I am to tend geese here at Joliet, and to watch my husband plow! He is wiser than we. I trust in him. And you must trust in him too, Thésée!

"He says," she went on, "Mazeppa says, that all that has happened to me has happened, perhaps, to teach me this one thing. And to teach me, too, something that it has been very difficult for me to learn. Lucan knew it all the time, and might have taught me, but I would not let myself be taught by her. Now Mazeppa tells me that you may know the way to teach me, and make me understand. But you are not to scold me, Thésée, you are not to say that you will never forgive me. Mazeppa swears that he has never been trained with hardness, and he says that I should be treated just like him. Nay, he tells me—he whispered to me a moment ago—that you will know of a better, a strange, wonderful way in which to school a wild, unruly foal, and also a wild, silly girl! And he has made me believe him, Thésée!"

The young man rose, seized the girl in his arms, and kissed

her. When at last he let her go, she looked at him, her smiling, radiant eyes filled with tears, and whispered, "Yes, he is right. It is so!"

The same evening, before the people in the drawing-room of Joliet parted to go to bed, Madame de Valfonds gently took Zosine's hand and led her up to a large painting on the wall. Between her vague and wandering moods, the old lady had moments of great clearness and dignity, in which she spoke as powerfully as a sibyl.

"Zosine," she said, "the day you came here, you talked about the mirrors of Joliet. Now I will show you the mirror in which you are to see yourself. It has been waiting for you here, before you were born. Must not that give it a right to guide and advise you? When, in the old days, this same face smiled and talked to it, Joliet, as you see, in return gave it all its flowers. Do you not believe that it may be so once more?"

Zosine gazed at the picture in the highest surprise. She had not been outside her own room since the day when she first arrived at the house, and at that hour she had hardly noticed anything round her. Now she kept standing in front of the picture for a long time. In it she saw herself, light-hearted and happy, in the summer-green garden of Joliet. When she turned to Madame de Valfonds, who was still holding her hand, it was the tender, arch, mysterious smile of the portrait itself which met the old lady's tear-filled eyes.

"Yes, I believe it, Grandmama!" she said. "Now it seems to me that I have known it all the time!"

18. now we shall never meet again

THE elegant carriage from Joliet, which was driving Sir Noël Hartranft and his young wife to Lunel, on the very first bit of their wedding trip, rolled down the avenue from the chateau. Farewell after farewell had been said in the rooms and on the stairs. Now Lucan sat back, after having for the last time waved her little handkerchief toward the terrace, from which there was a last view toward the road. She had wept in Zosine's arms. She was still weeping, and did not attempt to hide her tears from her husband. It seemed to her to be part of her new, inconceivable happiness that she might in this way give free vent to her tears at his side.

Three days ago a double wedding had been celebrated at Joliet.

Sir Noël had come from England to fetch his bride. He was going to take her with him to Italy and Greece, old fairways of his, before he brought her to her future home. The chaplain from the English consulate in Marseilles had married them in the very room in which Zosine's grandmother and her husband, on their flight to England, had been married, and into which Father Vadier had brought the girls on the morning after their last night at Sainte-Barbe.

On the same day Zosine had become Thésée de Valfonds' wife. She had written to her Papa, and had got his consent to her marriage, and she was now looking forward with the greatest joy to his arrival at Joliet. But she had wished to see him only after her destiny had been definitely settled, and when she herself was already tied to her new country and to her new, and old, family.

Madame de Valfonds had longed to collect all her relations in France to celebrate such a happy event as this marriage, and this miraculous union of two branches of the Valfonds family. Only reluctantly had she given in to the wish of her children. There had been but few witnesses to the wedding in the chapel of Joliet. But in the evening a big feast was given in its honor in the castle yard to all the peasants of the estate.

Zosine as a bride had worn her own grandmother's bridal veil and little bridal shoes, which had been brought to light from a chest. Old people of the neighborhood, who remembered, in distant, happy days, to have seen a girl with her face and her smile cantering along the forest paths, or kneeling in the chapel, were strangely moved to meet her again as the future mistress of the chateau. The happenings at Sainte-Barbe, of which much was talked, but little really known, formed a dark background for her light figure. The peasants of Joliet felt that she had been brought back to them by the unknown, winding paths of a fairy tale.

Sainte-Barbe stood empty. It was said that the house would be pulled down. It was also told that Baptistine Labarre, whom nobody had seen since the death of her foreign lessees, walked through the house at night like a restless, lost spirit which dared not show itself in the place where it belonged, and which yet could not leave it.

Now Lucan was going to Lunel in a traveling costume which Madame de Valfonds had ordered for her from her own dressmaker at Nîmes. The pretty frocks and bonnets, the only remnants of Zosine's former elegant wardrobe, in which she and Lucan had arrived in France, had forever vanished, no one knew where, and if they had been found, neither of the girls could have touched them. Lucan had seen herself in the mirror in a cashmere shawl, the like of which few ladies in England could boast of, and a bonnet which framed her sweet face like a cloud, and imparted to it a delicate, rose color. Behind her own figure that of Zosine clapped her hands and assured her that she had never been so lovely. "Like a rose," thought Sir Noël. He knew that he was not good at inventing poetic comparisons for the beauty of his young wife. "Like a flower, like a branch of a blossoming apple tree," he repeated, and felt himself like a big bumble-bee, dizzy in the flower-chalice, and too dark and heavy for this floral sweetness and loveliness.

In the carriage he took her hand. "What are you thinking of?" he asked her.

Lucan did not answer him at once. She thought of Zosine, but she could not have given words to her thoughts, not even to herself. Among all the adventures which had united the two girls, none had bound them together as strangely and fatally as this last: that they had been married on the same day. No old Nordic heroes, who, according to the Viking custom, had mingled blood, could ever have felt a more eternal and mysterious oneness than the two friends after their wedding day.

In the last days before it, Zosine had clung to Lucan, so that she had even neglected her fiancé for the sake of her friend. "Do you remember," she asked her, "what I said to you first of all when you came to Tortuga? I begged John to go in and tell Papa that something wonderful and joyful had happened to me: my best friend had come to help me! But how could I then foretell how much you were to help me, you dear, sweet girl!"

In the three days after the wedding Lucan and Zosine had hardly talked together. Their silence was not only due to the fact that their young husbands claimed their presence and attention. They both felt, with equal strength, that from now words were superfluous between them. The short, deep, gentle, happy glances, which from time to time they exchanged, expressed more than they had ever said, or would ever say to each other.

"I am thinking of Clon," said Lucan. The fate of the boy had been on her mind many times since she last saw him in the morning mist by the wall of Sainte-Barbe. She was happy to know that old Madame de Valfonds would take him in her service.

"And of Olympia," she went on with a smile. "How wonderfully she has come to feel at home at Joliet! After having slept for three full days, she begged Father Vadier to confess her. She had not, she said, been to confession for fifty years. Since then she has been happy and calm in quite a new way. She is as devoted to Zosine as ever, and very pleased with her husband, but it is of Father Vadier that she thinks and talks most, so that I think he is a little shy of her, and she is already looking forward to her next confession. Now she is cleaning up the pavilion in the garden for her old master. Zosine wants it to be her Papa's, and she thinks that he will be happy there, and quite content from time to time to turn his back on all his friends in England and to come and stay with her." She again smiled at her own thoughts as she remembered that Zosine had said to her with big, grave eyes, "Now Papa really ought to marry Aunt Arabella. For after all it was Aunt Arabella who saved both your life and mine!"

But once more her eyes filled with tears at the thought of Zosine. She remembered how, the day after his wedding, Thésée had wanted to set an old beautiful diamond ring on his young wife's finger, and had smiled to find there a small, childish ring, made of tiny colored glass beads, such as ladies use for their needlework. He had asked Zosine who had given it to her. Zosine raised her clear, dark eyes to his face. She took the ring from her finger and handed it to him. "Now I give it to you," she said. "It signifies something. It pleads the cause of the defenseless, the oppressed, and the wronged. It is right and fit that it should be with you." She paused. Suddenly a deep wave of her blood mounted to her face, and the moment after she grew very pale. "But do not let me see it again!" she exclaimed. "I must never see it again now!"

In front of the travelers in the carriage the sun broke through the clouds. "Now we are heading straight South," Noël said, "for Genoa, which was the first continental port where I went ashore as a little midshipman. You will like the Mediterranean, I think, for I am reminded of it when I look into your blue eyes. Within a week we are to see Mount Vesuvius, and to walk together among the old, big ruins of Rome. There you will have to go through my history with me, for I have forgotten all that I was ever taught about the old Romans."

His words awoke a faint, distant echo in Lucan's heart. Someone, somewhere, a long, long time ago, had talked to her of promenades among the ruins of Rome. She searched her memory, remembered her conversation with Mr. Armworthy, and grew very still. Noël saw that his wife blushed slowly and deeply beneath her rose bonnet, and the sight enchanted him, so that he would not disturb it by questioning her. In silence he carried her hand to his lips.

Lucan wondered whether she ought to tell her husband of what had happened to her at Fairhill, and whether she ought perhaps to have done so a long time ago. Could he blame her because a man had dared to make her an offer like Mr. Armworthy's? But if she told him of it, she thought, he would fire up in a dangerous way. She could not tell what terrible revenge he might take upon the man who had insulted her. "Alas," she thought, "revenge is not my affair." She knew herself that she had been blameless in the matter, yes, that it was because she had been too innocent and confident that Mr. Armworthy had dared to insult her. She had one more reason to conceal the whole thing from her husband. When she came back to England, she thought, she would be happy if things could ever come about so that she might again meet the blind boy from Fairhill. As Noël's wife, she might, face to face with Mr. Armworthy, wipe out what had happened between them, and what had once seemed to her so unforgettable, as if it had never taken place. She dwelt on the thought for a while, and her happiness was so great and her feeling of safety so strong that she told herself, "It *has* never taken place!"

It seemed to Lucan as if she had for many years been carrying an unseen burden, a trust that was both heavy and sweet. She had been in charge of a treasure. It belonged to Noël, it was his by right, and had been so from the beginning of things, and she would have died rather than ever to fail or betray him. Ever armed, vigilant and watchful, she had guarded his treasure for him behind cast down eyes and closed lips, as behind a veil and a seal. She had brushed her pretty hair, and hidden it in her bonnets, because it was his. She had preserved her heart from disturbance, hardness and bitterness, because it was his. She had kept her slim, delicate waist so firmly laced in whalebones, in order that it might fit into his arm. During the three days which had passed since her wedding, she had felt with dawning, happy surprise that she had been released from her post. She had handed over his rightful property, his buried treasure, to Noël. It was to make him rich for all his life, and it was he who must now keep watch over it. In his keeping she was not only safe, but wonderfully light and free. For a little while she would perhaps still be shy of raising her eyes, or her voice. But soon she would learn to gaze freely and dauntlessly to all sides, to listen to the voices of the world, and to answer them without diffidence. And now that she had become free from care, and light-hearted as a child, she was going to turn her young husband's zealous watch-service itself into a child's play.

"For these three days and nights since our wedding only," said Noël, when the rush of blood had again sunk back from her cheeks, "I owe you all that I own in this world. Into what debt shall I not run, if we live to celebrate our golden wedding! But you must tell me into what pretty ladies' things I am to turn that wealth, which is precious to me only because it may give you pleasure. You must tell me what lovely sights I am to show you first of all. With all your candidness, you are still so mysterious, my beloved girl." Lucan smiled to him.

"I ought to have met you fifteen years ago!" he exclaimed. "I ought to have followed your steps from the time when you were a little girl, so as to have learned all your tastes, and to have known what such a little girl as you may have longed and hoped for!"

His young wife looked up. "I myself," she said gently and slowly, "once, upon an evening in England, put that same question as you are now asking to my own heart. 'What is it,' I thought then, 'that I demand of life, and that I have always longed and hoped for?' And I could answer the question without doubt or hesitation. For it was love, Noël."

A moment before she would not have thought it possible that she could have pronounced these words. It was as if her heart had spoken on its own. Her lips quivered as her confession left them, like the string of a bow, when the strong hand behind it lets fly the arrow.

Noël could now no longer be content with her hand. He bent his face under the pretty bonnet and kissed her.

At this moment the coachman on the box pulled up the horses. Without turning round, or disturbing the young lady and gentleman in the carriage, with the whip-handle to his hat, he respectfully called their attention to the fact that from this place on the road one might, at a long distance, for the last time catch a glimpse of the white walls and the tall roof and towers of Joliet.

MORE ABOUT PENGUINS, PELICANS AND PUFFINS

A CHOICE OF PENGUINS

KING PENGUIN

☐ ***Selected Poems*** **Tony Harrison** £3.95

Poetry Book Society Recommendation. 'One of the few modern poets who actually has the gift of composing poetry' – James Fenton in the *Sunday Times*

☐ ***The Book of Laughter and Forgetting***
Milan Kundera £3.95

'A whirling dance of a book . . . a masterpiece full of angels, terror, ostriches and love . . . No question about it. The most important novel published in Britain this year' – Salman Rushdie in the *Sunday Times*

☐ ***The Sea of Fertility*** **Yukio Mishima** £9.95

Containing *Spring Snow, Runaway Horses, The Temple of Dawn* and *The Decay of the Angel*: 'These four remarkable novels are the most complete vision we have of Japan in the twentieth century' – Paul Theroux

☐ ***The Hawthorne Goddess*** **Glyn Hughes** £2.95

Set in eighteenth century Yorkshire where 'the heroine, Anne Wylde, represents the doom of nature and the land . . . Hughes has an arresting style, both rich and abrupt' – *The Times*

☐ ***A Confederacy of Dunces*** **John Kennedy Toole** £3.95

In this Pulitzer Prize-winning novel, in the bulky figure of Ignatius J. Reilly an immortal comic character is born. 'I succumbed, stunned and seduced . . . it is a masterwork of comedy' – *The New York Times*

☐ ***The Last of the Just*** **André Schwartz-Bart** £3.95

The story of Ernie Levy, the last of the just, who was killed at Auschwitz in 1943: 'An outstanding achievement, of an altogether different order from even the best of earlier novels which have attempted this theme' – John Gross in the *Sunday Telegraph*

KING PENGUIN

☐ ***The White Hotel*** **D. M. Thomas** £3.95

'A major artist has once more appeared', declared the *Spectator* on the publication of this acclaimed, now famous novel which recreates the imagined case history of one of Freud's woman patients.

☐ ***Dangerous Play: Poems 1974–1984***
Andrew Motion £2.95

Winner of the John Llewelyn Rhys Memorial Prize. Poems and an autobiographical prose piece, *Skating*, by the poet acclaimed in the *TLS* as 'a natural heir to the tradition of Edward Thomas and Ivor Gurney'.

☐ ***A Time to Dance*** **Bernard Mac Laverty** £2.50

Ten stories, including 'My Dear Palestrina' and 'Phonefun Limited', by the author of *Cal*: 'A writer who has a real affinity with the short story form' – *The Times Literary Supplement*

☐ ***Keepers of the House*** **Lisa St Aubin de Terán** £2.95

Seventeen-year-old Lydia Sinclair marries Don Diego Beltrán and goes to live on his family's vast, decaying Andean farm. This exotic and flamboyant first novel won the Somerset Maugham Award.

☐ ***The Deptford Trilogy*** **Robertson Davies** £5.95

'Who killed Boy Staunton?' – around this central mystery is woven an exhilarating and cunningly contrived trilogy of novels: *Fifth Business, The Manticore* and *World of Wonders*.

☐ ***The Stories of William Trevor*** £5.95

'Trevor packs into each separate five or six thousand words more richness, more laughter, more ache, more multifarious human-ness than many good writers manage to get into a whole novel' – *Punch*. 'Classics of the genre' – Auberon Waugh